By Kristin Hannah
Published by Ballantine Books

A Handful of Heaven

The Enchantment

Once in Every Life

If You Believe

When Lightning Strikes

Waiting for the Moon

Home Again

On Mystic Lake

Angel Falls

Summer Island

Distant Shores

Between Sisters

The Things We Do for Love

Comfort & Joy

Magic Hour

Firefly Lane

True Colors

Winter Garden

MAGIC HOUR

MAGIC HOUR

A Novel

KRISTIN HANNAH

BALLANTINE BOOKS TRADE PAPERBACKS
NEW YORK

2010 Ballantine Books Trade Paperback Edition

Copyright © 2006 by Kristin Hannah
Reading group guide copyright © 2010 by Random House, Inc.
Excerpt from *Angel Falls* copyright © 2000 by Kristin Hannah

Published in the United States by Ballantine Books Trade Paperbacks,
an imprint of The Random House Publishing Group,
a division of Random House, Inc., New York.

BALLANTINE and colophon are registered
trademarks of Random House, Inc.
RANDOM HOUSE READER'S CIRCLE & Design is a registered
trademark of Random House, Inc.

Originally published in hardcover in the United States by Ballantine Books,
an imprint of The Random House Publishing Group,
a division of Random House, Inc., in 2006.

LIBRARY OF CONGRESS CATALOGING-IN-PUBLICATION DATA
Hannah, Kristin.
Magic hour / Kristin Hannah.
p. cm.
ISBN 978-0-345-52218-4
1. Child psychologists—Fiction.
2. Northwest, Pacific—Fiction. I. Title.
PS3558.A4763M34 2006
813'.54—dc22
2005048342

Printed in the United States of America

www.randomhousereaderscircle.com

2 4 6 8 9 7 5 3 1

Book design by Julie Schroeder

This one is for my son, Tucker.
It seems like only a few years ago I could hold you in my arms.
Now we're touring colleges and talking about your future.
I am so proud of the boy you were and the man you are becoming.
Soon you will be leaving your dad and me to find your own way
in the world. Know that whatever you do, wherever you go,
we will always love you.

ACKNOWLEDGMENTS

Several people were instrumental in the writing
of this novel. Thanks go out to:

Lindsey Brooks, investigative manager/case
management department, Child Quest International;

Luana S. Burnett, police services officer,
city of Newport, Washington;

Kany Levine, criminal defense attorney and friend;

and Kim Fisk and Megan Chance,
who both helped more than they know.

"Real isn't how you are made," said the Skin Horse.
"It's a thing that happens to you. When a child loves you
for a long, long time, not just to play with, but REALLY loves
you, then you become Real."
"Does it hurt?" asked the Rabbit.
"Sometimes," said the Skin Horse, for he was always truthful.

—*The Velveteen Rabbit*
Margery Williams

MAGIC HOUR

ONE

I*T WILL ALL BE OVER SOON.*

Julia Cates had lost count of the times she'd told herself that very thing, but today—finally—it would be true. In a few hours the world would know the truth about her.

If she made it downtown, that was. Unfortunately, the Pacific Coast Highway looked more like a parking lot than a freeway. The hills behind Malibu were on fire again; smoke hung above the rooftops and turned the normally bright coastal air into a thick brown sludge. All over town terrified babies woke in the middle of the night, crying gray-black tears and gasping for breath. Even the surf seemed to have slowed down, as if exhausted by the unseasonable heat.

She maneuvered through the cranky, stop-and-go traffic, ignoring the drivers who flipped her off and cut in front of her. It was expected; in this most dangerous of seasons in Southern California, tempers caught fire as easily as backyards. The heat made everyone edgy.

Finally, she exited the freeway and drove to the courthouse.

Television vans were everywhere. Dozens of reporters huddled on the courthouse steps, microphones and cameras at the ready, waiting for the story to arrive. In Los Angeles it was becoming a daily event, it seemed; legal proceedings as entertainment. Michael Jackson. Courtney Love. Robert Blake.

Julia turned a corner and drove to a side entrance, where her lawyers were waiting for her.

She parked on the street and got out of the car, expecting to move forward confidently, but for a terrible second she couldn't move. *You're innocent,* she reminded herself. *They'll see that. The system will work.* She forced herself to take a step, then another. It felt as if she were moving through invisible wires, fighting her way uphill. When she made it to the group, it took everything she had to smile, but one thing she knew: it looked real. Every psychiatrist knew how to make a smile look genuine.

"Hello, Dr. Cates," said Frank Williams, the lead counsel on her defense team. "How are you?"

"Let's go," she said, wondering if she was the only one who heard the wobble in her voice. She hated that evidence of her fear. Today, of all days, she needed to be strong, to show the world that she was the doctor they'd thought she was, that she'd done nothing wrong.

The team coiled protectively around her. She appreciated their support. Although she was doing her best to appear professional and confident, it was a fragile veneer. One wrong word could strip it all away.

They pushed through the doors and walked into the courthouse.

Flashbulbs erupted in spasms of blue-white light. Cameras clicked; tape rolled. Reporters surged forward, all yelling at once.

"Dr. Cates! How do you feel about what happened?"

"Why didn't you save those children?"

"Did you know about the gun?"

Frank put an arm around Julia and pulled her against his side. She pressed her face against his lapel and let herself be pulled along.

In the courtroom, she took her place at the defendant's table. One by one the team rallied around her. Behind her, in the first row of gallery seating, several junior associates and paralegals took their places.

She tried to ignore the racket behind her; the doors creaking open and slamming shut, footsteps hurrying across the marble tiled floor, whispered voices. Empty seats were filling up quickly; she knew it without turning around. This courtroom was the Place to Be in Los Angeles today, and since the judge had disallowed cameras in the courtroom, journalists and artists were no doubt packed side by side in the gallery, their pens ready.

In the past year, they'd written an endless string of stories about her. Photographers had snapped thousands of pictures of her—taking out the trash, standing on her deck, coming and going from her office. The least flattering shots always made the front page.

Reporters had practically set up camp outside her condo, and although she had never spoken to them, it didn't matter. The stories kept coming. They reported on her small-town roots, her stellar education, her pricey beachfront condo, her devastating breakup with Philip. They even speculated that she'd recently become either anorexic or addicted to liposuction. What they didn't report on was the only part of her that mattered: her love of her job. She had been a lonely, awkward child, and she remembered every nuance of that pain. Her own youth had made her an exceptional psychiatrist.

Of course, that bit of truth never made it to press. Neither had a list of all the children and adolescents she'd helped.

A hush fell over the courtroom as Judge Carol Myerson took her seat at the bench. She was a stern-looking woman with artificially bright auburn hair and old-fashioned eyeglasses.

The bailiff called out the case.

Julia wished suddenly that she had asked someone to join her here today, some friend or relative who would stand by her, maybe hold her hand when it was over, but she'd always put work ahead of socializing. It hadn't given her much time to devote to friends. Her own therapist had often pointed out this lack in her life; truthfully, until now, she'd never agreed with him.

Beside her, Frank stood. He was an imposing man, tall and almost elegantly thin, with hair that was going from black to gray in perfect order, sideburns first. She'd chosen him because of his brilliant mind, but his demeanor was likely to matter more. Too often in rooms like this it came down to form over substance.

"Your Honor," he began in a voice as soft and persuasive as any she'd ever heard, "the naming of Dr. Julia Cates as a defendant in this lawsuit is absurd. Although the precise limits and boundaries of confidentiality in psychiatric situations are often disputed, certain precedents exist, namely *Tarasoff v. Regents of University of California*. Dr. Cates had no knowledge of her patient's violent tendencies and no information regarding specific threats to named individuals. Indeed, no such specific knowledge is even alleged in the complaint. Thus, we respectfully request that she be dismissed from this lawsuit. Thank you." He sat down.

At the plaintiff's table, a man in a jet-black suit stood up. "Four children are *dead*, Your Honor. They will never grow up, never leave for college, never have children of their own. Dr. Cates was Amber Zuniga's psychiatrist. For three years Dr. Cates spent two hours a week with Amber, listening to her problems and prescribing medications for her growing depression. Yet with all that intimacy, we are now to believe that Dr. Cates didn't *know* that Amber was becoming increasingly violent and depressed. That she had no warning whatsoever that her patient would buy an automatic weapon and walk into her church youth group meeting and start shooting." The lawyer walked out from behind the table and stood in the middle of the courtroom.

Slowly, he turned to face Julia. It was the money shot; the one that would be drawn by every artist in the courtroom and shown around the world. "She is the expert, Your Honor. She should have foreseen this tragedy and prevented it by warning the victims or committing Ms. Zuniga for residential treatment. If she didn't in fact know of Ms. Zuniga's violent tendencies, she should have. Thus, we respectfully seek to keep Dr. Cates as a named defendant in this case. It is a matter of justice. The slain children's families deserve redress from the person most likely to have foreseen and prevented the murder of their children." He went back to the table and took his seat.

"It isn't true," Julia whispered, knowing her voice couldn't be heard. Still, she had to say it out loud. Amber had never even hinted at violence. Every teenager battling depression said they hated the kids in their school. That was light-years away from buying a gun and opening fire.

Why couldn't they all see that?

Judge Myerson read over the paperwork in front of her. Then she took off her reading glasses and set them down on the hard wooden surface of her bench.

The courtroom fell into silence. Julia knew that the journalists were ready to write instantly. Outside, there were more of them standing by, ready to run with two stories. Both headlines were already written. All they needed was a sign from their colleagues inside.

The children's parents, huddled in the back rows in a mournful group, were waiting to be assured that this tragedy could have been averted, that someone in a position of authority could have kept their children alive. They had sued everyone for wrongful death—the police, the paramedics, the drug manufacturers, the medical doctors, and the Zuniga family. The modern world no longer believed in senseless tragedy. Bad things couldn't just happen to people; someone had to pay. The victims' families hoped that this lawsuit would be the answer, but Julia knew it would only give them something else to think about for a while, perhaps distribute some of their pain. It wouldn't alleviate it, though. The grief would outlive them all.

The judge looked at the parents first. "There is no doubt that what happened on February nineteenth at the Baptist church in Silverwood was a terrible tragedy. As a parent myself, I cannot fathom the world in which you have lived for the past months. However, the question before this court is whether Dr. Cates should remain a defendant in this case." She folded her hands on the desk. "I am persuaded that as a matter of law, Dr. Cates had no duty to warn or otherwise protect the victims in this set of circumstances. I reach this conclusion for several reasons.

First, the facts do not assert and the plaintiffs do not allege that Dr. Cates had any specific knowledge of identifiable potential victims; second, the law does not impose a duty to warn except to clearly identifiable victims; and finally, as a matter of public policy, we must maintain the confidentiality of the psychiatrist-patient relationship unless there is a specific, identifiable threat which warrants the undermining of that confidentiality. Dr. Cates, by her testimony and her records and pursuant to the plaintiffs' own assertions, did not have a duty to warn or otherwise protect the victims in this case. Thus, I am dismissing her from the complaint, without prejudice."

The gallery went crazy. Before she knew it, Julia was on her feet and enfolded in congratulatory hugs by her defense team. Behind her, she could hear the journalists running for the doors and down the marble hallway. "She's out!" someone yelled.

Julia felt a wave of relief. *Thank God*.

Then she heard the children's parents crying behind her.

"How can this be happening?" one of them said loudly. "She should have known."

Frank touched her arm. "You should be smiling. We won."

She shot a quick glance at the parents, then looked away. Her thoughts trailed off into the dark woods of regret. Were they right? Should she have known?

"It wasn't your fault, and it's time you told people that. This is your opportunity to speak up, to—"

A crowd of reporters swarmed them.

"Dr. Cates! What do you have to say to the parents who hold you responsible—"

"Will other parents trust you with their children—"

"Can you comment on the report that the Los Angeles District Attorney's Office has taken your name off the roster of forensic psychiatrists?"

Frank stepped into the fray, reaching back for Julia's hand. "My client was just released from the lawsuit—"

"On a technicality," someone yelled.

While they were focused on Frank, Julia slipped to the back of the crowd and ran for the door. She knew Frank wanted her to make a statement, but she didn't care. She didn't feel triumphant. All she wanted was to be away from all this . . . to get back to real life.

The Zunigas were standing in front of the door, blocking her path. They were paler versions of the couple she'd once known. Grief had stripped them of color and aged them.

Mrs. Zuniga looked up at her through tears.

"She loved both of you," Julia said softly, knowing it wasn't enough. "And you were good parents. Don't let anyone convince you otherwise. Amber was ill. I wish—"

"Don't," Mr. Zuniga said. "Wishing hurts most of all." He put an arm around his wife and drew her close to him.

Silence fell between them. Julia tried to think of more to say, but all that was left was *I'm sorry*, which she'd said too many times to count, and "Good-bye." Holding her purse close, she eased around them, then left the courthouse.

Outside, the world was brown and bleak. A thick layer of haze darkened the sky, obliterating the sun, matching her mood.

She got into her car and drove away. As she merged into traffic, she wondered if Frank had even noticed her absence. To him it was a game, albeit with the biggest stakes, and as the day's winner, he would be flying high. He would think about the victims and their families, probably tonight in his den, after a few Dewars over ice. He would think about her, too, perhaps wonder what would become of a psychiatrist who'd so profoundly compromised her reputation with failure, but he wouldn't think about them all for long. He didn't dare.

She was going to have to put it behind her now, too. Tonight she'd lie in her lonely bed, listening to the surf, thinking how much it sounded like the beat of her heart, and she'd try again to get beyond her grief and guilt. She *had* to figure out what clue she'd missed, what sign she'd overlooked. It would hurt—remembering—but in the end she'd be a better therapist for all this pain. And then, at seven o'clock in the morning, she'd get dressed and go back to work.

Helping people.

That was how she'd get through this.

GIRL CROUCHES AT THE EDGE OF THE CAVE, WATCHING WATER FALL FROM the sky. She wants to reach for one of the empty cans around her, maybe lick the insides again, but she has done this too many times already. The food is gone. It has been gone for more moons than she knows how to keep track of. Behind her the wolves are restless, hungry.

The sky grumbles and roars. Trees shake with fear, and still the water drips down.

She falls asleep.

She wakes suddenly and looks around, sniffing the air. There is a strange scent in the darkness. It should frighten her, send her back into the deep, black hole, but she can't quite move. Her stomach is so tight and empty it hurts.

The falling water isn't so angry now; it is more of a spitting. She wishes she could see the sun. Life is better when she is in the light. Her cave is so dark.

A twig snaps.

Then another.

She goes very still, willing her body to disappear against the cave wall. She becomes like the shadow of herself, flat and motionless. She knows how important stillness can be.

Him is coming. Already he has been gone too long. The food is no more. The sunny days are past, and though she is glad Him is gone, without Him, she is afraid. In a time—long ago now—Her would have helped some, but she is DEAD.

When the forest falls silent again, she leans forward, poking her face into the gray light Out There. The darkness of sleepnight is coming; soon it will be blackness all around. The falling water is gentle and sweet. She likes the taste of it.

What should she do?

She glances down at the pup beside her. He is on alert, too, sniffing the air. She touches his soft fur and feels the tremble in his body. He is wondering the same thing: would Him be back?

Always before Him was gone a moon or two at the most. But everything changed when Her got dead and gone. When Him left, he actually spoke to Girl.

YOUBEGOODWHILEI'MGONEORELSE.

She doesn't understand all of the words, but she knows Or Else.

Still, it is too long since he left. There is nothing to eat. She has freed herself and gone into the woods for berries and nuts, but it is the darkening season. Soon she will be too weak to find food, and there will be none anyway when the white starts falling and turns her breath into fog. Though she is afraid, terrified of the Strangers who live Out There, she is starving, and if Him comes back and sees that she has freed herself, it will be bad. She must make a move.

THE TOWN OF RAIN VALLEY, TUCKED BETWEEN THE WILDS OF THE Olympic National Forest and the roaring gray surf of the Pacific Ocean, was the last bastion of civilization before the start of the deep woods.

There were places not far from town that had never been touched by the golden rays of the sun, where shadows lay on the black, loamy soil all year, their shapes so thick and substantial that the few hardy hikers who made their way into the forest often thought they'd stumbled into a den of hibernating bears. Even today, in this modern age of scientific wonders, these woods remained as they had for centuries, unexplored, untouched by man.

Less than one hundred years ago, settlers came to this beautiful spot between the rain forest and the sea and hacked down just enough trees to plant their crops. In time they learned what the Native Americans had learned before them: this was a place that wouldn't be tamed. So they gave up their farming tools and took up fishing. Salmon and timber became the local industries, and for a few decades the town prospered. But in the nineties, environmentalists discovered Rain Valley. They set out to save the birds and the fish and the eldest of the trees. The men who made their living off the land were forgotten in this fight, and over the years the town fell into a quiet kind of disrepair. One by one the grandiose visions of the town's prominent citizens faded away. Those much-anticipated streetlights were never added; the road out to Mystic Lake remained a two-lane minefield of thinning asphalt and growing potholes; the telephone and electrical lines stayed where they were—in the air—hanging lazily from one old pole to the next, an invitation to every tree limb in every windstorm to knock out the town's power.

In other parts of the world, in places where man had staked his claim long ago, such a falling apart of a town might have dealt a death blow to the citizens' sense of community, but not here. The people of Rain Valley were hardy souls, able and willing to live in a place where it rained more than two hundred days a year and the sun was treated like a wealthy uncle who only rarely came to call. They withstood gray days and springy lawns and dwindling ways to make a living, and remained through it all the sons and daughters of the pioneers who'd first dared to live among the towering trees.

Today, however, they were finding their spirit tested. It was October seventeenth, and autumn had recently lost its race to the coming winter. Oh, the trees were still dressed in their party colors and the lawns were green again after the brown days of late summer, but no mistake could be made: winter was coming. The sky had been low and gray all week, layered in ominously dark clouds. For seven days it had rained almost nonstop.

On the corner of Wheaton Way and Cates Avenue stood the police station, a squat gray-stone building with a cupola on top and a flagpole on the grassy lawn out front. Inside the austere building, the old fluorescent lighting was barely strong enough to keep the gray at bay. It was four o'clock in the afternoon, but the bad weather made it feel later.

The people who worked inside tried not to notice. If they'd been asked—and they hadn't—they would have admitted that four to five consecutive days of rain was acceptable. Longer if it was only a drizzle. But there was something *wrong* in this stretch of bad weather. It wasn't January, after all. For the first few days, they sat at their respective desks and complained good-naturedly about the walk from their cars to the front door. Now, those conversations had been pummeled by the constant hammering of rain on the roof.

Ellen Barton—Ellie to her friends, which was everyone in town— stood at the window, staring out at the street. The rain made everything appear insubstantial. She caught a glimpse of herself in the water-streaked window; not a reflection, precisely, more of a feeling played out momentarily on glass. She saw herself as she always did, as the younger woman she'd once been—long, thick black hair and corn-flower blue eyes and a bright, ready smile. The girl voted Homecoming Queen and head cheerleader. As always when she thought about her youth, she saw herself in white. The color of brides, of hope for the future, of families waiting to be born.

"I gotta have a smoke, Ellie. You know I do. I've been really good, but it's reaching critical mass about now. If I don't light up, I'm heading to the refrigerator."

"Don't let her do it," Cal said from his place at the dispatch desk. He sat hunched over the phone, a lock of black hair falling across his eyes. In high school Ellie and her friends had called him the Crow because of his black hair and sharp, pointed features. He'd always had a bony, ill-put-together look, as if he wasn't quite at home in his body. At almost forty, he still had a boyish appearance. Only his eyes—dark and intense—showed the miles he'd walked in his lifetime. "Try tough love. Nothing else has worked."

"Bite me," Peanut snapped.

Ellie sighed. They'd had this same discussion only fifteen minutes ago, and ten minutes before that. She put her hands on her waist, resting her fingertips on the heavy gun belt that was slung across her hips. She turned to look at her best friend. "Now, Peanut, you know what

I'm gonna say. This is a public building. I'm the chief of police. How can I let you break the law?"

"Exactly," Cal said. He opened his mouth to say more, but a call came in and he answered it. "Rain Valley Police."

"Oh, right," Peanut said. "And suddenly you're Miss Law and Order. What about Sven Morgenstern—he parks in front of his store every day. Right in front of the hydrant. When was the last time you hauled his car away? And Large Marge shoplifts two boxes of freezer pops and a bottle of nail polish from the drugstore every Sunday after church. I haven't processed her arrest papers in a while. I guess as long as her husband pays the tab it doesn't matter. . . ." She let the sentence trail off. They both knew she could cite a dozen more examples. This was Rain Valley, after all, not downtown Seattle. Ellie had been the chief of police for four years and a patrol officer for eight years before that. Although she stayed ready for anything, she'd never processed a crime more dangerous than Breaking and Entering.

"Are you going to let me have a cigarette or am I going to get a doughnut and a Red Bull?"

"They'll both kill you."

"Yeah, but they won't kill us," Cal said, disconnecting his call. "Hold firm, El. She's the patrol clerk. She shouldn't smoke in a city building."

"You're smoking too much," Ellie finally said.

"Yeah, but I'm eating less."

"Why don't you go back to the salmon jerky diet? Or the grapefruit one? Those were both healthier."

"Stop talking and answer me. I need a smoke."

"You started smoking four days ago, Peanut," Cal said. "You hardly *need* a cigarette."

Ellie shook her head. If she didn't step in, these two would bicker all day. "You should go back to your meetings," she said with a sigh. "That Weight Watchers was working."

"Six months of cabbage soup to lose ten pounds? I don't think so. Come on, Ellie, you know I'm about ready to reach for a doughnut."

Ellie knew she'd lost the battle. She and Peanut—Penelope Nutter—had worked side by side in this office for more than a decade and been best friends since high school. Over the years their friendship had weathered every storm, from the ruination of Ellie's two fragile marriages to Peanut's recent decision that smoking cigarettes was the key to weight loss. She called it the Hollywood diet and pointed out all of the stick-figure celebrities who smoked.

"Fine. But just one."

Grinning at Cal, Peanut placed her hands on the desk and pushed herself to a stand. The fifty pounds she'd gained in the past few years made her move a little slower. She walked over to the door and opened it, although they all knew there'd be no breeze to suck the smoke away on such a wet and dismal day.

Ellie went down the hall to the office in the back that was technically hers. She rarely used it. In a town like this, there wasn't much call for official business, and she preferred to spend her days in the main room with Cal and Peanut. She dug past the signs from last month's pancake breakfast and found a gas mask. Putting it on, she headed back down the hall.

Cal burst out laughing.

Peanut tried not to smile. "Very funny."

Ellie lifted the mask to say, "I may want children someday. I'm protecting my uterus."

"If I were you, I'd worry less about secondhand smoke and more about finding a date."

"She's tried everyone from Mystic to Aberdeen," Cal said. "Last month she even went out with that UPS guy. The good-looking one who keeps forgetting where he parked his truck."

Peanut exhaled smoke and coughed. "I think you need to lower your standards, Ellie."

"You sure look like you're enjoying that smoke," Cal said with a grin.

Peanut flipped him off. "We were talking about Ellie's love life."

"That's all you two ever talk about," Cal pointed out.

It was true.

Ellie couldn't help herself: she loved men. Usually—okay, always—the wrong men.

Peanut called it the curse of the small-town beauty queen. If only Ellie had been like her sister and learned to rely on her brains instead of her beauty. But some things simply weren't meant to be. Ellie liked having fun; she liked romance. The problem was, it hadn't yet led to true love. Peanut said it was because Ellie didn't know how to compromise, but that wasn't accurate. Ellie's marriages—both of them—had failed because she'd married good-looking men with itchy feet and wandering eyes. Her first husband, former high school football captain Al Torees, should have been enough to turn her off men for years, but she'd had a short memory, and just a few years after the divorce she married another good-looking loser. Poor choices, to be truthful, but the divorces hadn't dimmed her hopes. She still believed in romance and was waiting to be swept away. She knew it was possible; she'd seen that true love with her parents. "Any lower, Pea, and I'd be dating out of my species. Maybe Cal here can set me up with one of his geek friends from the comic book convention."

Cal looked stung by that. "We're not geeks."

"Yeah," Peanut said, exhaling smoke. "You're grown men who think other men in tights look good."

"You make us sound gay."

"Hardly." Peanut laughed. "Gay men have sex. Your friends wear *Matrix* costumes in public. How you found Lisa, I'll never know."

At the mention of Cal's wife, an awkward silence stumbled into the room. The whole town knew she was a run-around. There was always talk; men smiled, women frowned and shook their heads at the mention of her name. But here in the police station, they never spoke about it.

Cal went back to reading his comic book and doodling in his sketch pad. They all knew he'd be quiet for a while now.

Ellie sat down at her desk and put her feet up.

Peanut leaned back against the wall and stared at her through a cloud of smoke. "I saw Julia on the news yesterday."

Cal looked up. "No kidding? I gotta turn on the TV more."

Ellie pulled off the mask and set it on the desk. "She was dismissed from the lawsuit."

"Did you call her?"

"Of course. Her answering machine had a lovely tone. I think she's avoiding me."

Peanut took a step forward. The old oak floorboards, first hammered into place at the turn of the century when Bill Whipman had been the town's police chief, shuddered at the movement, but like everything in Rain Valley, they were sturdier than they appeared. The West End was a place where things—and people—were built to last. "You should try again."

"You know how jealous Julia is of me. She especially wouldn't want to talk to me now."

"You think everyone is jealous of you."

"I do not."

Peanut gave her one of those *Who-do-you-think-you're-fooling?* looks that were the cornerstone of friendship. "Come on, Ellie. Your baby sister looked like she was hurting. Are you going to pretend you can't talk to her because twenty years ago you were Homecoming Queen and she belonged to the Math club?"

In truth, Ellie had seen it, too—the haunted, hunted look in Julia's eyes—and she'd wanted to reach out and help her younger sister. Julia had always felt things too keenly; it was what made her a great psychiatrist. "She wouldn't listen to me, Peanut. You know that. She considers me only slightly smarter than a pet rock. Maybe—"

The sound of footsteps stopped her.

Someone was *running* toward their office.

Ellie got to her feet just as the door swung open, hitting the wall with a *crack*.

Lori Forman skidded into the room. She was soaking wet and obviously cold; her whole body was shaking. Her kids—Bailey, Felicia, and Jeremy—were clustered around her.

"You gotta come," Lori said to Ellie.

"Take a breath, Lori. Tell me what's happened."

"You won't believe me. Heck, I've seen it and I don't believe me. Come on. There's something on Magnolia Street."

"Yee-*ha*," Peanut said. "Something's actually happening in town." She reached for her coat on the coatrack beside her desk. "Hurry up, Cal. Forward the emergency calls to your cell phone. We don't want to miss all the excitement."

Ellie was the first one out the door.

TWO

ELLIE PULLED HER CRUISER INTO AN EMPTY PARKING SLOT ON THE corner of Magnolia and Woodland and killed the engine. It sputtered a few times, coughing like an old man, then fell silent.

The rain stopped at the same time, and sunlight peered through the clouds.

Even Ellie, who'd lived here all of her life, was awed by the sudden change of weather. It was Magic Hour, the moment in time when every leaf and blade of grass seemed separate, when sunlight, burnished by the rain and softened by the coming night, gave the world an impossibly beautiful glow.

In the passenger seat, Peanut leaned forward. The vinyl seat squeaked at the movement. "I don't see nothin'."

"Me, either." This from Cal, who sat perfectly erect in the backseat, his tall, lanky body folded into neat thirds. His long, bony fingers formed a steeple.

Ellie studied the town square. Clouds the color of old nails moved across the sky, trying to diffuse the fading light, but now that the sun was here, it wouldn't be pushed aside. Rain Valley—all five blocks of it—seemed to glow with an otherworldly light. Brick storefronts, built one after another in the halcyon salmon-and-timber days of the seventies, shone like hammered copper.

There was a crowd outside of Swain's drugstore, and another one across the street in front of Lulu's hair salon. No doubt the patrons of The Pour House would come stumbling out any second, demanding to know what everyone was looking at.

"You there, Chief?" came a voice over the radio.

Ellie flicked the button and answered, "I'm here, Earl."

"Come on down to the tree in Sealth Park." There was a bunch of static, then: "Move slow. I ain't kiddin'."

"You stay here, Peanut. You, too, Cal," Ellie said as she got out of the car. Her heart was beating quickly. This was the most exciting call she'd ever had. Mostly, her job consisted of driving home folks who'd drunk too much or talking to kids at the local school about the dangers of drugs. But she'd prepared herself for anything. That was a lesson she'd learned from her Uncle Joe, who'd been the town's police chief for three decades. *Don't take peace for granted*, he'd said to her often. *It can shatter like glass.*

She'd believed him, and so, even though she'd become a cop in a kind of lackadaisical way, she'd grown into the job. Now she read up on all the newest information, kept her skills honed at the shooting range, and watched over her town with a sharp eye. It was really the only thing she'd ever been good at, besides looking good, which she took just as seriously.

She moved down the street, noticing how quiet the town was.

She could have heard a pin drop. It was unnatural for a town chock full of gossips.

She unclasped her holster and reached for her weapon. It was the first time she'd ever drawn it in the field.

With each step, she heard her heels click on the pavement. On either side of the street the ditches were rivers of boiling silver water. As she neared the four-way stop, she could hear whispering and see people pointing toward Chief Sealth City Park.

"There she is," someone said.

"Chief Barton will know what to do."

At the corner, she paused. Earl came running at her, his cowboy boot heels sounding like gunfire on the slick pavement. He moved like a marionette on slack strings, kind of akimbo and disjointed. Rain streaked his uniform.

"Shhh," she hissed.

Earl Huff's face scrunched into a ruddy fist. At sixty-four, he'd been a cop before Ellie was born, but he never failed to show her the utmost respect. "Sorry, boss."

"What's going on?" Ellie asked. "I don't see a damn thing."

"She showed up about ten minutes ago. Right after that big thunder crack. Y'all hear it?"

"We heard it," Peanut said, her voice wheezy from moving so fast. Cal was beside Peanut.

Ellie spun around. "I told you both to stay in the cruiser."

"You *meant* it?" Peanut said incredulously. "I thought that was one of them 'for legal reasons' orders. Hell, Ellie, we're not gonna miss the first real call in years."

Cal nodded, grinning. It made her want to smack him. She wondered if the captain of the LAPD had similar problems with his friends. With a sigh, she turned back to Earl. "Talk to me."

"After the thunder crack, the rain stopped. Just like that. One minute it was pourin', and then it wasn't. Then that amazin' sun came out. That's when old Doc Fischer heard a wolf howl."

Peanut shivered. "It's like that time on *Buffy* when she—"

"Keep going, Earl," Ellie said sharply.

"It was Mrs. Grimm who noticed the girl. I was getting my hair cut—and don't say 'What hair?'" He turned slowly and pointed. "When she climbed up that there tree, we called you."

Ellie stared at the tree. She'd seen it every day of her life, had played in it as a kid, stood beside it to smoke bummed menthol cigarettes as a teenager, and gotten her first kiss—from Cal, no less—beneath its green canopy. She didn't see a damn thing out of the ordinary now. "Is this some kind of joke, Earl?"

"Holy Mother o' God. Put your glasses on, El."

Ellie reached into her breast pocket and retrieved the over-the-counter glasses she still didn't admit to needing. They felt alien and heavy on her face. Squinting through the oval lenses, she stepped forward. "Is that. . . ?"

"Yes," Peanut said.

There was a child hidden high in the autumn-colored leaves of the maple tree. How could anyone climb that high on rain-slicked branches?

"How do you know it's a girl?" Cal whispered to Earl.

"All's I know is it's wearing a dress and has long hair. I'm makin' one of them education guesses."

Ellie took a step forward to see better.

The child was little, probably no more than five or six. Even from this distance, Ellie could see how spindly and thin she was. Her long dark hair was a filthy mat, filled with leaves and debris. Tucked in her arms was a snarling puppy.

Ellie reholstered her gun. "Stay here." She started forward then stopped and glanced back at Peanut and Cal. "I mean it, you two. Don't make me shoot you."

"I'm glue," Peanut said.

"Superglue," Cal agreed.

Ellie could hear a flurry of whispering as she strode through the four-way stop. As she neared her destination, she took her glasses off. She hadn't come to the point where she trusted the world as seen through a lens.

About five feet from the tree she looked up. The child was still there, curled on an impossibly high branch. Definitely a girl. She appeared completely at ease on her perch, with the pup in her arms, but her eyes were wide. She was watching every move. The poor kid was terrified.

And damn if that wasn't a *wolf* pup in her arms.

"Hey, little one," Ellie said in a soothing voice. It was one of the many times she wished she'd had children. A mother's voice would be good right about now. "What are you doing up there?"

The wolf snarled and bared its teeth.

Ellie's gaze locked on the child's. "I won't hurt you. Honestly."

There was no response; not the flinch of an eyelash or the movement of a finger.

"Let's start over. I'm Ellen Barton. Who are you?"

Again, nothing.

"I'm guessing you're running away from something. Or maybe playing some game. When I was a girl, my sister and I used to play pirates in the woods. And Cinderella. That was my favorite because Julia had to clean the room while I put on pretty dresses for the ball. It's always best to be the older kid."

It was like talking to a photograph.

"Why don't you come on down from there before you fall? I'll make sure you're safe."

Ellie talked for another fifteen minutes or so, saying everything she could think of, then she just ran out of words. Not once had the girl responded or moved. Frankly, it didn't even appear that she was breathing.

Ellie walked back to Earl and Peanut and Cal.

"How we gonna get her down, Chief?" Earl asked, looking worried. His pale, sweaty forehead pleated into folds. He nervously smoothed his almost bald head, reemphasizing the red comb-over that had been his look for more years than anyone could count.

Ellie had no idea what to do. She had all kinds of manuals and reference books at the station, and she'd memorized most of them for her captain's test. There were chapters on murder, mayhem, robberies, and kidnapping, but there wasn't a damn paragraph devoted to getting a silent child and her snarling wolf pup out of a tree on Main Street. "Anyone see her climb up?"

"Mrs. Grimm. She said the kid was up to no good—maybe lookin' to steal apples from the barrels out front at the market. When Doc Fischer yelled at her, the girl ran across the street and jumped into the tree."

"Jumped?" Ellie said. "She's twenty feet in the air, for God's sake."

"I didn't believe it either, Chief, but several witnesses agreed. They say she ran like the wind, too. Mrs. Grimm crossed herself when she was tellin' me."

Ellie felt the start of a headache. By suppertime the whole town would have heard the story of a girl who ran like the wind and jumped into the uppermost limbs of a maple tree. No doubt by then they'd say she could shoot fire from her fingertips and fly from branch to branch.

"We need a plan," Ellie said, more to herself than anyone else.

"The volunteer fire department got Scamper outta that Doug fir on Peninsula Road."

"Scamper's a *cat*, Earl," Peanut said, crossing her arms.

"I think I know that, Penelope. It ain't like we got a protocol for kids stuck in trees. With *wolves*," he added for good measure.

Ellie touched the officer's arm. "It's a good idea, Earl, but she's terrified. If she sees that big red ladder coming at her, she might fall."

Peanut tapped her long, star-spangled purple fingernail against her teeth. A sure sign of deep thought. Finally, she said, "I'll bet she's hungry."

"You think everyone's hungry," Cal said.

"I do not."

"Do, too. How 'bout if I try talking to her, El?" Cal said. "My Sarah is about her age."

"No. Let *me* talk to her," Peanut said. "I'm a mom, after all."

"I'm a dad."

"Shut up, you two," Ellie snapped. "Earl, go to the diner and order me a nice hot meal. Some milk, too. Maybe a slice of Barbara's apple pie."

"You're a genius, Ellie. Mrs. Grimm thought the girl was tryin' to steal food," Earl said, grinning broadly. "I seen something like this on one of them cop shows. I think it was—"

"*I* was the one who mentioned it," Peanut said, puffing up.

"You always mention food," Cal said. "It's hardly noteworthy."

"And clear the streets," Ellie cut in before they started up again. "I want everyone gone for a two-block radius."

Earl's smile faded. "They won't wanna go."

"We're the law, Earl. Make them go home."

He looked at her sideways. They both knew he didn't have much experience with being the law. Although he'd patrolled these streets for decades, he'd spent most of that time going for coffee and handing out parking tickets. "Maybe I should call Myra. Everyone listens to her."

"You don't need your wife to clear the streets, Earl. If you have to, start writing tickets. You know how to do that."

Earl slumped in a hangdog way and headed for the hair salon. When he reached the drugstore, a crowd immediately formed around him. After a moment they groaned loudly.

Peanut crossed her arms and made a clucking sound. "This is the biggest thing to hit town since Raymond Weller drove his car into Thelma's R.V. You aren't going to be Miss Popular for making them miss it."

Ellie looked at her best friend. "Them?"

Peanut's eyes rounded in disbelief. "Surely you don't mean *me*, too?"

"We've got a terrified girl up there, Pea, and by the looks of it, something isn't right with her. Entertaining the folks of Rain Valley—you included—is hardly my first priority. Now you and Cal go back to the station and get me some kind of net. I don't imagine its going to be easy to catch that poor thing. Call Nick in Mystic. And Ted over on the res. See if a kid got lost in the park today. Cal, you call Mel. He's probably out by the park entrance, trying to ticket tourists. Tell him to start canvassing the town. She's not a local kid, but maybe she's staying with someone."

"I, for one, can follow orders," Cal said, heading for the cruiser.

Peanut didn't move.

"*Go,*" Ellie said again.

Peanut sighed dramatically. "I'm going."

. . .

AN HOUR AND A HALF LATER THE STREETS OF DOWNTOWN RAIN VALLEY were quiet. The shops had all been locked up, and the parking slots were empty. Just out of sight there were two police barricades set up. No doubt Peanut and Cal were having the time of their lives as the official voices of Police Chief Ellen Barton.

"I guess you're thinking it's sorta weird that a woman is the chief of police," Ellie said, sitting as still as she could on the uncomfortable iron and wooden bench beneath the maple tree. She'd been here for almost an hour and it was becoming obvious that she wouldn't be able to talk the kid down. It wasn't entirely surprising. Ellie could drive safely at one hundred miles per hour, shoot a bird from five hundred feet away, and make a grown man confess to burglary, but what she knew about children wouldn't fill a thimble.

But Peanut and Cal—who did know kids—both thought talking was the ticket. It was the "A" plan. They all agreed it would be best if the girl came down on her own. So Ellie talked.

She glanced down at the platter at the base of the tree. Two perfectly roasted chickens were surrounded by apple and orange slices. A freshly baked apple pie rested on a separate plate. There were several paper plates and forks set in a neat stack. The glass of milk had long since warmed.

It should have been kid food—cheeseburgers and fries and pizza. Why hadn't she thought of that before?

Still, it smelled heavenly. Ellie's stomach grumbled, reminding her that it was past dinnertime, and she wasn't accustomed to missing meals. If it weren't for daily aerobics classes at the local dance studio, she would certainly have packed on the pounds since high school. And Lord knew a woman of her petite stature couldn't afford to gain weight. Not when she was unmarried and looking for love.

She cocked her head ever so slightly to the left and looked up.

The girl stared back at her with an unsettling intensity. Eyes the color of a shallow Caribbean sea looked out from beneath a dark fringe of lashes. For a split second Ellie was reminded of her second honeymoon, when she'd first seen a tropical ocean and the hordes of small, dark-skinned children who played in the waves. Those children, as thin as they were, had been full of smiles and laughter.

She glanced across the street to the huge rhododendron in front of the hardware store. Behind it, she knew, a man from Animal Control had his rifle trained in this direction. It was loaded with a tranquilizer dart for the wolf pup. Behind him, a worker from the local game farm was ready with a muzzle and a cage.

Keep talking.

She sighed. "I didn't really set out to become a cop. I just sort of bumped into it; that's how life works for me. Now my sister, Julia, she's a planner. By the time she was ten years old she wanted to be a doctor. Me, I just wanted her Barbie collection." She smiled ruefully. "I was twenty-one the second time I got married. When that marriage tanked, I moved back in with my dad. That is not a high point for a girl who can legally drink . . . and boy, did I drink. Margaritas and karaoke were my life back then. I meant to try out for a band, but somehow I never did. Story of my life. Anyway, my Uncle Joe was the chief of police. He made a deal with me: if I'd go to the Police Academy, he'd ignore my parking tickets." She shrugged. "I had nothing better to do, so I went. When I got home, Uncle Joe hired me on. Turns out I was born for this job." She shot a glance at the girl.

No movement. Nothing.

Ellie's stomach grumbled loudly.

"Aw, hell." She reached down for the chicken and tore off a leg.

As she bit into it, she couldn't help closing her eyes for just a second. She chewed slowly, swallowed.

The leaves rustled. The branch creaked.

Ellie stilled. She felt a breeze move through the park; it scratched the drying leaves.

The girl leaned forward. The pink tip of her tongue showed between her lips. Ellie noticed that the girl was missing one front tooth.

"Come on," she whispered. When there was no movement, Ellie

tried different words, hoping for a connection. The stories and sentences weren't working. Maybe simpler was the answer. "Down. Here. Chicken. Pie. Dinner. Food."

At that, the girl dropped from the branch, landing like a cat, quietly and on all fours, with the pup still in her arms.

Impossible. The child's bones should have snapped like twigs on impact.

Ellie felt something in her gut tighten. She wasn't a fanciful or superstitious woman, but just now, sitting here on this bench, staring at this filthy, scrawny child with her silent white wolf pup, she felt a kind of awe.

The girl's gaze locked on her. Those beautiful, eerie blue-green eyes seemed to see everything.

Ellie didn't move, didn't even breathe.

The girl tilted her chin and sniffed the air, then slowly released her hold on the wolf, who stayed close beside her. She took a cautious step toward the chicken.

Then another.

And another.

Ellie released her breath as quietly as she could. The girl moved like a wild animal, sniffing, sensing. The wolf pup shadowed her every move.

Finally the girl broke eye contact and went for the food.

Ellie had never seen anything like it. The two looked more like litter mates over a kill than anything else. The girl kept tearing off chunks of chicken and stuffing them in her mouth.

Ellie reached slowly behind her and gathered up her net.

Please God. Let this work. She didn't have a clue what Plan B was.

In a perfect cheerleader turn, Ellie pulled out the net and tossed it toward the girl. It settled over the child and the wolf pup and hit the ground. When they realized they'd been caught, all hell broke loose.

The girl went crazy. She threw herself to the ground and rolled to get free, her grimy fingers clawing at the nylon net. The more she struggled to be free, the tighter she was bound.

The wolf pup snarled. When the red dart hissed into his side, he let out a surprised yelp, then staggered and fell over.

The girl howled. It was a terrible, harrowing sound.

"It's okay, honey," Ellie said, finally moving toward them. "Don't be afraid. He's not hurt. I'm going to send him to a nice, safe place."

The girl pulled the sleeping pup into her lap and stroked him furiously, trying to waken him. At her failure, she howled again, another desperate, keening wail of pain that cut through the quiet and sent a flock of crows into the darkening sky.

Ellie inched around behind the child. As she approached, she noticed the smell. Dying black leaves and fecund, overripe earth; beneath it all was the ammonia scent of urine.

She swallowed hard and let the hypodermic slip down from its hiding place in her sleeve. Carefully, she stabbed the girl's rump and gave her the injection.

The child screamed in pain and twisted around to face her.

"I'm sorry," Ellie said. "It's just protective custody. You'll go to sleep for a minute or two. I won't let anyone hurt you."

The girl scrambled backward to avoid Ellie's touch and lost her balance. Another wailing howl came up her throat and then she collapsed. Lying there, coiled around the unconscious pup, the girl looked impossibly frail and young, and more helpless than any person Ellie had ever seen.

In the last few moments of the climb, the pale Pacific sky began to slowly turn from burnished gold to the palest salmon hue.

He paused in his descent, breathing hard, and swung around, dangling from his rope and harness, to take in the view.

From his perch on the granite face, some four hundred vertical feet above the crystalline blue beauty of an unnamed alpine lake, Max Cerrasin could see the world. All around him were the jagged, imposing peaks of the Olympic Mountains. The breathtaking, awe-inspiring landscape felt as far from civilization as anywhere on Earth. For all he knew, he was the first person to climb this jutting, dangerous slab of rock.

That was what he loved about this sport. When you were high above the world, anchored to a bit of stone by a piece of metal and your own courage, there was no outside world. No worries, no stresses, no memories of what you'd lost.

There was only the extreme beauty, the solitude, and the risk. He loved that most of all: the risk.

There was nothing like imminent danger to make a man know he was alive.

Still breathing hard, sweating, he climbed down slowly, finding his way inch by inch, caressing the granite, feeling it for weaknesses and instability.

His foot missed once and he started to fall. The rock crumbled beneath his hand and skittered away, pelting his face.

In the split second that he was free, he felt his stomach clench and his heart kick into overdrive. He reached out, grabbed hold.

And found purchase.

He laughed in relief and rested his forehead on the cool stone as his heartbeat settled back down to normal.

Then he wiped sweat from his brow and kept moving downward. As he got closer to the ground, he moved faster, more sure of himself. He was almost there—less than thirty feet from safety—when his cell phone rang.

He dropped to the ground, fished his phone out of his pack, and flipped it open. He knew before he saw the number that it was an emergency.

NEWS OF THE GIRL'S APPEARANCE SPREAD THROUGH RAIN VALLEY LIKE a spring shower. By nine o'clock that evening crowds had formed outside of the county hospital. Cal was answering one phone call after another. He'd surprised Ellie by offering to work late. Usually he raced home to make dinner for his wife and kids. But by now the story being told was of a flying wolf girl with magical powers over the weather, and everyone wanted to be part of it. Tomorrow morning there would be lines at the Olympic Game Farm; everyone wanted to see the wolf pup they'd captured.

Inside the hospital, the girl lay in a narrow bed. There were several electrodes attached to her head and another pair that monitored the beating of her heart. A single leather restraint coiled around her left wrist and anchored her to the bed rail, although in her unconscious state she certainly posed no threat to herself or others. It was the first time the restraints had been used in ten years; nurses had spent forever in the storage room, trying to find them.

Ellie stood back from the bed, her arms crossed. Peanut was beside her. For once, her friend wasn't talking. They both felt badly about leaving Earl to handle the crowd outside and Cal to handle the phones, but they had to delegate. Ellie needed to talk to the doctor, and Peanut . . . well, Peanut did not intend to miss one iota of this drama. She'd left the station for only thirty minutes since the girl's appearance—and that was to drop off dinner at home. Her daughter, Tara, was babysitting for Cal.

Now, Dr. Max Cerrasin was examining the child. Every now and then he murmured something under his breath; other than that, no one spoke.

Ellie had never seen him so serious. In the six years he'd lived in Rain Valley, Max had gathered quite a reputation—and it wasn't only for his doctoring skills. Ellie still remembered when he'd moved to town. He'd taken over Doc Fischer's practice and settled into a piece of lakefront property on the edge of town. The single women had been all aflutter; every woman between twenty and sixty—Ellie included—had been drawn to him. They'd arrived at his front door in a steady, chattering stream, always bringing a casserole.

Then they'd waited impatiently for him to choose one of them.

And waited.

Over the years, he'd dated—plenty, in fact—and he'd made friends with almost all of the available women in town, but no one could really lay claim to him. Although he was an outrageous flirt, his attention was spread out evenly.

Even Ellie had failed to coax love from him. Their affair had been like all the others—white-hot and blink-and-you'll-miss-it brief. Lately he'd been seen going out less and less, becoming that strangest of animals in a small town: a loner. It made no sense at all to Ellie. All those good looks gone to waste.

"Well," he said at last, shoving a hand through his steel gray hair.

Ellie eased away from the wall and went to him. When she looked up into Max's blue eyes, she saw how tired he was. No wonder. She'd heard they'd found him on some rock face only a few hours ago. He'd come straight from the mountains, not even bothering to change into work clothes or put on his white coat. He wore an old, faded pair of Levi's and a black tee shirt. His curly gray hair was slightly damp and messy, but—as always—it was his eyes that demanded attention. They were an electric blue, and when he looked at you, there seemed to be no one else in the room. Even now, looking tired and confused, he was the best-looking man she'd ever seen.

"What can you tell me, Max?"

"She's seriously malnourished and dehydrated. The hydration we can take care of pretty quickly, but the malnourishment is serious." He lifted the child's unbound wrist; his fingers easily encircled it. Next to his tanned skin, her dirty flesh looked splotchy and gray.

Ellie flipped open her notepad. "Native American?"

"I don't think so. I'm pretty sure that under all this filth, she's Caucasian." He let go of the girl's wrist and moved down the bed. He gently lifted her right leg at the knee. "You see those scars on her ankle?"

Ellie leaned closer. Beneath the grime she saw it: a thick, discolored band of scar tissue. "Ligature marks."

"Almost certainly."

Peanut made a gasping sound. "The poor thing was *tied?*"

"For a long time, I'd say. The scarring is not new tissue, although the cuts around it are fairly recent. Her X rays show a broken left forearm that healed badly, too."

"So, we're not looking at some ordinary kid who wandered off from her family in the park and got lost."

"I don't think so."

"Any evidence of sexual trauma?"

"No. None."

"Thank God," Ellie whispered.

He shook his head, sighing quietly. "I saw a lot of bad shit in the inner city, El, but I never saw anything like this."

"What can you do for her?"

"This isn't my area of expertise."

"Come on, Max . . ."

He looked down at the girl. Ellie saw something in his eyes—a sadness; or maybe fear. You could never tell with Max. "I could run some tests—brain waves, blood samples, that kind of thing. If she were conscious, I could observe her, but—"

"The old day care center is empty," Peanut said. "You could watch her through the window."

"Right. Put her there, Max. She might try to escape, so keep the door locked. By morning I'm sure we'll know more. Mel and Earl are canvassing the town. They'll find out who she is. Or when she wakes up, she'll tell us."

Max turned to her. "We're in the deep end here, Ellie, and you know it. Maybe you should call in the big boys."

Ellie looked at him. "It's my pool, Max. I can handle one lost girl."

THREE

JULIA STOOD IN FRONT OF THE FULL-LENGTH MIRROR IN HER BED-room, studying herself with a critical eye. She wore a charcoal gray pantsuit and a pale pink silk blouse. Her blond hair was coiled back in a French twist; the way she always wore it when seeing patients. Not that she had a lot of patients left. The tragedy in Silverwood had cost her at least seventy percent of them. Thankfully there had been those who still trusted her, and she would never let them down.

She grabbed her briefcase and went down to her garage, where her steel blue Toyota Prius Hybrid waited. The garage door opened, revealing the empty street outside.

On this warm, brown October morning there were no reporters out there waiting for her, clustered together and yet apart, smoking cigarettes and talking.

She was no longer part of the story.

Finally, after a year of nightmares, she had her life back. It took her more than an hour to reach the small, beautiful Beverly Hills office building that she'd leased for more than seven years.

She parked in her spot and went inside, closing the door quietly behind her. On the second floor, she paused outside her office, looking at the sterling silver plaque on the door.

DR. JULIA CATES

She pressed the intercom button.

"Dr. Cates's office," came the scratchy-voiced reply through the speaker. "May I help you?"

"Hey, Gwen, it's me."

"Oh!"

There was a buzzing sound, then the door eased open with a click.

Julia took a deep breath and opened it. The office smelled of the fresh flowers that were delivered every Monday morning. Though there were fewer patients now, she'd never cut back on the flower order. It would have been a sign of defeat.

"Hello, Doctor," said Gwen Connelly, her receptionist. "Congratulations on yesterday."

"Thanks." She smiled. "Is Melissa here yet?"

"You have no appointments this week," Gwen said gently. The compassion in her brown eyes was unnerving. "They all cancelled."

"All of them? Even Marcus?"

"Did you see the *L.A. Times* today?"

"No. Why?"

Gwen pulled a newspaper out of the trash can and dropped it on the desk. The headline was DEAD WRONG. Beneath it was a photograph of Julia. "The Zunigas gave an interview after the hearing. They blamed you for all of it."

Julia reached out for the wall to steady herself.

"I'm sure they're just trying to get out from under the lawsuit. They said . . . you should have committed their daughter."

"Oh." The word slipped out on a breath.

Gwen stood up and came around the desk. She was a small, compact woman who had run this office as she'd run her home, with discipline and caring. Moving forward, she opened her arms. "You helped a lot of people. No one can take that from you."

Julia sidestepped quickly. If she were touched right now, she'd fall apart. She might never put all the pieces back together.

Gwen stopped. "It's not your fault."

"Thank you. I . . . guess I'll take a vacation." She tried to smile. It felt heavy and wooden on her face. "I haven't gone anywhere in years."

"It'd be good for you."

"Yes."

"I'll cancel the flowers and call the building manager," Gwen said. "Let him know you'll be gone for . . . a while."

I'll cancel the flowers.

Funny how that, of all of it, broke the skin. Julia held on to her composure by the thinnest strand as she moved Gwen toward the door and said good-bye.

Then, alone in the office, she sank to her knees on the expensive carpeting and bowed her head.

She wasn't sure how long she knelt there in the darkness, listening to the strains of her own breathing and the beat of her heart.

Finally, she awkwardly got to her feet and looked around, wondering what she would do next. This practice was the very heart of her. In her pursuit of professional excellence, she'd put everything else on the back burner—friends, family, hobbies. She hadn't even had a date in almost a year. Not since Philip, in fact. She went to her phone and stood there, staring down at the speed dial list.

Dr. Philip Westover was still number seven. She felt an ache of need, a bone-deep desire to hear his voice, hear him say *It'll be okay, Julia,* in that lilting brogue of his. For five years he'd been her best friend and her lover. Now he was another woman's husband.

That was the thing about love—it was unreliable.

With a sigh, she pushed the number two button.

Her therapist, Dr. Harold Collins, answered on the second ring. She'd been seeing him once a month since her residency, when it had been required of all psychiatric students. In truth, he'd been more of a friend than a doctor.

"Hey, Harry," she said, leaning tiredly against the wall. "Did you see this morning's paper?"

He sighed heavily. "Julia. I've been worried about you."

"I'm worried about myself."

"You need to start giving interviews, tell your side of the story. It's ridiculous to shoulder the whole blame for this thing. We all think—"

"What's the point? They'll believe what they want to, anyway. You know that."

"Sometimes fighting is the point, Julia."

"I've never been good at that, Harry." She stared out the window at the bright blue-skied day and wondered what she would do now. They talked for a while longer, but in truth, Julia wasn't listening. Treating patients was all she had; all she was good at. She should have built herself a life instead of just a career. If she had, she wouldn't be alone now. And talking about her emptiness wouldn't help. She'd been wrong to reach out. "I better go, Harry. Thanks for everything."

"Julia—"

She hung up the phone and walked around her office. When she felt tears gathering, she stripped out of her suit and put on her workout clothes, then headed to the treadmill she kept in the next room.

She knew she'd been on it too much lately, that she'd lost so much weight she was down to nothing, but she couldn't seem to stop.

Staring into the murky darkness of her beloved office, she stepped on the black pad and set the incline button for hills. When she was running, she almost forgot her pain. It wasn't until much later, when she'd turned the machine off and driven back to her too quiet home, that she thought about what it meant to run and run and have nowhere to go.

IN THESE LATE EVENING HOURS THE HALLS OF THE COUNTY HOSPITAL were quiet. It was Max's least favorite time; he preferred the hustle and bustle of daily emergencies. There were too many thoughts that waited for him in the shadowy quiet.

He made a few last notes on the girl's chart, then looked down at her.

She lay perfectly still, breathing in the deep, even way of sedated sleep. On her left wrist, the brown leather restraint looked obscenely heavy and ugly.

He reached down for her free hand, picked it up and held it. Her fingers, clean now but still stained by blood and lined with scars, were thin and tiny against his palm. "Who are you, little one?"

Behind him the door opened and closed. He knew without looking that it was Trudi Hightower, the charge nurse of the swing shift. He could smell her perfume—gardenias.

"How is she?" Trudi asked, coming up close to him. She was a tall, good-looking woman with kind eyes and a loud voice. She claimed that the voice had come from raising three boys on her own.

"Not good."

She made a tsking sound. "The poor thing."

"Are we ready to move her?"

"The old day care center is all set up." She reached down and un-hooked the restraint. When she lifted the heavy strap, Max touched her wrist.

"Leave it here," he said.

"But—"

"I think she's been bound enough in her life."

He bent down and scooped the sleeping child up in his arms.

In silence, they walked down the brightly lit hallways to the old day care center.

There, he tucked the girl into the hospital bed they'd moved into the room. At the last second he had to stop himself from whispering, *Sleep tight, kiddo.*

"I'll stay with her awhile," he said instead.

Trudi touched his forearm gently. "I'm off in forty minutes," she said. "You want to come over to the house?"

He nodded. God knew he could use a distraction. Tonight, if he went home alone, the memories would be there, waiting to keep him company.

ELLIE STARED AT THE COMPUTER SCREEN UNTIL THE LETTERS BLURRED into little black blobs on a field of throbbing white. A headache opened its parachute at the back of her skull and floated down her spine. If she read one more report of a missing or abducted child, she was going to scream.

There were thousands of them.

Thousands.

Lost girls who had no voice to cry for help, no way to reach out. The few who were lucky enough to be alive somewhere were counting on professionals to find and save them.

Ellie closed her eyes. There had to be more she could do, but what? She'd already done everything she could think of. She and the town's other two officers had canvassed the streets. They'd notified the county sheriff's office that an unidentified child had been found. They'd also contacted the Family Crisis Network and Rural Resources, as well as every state and national agency. No one knew who the kid was, and it was becoming increasingly clear that this was Rain Valley's case. Her case. Other law enforcement and social agencies might be called upon to help, but the child had shown up in this town, and that made identifying the girl her job. The county sheriff had backed away so fast he'd practically left skid marks. His *Sorry, she's on city property* told Ellie plenty. No one would take responsibility for this girl until a positive ID was made.

She pushed away from the desk and got to her feet. Arching her back, she kneaded her aching neck.

She stepped over her sleeping dogs and went to the porch, looking out across her backyard. It was almost dawn. Here, on the edge of the rain forest, the world was both utterly still and deeply alive. As always, there was moisture everywhere; wet air blew in from the ocean and left millions of dew beads on the leaves. Come dawn, those drops would fall soundlessly to the ground. Invisible rain, her dad had called it, and Ellie always listened for it, if only to remember him.

"I wish you were here, Dad," she said, slipping her feet into the fleece-lined clogs by the back door. "You and Uncle Joe always knew how to run with the big dogs."

She crossed the porch and went down the back steps, then through the pink and violet morning toward the river. Mist coiled around her feet, rose up from the dark grass in vapors.

She was at the very edge of her property, standing by her dad's favorite Fall River fishing hole, when she realized why she was here.

His house was on the other side of the river and across a marshy field. From this distance it looked no bigger than a toolshed, but she knew better.

As a kid she'd hiked through this field every day and played in that yard.

For a minute she almost started for it. She had the idea to toss stones at his window again and call out to him. He would listen to her fears and understand them. He always had.

But those days were more than two decades old. Lisa certainly didn't want to be wakened at dawn by the sound of stones hitting her bedroom window, and though Cal would answer and sit outside with her (she was his boss; not just his friend), he wouldn't really be listening. He had his own life now, his own wife and children, and even though everyone knew that Lisa wasn't good enough for him, he loved his family.

Ellie knew she was on her own. She turned and went back to her house. With a tired sigh she sat back down at her desk and pulled up the missing children reports. The answer had to be in here. It *had* to be.

It was her last thought before falling asleep.

She was wakened by a car horn. She came awake with a start, realizing all at once that she'd fallen asleep at her computer.

"Shit."

She stumbled to her feet and went to the front door.

Peanut stood in the yard, waving good-bye to her husband as he drove away.

Ellie looked down at her watch. It was 7:55 in the morning. "What in the hell are you doing here?" she said in a voice that sounded like she smoked a pack a day.

"I heard you tell Max you'd meet him at eight at the hospital. You're going to be late."

"I didn't invite you to join us."

"I figured it was an oversight. Now hustle your ass."

Ellie fished the car keys out of her pocket and tossed them to Peanut, then went back into the house. There was no time to shower and no reason to change her clothes since she was still in her uniform. So she brushed her teeth, took off last night's makeup, and put on some new layers. In the kitchen, she took out a package of pork chops—of course there were two of them; no wonder she had to spend so much time exercising. Life came in twin packs. It wasn't exactly a help to the single woman. She put the package on a paper towel in the refrigerator to thaw.

It was eight on the dot when she got into her cruiser.

Peanut had turned the stereo on and put in an Aerosmith CD.

Ellie snapped off the music. "It's too early for that."

"You were up all night?"

"How can you tell?"

"You have a keyboard imprint on your cheek."

Ellie touched her cheek. "Shit. Is it noticeable?"

"Honey, you could see it from space." Peanut laughed, then sobered. "Did you find anything useful?"

"I was online all night, and called every precinct in five counties. No one has reported a missing girl in the area. Not lately, anyway. If we have to go national in the search, it means going through the files of *all* the girls reported missing in the past few years."

At the thought of that, they both fell silent. Ellie was trying to think of something ordinary to say when she turned into the hospital's parking lot and saw the crowd gathered at the front door.

"Damn it. They're turning this into a circus." Ellie parked in a visi-

tor's spot, grabbed her notebook, and got out of the car. Peanut followed in an uncharacteristic silence.

Like geese, the crowd surged into formation and flew at her. The
Grimm sisters—Daisy, Marigold, and Violet—led the charge.

As identical as prongs on a fork, the three old ladies matched each
other step for step.

Daisy, the eldest, was the first to speak. As always, she clutched an
old black urn that held her late husband's ashes. "We've come for word
of the child."

"Who is the poor dear?" Violet demanded, squinting up through
scratched glasses.

"Can she truly fly like a bird?" Marigold asked.

"Or jump like a cat?" This came from someone in the back.

Ellie had to remind herself that these people were her constituents.
More than that, they were her friends and neighbors. "We don't have
any answers yet. I'll let you all know when we do. For now, I could use
your help."

"Anything," Marigold said, pulling a flower-spangled notebook out
of her purple vinyl handbag.

Violet offered her sister a tulip pen.

"The child will need clothes and such. Maybe a stuffed animal or
two to keep her company," Ellie said. Before she'd even finished, the
Grimm sisters had taken over. The three ex-teachers corralled the
group and started delegating tasks.

Ellie and Peanut left the crowd. Together, they walked up the concrete path to the hospital's glass doors. The sliders whooshed open.

"Hey, Ellie," said the receptionist at their approach. "Dr. Cerrasin
is waiting for you at the old day care center."

"Thanks," Ellie said.

She and Peanut didn't speak as they walked down the hallway and
into the elevator. On the second floor, they went past the X-ray room
and turned left.

The last room on the right had once been a day care center for employees. It had been designated and designed years ago, when the city

coffers were full. In the time since the spotted owl and the dwindling salmon runs and the protection of old growth forests, those accounts had grown too thin to support luxuries like day care. The room had been empty and unmanned for more than two years.

Max stood in the hallway with his arms crossed. Fluorescent lighting tangled in his hair and made his ever-present tan look faded. She hadn't seen him look this bad since the time he fell forty feet down some mountain. Then, he'd had two black eyes and a split lip.

At their approach, he looked up and waved, but didn't bother smiling. He moved sideways to make room for them at the window.

The room beyond was small and rectangular, with red and yellow color-blocked walls and cubbyholes full of toys and games and books. A sink and counter took up one corner, used years ago, no doubt, for art projects and daily clean up. Several small tables surrounded by even smaller chairs filled the center of the room. Along the left wall were a single hospital bed and several empty cribs. There were two windows in the room. The one in front of them and a second, smaller one which overlooked the rear parking lot. To their left, a locked metal door was the only entrance.

Ellie sidled close, letting her shoulder touch his arm. "Talk to me, Max."

"Last night, after we finished the testing, we diapered her and tucked her into the bed. This morning when she woke up, she went crazy. There's no other word for it: crazy. Screaming, shrieking, throwing herself to the floor. She broke every lamp and smashed the mirror over the sink. When we tried to give her another injection, she bit Carol Rense hard enough to draw blood, then hid under the bed. She's been there almost an hour. Do you have an ID on her yet?"

Ellie shook her head, then turned to Peanut. "Why don't you go to the cafeteria? Get kid food for her."

"Sure, send the fat girl for food." Peanut sighed dramatically, but couldn't help smiling. She loved to be a part of things.

When she'd gone, Max said to Ellie, "I don't know what to tell you, Ellie. I've never seen a case like this."

"Tell me what you do know."

"Well . . . I think she's probably about six years old."

"But she's so small."

"Malnourished. Plus, she's had no dental or medical care, and her body is pretty scarred up."

"Scarred?"

"Little things mostly, although there's one that looks more serious. On her left shoulder. Maybe an old knife wound."

"Jesus."

"I drew blood and swabbed her mouth for DNA. If it were up to me, she'd still be sedated for hydration, but you wanted a diagnosis. . . ."

"Has she spoken?"

"No, but her vocal cords look unimpaired. I'd say—and this is just a guess—that she is physically able to speak, but I can't tell if she knows how."

"She doesn't know *how* to speak? What are you saying?"

"All I know is that her screams are unintelligible. I recorded it. There were no recognizable words. Her brain waves show no anomalies. She could well be deaf or mentally challenged or severely developmentally delayed or autistic. I can't be sure. I'm not even sure I know what tests to run for her mental state."

"What should we do?"

"Find out who she is."

"Gee, thanks. I meant right now."

He nodded toward Peanut, who was coming toward them with a tray of food. "That's a good start."

Ellie looked down at what Pea had chosen: a stack of pancakes, a pair of fried eggs, a waffle with strawberries and whipped cream, and a glass of milk. It made Ellie hungry.

Max said, "I'll get an orderly to crawl under the bed and get her—"

"Just leave it on the table," Peanut said. "She might be odd, but she's a kid. They do things in their own way and their own time. Hell, you can't make a two-year-old eat and they're tiny."

Ellie smiled at her friend. "Any other advice?"

"No more strangers. She knows you, so you should take the food in. Talk to her in a soothing voice, but don't stay. Maybe she wants to be alone to eat."

"Thanks." Taking the tray, Ellie went into the brightly painted room. The metal door clicked shut behind her. "Hey, little one. It's me again. I hope you don't hold that whole net thing against me." She moved cautiously forward and set the tray on one of the tables. At the movement, the keys on her belt jingled; she clamped her hand over them. "I thought you might be hungry."

Under the bed, the girl made a growling sound. It made the hairs on the back of Ellie's neck stand up. She tried to think of just the right thing to say, but nothing came to her, so she backed out of the room and closed the door behind her. The lock clicked loudly into place.

In the hall again, Ellie stood by Max at the window. "Will she eat it?"

He opened the girl's chart and got out his pen. "I guess we'll find out."

In silence, they stood there, looking through the glass at the room that appeared empty.

Several minutes later a tiny hand came out from underneath the bed.

Peanut gasped. "Lookee there."

More time passed.

Finally, a dark head appeared. Slowly, the child crawled out from her hiding place on all fours. When she looked up at the glass and saw them standing there, her nostrils flared.

Then she dashed to the table, where she froze again and bent low over the food, sniffing it suspiciously. She threw the whipped cream to the floor, then ate the pancakes and the eggs. She didn't seem to know what to make of the waffles and syrup. Ignoring both, she grabbed the strawberries and took them back to her hiding place under the bed. The whole incident took less than a minute.

"And I thought my kids had bad table manners," Peanut said. "She eats like a wild animal."

"We need a specialist," Max said quietly.

"I've contacted the authorities," Ellie answered. "The state, the FBI, and the Center for Missing and Exploited Children. They all need an identity or a crime to get in the action. I don't know how to find out her identity if she won't talk."

"Not that kind of specialist. She needs a psychiatrist."

Peanut drew in a sharp breath. "I can't believe we didn't think of it. She'd be perfect."

Max frowned. "Who?"

Ellie looked at Peanut. "She'd never do it. Her clients pay two hundred an hour."

"That was before. She can't have many patients left."

"God knows she's qualified for this," Ellie said.

"Who in the hell are you two talking about?" Max asked.

Ellie finally looked at him. "My sister is Julia Cates."

"The shrink who—"

"Yeah. That one." She turned to Peanut. "Let's go. I'll call her from the office."

IN THE PAST TWELVE HOURS JULIA HAD BEGUN AT LEAST A DOZEN PROJ-ects. She'd tried organizing her closet, rearranging her furniture, scrubbing her refrigerator, and deep cleaning her bathrooms. She'd also gone to the nursery to buy autumn plants and to Home Depot for deck stain and paint stripper. It was a good time to do all of the projects she'd been putting off for . . . ten years.

The problem was her hands.

She was fine when she started a project; more than fine. She was optimistic. Unfortunately, her optimism was as thin as an eggshell. All it took was a thought (it's time for Joe's appointment, or—worse yet—Amber's) and her hands would start to shake; she'd feel herself go cold. No temperature setting was high enough to keep her warm. Late last night, in the deepest hour of darkness, when the traffic behind her condo had dwindled to a drone as faded as a single mosquito's flight and the mighty Pacific Ocean out front had whooshed steadily toward the golden sand, she'd even tried to write a book.

Why not?

Every pseudofamous person went that route these days. And she wanted to tell her side of the story; maybe she even needed to. She'd slipped out of her comfortable queen-sized bed and dressed in fleece sweats and Ugg boots, then gone out onto her small deck. From her place on the sixth floor, the midnight blue ocean lay before her, always in motion. Moonlight cut the sea in half, tangled in the foamy surf.

Hours she'd sat there, her booted feet propped on the deck rail, her yellow pad in her lap, her pen in her hand. By midnight she was sur-rounded by balled-up yellow wads of paper. All any of them said were: *I'm sorry.*

Somewhere around four o'clock she fell into a fitful, nightmare-ridden sleep.

The phone wakened her.

Julia heard it as if from far away. She blinked her gritty eyes and sat up, realizing that she'd fallen asleep out on her deck. Wiping her face with one hand, she eased out of the chair and stepped over the piles of balled-up paper.

At the phone, she stopped.

The answering machine clicked on and she heard her own voice say cheerily: "You've reached Dr. Julia Cates. If this is a medical emer-gency, hang up and call 911. If not, please leave a message, and I'll get back to you as soon as I can. Thanks and good-bye."

There was a long beep.

Julia tensed. In the last months, most of her calls had come from reporters and victims' families and straight-out kooks.

"Hey, Jules, it's me. Your big sis. It's important."

Julia picked up the phone. "Hey, El."

There was an awkward pause, but wasn't that always the way it was between them? Though they were sisters, they were four years apart in age and light-years apart in personality. Everything about Ellie was larger than life—her voice, her personality, her passions. Julia always felt colorless beside her flamboyant Miss Popular sister. "Are you okay?" Ellie finally asked.

"Fine, thanks."

"You got released from the lawsuit. That's a good thing."

"Yeah."

There was another awkward pause, and then Julia said, "Thanks for calling, but—"

"Look, I need a favor."

"A favor?"

"There's a . . . situation up here. You could really help us out."

"You don't have to do it anymore, Ellie. I'm fine."

"Do what?"

"Try to save me. I'm a big girl now."

"I never tried to save you."

"Yeah, right. How about when you got Tod Eldred's little brother to ask me to the prom? Or when you brought all of your popular friends to my sixteenth birthday party?"

"Oh. That. Mom made me do all that stuff."

"Do you think I don't know that? None of your friends even talked to me at the party. And don't get me wrong: I appreciated it. Then and now. But it's not necessary. I'll be fine."

"I thought you said you *were* fine."

Julia was surprised by the perceptiveness of her sister's question. "Don't worry about me, El. Really."

"For a shrink, you're a shitty listener. I'm telling you I need you in Rain Valley. Specifically, I need a child psychiatrist."

"You're older than I usually take."

"Very funny. Will you fly up here? And I mean right now." There was a pause, a rustling of paper on the other end of the line. "Alaska has a flight in two hours. Another one in three. I can have a ticket waiting for you."

Julia frowned. This didn't sound like the ordinary super-sister-saving-loser-sister scenario that had set like concrete in their school years. "Tell me what's going on."

"There isn't time. I want you to catch the ten-fifteen flight. Will you trust me?"

Julia glanced out the huge floor-to-ceiling windows and tried to focus on the blue Pacific Ocean, but all she could really see were the yellow balls of paper that cluttered the deck floor.

"Jules? Please?"

"Why not?" Julia finally said.

She had nothing better to do.

FOUR

JULIA HADN'T BEEN BACK TO RAIN VALLEY IN YEARS, AND NOW SHE was returning on the wave of failure.

Perhaps she should have stayed in L.A. after all. There, she would have disappeared. Here, she would always be the other Cates girl. (*You know . . . the weird one . . .*) When a girl grew up in the shadow of the Homecoming Queen, there were two possible choices: disappear or make your own reputation. Unfortunately, when you were the tall, scarecrow-thin bookworm in a beloved, gregarious, larger-than-life family, there was no way to do either. From early on, she'd been the square peg, the kid who mediated every playground dispute but never joined in any of the games. The last kid picked for every sport; the girl at home, reading, during the senior prom. She was—or had been—that rarest of birds in a small, blue-collar town: a loner.

Only her mother had believed in a bright future for Julia. In fact, she'd encouraged her daughter to dream big. Unfortunately, her mother hadn't lived to see Julia's med school graduation. That loss had always been a sliver under Julia's skin, a phantom pain that came and went. The closer she got to Rain Valley, the more it was likely to hurt.

She stared out the plane's small window. Everything was gray, as if a cloud artist had painted the merest of washes over the green landscape. It made her feel lonely, all that gray; as if she, too, might disappear again in the Washington mist. The four white-capped volcanoes that stretched from northern Oregon to Bellingham looked like the spine of some mythic, sleeping beast. She heard the passenger behind her draw in a sharp breath and murmur, "Look, Fred, at that . . . is it Rainier?"

Suddenly she was thinking about the Zunigas and those lost children. *Dead wrong.* It didn't surprise her. In the past year, everything, every thought and deed, led her back to regret.

Don't think about that.

She closed her eyes and concentrated on her breathing until the emotions subsided. By the time the plane landed she was okay again.

She grabbed her bag from the overhead bin and merged into the line of passengers exiting the plane.

She was almost to the exit door when it happened.

One of the flight attendants recognized her. There was no mistaking the signs—the widening of the eyes, the slowly opening mouth. As Julia passed, she heard the woman whisper, "It's *her*. That doctor. The one who—"

She kept moving. By the end of the jetway she was almost running. She caught a glimpse of Ellie standing amid the crowd, dressed in her blue uniform, looking stunningly beautiful.

Julia knew she should stop, say hello and pretend everything was all right. That was the smart thing to do. The *fine* thing.

She kept moving, running.

She raced across the crowded concourse hallway toward the ladies' restroom sign. Ducking in, she disappeared into one of the stalls and slammed the door shut, then sat down on the toilet.

Calm down, Jules. Breathe.

"Are you in here, Julia?" Ellie sounded out of breath and irritated.

Julia released a slow, shaking breath. Having a panic attack was bad; having one in front of her sister was almost unbearable. She got slowly to her feet and opened the door. "I'm here."

Ellie put her hands on her hips and stared at her. It was a cop-assessing-the-situation look. "I haven't seen an airport sprint like that since the O.J. commercials."

"I had to go to the bathroom."

"You should see a urologist."

"It's not that. I . . ." Julia felt like an idiot. "The flight attendant recognized me. She looked at me as if *I* killed those kids." She felt her cheeks heat up, knowing she should say more. Explain. But her sister couldn't understand a thing like this. Ellie was like one of those pioneer wives who could give birth in the field and go back to work. Her sister knew little about being fragile.

Ellie's hard look softened. "Fuck 'em all. You can't let it get to you."

Julia wished she could do that, but she'd always needed to be accepted. As a shrink, she knew the hows and whys of her need—how her popular, in-the-spotlight family had somehow made her feel marginalized and unimportant, how her father's withheld love had made her believe she was unlovable—but knowledge didn't soften the need. She wasn't even sure how it had come to matter so much. All she knew was that her profession, her ability to help people, had filled the frightened place inside of her with joy, and now she was scared again. "It's not that easy for me. You can't understand."

Ellie leaned against the pale green tile wall. "Because you think I'm only slightly smarter than an earthworm or because I have nothing in my life worth losing?"

Julia wished suddenly that she had a better memory reservoir. Surely there were times when they'd played together, she and Ellie, when they'd counted secrets instead of slights, when laughter had followed their conversations instead of awkward pauses. But if all that had happened, Julia didn't recall it. What she remembered was being the "smart" sister, the "weird" one who grew too tall in a petite family and wanted things no one else understood. The mushroom in a family of orchids. She'd always been able to say the right things to strangers, but the wrong thing to her sister. She sighed. "Let's not do this, El."

"You're right. Come on."

Before Julia could answer, Ellie headed out of the bathroom. Julia had no choice but to follow.

At the car—an ugly white Suburban with wood-grain door panels— Ellie stopped at the back door just long enough to toss her purse in, then she strode around to the driver's side.

Julia struggled with her suitcase. It took her two tries to stow it. She slammed the back door shut, then went to the passenger side and climbed into the front seat.

Ellie backed the car out of the stall and headed for the exit. The minute the engine roared to life, the stereo came on. Some guy with a twangy voice was singing about the pocket of a clown.

Neither one of them said anything. As the landscape changed, going from city gray to country green, Julia began to feel like an idiot for sparring with her sister. How was it that, even after all these distant and separate years, they immediately fell into their childhood roles? One look at each other and they were adolescents again.

They were *family*, as specious as that connection sometimes felt, and they ought to be able to get along. Besides, she was a psychiatrist, for God's sake, a specialist in interpersonal dynamics, and here she was acting like the younger sister who wasn't invited to play with the big kids.

"Why don't you tell me why I'm here," she finally said.

"I'll tell you at the house. I have a lot of photographs to show you. I'm afraid you won't believe me otherwise."

Julia glanced at her. "So it *is* a rescue mission. There's no real reason I'm here."

"Oh, there's a reason. We have a little girl who needs help. But it's . . . complicated."

Julia didn't know if she believed that, but she knew that Ellie did things in her own way and in her own time. There was no point in asking further questions. The better course of action was a neutral topic. Small talk. "How's your friend Penelope?"

"She's good. Raising teenagers is killing her, though." Ellie immediately winced, as if realizing she shouldn't have paired teenager and killing in the same sentence. "Sorry."

"Don't sweat it, El. Teenagers are difficult. How old are they?"

"A fourteen-year-old boy and a sixteen-year-old girl."

"Tough ages."

Ellie smiled. "The girl—Tara—keeps wanting to pierce body parts and get tattoos. It's making Pea's husband insane."

"And Penelope? How's she handling it?"

"Great. Well . . . unless you consider her weight gain. In the past year, she's gone on every diet known to man. Last week she started smoking. She says it's how the stars do it."

"That and throwing up," Julia said.

Ellie nodded. "How's Philip?"

Julia was surprised by the swift pain that came with his name. If only she could say: *He stopped loving me.* Maybe Ellie could get her to laugh about her broken heart. As a shrink, she knew it would be a good move, that kind of honesty. It might open a door that had been closed for most of their lives. Instead, she said, "We broke up last year. I'm too busy—I mean, I *was* too busy—for love."

Ellie laughed at that. "Too busy for love. Are you crazy?"

For the next two hours they alternated between meaningless conversation and meaningful silences. Julia worked hard to find questions that brought them together and stayed away from answers that caused separation. They barely mentioned their father, and stayed away from memories of Mom.

They came to the Rain Valley exit and turned off the highway. On the long, winding forest road that led to childhood, Julia found herself tensing up. Here, amidst the towering trees, she started to feel small again. Insignificant.

"I was going to sell the place, move closer to town, but every time I get close to listing it, I find another repair that needs to be done,"

Ellie said on the way out of town. "I don't need a shrink to tell me I'm afraid to leave it."

"It's just a house, El."

"I guess that's how we're different, Jules. To you, it's three bedrooms, two baths, and a kitchen-dining-living room. To me, it's the best childhood ever. It's where I caught dragonflies in a glass jar and let my little sister braid my hair with flowers." Her voice dropped a little. She gave Julia a meaningful look, then turned onto their driveway. "It's where my parents loved each other for almost three decades."

Julia wouldn't let herself disagree with that, although they both knew it was a lie. A fable. "So, quit threatening to sell it. Admit that it's where you want to be. Hand the memories down to your own kids."

"As you may have noticed, I don't have kids. But thanks for pointing it out." Ellie drove into the yard and stopped hard. "We're here."

Julia realized she had said the wrong thing again. "You don't need a husband, you know. Especially not the kind *you* pick," she said. "You can have a baby on your own."

Ellie turned to look at her. "That might be how it is in the big city, but not here, and not for me. I want it all—the husband, the baby, the golden retriever." She smiled. "Actually, I've got the dogs. And I'd appreciate it if you didn't mention my husbands again."

Julia nodded. Time to change the subject. "So, how are Jake and Elwood? Still go straight for a girl's crotch?"

"They're males, aren't they?" Ellie smiled and Julia was struck by how beautiful her sister still was. Though Ellie was thirty-nine years old, there wasn't a line around her eyes or a pleating of skin around her mouth. Those startling green eyes shone against the milky purity of her skin. She had strong cheekbones and full, sensuous lips. Even her small-town, poorly layered haircut couldn't dim her beauty. She was petite and surprisingly curvy, with a smile like a halogen spotlight. No wonder everyone loved her.

"Come on." Ellie got out of the Suburban and slammed the door shut behind her.

Julia meant to move. Instead she sat there, looking through the dirty windshield at the house in which she'd grown up. The late afternoon sunlight made everything appear golden and impossibly softened except for the fringe of dark green trees.

This was only the second time she'd been back since her mother's funeral; then, she'd stayed only as long as she absolutely had to. Medical school had provided an excellent excuse. She'd said *I have to get back for tests*, and no one questioned her. In retrospect, she should have stayed. That time might have built a bridge between her and her sister, given them a common ground. As it was, however, the opposite had occurred. They had moved through the shoulder-to-shoulder crowd separately. No one in Rain Valley had known what to say to Julia in good times; in bad, they were even more confused. All they'd said over and over again was how proud her mother had been of Julia's education. By the third mention of it, Julia couldn't stop crying. It hadn't helped to see how much comfort Ellie got from her friends, while she had stood alone all night, waiting for her father's attention to turn her way. Of course, she'd been disappointed. He'd been the star that night, the widower laid low by grief. Everyone held him, kissed his cheek, and promised that Brenda was in a better place. Only Julia seemed to see the lie in all of it, the act. When at last her father broke down and wept, everyone except Julia rushed to comfort him. She had seen even as a child what no one else, especially Ellie, ever had: that her father's selfishness had crushed his wife's spirit, just as he'd crushed his younger daughter's. Only Ellie had flourished in the white-hot light of her father's self-absorption.

Julia reached for the door handle and wrenched it hard, then stepped down. Everything was exactly as it should be in October. Maple trees were dropping their leaves, creating that autumn song that was as familiar to her as the rushing whisper of the nearby river. She heard her mother's voice in that sound, in the falling leaves and crackling twigs and whispering wind. Softly, she whispered, "Hey, Mom." Part of her even waited for a reply. But there was only the chattering of the river and the breeze through the leaves.

She followed Ellie across the marshy lawn toward the house.

In the glorious light, the old house appeared to be made of ham-

mered strips of silver. The grayed clapboards shone with a hundred secret colors. White trim, peeled in places to reveal patches of wood,
outlined the windows and doors. Rhododendrons the size of house
trailers dotted the yard.

Ellie opened the door and led the way inside.

Everything looked as it always had. The same slip-covered
furniture—pale beige with pink cabbage roses and faded green
leaves—graced the living room. Pine antiques were everywhere—an
armoire that was probably still filled with Grandma Whittaker's doilies
and table linens, a dining table scarred by three generations of Cateses
and Whittakers, a credenza that was decorated with dusty silk flowers
in ceramic vases. French doors flanked a river-rock fireplace; through
the silvery glass panes, a ghostly ribbon of river shone in the sunlight.
Ellie hadn't changed a thing. It wasn't surprising. In Rain Valley things
and people either belonged or they didn't. If they belonged, they were
loved and kept forever.

Ellie shut the door. Just as she said, "Brace yourself," two full-grown
golden retrievers came thundering down the stairs. At the bottom, on
the slick wooden floors, they skidded together and slid sideways, then
found their footing. They barreled across the room and hit Julia like
the Seahawks' front line.

"Jake! Elwood! *Down*," Ellie yelled in her best police voice.

The dogs were clearly deaf.

Julia gave them a giant shove and spun away. The dogs turned
their lavish attention on Ellie, who threw herself into loving them.

Julia watched the three of them roll around on the floor. "Please
tell me they sleep outside."

Ellie sat up, laughing, and pushed the hair out of her eyes. The dogs
licked her cheeks. "Okay, they sleep outside." At Julia's relieved sigh, her
sister said: "*Not!* But I'll keep them out of your room."

"That's as good as it's going to get, I suppose."

"It is." Ellie told the dogs to sit. On about the twelfth command
they obeyed, but as soon as Ellie looked away, they started to belly
crawl toward the door.

"Come on," Ellie said, leading the way to the stairs.

Julia dragged her suitcase up the narrow, creaking stairway. At the top she turned right and followed her sister down the hallway to their childhood bedroom.

A pair of twin beds, swaddled in pink chiffon, a pair of white-painted French provincial student desks with gold trim, a lime green bean bag chair. Trolls and Barbies lined the white shelving; dozens of blue-and-yellow Nancy Drews reminded her of nights spent reading with a flashlight. A faded, dusty poster of Harrison Ford as Indiana Jones was tacked to the wall.

On her bed, a pair of cats lay sleeping, twined together like a French braid.

"Meet Rocky and Adrienne," Ellie said as she crossed the room and scooped up the apparently boneless animals. The cats hung lazily from her arms, yawning. She tossed them into the hallway, said, "Go to Mommy's room," and then turned to Julia. "The sheets are clean. There are towels in your bathroom. The hot water still takes decades, and don't flush the toilet before you shower." Ellie stepped closer. "Thanks, Jules. I really appreciate your coming. I know things have been . . . bad for you lately, and . . . well, thanks."

Julia looked at her sister. If she'd been another kind of woman, or if they'd been different sisters, she might have admitted: *I had no where to go, really.* Instead, she said, "No problem," and tossed her suitcase into the room. "Now tell me why I'm here."

"Let's go downstairs. I'll need a beer for this story." Ellie started for the stairs, then turned back to Julia. "So will you."

JULIA SAT IN HER MOTHER'S FAVORITE CHAIR AND LISTENED TO HER SISTER in growing disbelief. "She leaps from branch to branch like a cat? Come on, El. You're getting caught up in some country myth. It sounds like you've found an autistic child who simply wandered away from home and got lost."

"Max doesn't think it's that simple," Ellie said, sipping her beer. They'd been in the living room for the better part of an hour now. There were papers spread out across the coffee table. Photographs and fingerprint smudge sheets and missing-children reports.

"Who's Max?"

"He took over Doc Fischer's practice."

"He's probably just over his head with this girl. You should have called the University of Washington. They'll have dozens of autism experts."

"Yeah, God forbid someone *smart* should live in Rain Valley," Ellie said, her voice spiking up. "You're not even listening to me."

Julia made a mental note to temper her comments. "Sorry. So, there's more to the story than dirty hair and prodigious tree-climbing skills. Hit me."

"She won't speak. We think—Max thinks, anyway—that maybe she doesn't know how."

"That's not unusual for an autistic. They seem to operate in a different world. Often, these kids—"

"You didn't see her, Jules. When she looked at me, I got chills. I've never seen such . . . terror in a child."

"She looked at you?"

"Stared is more like it. I think she was trying to communicate something to me."

"She made direct, purposeful eye contact?"

"Hel-*lo*, I just said that."

It was probably nothing, or maybe Ellie had it wrong. Autistics rarely made purposeful eye contact. "What about her physical mannerisms? Hand movements, way of walking; that sort of thing?"

"She sat in that tree for hours and never moved so much as an eyelash. Think reptile stillness. When she did finally jump down, she moved with lightning speed. Daisy Grimm claimed she ran like the wind. And she sniffed everything in this weird, doglike way."

In spite of herself, Julia was intrigued. *Perhaps she's mute. And deaf.*

That would also explain her getting lost. Maybe she didn't hear people calling for her."

"She's not mute. She screamed and growled. Oh, yeah, and when she thought we'd killed her wolf, she howled."

"Wolf?"

"Did I forget that part? She had a wolf pup with her. He's out at the game farm now. Floyd says he just sits at the gate and howls all day and all night."

Julia leaned back and crossed her arms. Enough was enough. This had all been a ruse, another of her sister's misguided attempts to save poor little Julia. "You're making this up."

"I wish I were. Unfortunately, it's all true."

"She *really* has a wolf pup?"

"Yes. And are you ready for the kicker?"

"There's more?"

"She has a lot of scarring."

"What kind of scarring?"

"Knife wounds. Maybe some . . . whipping marks. And on her ankle—ligature-type scarring."

Julia uncrossed her arms and leaned forward. "You better not be pulling my chain. This is a big deal."

"I know."

Julia's mind ticked through dozens of possibilities. Autism. Mental or developmental delays. Early onset schizophrenia. Those were the easy, purely internal answers. But there could be something darker here, something infinitely more unique and dangerous. It could be that this child had escaped from some terrible captor. Elective mutism would be a common response to that kind of trauma. In any case, the kid would need help. And not just any psychiatrist could handle this sort of diagnosis and treatment. Only a handful of people on the West Coast specialized in this sort of thing. Fortunately, she was one of them.

"She really touched me, Jules. I'm afraid that when the bigwig authorities get involved, we'll lose her. They'll warehouse her in some state institution until we find her parents. I don't think I could live with that. There's something so . . . broken and sad about this kid. I don't know if anyone has ever fought for her. With you, we could make a case for treating her while we search. No one could deny your credentials."

And there it was: the reminder.

Julia said softly, "Have you been watching the news, El? I'm hardly at the top of anyone's list. Your state bigwigs might not be too impressed with me."

Ellie looked at her. As always, there was a directness in Ellie's eyes that was vaguely disconcerting. Her sister was one of those rare people who made up her mind easily, stuck with her decision, and fought to the end for her beliefs. Actually, it was one of the few things they had in common. "Since when have I cared what other people think? You're the one we want to save this girl."

"Thanks, El." Julia's voice was quieter than she'd expected, less certain than usual. She wished she could tell Ellie what this meant to her.

Ellie nodded. "I just hope you're as good as you think you are."

"I am."

"Excellent. Now go take a shower and unpack. I told Max we'd meet him at the hospital before four."

THIRTY MINUTES LATER JULIA WAS SHOWERED, MADE UP, AND DRESSED in a well-worn pair of flare-legged jeans and a pale green cashmere sweater. She was trying not to be too excited about seeing the so-called Flying Wolf Girl, but she couldn't quite manage her usual calm. She'd felt on the outside for so long now that even this glimpse into her old life was enough to rev her engines.

She got a Diet Coke from the fridge and sat down in the living room. Glancing at the dusty piano in the corner, she was blindsided by

a memory. She saw her mom, sitting on the black bench, smoking a
Virginia Slim menthol and pounding out a raucous version of "That
Old Time Rock 'n' Roll." There was a crowd of friends clustered
around the piano, singing along.

"Come on girls," Mom said, waving them over. "Sing along."

Julia turned her back on the piano. She didn't want to think about
Mom, not yet, but here, in this house, time unraveled somehow. If she
stayed too long, she'd become the gawky bookworm with the bad haircut and thick glasses again.

Ellie came downstairs, dressed in her blue-and-black uniform. The
three gold stars on her collar winked in the light. Even in the bulky
outfit, she looked petite and beautiful. "You ready?"

Julia nodded and grabbed her purse. The few miles passed in a surprisingly companionable conversation. Julia remarked on the changes
that had taken place—the stoplight, the new bridge, the closure of
Hamburger Haven; Ellie pointed out how much had stayed the same.

Finally, they turned a corner and the county hospital came into
view. The modest cement building was tucked at the back of a midsized
gravel parking lot. A single ambulance was parked to the left of the
emergency entrance. The two-story building was dwarfed by the bank
of magnificent evergreen trees behind it. Right now, the streetlamps
were coming on; every few seconds a beam of light pulsed through the
parking lot, illuminating the tiny droplets of mist that couldn't quite be
called rain. The air smelled sweet and green, like freshly cut grass.

As soon as they parked, Julia was out of the car. The closer she got
to the door, the more confident she felt.

She and Ellie walked side by side through the double doors and
past the receptionist, who waved. The nurses and aides who passed her
wore pale, salmon-hued uniforms that appeared to once have been
bright orange. Their crepe soles made a squeaking sound on the
linoleum-tiled floor.

At a closed door, Ellie paused. She smoothed her clothes and
tucked her hair behind her ears, then quickly checked her makeup in
a hand mirror.

Julia frowned. "What is this, a photo shoot?"

"You'll see." Ellie knocked on the door.

A voice said: "Come in."

Ellie opened the door. They walked into a small, cramped office with a ground-level window view of a gargantuan rhododendron.

He stood in the corner of the room, still as a blade of grass on a windless day, wearing faded Levi's and a black cable-knit sweater. His hair was steely gray. Not salt-and-pepper, either, but a perfect Richard Gere, going-gray-all-at-once kind of color. He had the rugged, tanned look of a man who spent a lot of his time in the sun and the wind. But it was his eyes that caught her attention. They were searingly blue, and intense.

He was the best-looking man Julia had ever seen.

"You must be Dr. Cates," he said, moving toward her.

"Please, call me Julia."

The smile he gave her was literally dazzling. "Only if you'll call me Max."

She recognized instantly the kind of man he was. A player, like Philip, a man who wore his sexuality like a sport coat. Los Angeles was full of men like him. On several occasions she'd fallen into their trap. When she was younger, of course. She wasn't surprised at all to see that one of his ears was pierced. She gave him a professional smile. "Why don't you tell me about your patient? I understand the girl is . . . what, autistic?"

Surprise flickered across his handsome face. He reached down for a folder that lay on his desk. "A diagnosis is your job. Adolescent minds are hardly my specialty."

"And what is your specialty?"

"Writing prescriptions, if I had to choose. I went to Catholic school." That smile again. "Thus, my penmanship is excellent."

She glanced at the framed diplomas that hung on his wall, expecting to see degrees from little known, out-of-the-way schools. Instead he had an undergraduate degree from Stanford and a medical degree from UCLA. She frowned.

What in the world was this guy doing *here*?

Running away. That had to be it. Rain Valley newcomers pretty much fell into two groups: people running away from something, and people running away from everything. She couldn't help wondering which category he fell into.

She looked up suddenly and found him studying her closely. "Come with me," he said, taking her by the arm.

Julia let him lead her down the wide, white hallway. Ellie was on his other side. After a few more turns they came to a big picture window that showcased some kind of child care center. There, they stopped. Max stood so close to Julia they were nearly touching. She took a step sideways to put space between them.

The room beyond the glass was an ordinary looking playroom with a small table and chairs, a wall of cubbies filled with toys and games and books, a sink and counter area, a row of empty cribs and a hospital bed. "Where is she?"

Max nodded. "Watch."

In silence, they waited for something. Finally, a nurse walked past them and entered the playroom. She set a tray of food down on the table, then left.

Julia was about to ask a question when she saw a flash of movement under the bed.

She leaned forward. Her breath clouded the glass. She wiped it away impatiently and eased back.

Fingers appeared beneath the bed, then a hand. After a few more long moments, a child crawled out from under the bed. She wore a faded hospital gown that was too big for her.

The child—girl—had long, tangled black hair and deeply tanned skin. Even from this distance the silvery network of scars along her arms and legs were visible. Her body was hunched over, as if she'd be more comfortable on all fours. After every step she paused, going utterly still except for a quick, furtive cocking of her head. She sniffed the air, seeming to follow the scent to the food. Once there, at the table, she descended on the food like a wild animal; while she ate, she never relaxed, never stopped scanning the room and sniffing the air.

Julia felt a chill move down her spine. She reached down and quietly opened her briefcase, pulling out a notepad and pen. As she observed the girl, she began making notes. "What do we know about her?"

"Nothing," Ellie answered. "She just walked into town one day. Daisy Grimm thinks she came looking for food."

"From which direction?"

It was Max who answered. "From the woods."

The woods. Julia remembered the Olympic National Forest. Hundreds of thousands of acres of mossy darkness; much of it was still unexplored. It was the realm of myth and legend, where signs and wonders existed. Land of the Sasquatch.

"We think she was lost there for a few days," Ellie said.

Julia didn't respond. This was more than a lost day or two in the national park. "Has she spoken?"

Max shook his head. "No. We don't think she understands us, either. She spends all her time under the bed. We bathed and diapered her when she was unconscious, but we haven't been able to get close enough to change the diapers. She's made no attempt to use the toilet."

"Well," Julia said, feeling a rush of adrenaline. "Let's see what we're dealing with, shall we?" She turned to her sister. "Go to the cafeteria. Get me a sampling of chocolates and fudges. Also, a slice of apple pie and a piece of chocolate cake."

"Anything else?"

"Dolls. Lots of them. Preferably with clothes that come on and off, but not Barbies. Cuddly dolls. And a stuffed animal. You said she was with a wolf pup, right? Get me a stuffed wolf."

"Gotcha. Back in a bit." Ellie turned and hurried off.

To Max, she said, "Tell me about those ligature marks on her ankle."

"I think—" He was interrupted by the hospital intercom system paging him to the E.R., stat.

He handed her the file. "It's all in here, Julia, and it isn't pretty. If you want to get together later to discuss—"

"The chart is fine for now. Thank you." She flipped open the folder and began reading. She barely noticed when Max left her.

The entire first page was a catalogue of the child's extensive scarring, including what appeared to be a poorly healed knife wound on her left shoulder.

Max was right. Whatever had happened to this child, it wasn't pretty.

FIVE

O

N LEAVING THE HOSPITAL, ELLIE WASN'T SURPRISED TO FIND a crowd outside.

They were standing in formation, like a landing party from a distant era, with the Grimm sisters positioned at the front in a loosely formed triangle. As always, Daisy was in the lead. Today she wore a floral housedress beneath a heavy sweater. Green rubber boots ended an inch below her knees and two inches below the eyelet hem of the dress. Her dove gray hair was pulled back into a bun so tight it caused her eyes to tilt slightly up. The ever-present daisy necklace and earrings dwarfed her pale, wrinkled face.

"Chief Barton," Daisy said, moving regally forward—or, at least as regally as one could move in rubber boots, carrying her dead husband's ashes in an urn. The cowichan sweater she wore—a bulky gray and white Native American design—was at least two sizes too big. "We heard you were headed this way."

"Ned saw you turn off the highway. He called Sandi, who saw you turn onto Bay Road," Violet said, nodding with each word, as if the motion were necessary punctuation.

"What's the story, Chief?" someone yelled from the back of the crowd.

Ellie was pretty sure it was Mort Elzik, the local reporter who'd broken the story in this morning's paper.

"Hush, Mort," Daisy said sternly, using her former principal's voice to full effect. "We've rallied the town, Chief, just like you ordered. Folks really came through. We have toys and books and games and clothes. Even a scooter. That child will want for nothing. Shall I take them to her hospital room? Where is she, poor thing?"

Marigold stepped forward, lowering her voice as she said, "Psych ward?" She glanced at the crowd around her, got them all nodding. "On *ER*, they *always* get a consult from psych."

"What happened to the wolf?" It was Mort again, trying now to push through the crowd.

Suddenly everyone was talking. Daisy couldn't stop them and Ellie didn't try. They'd lose steam soon enough on their own. It was, after all, almost Happy Hour.

One by one they'd check their watches, mumble something, and head back to their cars. Daisy Grimm would lead the pack. No one could remember a day when she hadn't been at the Bigfoot Bar at the start of Happy Hour, with the black urn on the stool beside her. Half-price boilermakers were her favorite poison. She proudly said that she never had more than two. Or less.

"Who is she?" Mort asked in a loud, exasperated voice.

That shut everyone up.

"That's the sixty-four-thousand-dollar question, Mort. Peanut is back at the station, doing everything she can to find out."

"You see my article today? It was the front page."

"I haven't seen the paper yet, Mort. Sorry. What's your headline?"

"Mowgli lives." He swelled up with pride. "I love referencing the classics. Anyhoo, it got me a call from the *National Enquirer*."

Ellie winced. She hadn't thought about the sensational angle to this story. *Flying Wolf Girl Lands in Rain-Forest Town*. This wasn't just local news.

And now Julia was involved.

Oops.

"Did you ask people to contact us with information on her possible identity?"

Mort looked stung. "Of course. I'm a professional, you know. I'd like to interview her."

"Wouldn't we all? I've got a psychiatrist in with her now. I'll let you know if we get any information. As to the items you've all gathered—"

"It's Julia!" Violet yelled, clapping her hands together.

"Of course!" Marigold chimed in. "Ned wondered who the blond woman was."

"I can't believe I missed the obvious. You went to the airport to fetch her," Daisy said.

"Dogs fetch," Marigold said with a sniff. Once a high school English teacher, always a high school English teacher.

Mort started to bounce up and down like a kid at the front of the *Pirates of the Caribbean* line. "I want to interview your sister."

"I have not confirmed that Julia Cates has been contacted in this case, *nor* that she is here." Ellie looked directly at Mort. "Is that clear? I don't want to see her name in print."

"Maybe if you promised me an exclusive—"

"Stop talking."

"But—"

Daisy whopped him in the back of the head. "Mort Elzik, don't you even *think* of disobeying Ellie. Your mother would turn in her grave at the very thought. And Lord knows I'll call your daddy."

"Don't break that story, Mort." Ellie added, "Please," because they both knew he could do what he wanted. But they had decades of history between them. At times like this they were more high school newspaper geek and Homecoming Queen than reporter and police chief. In small towns, the social dynamic was like concrete; it set early and hard.

"Okay," he said, drawing the word out into a whine.

Ellie smiled. "Good."

Daisy said, "What do we do with the supplies, Chief?"

"Thank you, Daisy. Why don't you put everything in my carport? Be sure and get every donor's name. I'll want to tell them thanks."

Marigold patted her vinyl notebook. "Already done."

Ellie nodded. "Good. I knew I could count on you all. Now, I'd best get to work. We've got an identity to track down. Thanks for all your help. That kid was lucky to stumble into our town."

"We'll take care of her," someone said.

Ellie headed across the parking lot. She could hear the buzz of gossip behind her; it grew softer with each step. Tonight, at both the Bigfoot and The Pour House, speculation would be served more often than pitchers of Olympia beer. The subjects would be Julia and the wolf girl in equal proportions. She should have seen it coming.

Julia had always been different in a town that prized sameness. A quiet, gawky girl who'd somehow been born into the wrong family, and then—unimaginably—proven that she was practically a genius. The townspeople hadn't known what to make of her when she belonged here; God knew they wouldn't know what to say to her now.

Ellie climbed up into her mom's old Suburban—"Madge" to those in the know—and drove back to the station house. All the way there she added things to her mental to-do list. Today was the day she'd find the girl's identity. It *had* to be. Either someone would read a newspaper and come forward or (and this was the best answer) she would find the answer in the cold case files and become a hero.

Ellie parked in her spot and went into the station.

Viggo Mortensen stood in her office. Not in the flesh, of course. A cardboard cutout of him in full Lord of the Rings regalia. A white construction-paper dialogue bubble had been taped next to his lips. It read: *Forget Arwen. It's you I want.*

Ellie burst out laughing.

Peanut came around the corner and walked into the office, holding two cups of coffee.

"How did you know I'd need this today?" Ellie said.

Peanut handed her a cup of coffee. "A good guess."

"And Aragorn? Where was he hiding?"

"In the projection booth at the Rose Theater. Ned loaned him to me."

"So I have to return him?"

Peanut grinned. "Tomorrow. Maybe the next day. I told Ned it'd be a while, seeing how badly you need a man in your bedroom. Ned said cardboard was better than nothing."

Ellie couldn't help smiling. "Thanks, Peanut." Then she thought of her to-do list and it was easy to let go of that smile. "Well, I guess we'd best get to work."

Peanut reached down to her cluttered desk and pulled up a single sheet of paper from the mess. "Here's where we are so far." She put on her rhinestone-encrusted Costco reading glasses. "The Center for Lost and Missing Children is running a database search. Their first pass brought up over ten thousand potential matches. They're trying to narrow it down. Her exact age would help."

Ellie slowly sat down. Her dream of heroism fizzled like an old balloon. "Ten thousand missing girls. God help us, Peanut. It would take us decades to go through all the information."

"Get this, El. There are eight hundred thousand missing children cases a year in this country. That's almost two thousand a day. Statistically, fifty percent of them will be white girls, kidnapped by someone they know. Is she white for sure?"

"Yes." Ellie felt overwhelmed suddenly. "Did the FBI get back to us?"

"They're waiting for proof of kidnapping or a solid identification. It could just be a lost girl from Mystic or Forks. Technically we have no proof of a crime yet. They recommend we canvass the town . . . again. And the DSHS is putting pressure on us to identify a temporary foster parent. We'll need to get on that. She can't stay in the hospital forever."

"Did you call the Laura Recovery Center?"

"And *America's Most Wanted*. And the attorney general. By tomorrow this girl is going to be front page news." Peanut's face pleated into worried folds. "It won't be easy to hide Julia."

This story was going to be a hurricane of publicity, no doubt about it. And once again, Dr. Julia Cates would be in the eye of the storm.

"No," Ellie said, frowning. "It won't."

GIRL IS COILED UP LIKE A YOUNG FERN IN THIS TOO-WHITE PLACE. THE ground is cold and hard; it makes her shiver sometimes and dream of her cave. While she was asleep, the Strangers changed her. She smells now of flowers and rain. She misses her own scent.

She wants to close her eyes and go to sleep, but the smells in here are all wrong. Her nose itches most of the time and her throat is so dry it hurts to swallow. She longs for her river and the roar of the water that is always leaking over the steep cliff not far from her cave. She can hear the Sun-Haired Her breathing, and her voice. It is like a thunderstorm, that voice; dangerous and scary. It makes her scoot closer to the end of the place. If she were a wolf, she could burrow through it and disappear. The idea of that makes her sad. She is thinking of Her . . . of Him, even. Of Wolf.

Without them she feels lost. She can't live in this place where nothing green is alive and the air stinks.

She shouldn't have run away. Him always told her it was cold and bad beyond their wood, that she had to stay hidden because in the world there were people who hurt little girls worse than Him did. Strangers.

She should have listened, but she'd been so scared for so long.

Now she will be hurt worser than the net.

They are waiting to hurt her when she comes out, but she will be too small for them to see. Like a green bug on the leaf, she will disappear.

. . .

SITTING ON AN UNCOMFORTABLE PLASTIC CHAIR IN THE CHEERILY
decorated playroom, Julia stared down at the notebook in her lap. In
the last hour she'd talked endlessly to the girl hidden beneath the bed,
but had received no response. Her notebook remained full of questions
without answers.

> *Teeth—dental work?*
> *Deaf?*
> *Stool—any evidence of diet?*
> *Toilet trained?*
> *Scars—age of*
> *Ethnicity*

In the early years of her residency it had become clear to everyone
that Julia had a true gift for dealing with traumatized and depressed
children. Even the best of her teachers and colleagues had come to her
for advice. She seemed innately to understand the extreme pressures
on today's kids. All too often they ended up on the dark, back streets
of downtown wherever, selling their thin bodies to pay for food and
drugs. She knew how exploitation and abuse and alcohol marked a
child, how families lost their elasticity and snapped apart, leaving each
member adrift and searching. Most importantly, she remembered how
it felt to be an outsider, and though she'd grown up and merged into
the traffic of adulthood, those painful childhood memories remained.
Kids opened up to her, trusted her to listen to them, to help them.

Although she hadn't specialized in autism or brain damage reha-
bilitation or mental challenges, she'd dealt with those patients, of
course. She knew how autistics functioned and reacted.

She knew, too, how profoundly deaf children acted before they'd
learned sign language. Astoundingly, there were still places in this
country—backwoods settlements and such—where deaf/mute children grew up with no ability to communicate.

But none of that seemed relevant to this case. The child's brain
scan showed no lesions or anomalies. The girl under the bed could be

a perfectly normal child who'd been lost on a day hike and was now too terrified to speak up.

A perfectly normal girl who traveled with a wolf

—and howled at the moon

—and seemingly didn't know what a toilet was for.

Julia put down her pen. She'd been silent for too long. Her best hope with this child lay in *connecting*. That meant communication. "I guess I can't write my way to understanding you, can I?" she said in gentle, soothing tones.

"That's too bad, because I enjoy writing. Probably you prefer drawing. Most girls your age do. Not that I know your age, exactly. Dr. Cerrasin believes you're about six. I'd say you're a little younger, but I haven't really gotten a good look at you, have I? I'm thirty-five. Did I tell you that? I'm sure it seems old to you. Frankly, in the last year, it's started to feel old to me, too."

For the next two hours Julia talked about nothing. She told the girl where they were and why they were here—that everyone wanted to help her. It didn't matter so much what she said as how she said it. The subtext on every word was *Come on out, honey, I'm a safe place.* But there had been no response whatsoever. Not once had so much as a finger appeared out from beneath the bed. She was about to start talking about how lonely the world could sometimes feel when a knock at the door interrupted her.

There was a scuffling sound under the bed.

Had the girl heard the knock?

"I'll be right back," Julia said in a quite ordinary oh-there's-someone-at-my-door voice. She went to the door and opened it.

Dr. Cerrasin cocked his head to the right, where two white-clad male orderlies stood. One held a large box; the other held a tray of food. "The food and toys are here."

"Thanks."

"No response yet?"

"No, and it's impossible to diagnose her this way. I need to *study* her. Actions, reactions, movements. That damn bed makes it impossible."

"Whatcha want us to do with this stuff?" asked one of the orderlies.

"I'll take the stuffed animals. Store the rest of the toys for now. She's hardly ready for that kind of play. The food can go on the table. And be quiet. I don't want to scare her any more than she already is." To Max, she said, "Does this town still have a library the size of my car?"

"It's small," he admitted, "but with the Internet, you have access to everything. The library went online last year." He smiled charmingly. "There was a parade."

She felt a moment's connection to him then. They were the outsiders, laughing at small-town customs. When she realized that he'd made her smile, she stepped back. "There always is." She started to say something else—she wasn't even sure what, when it struck her.

Move the bed. How had she missed the obvious?

She spun around and shut the door, realizing a moment too late that she'd shut it in Max's face. Oops. Oh, well. She went to the nearest orderly, who was just setting down a tray of food, and said, "Take the bed out of here, please, but leave the mattress."

"Huh?"

"We're not furniture movers, miss," the other man said.

"Doctor," she pointed out. "Are you telling me that you two aren't strong enough to help me?"

"Of course we're strong enough," the taller man sputtered as he set down the box of stuffed animals.

"Good. Then what's the problem?"

"Come on, Fredo. Let's move the bed before the doc here starts wantin' a fridge."

"Thank you. There's a child under there. Try not to scare her."

One of the men turned to her. "Why don't you tell her to come out?"

"Just move the bed, please. Carefully. Put the mattress in the corner."

They placed the mattress where she'd indicated, lifted the bed off the floor, and backed out of the room. The door clicked shut behind them, but Julia didn't notice. All she saw was her patient.

Crouched low, the girl opened her mouth to scream.

Come on, Julia thought, *let me hear you.*

But there was no sound as the child scrambled back to the wall and froze. She went perfectly still.

Julia was reminded of a chameleon settling into its environment. But the poor kid couldn't change color, couldn't disappear. She was all-too-noticeable against the speckled gray linoleum floor and bright yellow wall. So still she seemed to be carved of pale wood, her only sign of life was her nostrils, which flared as if to pick up every scent.

For the first time, Julia noticed the child's beauty. Though the girl was wretchedly thin, she was still striking. She stared near Julia, but not quite at her, as if there were a dangerous animal to Julia's left that bore watching. Her expression was both bland and strangely obsessive; it gave nothing away but missed nothing, either. There was no curve to her mouth at all; no indication of displeasure or curiosity, and her eyes—those amazing, blue-green eyes—were serious and watchful.

Julia was surprised by the lack of fear in those eyes. Perhaps she was looking at the other side of fear. What happened to a child when fear had been the norm forever . . . did it melt into watchfulness?

"You're almost looking at me," she said in as conversational a tone as possible. Eye contact was important. Autistics routinely didn't make eye contact until or unless they'd undergone significant therapy. On her pad, she wrote: *Mute?* Her sister had said the girl made noises, but Julia hadn't heard it for herself. Besides, her sister had also implied prodigious jumping and tree-climbing skills. "I imagine you're scared. Everything that's happened to you since yesterday has been frightening. It would make anyone cry."

There was no reaction at all.

For the next twelve hours Julia sat quietly in a chair. She observed everything she could about the girl, but that wasn't much, to be truthful. In all those early hours, the child was almost completely motionless. Sometime around midnight she fell asleep, still crouched against the wall. When she finally slumped to the floor, Julia cautiously moved toward her, picking her up gently and transferring her to the mattress.

All through the night Julia watched the girl sleep, noticing how often she seemed seized by bad dreams. At some point Julia fell asleep, too, but by seven the next morning she was awake again, ready to go. She called home to tell Ellie that she'd probably spend the day at the hospital, then went back to work.

When the girl finally woke, Julia was ready. Smiling easily, she began talking again. In her voice, she made sure the girl heard acceptance and caring, so that the meaning was clear even if the words were unknown. Hour after hour Julia talked, all through the breakfast and lunch, which went uneaten. By late afternoon two things had become true: Julia was exhausted and the girl *had* to be hungry.

Julia moved very slowly over to the box that had been delivered yesterday. She was careful to make no sudden moves. She talked in a steady, soothing cycle of words, as if the child's silence were the most natural thing in the world. "How about if we look through this stuff now, see if you like any of it." She opened the box. A stuffed gray wolf pup lay on a pile of other plush toys and folded clothes. She picked it up and then went to the next box. Still smiling, she started to unpack it. "The people of Rain Valley sent you this stuff because they're worried about you. I'm sure your parents are worried, too. Maybe you got lost. That wouldn't be your fault, you know, and no one would be mad at you."

She glanced back at the girl, who was sitting up on the mattress now, perfectly still, staring just past Julia.

The window, Julia realized. The girl hadn't taken her gaze away from the window. Though the glass wasn't big and didn't reveal much of the outside world, there was a patch of blue sky and the green tip of a fir branch. "You're wondering how to get out there, aren't you? I'd like to help you get home. Would you like that?"

There was no reaction, not even to the word *home*.

Julia grabbed a big book off the shelf and dropped it on the floor. It hit with a loud *thwack*.

The girl flinched; her eyes widened. She glanced at Julia for a heartbeat, then scurried over to the corner.

"So you can hear. That's good to know. Now I need to figure out if you can understand me. Are you hearing words or sounds, little girl?" Cautiously, she moved toward the child. All the while she was waiting for a flicker in the eyes, an acknowledgment that she was being approached. There was none, but when Julia was about eight feet away, the girl's nostrils flared. A tiny, whimpering sound leaked past her lips. The tension in her laced fingers turned the tanned skin almost white.

Julia stopped. "That's close enough, huh? I'm scaring you. That's good, actually. You're responding normally to this strange environment." She bent down very slowly and tossed the stuffed animal to the girl. It landed right by her side. "Sometimes a soft toy can make us feel better. When I was a girl, I had a pink teddy bear named Tink. I took her everywhere." She went back to the table and set the box on the floor, then sat down.

A moment later there was a knock at the door. At the sound, the girl scrambled farther into the corner, crouching down to appear as small as possible.

"It's just your dinner. I know it's early, but you have to be hungry. I'm not leaving you to eat alone; you might as well understand that now." She opened the door, thanked the nurse for the food, then returned to the table.

The door clicked shut again, leaving Julia and the child alone.

As Julia unpacked the food, she kept up a steady stream of conversation. Nothing too personal or intense, just words; each one of them was an invitation that came back unopened. Finally, she pushed the box aside. On the table there was now an array of kid-friendly food. Macaroni and cheese—from a box, just the way kids liked it; glazed doughnuts, brownies, chicken tenders with ketchup, milk, Jell-O with fruit chunks, cheese pizza, and a hot dog with fries. The tempting aromas filled the small room. "I didn't know what you liked so I pretty much ordered everything."

Julia reached over and plucked a doughnut off the red plastic plate. "I can't remember the last time I had a glazed doughnut. They're not good for you, but oh man, are they good." She took a bite. The flavor exploded in her mouth. Savoring it, she looked directly at the girl. "I'm sorry. Are you hungry? Maybe you'd like a bite."

At the word *hungry*, the girl flinched. For just a moment her gaze skittered across the room and came to rest on the table of food.

"Did you understand that?" Julia said, leaning ever so slightly forward. "Do you know what hungry means?"

The girl looked at her for a moment. It lasted less than a breath, but Julia felt its impact all the way to her toes.

Understanding.

She'd bet her degrees on it.

Very slowly Julia reached for a second doughnut. She placed it on a red plastic plate and then stood up. She walked closer to the girl than she'd been before—this time there was about six feet between them. Once again the child snorted and whimpered and tried to back up, but the wall pinned her in place.

Julia set the plate on the floor and gave it a little push. It skidded across the linoleum. Close enough to the child that she could smell its vanilly sweetness; far enough away that she had to move forward to take it.

Julia returned to her seat. "Go ahead," she said. "You're hungry. That's food."

This time the girl looked right at her. Julia felt the desperate intensity of those blue-green eyes. She wrote down: *Food*.

"No one will hurt you," Julia said.

The girl blinked. Was that a reaction to the word *hurt*? She wrote it down.

Minutes passed. Neither one of them looked away. Finally Julia glanced at the window by the door. Dr. Better-looking-than-God was there, watching them.

The second Julia glanced away, the girl ran for the food, snatched it up and returned to her spot, like a wild animal returning to its lair to feed.

And the way she ate . . .

The girl put most of the doughnut into her mouth and started to chew loudly.

Julia could tell when the taste kicked in. The girl's eyes widened.

"Can't beat a good doughnut. You should taste my mom's brownies. They were delicious." Julia stumbled slightly over the past tense of the word. The odd thing was, she would have sworn the child noticed, though she couldn't have said why she thought so. "You'd better have some protein with that, kiddo. Too much sugar isn't good." She got a hot dog and doctored it up with ketchup and mustard then set it down on the floor about two feet closer to the table than before.

The girl looked at the empty plate where the doughnut had been. It was obvious that she recognized the difference. She seemed to be gauging the additional distance, calculating additional risk.

"You can trust me," Julia said softly.

No response.

"I won't hurt you."

The girl's chin slowly came up. Those blue-green eyes fixed on her.

"You understand me, don't you? Maybe not everything, but enough. Is English your first language? Are you from around here?"

The girl glanced down at the hot dog.

"Neah Bay. Joyce. Sequim. Forks. Sappho. Pysht. La Push. Mystic." Julia watched closely for a reaction. None of the local towns prompted a response. "A lot of families go hiking in the forest, especially along Fall River."

Had the girl blinked at that? She said it again: "Fall River."

Nothing.

"Forest. Trees. Deep woods."

The girl looked up sharply.

Julia got up from her seat and very slowly moved toward the girl. When she was almost close enough to make contact, she squatted down so that she and the child were at eye level. Reaching behind her, she felt around for the hot dog plate. Finding it, she grasped the plastic rim and held the plate of food forward. "Were you lost in the woods, honey? That can be so scary. All that darkness, all those sounds. Did you get separated from your mommy and daddy? If you did, I can help you. I can help you go back where you belong."

The girl's nostrils flared, but whether from the words or the scent of the hot dog, Julia couldn't be sure. For a moment there—maybe at the word *back* or *help*—there had been a flash of fear in those young eyes.

"You're afraid to trust me. Maybe your mom and dad told you not to talk to strangers. That's normally good advice, but you're in trouble, honey. I can only help you if you'll talk to me. How else can I get you home? You can trust me. I won't hurt you," she said again. "No hurt."

At that the girl inched slowly forward. Not once did her gaze waver or lower. She stared directly at Julia as she scuttled forward in her awkward crouch.

"No hurt," Julia said again as the girl neared.

The child was breathing fast; her nostrils were blowing hard. Sweat sheened her forehead. She smelled vaguely of urine because of the diapers they'd been unable to change. The hospital gown hung slack on her tiny body. Her toenails and fingernails were long and still slightly grimy. She reached for the hot dog, grabbed it in her hands.

She brought it to her nose, sniffed it, frowning.

"It's a hot dog," Julia said. "Your parents probably brought them on the camping trip. Where did you go on that trip, do you remember? Do you know the name of your town? Mystic? Forks? Joyce? Pysht? Where did your daddy say you were going? Maybe I could go get him."

The girl attacked her. It happened so fast that Julia couldn't respond. One second she was sitting there, talking softly, the next, she felt herself falling backward, hitting her head on the floor. The girl jumped on Julia's chest and clawed at her face, screaming unintelligible words.

Max was there in an instant, pulling the girl off Julia.

Dazed, Julia tried to sit up. She couldn't focus. When the world finally righted itself she saw Max sedating the child.

"No!" Julia cried, trying to get to her feet. Her vision blurred. She stumbled.

Max was back at her side, steadying her. "I've got you."

Julia wrenched away from him and fell to her knees. "I can't *believe* you sedated her. Damn it. Now she'll never trust me."

"She could have hurt you," he said in an irritatingly matter-of-fact voice.

"She's all of what—forty-five pounds?"

Her cheeks hurt. So did the back of her head. She couldn't believe how fast the attack had come on. She let out a shaky breath and glanced around the room. The girl lay on a mattress by the back wall, asleep. Even in slumber she was curled into a tight ball, as if the whole world could hurt her. *Damn it.* "How long will she sleep?"

"Not more than a few hours. I think she was looking for a weapon when I came in. If she'd found one, she could have really hurt you."

Julia rolled her eyes. No doubt he was one of those people whose lives had never been touched by violence of any kind. "It's hardly the first time I've been attacked by a patient. I doubt it'll be the last. Part of the job description. Next time don't sedate her without asking me, okay?"

"Sure."

She frowned. The movement hurt. "The question is: what did I say?"

"What do you mean?"

"You saw her. She was fine. I thought maybe she was even understanding a few words. Then: *bam!* I must have said just the wrong thing. I'll listen to the tapes tonight. Maybe that will give me a clue." She looked back at the girl. "Poor baby."

"We should get you cleaned up. Those scratches on your cheek are pretty deep, and God knows what kind of bacteria is under her fingernails."

Julia could hardly disagree.

As they walked down the hallway, she realized how much her head hurt. So much that she felt queasy and unsteady. "I've never seen anyone move so fast. She was like a cat."

"Daisy Grimm swears she flew into the maple tree on Sealth Park."

"Daisy still carrying Fred's ashes around with her?"

"She is."

"Fred died when I was in seventh grade. Need I say more?"

Max guided her into an empty examining room. "Sit."

"Let me guess: you have dogs."

He smiled. "Just sit down. I need to look at your injuries."

She was too weak to argue, so she sat on the end of the table; paper rustled beneath her butt. Other than their breathing, it was the only sound in the room.

His touch was surprisingly gentle on her face. She'd expected him to be clumsier, a little uncertain. This was nurse's work, after all.

She winced when he dabbed the antiseptic on her wounds.

"Sorry."

"It's not your fault." He was too close. She shut her eyes.

That was when she felt his breath on her cheek, a little stream of it that smelled of Red Hot gum.

She opened her eyes. He was right there, looking at her, blowing cool breath on her cuts. Her heart skipped a beat. "Thanks," she said, jerking backward, trying to smile. *Oh, for God's sake, Julia.* She'd always been uncomfortable around good-looking men.

"Sorry." He didn't seem sorry at all. "I just wanted to help."

"Thanks. I'm fine."

He closed up the supplies and stowed everything back in the overhead cabinets. When he turned back to face her, he kept a certain distance between them. "You should take the rest of the day off. Have Ellie watch you. Concussions—"

"I know the risks, Max, and the symptoms. I'm sure I don't have a concussion, but I'll be careful."

"It wouldn't hurt to lie down for a while."

She saw the way he smiled when he said *lie down*, and it hardly surprised her. No doubt he was the type of man who could find a sexual innuendo in every conversation. "That little girl is counting on me, Max. I need to go to the police station and then to the library, but I'll take it easy."

"Why do I think you don't know how to take it easy?"

She frowned. That *did* surprise her. She wouldn't have pegged him as the kind of man who really understood women. Loved them, yes.

Used them, certainly. But understood them, no. Philip had never been very intuitive. "Am I that transparent?"

"As glass. How are you getting to the station?"

"I'll call Ellie. She'll—"

"I could give you a ride."

She slid off the table. This time when she stood, she felt a little steadier. She was about to say *That's not necessary* when she caught a glimpse of herself in the mirror.

"Wow." She moved closer. Four angry, seeping claw marks slashed across her left cheek. Already the skin was swelling, and it looked like she was going to wake up tomorrow morning with a black eye. "She really got me."

He handed her a tube of antibiotic ointment. "Keep—"

"I know. Thanks." She took it from him and slipped it in her pocket.

"Come on. I'll take you to the station."

Instead of arguing, she fell into step beside him.

But not too close.

SIX

"ARE YOU SURE THIS IS HOW IT'S DONE?" PEANUT ASKED FOR AT least the tenth time in as many minutes.

"Do I *look* like Diane Sawyer?" Ellie responded sharply. Whenever she got nervous, she got snippy, and this was her first press conference. She needed to do everything right or she'd come off looking like an idiot. And if there was one thing Ellie hated, it was looking and feeling stupid. That was why she'd left college; it was better to quit than to fail.

"Ellie? Are you having a meltdown?"

"I'm fine."

The police station had been transformed into a makeshift press room. They'd pushed their desks to the perimeter of the room.

Ten chairs had been set up in two rows of five each in the middle. A podium—dragged from the Rotary Club storeroom—had been placed in front of them.

Cal sat at his desk, answering the phones. Peanut stood in the hallway, surveying the setup. For some bizarre reason, she was certain she knew how to manage this.

As if.

Ellie at least had some media experience. Her Uncle Joe had held a press conference once, back when she was a new recruit. Her ex, Alvin, had sworn he'd seen Bigfoot. A few local papers and one tabloid had shown up. So had Alvin—drunk as a parolee.

Ellie checked the chairs again. On each metal seat was a flyer held in place by a small stone. She was rereading the statement she'd prepared when Earl walked into the station. He was in full dress uniform, with his few remaining strands of hair shellacked in place. He seemed taller.

Lifts in his shoes.

The realization made her smile. Not that she could tease him much. She'd applied a pretty healthy amount of makeup herself. It was her first time on television, and she wanted to look good. "Hey, Earl. You ready for the hoopla?"

He nodded. His Adam's apple bobbed up and down his thin throat. "Myra pressed my uniform. She said a man on television needed knife pleats on his pants."

"That's a good woman you married, Earl."

"Yes, it is."

Ellie went back to reading. She concentrated on each word, trying to memorize her lines. She barely looked up as reporters streamed in and sat down. By six o'clock all of the chairs were filled. Photographers and videographers stood behind the rows of chairs.

"It's time," Peanut said, coming up to her. "And you have lipstick on your teeth."

Perfect. Ellie wiped her teeth and leaned forward, tapping the microphone. It thumped and whined. Sound ricocheted through the room. Several people covered their ears.

"Sorry." She eased back a little bit. "Thank you all for coming. As most of you know, we need your help. A young girl has arrived in Rain Valley. We have no idea who she is or where she is from. Our best estimates put her age at somewhere between five and seven years. On your seats, you'll find an artist's sketch. She has black hair and blue-green eyes. Dental records are not yet available, but she appears to have had no fillings or other work done. She has naturally lost a number of baby teeth—such a loss is consistent with our age assertions. We have consulted with all available state and local agencies, as well as the Center for Missing Children, and have—as yet—been unable to identify her. We're hoping that you all run this as front page news to get the word out. Someone must know who she is."

"A *drawing*? What the hell is that about?" someone said.

"We're in the process of getting a photograph. For now, this is what's available," Ellie answered.

Mort from the *Rain Valley Gazette* stood up. "How come she doesn't just tell you her name?"

"She hasn't spoken yet," Ellie answered.

"*Can* she speak?"

"We don't have a definitive answer to that yet. Early indications, however, lead us to believe there is no physical barrier to speech."

A man wearing a *Seattle Times* baseball hat stood up. "So she's clammed up on purpose?"

"We don't know yet."

"Is she wounded or ill?"

"Or crazy?"

Ellie was formulating her answer when Earl stepped to the microphone and said, "We've got a famous psychi—"

Ellie kicked him hard. "Our very best doctors are taking care of her," she said. "That's all we have for now. Hopefully someone will come forward who can answer some of these thorny questions for us."

"I heard she had a wolf pup with her." This from a woman near the back.

"And that she jumped from a branch that was forty feet in the air," someone else added.

Ellie sighed. "Let's not get carried away by small-town rumors. The point is the identification of this child."

"You're not giving us much to go on," someone said.

Ellie had said everything she had to say, but the questions just kept on coming. Her personal favorite (this from Mort): "Are you sure she's human?"

From there it was all downhill.

"YOU'RE LUCKY IT WAS RAINING THIS MORNING WHEN I LEFT THE HOUSE. Otherwise I'd have my motorcycle," Max said, opening the passenger door of his truck for her.

"Let me guess," she said as he got into the driver's seat and started the engine, "Harley-Davidson."

"How'd you know?"

"The pierced ear. I'm a shrink, remember? We tend to notice the little things."

He drove out of the parking lot. "Oh. Do you like bikes?"

"The ones that go seventy miles an hour? No."

"Too fast, too free, huh?"

She stared out the window at the passing trees, wishing he would slow down. "Too many organ donors."

Several blocks passed between them in silence. Finally, Max said, "So, have you formed any specific conclusions about her yet?"

It was the sort of question medical professionals always asked psychiatrists. They didn't understand how much time an accurate diagnosis could take, but she appreciated the return to professionalism. "I can tell you what I *don't* think. Ruling out is always a good place to start. I don't believe she's deaf; at least not completely. I also don't believe she's profoundly mentally challenged; however, that's a hunch. As to autism, that's certainly the best guess for now, although if she is autistic, she's high functioning."

"You sound like you don't really believe that diagnosis, either."

"I need a lot more time to run tests. When she looked at me . . ." Her words trailed off. She was hesitant to speculate without more information. It was yet another ramification of her recent problems. She was, for the first time in her life, afraid to be wrong.

"What?"

"She looked at me. That's the point. Not near me or through me or beside me, but at me. And sometimes she appeared to understand words. Hurt. Food. Hungry. Those I'd swear she understood."

"Do you think a word set her off?"

"I have no idea. Honestly, I can't remember what I said to her."

"Can she speak?"

"So far it's only sounds. Expressions of the purest emotions. I can tell you this: elective mutism is a common response to childhood trauma."

"And there's been some serious trauma in her life."

"Yes."

The weight of those words made the air between them feel heavy suddenly, and sad.

"Maybe she was kidnapped," Max said quietly.

It had been on Julia's mind all day, that thought; it was the dark shadow that lay behind all her questions.

"That's what I'm afraid of, too. This girl's physical scars could be nothing compared to her emotional trauma."

"She's lucky you're here, then."

"Actually, I'm the lucky one." The minute the words were out, Julia wished them back. She wasn't sure why she'd revealed something so personal, and to this man she hardly knew. Thankfully, he didn't respond.

He turned left onto Azalea Street and found it barricaded. "That's odd. Another broken water main, most likely." He backed out and drove a block down Cascade, then parked. "I'll walk you in."

"That's hardly necessary."

"I don't mind."

Julia didn't want to make a big deal out of it, so she nodded.

They walked down the quiet tree-lined street toward the police station. "It's beautiful here," she said. "I'd forgotten. Especially in the fall." She was just about to remark on the brightly colored leaves when she turned the corner and saw the reason for the barricade.

The street was clotted with news vans. Dozens of them.

"Stop!" she said quickly, realizing a moment too late that she'd screamed the word at Max. She spun around so fast she ran into him. His arms curled around her, steadied her. If the press saw her now, with her battered face, they'd have a field day. Especially when they found out that her own patient had injured her.

"The station's right there. The front door—"

"I know where the damned front door is. I need to get out of here. Now."

He saw the news vans and made the connection. When he looked at her, she was *that doctor.*

"Let me go," she said, wrenching out of his arms.

He pointed across the street. "That's the Lutheran church. Go on in. I'll send Ellie."

"Thanks." She'd taken only a step or two when he called out her name.

She turned back to him. "What?"

He took a step toward her but didn't say anything.

She rolled her eyes. "Just say what's on your mind, Max. Everyone has a damned opinion. I'm used to it."

"Do you want me to stay with you?"

Julia drew in a sharp breath and looked up at him. She was reminded suddenly of how long she'd been alone. "No . . . but thanks." Without looking at him again, she walked away.

MAX WALKED UP THE CONCRETE STEPS TOWARD THE POLICE STATION. As he stepped inside, the reporters turned on him like a school of barracuda. When they realized he was a nobody, they turned away.

He stood by the door, waiting for the press conference to end, and thinking about Julia.

In that moment when she'd seen the news vans, he'd seen the emotions flash through her green eyes—fear, hope, despair. Her vulnerability lasted for a heartbeat, maybe less, but he saw it, and he understood. Remembered. When the media turned their white-hot light on you, there was nowhere to hide.

He pushed through the waning crowd.

Ellie was at the podium, standing between Earl and Peanut.

He pulled her aside, said sharply, "Your sister is waiting for you in the Lutheran church."

Ellie winced. "She was here?"

"She was."

"Shit."

Max was surprised by a bolt of anger. "Here's a hint. Next time you gather the press, give her fair warning."

"I didn't think—"

"I know."

"What's *your* problem?"

He could hardly answer that. "Just be more careful next time."

Before she could say anything else, he walked away.

Outside, he paused on the concrete steps of the city hall. All around him, reporters were talking among themselves and packing up their gear. An American flag flapped in the breeze overhead.

Across the street, the white stone church sat huddled in the shade of a mammoth fir tree. When he looked closely, he saw the silhouette of a woman in the window.

Julia.

He used to be the kind of man who would cross the street now, go to her and offer help.

Instead, he went to his truck, climbed in, and headed for home.

As he drove down Lakeshore Drive, the sun began its slow descent toward the lake. At his battered mailbox, he withdrew the usual stack of junk mail and bills, then turned onto his driveway, which was a ribbon of potholed gravel road that unspooled through a nearly impenetrable forest. These were the acres his great-great-grandfather had homesteaded more than one hundred years ago, with the grandiose idea of building a world-class fishing and hunting lodge, but a single year in the wet, green darkness had changed the old man's mind. He'd cleared two acres out of the one hundred he owned, and that was as far as he got. He moved to Montana and built his fishing lodge; in time he forgot about these wild acres tucked deep in the woods along Spirit Lake. They were passed from eldest son to eldest son as wills were read, until at last they came to Max. It was anticipated by the whole of his family that he would do with this land what had always been done with it: nothing. Each generation had checked on the value of the acreage; each had been surprised by how little it was worth. So they'd kept paying the taxes and ignoring their ownership of the land.

If his life had unfolded as he'd expected, no doubt Max would have done the same.

He parked in the garage, beside the Harley-Davidson "fat boy" motorcycle that was his favorite toy, and went into the house.

Inside, he flipped the light switches.

Emptiness greeted him.

There were precious few pieces of furniture in the great room: to the left was a huge pine table with a single chair at one end. A gorgeous river-rock fireplace covered the eastern wall, its mantel empty of decoration. In front of it was an oxblood leather sofa, a battered coffee table, and a beautiful wooden cabinet.

Max tossed his coat on the sofa, then felt beneath the cushions for a remote.

Within moments a plasma TV screen rose up from the custom-made rosewood cabinet. He clicked it on. It didn't matter what was on the screen. All he cared about was the noise. He hated a quiet house.

He went upstairs, took a quick shower, and changed his clothes.

He was at the steamy mirror, shaving, when he thought about her again.

The pierced ear.

He put down his razor slowly, staring at the tiny dot in his ear. It was barely visible anymore; he hadn't worn an earring in more than seven years.

But she'd seen it, and in seeing it, she'd glimpsed the man he used to be.

"You decided to hold a press conference without warning me?" Julia couldn't help yelling at her sister. "Why not just tie a yellow ribbon around my throat and toss me to the wolves?"

"How was I supposed to know you'd stop by? You never came home last night, but I'm supposed to plan around your movements. Who am I? Carnac the Magnificent?"

Julia sat back in the car seat and crossed her arms. In the sudden silence, rain pattered the windshield of the police cruiser.

"Maybe the media *should* know you're here. I'll tell them how much we believe—"

"You think it would be a *good* thing to show my face on camera? Now? My patient—a kid, mind you—beat me up. It hardly is a ringing endorsement of my skills."

"That's not your fault."

"*I* know that," Julia snapped. "Believe me when I tell you they won't."

It was the same thing she'd told herself a dozen times in the last thirty minutes. For a moment there, when she'd seen those reporters, she'd considered revealing herself as the doctor on this case. But it was too early. They no longer trusted her. She needed to do something right or they'd ruin her. Again.

She had to get the girl talking. And fast.

This was obviously going to be a big story for a few days. Headlines would be everywhere; people would be speculating about the girl's identity. The story would probably run that she was incapable of intelligible speech because of brain damage or unwilling to talk because of fear or trauma. Nothing seized the public attention like a mystery; the press would pull at every strand. Sooner or later, Julia knew, she would be part of the story.

Ellie pulled up in front of the library. The building, an old converted taxidermy shop, sat tucked up against a stand of towering Douglas fir. Night was falling fast, so the gravel path to the door could barely be seen. "I sent everyone home for the night," Ellie said, reaching into her breast pocket for the key. "Just like you asked. And Jules . . . I am sorry."

"Thanks." Julia heard the wobble in her voice. It revealed more than she would have liked. And Ellie heard it.

If things had been different between them, this was the moment when she would reach out to her sister and say *I'm scared to face the media again.* Instead, she cleared her throat and said, "I need somewhere private to work with the child."

"As soon as we find a temporary foster parent, we can move her. We're looking for—"

"I'll do it. Call DSHS. There shouldn't be any problem getting me approved. I'll get the paperwork filled out tonight."

"Are you sure?"

"I'm sure. I can't help her an hour a week, or even an hour a day. She'll be a full-time job for a while. Get the paperwork started from your end."

"Okay."

Headlights came up behind them, illuminating the cab. Moments later there was a knock at the car window that sounded like gunfire.

Julia opened the car door.

Penelope stood alongside the passenger door, waving happily. Behind her was a battered old pickup truck. She was already into her sentence when Julia stepped out. "—said you could borrow old Bertha for a while. She was his daddy's hay truck when they lived in Moses Lake. The keys are in it."

"Thank you, Penelope."

"Call me Peanut. Heck, we're practically related, with Ellie being my best friend and all."

Julia had a sudden memory of Penelope at Mom's funeral. She'd taken care of everything and everyone like a den mother. When Ellie had started to cry, Penelope bustled her out of the room. Later, Julia had seen her sitting beside Ellie on the end of her parents' bed, rocking a sobbing Ellie as if she were a child.

Julia could have used a friend like that in the past year. "Thanks, Peanut."

Ellie got out of the cruiser and came around to where they stood. Her police-issue black heels crunched the gravel. As they stood there, the clouds drifted away to reveal a watery moon. "Get in the car, Pea. I'll walk her to the front door."

Peanut fluttered her fingers in a sorority girl wave and lowered herself into the cruiser, slamming the door shut.

Julia and Ellie walked up the gravel path to the library. As they neared the entrance, moonlight fell on the READING IS FUN! poster that filled the front window.

Ellie unlocked the door and opened it, leaning forward to flick on the lights. Then she looked at Julia. "Can you really help this girl?"

Julia's anger slipped away, along with the residue of her fear. They were back on track, talking about what mattered. "Yes. Any progress on her identity?"

"No. We've input her height, weight, eye and hair color into the system, so we're narrowing the possibilities down. We've also photographed and logged the scarring on her legs and shoulder. She has a very particular birthmark on her back left shoulder, too. That's the one identifying mark we know has always been on her. The FBI advised me to keep it secret—to weed out the kooks and crackpots. Max sent her dress to the lab, to look for fibers, but I'm sure the dress is homemade, so it won't give us a factory. Maybe DNA, but that's a real long shot. Her fingerprints don't match any recorded missing kids. That's not unusual, of course. Parents don't routinely fingerprint their kids. We've got her blood, so if someone comes forward, we can run a DNA test." Ellie sighed. "In other words, we're hoping that her mother reads tomorrow's newspaper and comes forward. Or that you can get her to tell us her name."

"What if it was her mother that tied her up and left her to die?"

Ellie's gaze was steady. It was obvious that she'd thought the same thing. They both knew that the overwhelming number of child abductions were by family members. Cases like Elizabeth Smart were incredibly rare. "Then you'd better get the truth out of her," she said quietly. "It's the only way we can help her."

"Nothing like a little pressure."

"On both of us, believe me. Until this week, my toughest law enforcement job was taking car keys from people at The Pour House on Friday night."

"We'll take it one step at a time, I guess. First off, I need a place to work with her."

"I'm on it."

"Good." Julia smiled. "Don't wait up for me. I'll be home late." She stepped over the threshold and onto the serviceable brown carpeting.

Ellie touched her shoulder. "Jules?"

Julia turned. Her sister's face was half in shadow and half in light. "Yes?"

"I believe you can do it, you know."

Julia was surprised by how much that meant to her. She didn't trust her voice to sound normal, so she didn't say thank you. Instead, she nodded, then turned on her heel and went into the brightly lit library. Behind her, she heard Ellie sigh heavily and say, "I believe in you, too, big sis. I know you can find the kid's family." Then the door banged shut.

Julia winced. It had never occurred to her to return the sentiment. She'd always seen her sister as indestructible. Ellie had never needed approval the way she had. Ellie always expected the world to love her, and the world had complied. It was unsettling to get a glimpse of her sister's inner nature. There was a vulnerability in there somewhere, a fragility that belied the tough-girl-meets-beauty-queen exterior. So, they had something else in common after all.

Julia walked around a grid of tables to the row of computers. There were five of them—four more than she'd expected—sitting on individual desks beneath a cork bulletin board studded with book covers and flyers announcing local events.

She pulled a legal-sized yellow tablet and a black pen out of her briefcase, then scouted through the interior pockets for her handheld tape recorder. Finding it, she added new batteries, turned it on and said: "Case file one, patient name unknown."

Clicking the Stop button, she sat down on the hard wooden chair and scooted closer to the screen. The computer came on with a *thump-buzz*. The screen lit up. Within seconds she was surfing the Net and making notes. While she wrote, she also talked into the recorder.

> *"Case number one, patient: female child, age unknown. Appears to be between five and seven years of age. Name unknown.*
>
> *Child presents with limited or no language ability. Physical assessment is severe dehydration and malnutrition. Extensive ligature-type scarring on body suggests some serious past trauma. Socialization impairment appears to be marked, as does her ability to interact in an age appropriate manner. Child exhibited utter stillness for hours, broken by period of high excitability and irritation. Additionally, she appears to be terrified of shiny metal objects.*
>
> *Initial diagnosis: autism."*

She clicked the recorder off, frowning. It didn't feel right. She Googled *autism, symptoms of,* and read through the list of behaviors typically associated with autism. None of it was new information.

- Language delay
- Some never acquire language
- Lack of pleasure at being touched
- Unable/unwilling to make eye contact
- Ignores surroundings
- May appear deaf, due to ignoring of sounds/world around him/her
- Repetitive physical behaviors common, i.e., hand clapping, toe tapping
- Severe temper tantrums
- Unintelligible gibberish

- Savant abilities may develop, often in math or music or drawing
- Failure to develop peer relationships appropriate to age level

The list went on. According to the DSM IV criteria, a patient who exhibited a set number of the symptoms could reasonably be diagnosed as autistic. Unfortunately, she hadn't observed the child fully enough to answer many of the behavioral questions. Like: did the girl like to be touched? Could she exhibit reciprocal emotions? To these, Julia had no concrete answers.

But she had a gut response.

The girl *could* speak, at least some, and she could hear and understand some limited amount. Strangely, Julia was convinced that the girl's responses were normal; it was the world around her that was wrong.

There was no point in running through the related diagnoses—Asperger's syndrome, Ratt's syndrome, childhood disintegrative disorder, or PDD NOS. She simply didn't have enough information. On her pad, she wrote: *Tomorrow: study social interaction, patterns of behavior (if any), motor skills.*

She clicked the pen shut, tapped it on the table.

There was something she was missing. She went back to the computer and started searching. She had no idea what she was looking for.

For the next two hours she sat there taking notes on whatever childhood behavioral and mental disorders she could find, but none of them gave her that *Aha!* moment. Finally, at around eleven, she ran a Google search on *lost children.* That took her to a lot of television movies and kidnapping sites. That was her sister's job. She added *woods* to the search to see how many similar cases there were of children lost or abandoned in a forest or national park.

Feral children came up. It was a phrase she hadn't seen in print since her college days. Below it was the sentence fragment: . . . *lost or abandoned children raised by wolves or bears in the deep woods may seem* . . .

She moved the cursor and clicked. Text appeared on the screen.

Feral children are lost, abandoned, or otherwise forgotten chil-
dren who survive in completely isolated conditions. The idea
of children raised by wolves or bears is prevalent in legend, al-
though there are few scientifically documented cases. Some of
the more celebrated such children include:
- The three Hungarian bear boys (17th century)
- The girl of Oranienburg (1717)
- Peter, the wild boy (1726)
- Victor of Aveyron (1797)
- Kaspar Hauser (1828)
- Kamala and Amala of India (1920)
- Genie (1970)

The second most recent case listed had been in the 1990s. It fea-
tured a Ukrainian child named Oxana Malaya, who was said to have
been raised by dogs until the age of eight. She never mastered normal
social skills. Today, at the age of twenty-three, she lived in a home for
the mentally disabled. In 2004, a seven-year-old boy—also reportedly
raised by wild dogs—was found in the deep woods of Siberia. To date
he had not learned to speak.

Julia frowned and hit the Print key.

It was unlikely as hell that this girl was a true wild child. . . .

The wolf pup

The way she eats

But if she were . . .

This child could be the most profoundly damaged patient she
would ever treat, and without extensive help, the poor girl could be as
lost and forgotten in the system as she'd been in the woods.

Julia leaned over and took the stack of papers from the printer. On
top lay the last page she'd printed. A black-and-white photograph of a
little girl stared up at her. The child looked both frightened and
strangely fixated. The caption below it read: *Genie. After twelve years
of horrific abuse and isolation, she became a media sensation. The modern
equivalent of the wild child raised in a California suburb. Saved from this*

nightmare, she was brought into the light for a short time until, like all the wild children before her, she was forgotten by the doctors and scientists and shuffled off to her shadowy fate; life in an institution for the mentally disabled.

Julia couldn't imagine being the kind of doctor that would use a traumatized child for career advancement, but she knew that sooner or later those kinds of people would come for the girl. If the true story were as bad as she thought it could be, it would make front page news.

"I won't let anyone hurt you again," Julia vowed to the little girl asleep in the hospital. "I promise."

SEVEN

BY EIGHT O'CLOCK THAT EVENING THE PHONES FINALLY STOPPED ringing. There had been dozens of press-conference-related, fact-checking calls and faxes and queries from the reporters who'd been here and those who hadn't bothered to come but had somehow gotten wind of the story. And, of course, the locals had arrived in a steady stream until the dinner hour, begging for any scrap of news about Rain Valley's most unexpected guest.

"The quiet before the storm," Peanut said.

Ellie looked up from the stack of papers on her desk just in time to see her friend light up a cigarette.

"I asked. You grunted," Peanut said before Ellie could argue.

Ellie didn't bother fighting. "What about the storm?"

"It's the quiet before. Tomorrow all hell is gonna break loose. I watch Court TV, I know. Today there were a few local channels and papers here. One Flying Wolf Girl headline and that will change. Every reporter in the country will want in on the story." She shook her head, exhaling smoke and coughing. "That poor kid. How will we protect her?"

"I'm working on that."

"And how will we trust whoever comes to claim her?"

It was the question that haunted Ellie, the root of her disquiet. "That's been bothering me from the get-go, Pea. I don't want to hand her over to the very people who hurt her, but I have damned little evidence. Gut instinct doesn't go far in today's legal system. I'm actually hoping there's a kidnapping report; how sad is that? I'd love to return a little girl who was outright stolen from her home. Then there might be blood samples and a suspect. If it's not that simple . . ." She shrugged. "I'll need some help from the big boys."

"Without a crime, they'll stay away like thieves from a lineup. They'll want you to do all the hard work. The state might step in, but only to warehouse her. They've already told us as much."

Ellie had ridden this merry-go-round of worries and outcomes all night. She was no closer to an answer now than when she climbed aboard. "It's all up to Julia, I guess. If she can get a story out of the girl, we have a starting place."

"If the girl *can* talk, you mean."

"That's Julia's side of the problem, and if anyone can help that girl, it's my sister. Right now our job is to find her a place to work." Ellie tapped her pen on the desk.

Peanut started coughing again.

"Put that thing out, Pea. You're the worst smoker I've ever seen."

"And I've actually gained a pound this week. I'm going back to eating only cabbage soup. Or maybe carrot sticks." Peanut put out her cigarette. "Hey, how about the old sawmill? No one would look for her there."

"Too cold. Too indefensible. Some wily tabloid photographer would find a way in. Four roads lead up to it; at least six doors would need to be guarded. And it's public property."

"County hospital?"

"Too many employees. Sooner or later someone would sell the story." Ellie frowned. "What we need is a secret location and a cone of silence."

"In Rain Valley? You must be joking. This town lives for gossip. Everyone will want to talk to the press."

Of course. The answer was so obvious, she didn't know how she'd missed it. This was just like that time in high school when they'd stolen the attendance sheet on senior skip day. Ellie had planned the whole thing. "Call Daisy Grimm."

Peanut glanced at the clock. "*The Bachelor* is on."

"I don't care. Call her. I want everybody who is anybody in this town at a six A.M. meeting at the Congregational church."

"A town meeting? About what?"

"It's top secret."

"A *secret* town meeting, and at dawn. How dramatic." Peanut pulled a pen out from the ratted coil of her auburn hair. "What's the agenda?"

"The Flying Wolf Girl, of course. If this town wants to gossip, we'll give them something to talk about."

"Oo-ee. This is going to be fun."

For the next hour Ellie worked on the plan, while Peanut called their friends and neighbors. By ten o'clock they were done.

Ellie looked down at the contract she'd devised. It was perfect.

I _____ agree to keep any and all informa-tion about the wolf girl completely confidential. I swear I won't tell anyone anything that I learned at the town meeting in October. Rain Valley can count on me.

_____ (signature required)

"It won't hold up in court," Peanut said, coming over to her.

"Who are you? Perry Mason?"

"I watch *Boston Legal* and *Law & Order*."

Ellie rolled her eyes. "It doesn't need to be legally binding. It just needs to seem like it is. What does this town love more than any-thing?"

"A parade?"

Ellie had to concede that point. "Okay, second most."

"A two-for-one sale?"

"Gossip," she said, realizing Peanut could make guesses until dawn. "And secrets." She stood up and reached for her coat. "The only problem will be Julia."

"Why's that?"

"She's not going to like the idea of a town meeting."

"Why not?"

"You remember how it was for her in town. No one knew what to make of her. She walked around with her nose in a book. She never talked to anyone but our mom."

"That was a long time ago. She won't care what people think of her now. She's a *doctor*, for cripe's sake."

"She'll care," Ellie said with a sigh. "She always did."

He is deep in a green darkness. Overhead, leaves rustle in an invisible breeze. Clouds mask the silvery moon; there is only the sheen of light. Perhaps it is a memory.

The girl is crouched on a branch, watching him. She is so still that he wonders how his gaze found her.

Hey, he whispers, reaching out.

She drops to the leaf-carpeted floor without a sound. On all fours, she runs away.

He finds her in a cave, bound and bleeding. Afraid. He thinks he hears her say "Help," and then she is gone. There is a little boy in her place, blond-haired. He is reaching out, crying—

Max came awake with a start. For a moment he had no idea where he was. All he saw around him were pale pink walls and ruffles . . . a collection of glass figurines on a shelf . . . elves and wizards . . . there was a vase full of silk roses on the bedside table and two empty wineglasses.

Trudi.

She lay beside him, sleeping. In the moonlight her naked back looked almost pure white. He couldn't help reaching out. At his touch, she rolled over and smiled up at him. "You're going?" she whispered, her voice throaty and low.

He nodded.

She angled up to her elbows, revealing the swell of her bare breasts above the pink blanket. "What is it, Max? All night you were . . . distracted."

"The girl," he said simply.

She reached out, traced his cheekbone with her long fingernail. "I thought so. I know how much hurt kids get to you."

"Picked a hell of a career, didn't I?"

"Sometimes a person can care too much." In the uncertain light, he thought she looked sad, but he couldn't be sure. "You could talk to me, you know."

"Talking isn't what we do best. That's why we get along so well."

"We get along because I don't want to be in love."

He laughed. "And I do?"

She smiled knowingly. "See you, Max."

He kissed her shoulder, then bent down for his clothes. When he was dressed, he leaned closer to her and whispered, " 'Bye," and then he left.

Within minutes he was on his motorcycle and racing down the black, empty expanse of road. He almost turned onto the old highway; then he remembered why he'd left Trudi's house in the first place. The dream he'd had.

His patient.

He thought about that poor girl, all alone in her room.

Kids were afraid of the dark.

He changed directions and hit the gas. At the hospital, he parked beside Penelope Nutter's battered red pickup and went inside.

The hallways were empty and quiet, with only a few nighttime nurses on duty. The usual noises were gone, leaving him nothing to hear save the metronome patter of his footsteps. He stopped by the nurses' station to get the girl's chart and check on her progress.

"Hey, Doctor," said the nurse on duty. She sounded as tired as he felt.

Max leaned against the counter and smiled. "Now, Janet, how many times have I asked you to call me Max?"

She giggled and blushed. "Too many."

Max patted her plump hand. Years ago, when he'd first met Janet, all he'd seen was her Tammy Faye fake eyelashes and Marge Simpson hair. Now, when she smiled, he saw the kind of goodness that most people didn't believe in. "I'll keep hoping."

Listening to her girlish laughter, he headed for the day care center. There, he peered through the window, expecting to see the girl curled up on the mattress on the floor, asleep in the darkness. Instead, the lights were on and Julia was there, sitting on a tiny chair beside a child-sized Formica table. There was a notebook open on her lap and a tape recorder on the table near her elbow. Although he could only see her profile, she appeared utterly calm. Serene, even.

The girl, on the other hand, was agitated. She darted around the room, making strange, repetitive hand gestures. Then, all at once, she stopped dead and swung to face Julia.

Julia said something. Max couldn't hear it through the glass. The words were muffled.

The girl blew snot from her nose and shook her head. When she started to scratch her own cheeks, gouging the flesh, Julia lunged at her, took her in her arms.

The girl fought like a cat, but Julia hung on. They stumbled sideways, fell down on the mattress.

Julia held the girl immobile, ignoring the snot flying and head shaking; then Julia started to sing. He could tell by the cadence of her voice, the way the sounds blended into one another.

He went to the door and quietly opened it. Just a crack.

The girl immediately looked at him and stilled, snorting in fear.

Julia sang, ". . . *tale as old as time . . . song as . . . old as rhyme . . .*"

He stood there, mesmerized by the sound of her voice.

Julia held the girl and stroked her hair and kept singing. Not once did she even glance toward the door.

Slowly, the minutes ticked by. "Beauty and the Beast" gave way to other songs. First it was "I'm a Lonely Little Petunia in an Onion Patch," and then "Somewhere Over the Rainbow," and then "Puff the Magic Dragon."

Gradually, the girl's eyelashes fluttered shut, reopened.

The poor thing was trying so hard to stay awake.

Julia kept singing.

Finally, the girl put her thumb in her mouth, started sucking it, and fell asleep.

Very gently, Julia tucked her patient into bed and covered her with blankets, then went back to the table to gather her notes.

Max knew he should back away now, leave before she noticed him, but he couldn't move. The sound of her voice had captured him somehow, as had the glimmer of pale moonlight on her hair and skin.

"I guess this means you like watching," she said without looking at him.

He would have sworn that she'd never once glanced at the door, but she'd known he was there.

He stepped into the room. "You don't miss much, do you?"

She put the last of the papers in her briefcase and looked up. Her skin appeared ashen beneath the dim lighting; the scratches on her cheeks were dark and angry. A yellow bruise marred her forehead. But it was her eyes that got to him. "I miss plenty."

Her voice was so soft, it took him a second to really hear what she'd said.

I miss plenty.

She was talking about that patient of hers, the one that killed those children in Silverwood and then committed suicide. He knew about that kind of guilt. "You look like a woman who could use a cup of coffee."

"Coffee? At one o'clock in the morning? I don't think so, but thank you." She sidled past him, then herded him out of the day care center and shut the door behind him.

"How about pie?" he said as she headed down the hallway. "Pie is good any time of the day."

She stopped, turned around. "Pie?"

He moved toward her, unable to keep from smiling. "I knew I could tempt you."

She laughed at that, and though it was a tired, not-quite-genuine sound, it made his smile broaden. "The pie tempted me."

He led her to the cafeteria and flipped on the lights. In this quiet time of night, the place was empty; the cases and buffets were bare. "Take a seat." Max eased around the sandwich counter and went back into the kitchen, where he found two pieces of marionberry pie, which he covered with vanilla ice cream. Then he made two cups of herb tea and carried a tray out into the dining room and set it down on the table in front of Julia.

"Chamomile tea. To help you sleep," he said, sliding into the booth seat opposite her. "And marionberry pie. A local favorite." He handed her a fork.

She stared at him, frowning slightly. "Thanks," she said after a pause.

"You're welcome."

"So, Dr. Cerrasin," she said after another long silence, "do you make a habit of luring colleagues down to the cafeteria for early morning pie?"

He smiled. "Well, if by colleagues you mean doctors, there aren't exactly a lot of us. To be honest, I haven't taken old Doc Fischer out for pie in ages."

"How about the nurses?"

He heard a tone in her voice and looked up. She was eyeing him over the beige porcelain of her cup. Assessing him. "It sounds to me like you're asking about my love life." He smiled. "Is that it, Julia?"

"Love life?" She put a slight emphasis on *love*. "Do you have one of those? I would be surprised."

He frowned. "You sure think you know me."

She took a bite of pie. "Let's just say I know your kind."

"No. Let's not say that. Whoever you're confusing me with is not sitting at this table. You just met me, Julia."

"Fair enough. Why don't you tell me about yourself, then? Are you married?"

"An interesting first question. No. Are you?"

"No."

"Ever been married?"

"No."

"Ever get close?"

She glanced down for a second. It was all he needed to know. Someone had broken her heart. He'd bet that it was fairly recent. "Yes."

"How about you? Have you ever been married?"

"Once. A long time ago."

That seemed to surprise her. "Kids?"

"No."

She looked at him sharply, as if she'd heard something in his voice. Their gazes held. Finally, she smiled. "So I guess you can have pie with anyone you'd like."

"I can."

"You've probably had pie with every woman in town."

"You give me too much credit. Married women make their own pie."

"And how about my sister?"

His smile faded. Suddenly the flirting didn't seem so harmless. "What about her?"

"Have you . . . had pie with her?"

"A gentleman wouldn't really answer that, now would he?"

"So you're a gentleman."

"Of course." He was becoming uncomfortable with the course of their conversation. "How is your face feeling? That bruise is getting uglier."

"We shrinks get popped now and then. Hazards of the trade."

"You can never quite know what a person will do, can you?"

Her gaze met his. "Knowing is my job. Although by now the whole world knows I missed something important."

There was nothing he could say, no real comfort he could give, so he stayed quiet.

"No platitudes, Dr. Cerrasin? No 'God doesn't give you more than you can bear' speech?"

"Call me Max. Please." He looked at her. "And sometimes God breaks your fucking back."

It was a long moment before she said, "How did He break you, Max?"

He slid out of the booth and stood beside her. "As much as I'd love to keep chatting, I have to be at work at seven. So . . ."

Julia put the dishes on the tray and slid from the booth.

Max took the tray to the kitchen and put the dishes in the dishwasher, then they walked side by side through the quiet, empty hallways and out to the parking lot.

"I'm driving the red truck," she said, digging through her purse for the keys.

Max opened the door for her.

She looked up at him. "Thanks."

"You're welcome."

She paused, then said, "No more pie for me. Just so you know. Okay?"

He frowned. "But—"

"Thanks again." She got in the truck, slammed the door shut, and drove away.

EIGHT

J ULIA REFUSED TO LET HERSELF THINK ABOUT MAX. SHE HAD enough on her mind right now without obsessing over some small-town hunk. So what if he intrigued her? Max was definitely a player, and she had no interest in games or the kind of man who played them. That was a lesson Philip had taught her.

She turned onto Olympic Drive. This was the oldest part of town, built back in the thirties for the families of mill workers.

Driving through here was like going back in time. She came to a stop at the T in the road, and there it was, caught in her headlights.

The lumber store. In this middle-of-night hour she couldn't read the orange banner that hung in the window. Still, she knew the words by heart: *This community is supported by timber*. Those same banners had been strung throughout town since the spotted owl days.

This store was the heart of the West End. In the summer it opened as early as three o'clock in the morning. And at that, men like her father were already there and waiting impatiently to get started on their day.

She eased her foot off the accelerator and coasted through a haze of fog. So often she'd sat in her dad's pickup outside this store, waiting for him.

He'd been a cutter, her dad. A cutter was to an ordinary logger what a thoracic surgeon was to a general practitioner. The cream of the crop. He'd gone into the woods early, long before his buddies; alone. Always alone. His friends—other cutters—died so often it stopped being a surprise. But he'd loved strapping spurs onto his ankles, grabbing a rope, and scaling a two-hundred-foot-tall tree. Of course, it was an adventurer's job. Near death every day and the money to match the risk.

They'd all known it was only a matter of time before it killed him.

She hit the gas too hard. The old truck lurched forward, bucked, and died. Julia started it up again, found first gear, and headed out to the old highway.

No wonder she'd stayed at the hospital so late. She'd told herself it was about the girl, about doing a great job, but that was only part of it. She'd been putting off going back to the house where there were too many memories.

She parked the truck and went inside. The house was full of shapes and shadows, all of which were familiar. Ellie had left the stairwell light on for her; it was the same thing Mom had always done, and the sight of it—that soft, golden light spilling down the worn oak stairs—filled her heart with longing. Her mother had always waited up for her. Never in this house had she gone to bed without a nighttime kiss. No matter how badly Mom and Dad were fighting, she always got her kiss from Mom. Julia was thirteen years old the first time she'd seen through the veil; at least that was how she now thought of it. In one day she'd gone from believing her family was happy to knowing the truth. Her mother had come in that night with bloodshot eyes and tearstained cheeks. Julia had only asked a few questions before Mom started to talk.

It's your father, she'd whispered. *I shouldn't tell you, but* . . .

Those next few words were like well-placed charges. They blew

Julia's family—and her world—apart. The worst part was, Mom never told Ellie the same things.

Julia went up the stairs. In the tiny second-floor bathroom that attached to her girlhood bedroom, she brushed her teeth, washed her face, and slipped into the silk pajamas she'd brought with her from Beverly Hills, then went into her old room.

There was a note on her pillow. In Ellie's bold handwriting, it read: *Meeting at Congregational church at six a.m. to discuss girl's placement. Be ready to leave at 5:45.*

Good. Her sister was working on it.

Julia stayed up another hour, filling out all the paperwork required to be appointed temporary foster parent for the child, then she climbed into bed and clicked off the light. She was asleep almost instantly.

At four o'clock she woke with a start.

For a second she didn't know where she was. Then she saw the ballerina music box on her white desk and it all came back to her. She remembered her dream, too. She'd been a girl again—*that* girl. The scarecrow-thin, socially awkward daughter of Big Tom Cates.

She threw the covers off her and stumbled out of bed. Within minutes she was in her jogging clothes and outside, running down the old highway, past the entrance to the national park.

By five-fifteen she was back home, breathing hard, feeling like her grown-up self again.

Pale gray predawn light, as watery as everything else in this rainforest climate, shone in flashlight beams through the stand of hemlock trees that grew along the river.

She didn't decide to move, didn't want to, but before she knew it, she was walking across the yard toward her father's favorite fishing hole.

Move back, Little Bit. Outta my way. I can hardly concentrate on my fishin' with you skulkin' beside me.

No wonder she had moved away from here and stayed away. The memories were everywhere; like the trees, they seemed to draw nutrients from the land and the rain.

She turned and went back into the house.

.   .   .

JULIA AND ELLIE WERE THE FIRST TO ARRIVE. THEY PULLED UP INTO A
spot near the church's front door and got out of the car.

Ellie started to say something, but the words were lost in the
crunching sound of wheels on gravel. A snake of cars rolled into the
parking lot, lining up side by side. Earl and Myra were the first people
out of their car. Earl was in full dress uniform, but his wife had on fuzzy
pink sweats. Her hair was up in rollers and covered by a bright scarf.

Ellie took Julia by the arm and hurried her into the church. The
door clanged shut behind them.

Julia couldn't help feeling a twinge of nerves. It pissed her off, that
weakness. None of this old crap should bother her now. It wouldn't
have if she'd come home in triumph instead of shame. "I don't care
what they think anymore. I really don't. So why—"

"I never understood why you let it all get to you. Who cares if they
don't like you?"

"Girls like you can't understand," Julia said, and it was true. Ellie
had been popular. She didn't know that some hurts were like a once-
broken bone. In the right weather, they could ache for a lifetime.

The doors banged open, and people rushed into the church, took
their places in the rows of oak pews. Their voices combined, rose,
sounded like a Cuisinart on high, crushing ice. Max was one of the last
to arrive. He took a seat in the back.

Ellie went to the pulpit. She waited until six-ten, then motioned
for Peanut to shut and lock the doors. It took her another five minutes
to quiet the crowd.

"Thank you all for coming," she said finally. "I know how early it is
and I appreciate your cooperation."

"What's this all about, Ellie?" someone asked from the back of the
room. "Our shift starts in forty minutes."

"Shut up, Doug," yelled someone else. "Let 'er talk."

"You shut up, Al. It's about the Flying Wolf Girl, right, Ellie?"

Ellie held up her hands for silence. They quieted. "It is about the girl who arrived recently."

The crowd erupted again, hurling questions at the podium.

"Can she really fly?"

"Where is she?"

"Where's the wolf?"

Julia was awed by her sister's patience. There was no eye rolling, no sneering, no fist pounding. She simply said, "The wolf is with Floyd at the Olympic Game Farm. He's being well cared for."

"I heard the girl eats with her feet," someone called out.

"And only raw meat."

Ellie took a deep breath. It was the first sign that she was losing her cool. "Look. We don't have long to get ourselves together. The point is this: Do we want to protect this child?"

A resounding *yes* rose from the crowd.

"Good." She turned to Peanut. "Hand out the contracts." To the crowd, she said, "I'm going to read off your names. Please answer so I know you're here."

Ellie read off the names in alphabetical order, starting with Herb Adams. One by one people responded until she came to Mort Elzik.

There was no answer.

"He ain't here," Earl yelled.

"Okay," Ellie said. "We don't mention this meeting or the girl to Mort, or to anyone else who isn't at this meeting. Agreed?"

"Agreed," they responded in unison.

"But what is it we ain't sayin', Ellie?"

"Yeah. Speed it up. I got a charter in thirty minutes."

"And the mill's gonna open."

Ellie held up her hands for silence. "Fair enough. As you all know by now, my sister, Julia, has come home to help. What she needs is peace and quiet, and a place to work away from the media."

Daisy Grimm stood up. She wore denim overalls that were covered with appliquéd daisies. Her drugstore makeup was so bright against her powdered cheeks that it probably glowed in the dark. "Can your sister really help this poor girl? I mean . . . after what happened in California, I just wonder . . ."

The crowd went still, waiting.

"Sit down, Daisy," Ellie said sharply. "Now, here's the plan. It's a version of Hide-the-Walnut. You—We—are all going to talk to the media. When asked, we're going to secretly and *off-the-record* tell where the girl is staying. You can tell them anyplace you want—except my house. That's where she'll be. They won't trespass on the police chief's land, and if they do, Jake and Elwood will give us warning."

"We're *lying* to the press?" Violet said in awe.

"We are. Hopefully we can send them all on wild-goose chases until we know the girl's name. And one other thing: no one mentions Julia. No one."

"Lying," Marigold said, trembling like an excited puppy and clapping her hands together. "This will be fun."

"Just remember," Ellie said, "until you hear differently from me, we're lying to Mort, too. No one outside this building gets to know the truth."

Violet burst out laughing. "You can count on us, Ellie. Those reporters will be looking for the girl as far north as the Yukon. And I don't know about the rest of you, but I never *heard* of Dr. Julia Cates. I believe the poor child is seeing Dr. Welby."

NINE

WHILE ELLIE WAS PARKING THE CAR, JULIA WENT INTO THE hospital. She was almost at the old day care center when she turned the corner and ran into a man.

He stumbled back from her, sputtering, "Watch where you're going, I'm—"

Julia bent down for the black canvas bag he'd dropped. "I'm sorry. I'm in a bit of a hurry. Are you okay?"

He snatched the bag from her and then looked up.

She frowned. He looked vaguely familiar, with his rust-colored crew cut and Coke-bottle glasses. "Do I know you?"

"No. Sorry," he mumbled, glancing away quickly. Without another word, he took off running down the hallway.

She sighed. People had been doing that a lot lately. No one quite knew how to treat her since the media frenzy and the Silverwood tragedy.

She picked up her briefcase and walked down the hallway to the day care center.

A few minutes later Peanut, Max, and Ellie arrived.

They stood at the window outside the day care center, looking in. The room was full of shadows. Pockets of light grew like mushrooms above the nightlights in the various outlets, and a pale golden haze fanned down from the only ceiling fixture they'd left on.

The girl lay on the floor, curled up, with her arms wrapped around her shins. The mattress, empty save for the pile of unused blankets, was beside her. From this distance, and without benefit of good lighting, she appeared to be asleep.

"She knows we're watching her," Peanut said.

Ellie said, "She looks asleep to me."

"She's too still," Julia said. "Peanut's right."

Peanut made a tsking sound. "Poor thing. How do we move her without terrifying her?"

"We put a sedative in her apple juice," Max said. He turned to Julia. "Can you get her to drink it?"

"I think so."

"Good," he said. "Let's try that. If it doesn't work, we'll go to Plan B."

"What's Plan B?" Peanut asked, her eyes wide.

"A shot."

Thirty minutes later Julia went into the day care center, flipping on the lights as she went. Although the "team" had moved away from the window, she knew they were standing in the shadows, watching her through the glass.

The girl didn't move a finger or bat an eyelash. She simply lay there, coiled up like a snail, holding her legs close to her chest.

"I know you're awake," Julia said conversationally. She set down her tray on the table. On it was a plate filled with scrambled eggs and toast. A green plastic sippee cup held apple juice.

She sat down on the child-sized chair and ate a bite of toast. "Um- um. This is good, but it makes me thirsty." She pretended to take a sip. Nothing. No reaction.

Julia sat there for almost thirty minutes, pretending to eat and drink, talking out loud to the child who didn't respond. Every second bothered her. They needed to move this girl *fast*, before the press came looking for her here.

Finally, she pushed back from the table. The chair legs screeched against the linoleum floor.

Before Julia knew what had happened, all hell broke loose. The girl screamed; she jumped to her feet and started clawing at her face and blowing her nose.

"It's okay," Julia said evenly. "You're upset. Scared. You know that word? You're scared, that's all. It was a loud, ugly noise and it scared you. That's all. You're fine. See how quiet everything is?" Julia moved toward the girl, who was standing in the corner, thumping her forehead against the wall.

Thud. Thud. Thud.

Julia winced at each blow. "You're upset. Scared. That's okay. The noise scared me, too." Very slowly, Julia reached out, touched the child's rail-thin shoulder. "Shhh," she said.

The girl went totally still. Julia could feel the tension in the girl's shoulder and back, the tightening up. "You are okay now. Okay. No hurt. No hurt." She touched the girl's other shoulder and gently turned her around.

The girl stared up at her through wary blue-green eyes. A purplish bruise was already forming on her forehead and the scratches on her cheeks were bleeding. At this proximity the smell of urine was almost overwhelming.

"No hurt," Julia said again, expecting the girl to pull free and run.

But she stood there, breathing like a deer caught between two headlights, too fast, her whole body trembling. She was weighing the situation, cataloguing her options.

"You're trying to read me," Julia said, surprised. "Just like I'm trying to read you. I'm Julia." She patted her chest. "Julia."

The girl glanced away, disinterested. The trembling in her body eased, her breathing regulated.

"No hurt," Julia said. "Food. Hungry?"

The girl looked at the table, and Julia thought: *Bingo! You know what I said. What I meant, anyway.*

"Eat," she said, finally letting go and stepping aside.

The girl sidled past her, moving cautiously, never taking her gaze off Julia's face. When there was a safe distance between them, the girl pounced on the food. She washed it all down with the apple juice.

After that, Julia waited.

THEIR EARLY MORNING JOURNEY FROM TOWN TO THE EDGE OF THE DEEP woods had the hazy feel of a dream.

In the miles from the hospital to the old highway, no one spoke. For Max, there was something about this clandestine rescue that precluded the luxury of talk. He assumed it was the same for his co-conspirators, for although they told themselves this move was in the girl's best interest— and indeed believed it—there was still a nagging worry, an unbound thread. At least at the hospital she was safe. The door locked; the glass was too thick to break. Here, in the last stretch of valley before the big trees, the world outside was too close; none of them doubted that those woods would beckon her.

He was in the backseat of the police cruiser, with Julia seated to his right. The girl lay between them with her head in Julia's lap, her bare feet in his. In the front seat, Ellie and Peanut sat in silence. Except for the sound of their breathing and the crunching of the tires on thick gravel, the only sound came from the radio. It was turned down so quietly it could hardly be heard at all, but every now and then Max caught a stanza or two and recognized a song. Right now it was "Superman" by Crash Test Dummies.

He looked down at the girl in his lap. She was so incredibly thin and frail. Today's scratches marred her cheeks, but even in this half-light he could see the silvery scars of older scratches. Evidence that she'd often attacked herself or been attacked. The bruise on her forehead was purple now, angry-looking. But it was the scarring on her left ankle that made his stomach tighten. The ligature marks.

"We're here," Ellie said from the front seat as she parked beneath an old shake lean-to. Moss turned the slanted roof into a patch of green fur.

Max scooped the sleeping child into his arms. Her arms curled around his neck; she pressed her wrecked cheek against his chest. Her black hair fell sideways, over his arm, almost to his thighs.

He knew exactly how to hold her. How was it that even after all these years, it still felt as natural as breathing?

Ellie hurried on ahead and turned on the exterior lights.

Max carried the girl toward the house. Julia fell into step beside him.

"You're still safe," she said to the girl. "We're outside now. At my parents' house. Safe here. I promise."

From somewhere, deep in the woods, a wolf howled.

Max stopped; Julia did the same.

Peanut made the sign of the cross. "I am not feeling good about this."

"I've never heard a wolf out here," Ellie said. "It can't be her wolf. He's over in Sequim."

The girl moaned.

The wolf howled again; an undulating, elegiac sound.

Julia touched his shoulder. "Come on, Max. Let's get her inside."

No one spoke as they walked through the house, up the stairs, and into the bedroom. Max put the child on the bed and covered her with blankets.

Peanut glanced nervously at the window, as if the wolf were out there, pacing the yard, looking for a way in. "She's gonna try to escape. Those are her woods."

So they were all thinking the same thing. Somehow, as impossible as it sounded, the child belonged out there more than she did in here.

"Here's what we need, and fast," Julia said. "Bars—skinny ones—on the window, so she can see outside but can't escape, and a dead bolt for the door. We need to cover every scrap of shiny metal with adhesive tape—the faucet, the toilet handle, the drawer pulls; everything except the doorknob."

"Why?" Peanut asked.

"I think she's afraid of shiny metal," Julia answered distractedly. "And we'll need a video camera set up as surreptitiously as possible. I'll need to record her condition."

"I thought you said no pictures," Ellie said, frowning.

"That was for the tabloids. This is for me. I need to observe her 24/7. We need food, too. And lots of tall houseplants. I want to turn one corner of the room into a forest."

"*Where the Wild Things Are*," Peanut said.

Julia nodded, then went to the bed and sat down beside the girl.

Max followed her. Kneeling beside the bed, he checked the girl's pulse and breathing. "Normal," he said, sitting back on his heels.

"If only her mind and her heart were as easy to read as her vital signs," Julia said.

"You'd be out of a job."

Julia surprised him by laughing.

They looked at each other.

The bedside lamp flickered on and off, sparking electricity. The girl on the bed made a whining, desperate sound.

"There's something weird going on here," Peanut said, stepping back.

"Don't do that," Julia said quietly. "She's just a child who has been through hell."

Peanut fell silent.

"We should go to town. Get supplies from the lumber store," Ellie said.

Max nodded. "I have time to put up the bars before my shift."

"Good. Thanks," Julia said. When they were gone, she remained at her place by the bed. "You're safe here, little one. I promise."

Julia said it over and over again, keeping her voice as gentle as a caress, but through it all, there was one thing she knew for certain.

This girl had no idea what it meant to be safe.

. . .

GONE IS THE BAD SMELL AND THE WHITE, HISSING LIGHT THAT STINGS her eyes. Girl opens her eyes slowly, afraid of what she will see. There have been too many changes. It is as if she has fallen in the dark water past her place, that pool in the deep forest that Him said was the start of Out There.

This cave is different. Everything is the color of snow and of the berries she picks in early summer. It is morning outside; the light in the room is sun-colored. She starts to get up but can't move. Something is holding her down. She panics, kicking and flailing to be free.

But she is not tied.

She moves out of the soft place and crouches on the ground, sniffing the scents of this strange place. Wood. Flowers. There is more, of course, many smells, but she doesn't know them.

Somewhere, water is dripping; it sounds like the last rain falling from a leaf to the hard summer's ground. There is a banging, clanging sound, too. The entrance to this cave is like the last one, a thick brown thing. There is something about the shiny ball on it that is the source of its magic; she is afraid to touch it. The Strangers would know then that she was wide-eyed. They would come for her again with their nets and their sharp points. She is safe from them only in the dark time when the sun sleeps.

A breeze floats past her face, ruffles her hair. On it is the scent of her place. She looks around.

There it is. The box that holds the wind. It is not like the other one, the trickster box that kept the outside out, through which you couldn't touch.

She moves forward, holding her stomach tightly.

Sweet air comes through the box. She carefully puts her hand through the opening. She moves slowly, a bit at a time, ready to pull back at the first sharp pain.

But nothing stops her. Finally, her whole arm is Out There, in her world, where the air seems to be made of raindrops.

She closes her eyes. For the first time since they trapped her, she can breathe. She lets out a long, desperate howl.

Come for me, that noise means, but she stops in the middle of it. She is so far away from her cave. There is no one to hear her.

This is why Him always told her to *stay*. He knew the world beyond her chain.

Out There is full of Strangers who will hurt Girl.

And she is alone now.

YEARS AGO, ELLIE HAD GONE TO THE DRIVE-IN WITH HER THEN-boyfriend, Scott Lauck, and seen a movie called *Ants*. Or maybe it had been *Swarm*. She wasn't entirely sure now. All she really remembered was a scene with Joan Collins being swarmed by Volkswagen-sized ants. Ellie, of course, had been more interested in making out with Scotty than watching the movie. Still, it was those long-ago film images that came to her now as she stood in the hallway outside the lunchroom, sipping her coffee and looking out at the melee in the station.

It was a hive of people. From her place at the end of the hall, she couldn't see a patch of floor or a sliver of wall. It was the same way outside and down the block.

The story had broken this morning under a variety of headlines.

THE GIRL FROM NOWHERE
WHO AM I?
REMEMBER ME?

And Ellie's particular favorite (this from Mort in the *Gazette*): FLY-ING MUTE LANDS IN RAIN VALLEY. His first paragraph described the girl's prodigious leaping capabilities and, naturally, her wolf companion. His description of her was the only accurate report. He made her sound crazy, wild, and heartbreakingly pathetic.

At eight A.M. the first call had come in. Cal hadn't had a moment's peace since then. By one o'clock the first national news van had pulled into town. Within two hours the streets were jammed with vans and reporters demanding another press conference. Everyone from journalists to parents to kooks and psychics wanted to get the scoop firsthand.

"So far nothing has panned out," Peanut said, coming out of the lunchroom. "No one knows who she is."

Ellie sipped her coffee and eyed the crowd.

Cal looked up from his desk and saw the two of them. He was talking into the dispatch headset at the same time he fielded questions from the crowd of reporters in front of him.

Ellie smiled at him.

He mouthed, *Help me*.

"Cal's losing it," Peanut said.

"I can hardly blame him. He didn't take this job to actually work."

"Who did?" Peanut said, laughing.

"That would be me." Ellie looked at her friend, said, "Wish me luck," and then waded back into the sea of clamoring, shouting reporters. In their midst, she raised her hands in the air. It took a long time to quiet them. Finally, she got their attention.

"There will be no more comments—either on or off the record—by anyone in this office today. We'll conduct a press conference at six o'clock and answer everything then."

Chaos erupted.

"But we need photos!"

"These artist renderings are crap—"

"Drawings don't sell papers—"

Ellie shook her head, exasperated. "I don't know how my sister—"

"That's it!" Peanut barreled into the crowd, using the come-to-Jesus voice she'd perfected when Tara, her daughter, turned thirteen. "You heard the chief. Everyone *out*. Now."

Peanut herded them out, then slammed the door shut.

It wasn't until Ellie turned toward her desk that she saw him.

Mort Elzick was standing in the corner, wedged between two industrial green metal file cabinets. He was pale and sweaty-looking in his brown, wide-wale corduroy pants and navy blue golf shirt. His red crew cut was so long it looked like a fringed pompadour. Behind thick glasses, his eyes looked huge and watery. When he saw her looking at him, he moved forward. His worn white-and-gray tennis shoes squeaked with every step. "Y-You need to give me an exclusive, Ellie. This is my big break. I could get a job with the *Olympian* or the *Everett Herald*."

"With a 'Mowgli Lives' headline? I doubt it."

He flushed. "What would a junior college dropout know about the classics? I know Julia is helping on this case."

"You think she is. Put it in print and I'll bury you."

His pale eyebrows beetled; his face turned red. "Give me an exclusive, Ellie. You owe it to me. Or . . ."

"Or what?" She moved closer.

"Or else."

"Mention my sister and I'll get you fired."

He stepped back. "You think you're something special. But you can't get your way all the time. I gave you a chance. You remember that."

On that, he pushed past her and ran out of the station.

"Praise Jesus and pass the ice," Cal said. He went down to the lunchroom and came back with three beers.

"You can't drink in here, Cal," Ellie said tiredly.

"Bite me," he said. "And I mean that in the nicest possible way. If I'd wanted an actual job, I wouldn't have answered your ad. I haven't been able to read a comic book in peace all week." He handed her a Corona.

"No, thanks," Peanut said when he offered her a beer. She went into the lunchroom, then came back out holding a mug.

Ellie looked at her friend.

"Cabbage soup," Peanut said, shrugging.

Cal sat on his desk, feet swinging, and drank his beer. His Adam's apple slid up and down his throat like a swallowed fishbone. His black hair reflected the light in waves of blue. "Good for you, Pea. I was afraid you were going to try the heroin diet next."

Peanut laughed. "To be honest, that smoking really sucked. Benji wouldn't even kiss me good-night."

"And you two are always making out," Cal said.

Ellie heard something in Cal's voice, a rawness that confused her. She looked at him. For a moment she saw him as he used to be—a gawky kid with features too sharp for childhood. His eyes had always been shadowed then, full of wariness.

He set his beer down and sighed. For the first time, she noticed how tired he looked. His mouth, usually curled in an irritatingly buoyant smile, was a thin pale line.

She couldn't help feeling sorry for him. She knew exactly what the problem was. Cal had worked for her now for two-and-a-half years fulltime; before that he'd been an at home dad. His wife, Lisa, was a sales rep for a New York company and was gone more than she was home. When the kids were all in school, Cal took the dispatch job to fill the empty hours while they were gone. Mostly, he read comic books during the day and drew action figures in his sketch pad. He was a good dispatcher, as long as the biggest emergency was a cat stuck in a tree. The past few days seemed to have undone him. She realized how much she missed his smile. "I'll tell you what, Cal. I'll handle the press conference. You go on home."

He looked pathetically hopeful. Still, he said, "You need someone to answer the emergency calls."

"Forward the calls to the service. If something's important, they'll radio me. It'll only be the 911 calls anyway."

"You're sure? I could come back after Emily's soccer game."

"That would be great."

"Thanks, Ellie." He finally grinned; it made him look about seventeen years old again. "I'm sorry I gave you the finger this morning."

"It's fine, Cal. Sometimes a man just has to make his point." It was what her father used to say whenever he banged his fist on the kitchen table.

Cal plucked his department issue rain slicker off the antler hook and left the station.

Ellie returned to her desk and sat down. To her left was a stack of faxes at least two inches tall. Each sheet of paper represented a lost child, a grieving family. She'd gone through them carefully, highlighted the similarities and the distinctions. As soon as the press conference was over, she'd start calling the various agencies and officers back. No doubt she'd be on the phone all night.

"You're getting that faraway look again," Peanut said, sipping her soup.

"Just thinking."

Peanut set down her mug. "You can do it, you know. You're a great cop."

Ellie wanted to agree with that wholeheartedly. On any other day she would have. But now she couldn't help glancing at the small stack of "evidence" they'd gathered on the girl's identity. There were four photographs—a face shot, a profile close-up, and two body shots. In each, the girl was so sedated she looked dead. The press would have a field day with them. Below the stack of eight-by-tens was a list of the girl's scars, identifying moles, and, of course, the birthmark on her back shoulder. In the photograph that accompanied the list, the birthmark looked remarkably like a dragonfly. The record also included X rays; Max estimated that her left arm had been broken when she was quite young. He believed it had healed without professional medical treatment. Each injury, scar, and birthmark had been marked on a diagram of her body. They had taken blood samples—she was type AB—fingerprints, and dental X rays; her blood had been sent off for DNA analysis, but that report wasn't back yet. Her dress had also been sent away for analysis.

There was nothing for them to do now except wait. And pray that someone came forward to identify the girl.

"I don't know, Pea. This is a tough one."

"You're up to it."

Ellie smiled at her friend. "Of all the decisions I've made in this job, you know what was the best one?"

"The 'Drive a Drunk Home' program?"

"Close: it was hiring you, Penelope Nutter."

She grinned. "Every star needs a sidekick."

Laughing, Ellie went back to work, reading through the pile of documents on her desk.

A few moments later there was a knock at the door. Peanut looked up. "Who knocks at a police station?"

Ellie shrugged. "Not a reporter. Come in," she said loudly.

Slowly, the door opened. A couple stood on the front step, peering inside. "Are you Chief Barton?" asked the man.

They weren't reporters, that much was certain. The man was tall and white-haired, thin to the point of gauntness. He wore a pale gray cashmere sweater and black pants with knife-sharp pleats. And big city shoes. The woman—his wife?—was dressed in black, from head to toe. Black coatdress, black hose, black pumps. Her hair, an expensive trio of blonds, was drawn back from her pale face and coiled in a French twist.

Ellie stood. "Come on in."

The man touched the woman's elbow, guided her to Ellie's desk. "Chief Barton, I'm Dr. Isaac Stern. This is my wife, Barbara."

Ellie shook both of their hands, noticing how cold their skin was. "It's nice to meet you."

A blast of wind hit the open door, made it smack hard against the wall.

"Excuse me." Ellie went to shut the door. "How can I help you?"

Dr. Stern looked at her. "I'm here about my daughter, Ruthie. *Our* daughter," he corrected, looking at his wife. "She disappeared in 1996. There are many of us here. Parents."

Ellie glanced outside. The reporters were still congregated in the street, talking among themselves and waiting for the press conference, but it was the line of people that caught her attention.

Parents.

There had to be one hundred of them.

"Please," said a man standing on the steps. "You threw us out with the press, but we need to talk to you. Some of us have come a long way."

"Of course I'll talk to you," Ellie said. "One at a time, though. Pass the word down the line. We'll be here all night if we need to."

While the news was being spread, Ellie heard several women burst into quiet sobs.

She shut the door as gently as she could. Steeling herself, she headed back to her desk and took her seat. "Sit down," she said, indicating the two chairs in front of the desk.

"Penelope," she said, "you can interview people, too. Just take down names, contact numbers, and any information they have."

"Sure, Chief." Peanut immediately headed for the door.

"Now," Ellie said, leaning forward. "Tell me about your daughter."

Grief stared back at her, stark as blood on snow.

Dr. Stern was the first to speak. "Our Ruthie left for school one day and never arrived there. It was two blocks from our house. I called the policeman who has been our friend in this, and he tells me this girl you have found cannot be my—our—Ruthie. I tell him our people believe in miracles, so we've come here to see you." He reached into his pocket and pulled out a small worn photograph. In it, a beautiful little girl with sandy brown ringlets held on to a bright pink Power Rangers lunch box. The date in the lower right corner was September 7, 1996.

Today, Ruthie would be at least thirteen. Maybe fourteen.

Ellie took a deep breath. It was impossible not to think suddenly of the line of hopeful parents outside, all of them waiting for a miracle. This would be the longest day of her life. Already she wanted to cry.

She took the photo, touched it. When she looked up again, Mrs. Stern was weeping. "Ruthie's blood type?"

"O," Mrs. Stern said, wiping her eyes and waiting.

"I'm sorry," Ellie said. "So very sorry."

Across the room, Peanut opened the door. Another couple walked in, clutching a color photograph to their chest.

Please God, Ellie prayed, closing her eyes for just a moment, a heartbeat, *let me be strong enough for this*.

Then Mrs. Stern started to talk. "Horses," she said in a throaty voice. "She loved horses, our Ruthie. We thought she wasn't old enough for lessons. Next year, we always said. Next year . . ."

Dr. Stern touched his wife's arm. "And then . . . this." He took the picture from Ellie, staring down at it. Tears brightened his eyes. He looked up finally. "You have children, Chief Barton?"

"No."

Ellie thought he was going to say something to that, but he remained silent, helping his wife to her feet.

"Thank you for your time, Chief."

"I'm sorry," she said again.

"I know," he said, and Ellie could see suddenly how fragile he was, how hard he was working to keep his composure. He took his wife's arm and steered her to the door. They left.

A moment later a man walked in. He wore a battered, patched pair of faded overalls and a flannel shirt. An orange Stihl chainsaw baseball cap covered his eyes, and a gray beard consumed the lower half of his face. He clutched a photograph to his chest.

It was of a blond cheerleader; Ellie could see from here.

"Chief Barton?" he said in a hopeful voice.

"That's me," she answered. "Please. Come sit down . . ."

TEN

L AST NIGHT JULIA HAD TRANSFORMED HER GIRLHOOD BEDROOM into a safety zone for her and her patient. The two twin beds still graced the left wall, but now the spaces beneath them were filled to block hiding places. In the corner by the window, she'd gathered almost one dozen tall, potted plants and created a mini-forest. A long Formica table took up the center of the room, serving as a desk and study space. Two chairs sat tucked up beside it. Now, however, she realized what she'd missed: a comfortable chair.

For the past six hours the child had stood at the barred, open window, with her arm stuck outside. Come rain or shine, she held her hand out there. Somewhere around noon a robin had landed on the windowsill and stayed there. Now, in the pale gray sunlight that followed the last hour's rain, a brightly colored butterfly landed on her outstretched hand, fluttering there for the space of a single breath, then flew off.

If Julia hadn't written it down, she would have stopped believing she'd seen it. After all, it was autumn; hardly the season for butterflies, and even in the full heat of summer, they rarely landed on a little girl's hand, not even for an instant.

But she *had* written it down, made a note of it in the permanent file, and so there it was now. A fact to be considered, another oddity among the rest.

Perhaps it was the girl's stillness. She hadn't moved in hours.

Not a shifting of her weight, not a changing of her arm, not a turn of her head. Not only did she evidence no repetitive or obsessive movements, she was as still as a chameleon. The social worker who had come this morning to conduct the home study to determine Julia's fitness as a temporary foster parent had been shocked, though she tried to hide it. As she closed her notebook, the woman had thrown a last, worried glance at the girl before whispering to Julia, "Are you sure?"

"I am," Julia had said. And she was. Helping this child had already become something of a quest.

Last night after preparing the bedroom, she had stayed up late, sitting at the kitchen table, making notes and reading everything she'd been able to find on the few true wild children on record. It was both fascinating and wrenchingly sad.

Their cases all followed a similar pattern, whether they'd been found three hundred years ago in the dense woods of Bavaria or in this century in the wilds of Africa. All of them were discovered—usually by hunters—hiding in deep, dark forests. More than a third of them ran on all fours. Very few had been able to speak. Several of them—including Peter, the wild boy in 1726; Memmie, the so-called Savage Girl in France; and most famously, Victor, the wild boy of Aveyron in 1797— had become media sensations in their day. Scientists and doctors and language theorists flocked to their sides, each hoping their wild child would answer the most elemental human nature questions. Kings and princesses brought them to court as oddities, entertainments. The most recent case, that of a girl named Genie, who, though not raised in the wild, had been subjected to such systematic and horrific abuse that she had never learned to speak or move around or play, was yet another case of media attention.

Most of the documented cases had two things in common. First, the children possessed the physical ability to speak, but never acquired actual language to any great degree. Secondly, almost all of these former wild children lived out their lives in mental institutions, forgotten and alone. Only two cases, Memmie and a Ugandan boy found living among the monkeys in 1991, ever truly learned to speak and function in society, and Memmie still died penniless and alone, forgotten. She had never been able to tell people what had happened to her in her youth, how she'd ended up in the dark woods.

One after another, scientists and doctors had been drawn to the challenge these children presented. The so-called professionals wanted to know and understand—and yes, to "save"—a human being totally unlike all others, one who could be seen as more pure, more untouched than anyone born in a thousand years. A person unsocialized, uncorrupted by man's teachings. One by one they had failed in their quest. Why? Because they cared too little about their patients.

It was not a mistake she would make.

She wouldn't be like the doctors who'd gone before her, who'd sucked the soul from their patients, furthered their own careers, and then moved on, leaving their silent, broken patients locked behind bars, more confused and alone than they'd been in the woods.

"It's your heart that matters, isn't it, little one?" she said, looking up again. As Julia watched, another bird landed on the windowsill by the girl's outstretched hand. The bird cocked its head and warbled a little song.

The girl imitated the sound perfectly.

The bird appeared to listen, then sang again.

The girl responded.

Julia glanced at the video camera set up in the corner. The red light was on. This bizarre "conversation" was being recorded.

"Are you communicating with him?" Julia asked, making a note of it in her records. She knew it would sound ridiculous, but she was seeing it. The girl and the bird seemed to understand each other. At the very least, the child was an accomplished mimic.

Then again, if she'd grown up in the woods, alone or among a pack of animals, she wouldn't necessarily make the distinctions between man and animals that were commonplace in our civilized world.

"Do you know the difference between man and animal, I wonder?" She tapped her pen on the pad of paper. At the gentle thudding sound, the bird flew away.

Julia reached sideways for the books on the table that served as her makeshift desk. There were four of them. *The Secret Garden, Andersen's Fairy Tales, Alice in Wonderland,* and *The Velveteen Rabbit.* These were only four of the many books donated by the generous townspeople. Early this morning, while the girl was still asleep, Julia had changed her diaper and then searched the boxes for anything that might help her communicate with her patient. She'd chosen crayons and paper, a pair of old Barbie dolls, still dressed for disco, and these books.

She opened the top one, *The Secret Garden,* and began to read out loud. "When Mary Lennox was sent to Misselthwaite Manor to live with her uncle, everybody said she was the most disagreeable-looking child ever seen. . . ."

For the next hour Julia read the beloved children's story aloud, concentrating on giving her voice a gentle, singsong cadence. There was no doubt in her mind that her patient didn't know most of these words and thus couldn't follow the story, and yet, like all preverbal children, the girl liked the sound of it.

At the end of a chapter, Julia gently closed the book. "I'm going to take a short break here. I'll be right back. *Back,*" she repeated in case the word was familiar.

She stood slowly, stretching. Long hours spent sitting in this chair, tucked up to a makeshift desk at the end of her girlhood bed, had left her with a crick in her neck. She took her pen—it could be a weapon, after all—and headed for the tiny bathroom that had been built for her and Ellie when they were preteens. It connected to their bedroom through a door by the dresser.

Julia went into the bathroom and closed the door just enough for privacy. She didn't want her voice to be lost. Pulling down her pants, she sat on the toilet and said, "I'm just going to go to the bathroom, honey. I'll be right back. I want to know what happens to Mary, too. Do you think she really hears crying? Do *you* cry? Do you know what—"

The girl skidded to a stop in the doorway and shoved the door open, wincing when it banged against the wall. She slapped her cheeks and shook her head. Snot flew from her nose as she blew it, hard.

"You're upset," Julia said in a soothing voice. "Upset. You're getting angry. Did you think I was leaving?"

At the sound of Julia's voice, the girl quieted. She looked nervously at the door, sidling away from it.

"We'll keep the door open from now on, but I need to go potty. You know that word? Potty?"

Perhaps there was the merest flinch at the word, a flash of recognition. Perhaps not.

The girl just stood there, watching her.

"I need privacy. You should . . . aw, hell." None of the social niceties mattered here.

The girl frowned and took a step closer. She cocked her head in the same way the blue jay had, as if to see things from a preferable angle.

"I'm peeing," Julia said matter-of-factly, reaching for the toilet paper.

The girl was intent now, utterly focused. Once again she'd gone completely still.

When Julia was done, she stood and pulled up her pants, and then flushed the toilet.

At the noise, the girl screamed and threw herself backward so fast she stumbled and fell. Sprawled on the floor, she started to howl.

"It's okay," Julia said. "No hurt. No hurt. I promise." She flushed the toilet again and again, until the girl finally sat up. Then Julia washed her hands and moved slowly toward her little patient. "Would you like me to keep reading?" She knelt down. They were eye level now, and close. She could see the remarkable turquoise color of the child's eyes; the irises were flecked with amber. Thick black lashes lowered slowly, then opened.

"Book," Julia said again, pointing at the novel on the table.

The girl walked over to the table and sat down on the floor beside it.

Julia drew in a sharp breath, but other than that, she didn't react. She went to the nearest chair and sat down. "I think Ellie and I should move Mom's old love seat in here. What do you think?"

The girl moved a little closer. Sitting cross-legged, she looked up at Julia.

Just then, even with her food-stained face and tangled hair, the girl looked like every kindergartner in every classroom at story time.

"I bet you're waiting for me to start."

As always, the only answer was silence. Those eerie blue-green eyes stared up at her. This time, maybe, there was a hint of anticipation, impatience, even. An ordinary kid would have said *Read* in an imperious tone. This girl simply waited.

Julia returned to the story. On and on she read, about Mary and Dicken and Colin and the secret garden that had belonged to Mary's lost mother. She read chapter after chapter, until night began to press against the window in strips of pink and purple. She was approaching the final chapters when a knock sounded at the door. The dogs started barking.

At the noise, the girl raced to her potted plant sanctuary and hid behind the leaves.

The door opened slowly. Behind it, the golden retrievers were crazy to get inside. "Down, Jake. Elwood. What's wrong with you two?" Ellie slipped past them and slammed the door shut with her hip. In the hallway, the dogs howled pitifully and scratched at the door.

"You need to get those dogs trained," Julia said, closing her book.

Ellie, who had a tray of food, set it down on the table. "I thought getting rid of their balls would make them trainable. No such luck. It's in the dick." She sat down on the end of her old bed. "How's the girl doing? I see she still thinks I'm Nurse Ratchett."

"She's doing better, I think. She seems to like being read to."

"Has she tried to escape?"

"No. She won't go near the door. I think it's the doorknob. Shiny metal really sets her off."

Ellie leaned forward and put her forearms along her thighs. "I wish I could say I was making progress on my end."

"You are. This story is making headlines. Someone will come forward."

"People *are* coming forward. I had seventy-six people in my office today. All of them had lost daughters in the last few years. Their stories . . . their pictures . . . it was awful."

"It's incredibly painful to sit witness to such grief."

"How do you do it, listen to sad stories all day long?"

Julia had never seen her job that way. "A story is only sad if there's no happy ending. I guess I always believe in that ending."

"A closet romantic. Who'd have thought?"

Julia laughed. "Hardly. So, how did the press conference go?"

"Long. Boring. Full of stupid questions. The national networks are just as bad. And I learned this about reporters: if a question is too ridiculous to be answered, they'll ask it again. My personal favorite was from the *National Enquirer.* They were hoping she had wings instead of arms. Oh, and *The Star* wondered if she'd lived with the wolves."

Thankfully it was a tabloid. No one would lend the story any credence. "What about an identification?"

"Not yet. Between the X rays, the birthmarks, the scarring, and her age range, we're narrowing the possibilities down, though. Oh, and your approval came through from DSHS. You're officially her temporary foster parent."

The girl crept out from her hiding place. Nostrils flaring, she paused, smelled the air, then streaked across the room, running low to the ground. Julia had never seen a kid move so fast. She disappeared into the bathroom.

Ellie whistled. "So that's what Daisy meant when she said the girl ran like the wind."

Julia slowly walked toward the bathroom.

Ellie followed her.

The girl was sitting on the toilet, with her pull-up big-kid diaper around her ankles.

"Holy cow," Ellie whispered. "Did you teach her that?"

Julia couldn't believe it herself. "She walked in on me today, when I was going to the bathroom. The sound of the flushing scared her to death. I would have *sworn* she'd never seen a toilet before."

"You think she taught herself? By seeing you once?"

Julia didn't answer. Any noise could ruin this moment. She inched into the room and gathered up some toilet paper. She showed the girl what to do with it, then handed it to her. The child frowned at the wadded up paper for a long time. Finally, she took it and used it. When she was finished, she slithered off the toilet, pulled up her diaper/underwear, and hit the white tape-covered lever. At the flushing noise, she screamed and ran, ducking between Julia's and Ellie's legs.

"Wow," Ellie said.

They both stared at the girl hiding in the forest of potted plants.

In the quiet room, the girl's breathing was loud and fast.

"This whole thing just gets stranger and stranger," Ellie said.

Julia couldn't disagree with that.

"Well," Ellie said at last, "I need to get back to the office. I don't know how long I'll be." She pulled a piece of paper out of her back pocket and handed it to Julia. "These are Peanut's and Cal's home numbers. If you need to go to the library again, they'll stay at the house with the kid."

"Thanks."

Julia walked Ellie to the door, let her out, then shut it again. She didn't bother locking it. So far, the girl seemed terrified of the door-knob.

She went to the table, where she made a few more notes, then set her paper and pen away.

"It's dinnertime."

The girl remained hidden in the plants, watching her.

"Food." She tapped the tray Ellie had left.

This time the girl moved. She crept out from the cover of green leaves and came to the table, where she started to attack the food in her usual way.

Julia grabbed her wrist. "No."

Their gazes clashed.

"You're too smart for this, aren't you?" Julia got up, still holding the bird-thin wrist, and moved around to stand beside the girl. "Sit." She pulled out a chair and patted the seat. "Sit."

For the next thirty minutes they stood there, locked in a battle with a one-word soundtrack.

Sit.

At first the girl howled and snorted and shook her head, trying to pull free.

Julia simply held on to her, shaking her head, saying, "Sit."

When the histrionics didn't work, the girl shut up. She stood perfectly still, staring at Julia through slitted, angry eyes.

"Sit," Julia said, patting the chair again.

The girl sighed dramatically and sat down.

Julia released her instantly. "Good girl." She washed the child's hands with baby wipes, then walked back around to the other side of the table and took her seat.

The girl attacked the food, eating as if it were a recent kill.

"You're at the table," Julia said. "That's a start. We'll work on manners tomorrow. After your bath." She reached down for her notebook and put it in her lap, flipping through the pages while the child ate. Maybe there was an answer in here, but she doubted it. This was a case of questions.

A paragraph she'd written this afternoon caught her eye.

A perfect mimic. The child can repeat birdsong note for note. It almost seems as if they're communicating, she and the bird, although that's not possible.

"Is that the answer, little one? Did you see me using the toilet and simply mimic me? Was that a skill you needed to learn in the wild?"

She wrote down: *In the absence of people, or society, how do we learn? By trial and error? By mimicry of other species? Perhaps she learned to learn fast and by observation.*

Julia lifted her pen from the page.

It felt like half an answer at best. A child who'd grown up in the wild, within a wolf pack or among other animals, would have learned to mark territory with urine. She wouldn't see the point in using a toilet.

Unless she'd seen one before, however long ago. Or she recognized a new pack leader in her and wanted to belong. "Who are you, little one? Where do you come from?"

As always, there was no answer.

WHILE THE GIRL WAS EATING, JULIA SLIPPED OUT OF THE ROOM AND went downstairs.

The house was quiet.

In the carport she found the two cardboard boxes that held the town's donations. One was filled with clothes. The other held all kinds of books and toys.

Julia went through everything again, condensing the best, most useful items into one box, which she carried back upstairs and set down on the floor with a thud.

The girl looked up sharply.

Julia almost laughed at the sight of her. There was as much food on her face and hospital gown as had been on her plate. The whipped cream/coconut ambrosia fruit salad clung to her nose, her cheeks, and her chin in a white beard.

"You look like Santa's mini me."

Julia bent down and opened the box. Three items lay on top. A beautiful, lacy white nightdress with pink bows on it, a doll in diapers, and a brightly colored set of plastic blocks.

She stepped back. "Toys. Do you know that word?"

No reaction.

"Play. Fun."

The girl stared at her, unblinking.

Julia bent down and picked up the nightgown. The worn cotton felt soft to the touch.

The girl's eyes widened. She made a sound, a low, growling noise that came from deep in the back of her throat. In a movement almost too fast and silent to be believed, she got out of her chair, ran around the table and yanked the nightdress out of Julia's grasp. Clutching it to her breast, she returned to her hiding place behind the potted plants and crouched down.

"Well, well, well," Julia said. "I see someone likes pretty things."

The girl started to hum. Her fingers found a tiny pink satin bow and began stroking it.

"You'll need to get clean if you want to wear the pretty dress."

Julia went into the bathroom and turned on the bathwater, then sat on the edge of the tub. "When I was your age I loved taking baths. My mom used to add lavender oil to the water. It smelled so good. Oh, look, here's a little bottle of it left in the cabinet. I'll add some for you."

When she turned around again, the girl was there, standing just inside the open door, looking in.

Julia held out a hand. "No hurt," she said gently, turning off the water. "No, hurt." Then: "Come."

No response.

"It feels so good to be clean." Julia skimmed her other hand through the water. "Nice. Come on."

The girl's steps forward were so small as to be almost nonexistent, and yet she was moving. Her gaze ping-ponged between the adhesive-tape-covered faucet and Julia's hand.

"Have you seen running water before?" Julia let the water stream from her fingers. "Water. Wa-ter."

The girl was at the bathtub's edge now. She was staring at the water with a mixture of fear and fascination.

Very slowly, Julia bent down to undress the girl, who offered no opposition at all. It surprised Julia, that easy compliance. What did it mean, if anything? She took the hospital gown away, looped it over the towel rack, then took hold of the girl's bird-thin wrist and gently urged her toward the tub. "Touch the water. Just try." She showed her how, hoping the action would be mimicked.

It took a long time, but the girl finally dipped her hand in the water.

The girl's eyes widened. She made a sound that was half sigh and half growl.

Julia stripped down to her bra and panties, then got into the tub. "You see?" she said, smiling. "This is what I want you to do." When the girl stepped closer, Julia got out of the tub and sat on the cool porcelain edge. "Your turn. Go ahead."

Cautiously, the girl climbed over the tub's porcelain edge and lowered herself into the water. The minute she was in, she made a sound, almost like a purr, and looked up at Julia. Then she slapped at the water and kicked her feet and splashed around, and set about exploring. She licked the tiles and touched the grout and sniffed the faucets. She cupped water in her hands and drank it (a habit to be broken, of course, but later).

Finally, Julia reached for the bar of lavender-scented soap in the dish. This, she handed to the girl, who smelled it, then tried to eat it.

Julia couldn't help laughing. "No. Icky." She made a face. "Icky."

The child frowned, tried to grab it.

Julia rubbed her hands together to make a soapy foam. "Okay. I'm going to bathe you now. Clean. Soap." Very slowly she reached out, took the girl's hand in hers and began washing.

The girl watched her with the intensity of a magician's apprentice trying to learn a new trick. Slowly, as Julia kept washing her hands the girl began to relax. She was pliable when Julia gently turned her around in the tub and began washing her hair. As Julia massaged her scalp, the child began to hum.

It took Julia a moment to realize that there was a tune within the notes.

Twinkle, twinkle, little star.

Julia straightened. Of all the unexpected twists today, this one was the most important. "Somebody sang that to you, little one. Who was it?"

The girl kept humming, her eyes closed.

Julia rinsed the long black hair, noticing how thick and curly it was. Tendrils coiled around her fingers like vines. She saw, too, the network of scars that crisscrossed the tiny back; there was one near her shoulder that was especially ugly.

Where have you been?

The song was a glimpse into a part of this girl's true history; the first one they'd seen. More questions were unlikely to solicit answers. Julia knew what she needed was more primal than that.

She decided to sing along with the humming. "How I wonder what you are."

The girl splashed around until she was facing Julia. Her blue-green eyes were so wide they seemed too big for her small, pointed face.

Julia finished the song, then planted a hand to her chest and said, "Julia. Ju-li-a. That's me." She grabbed the girl's hand. "Who are you?"

The only answer was that intense stare.

With a sigh, Julia stood and reached for a towel. "Come on."

To her amazement, the girl stood up and got out of the tub.

"Did you understand me? Or did you stand up because I did?" Julia heard the wonder in her voice. So much for professional detachment. This girl kept throwing curveballs. "Do you know how to speak? Talk? Words?" She touched her chest again. "Julia. Ju-li-a." Then she touched the girl's chest. "Who? Name? I need to call you something."

Nothing but the stare.

Julia dried the girl off, then dressed her. "I'm putting you in pull-up diapers again. Just to be safe. Turn around. I'll braid your hair. That's what my mom always did to me. But I'll be gentler, I promise. Mom used to pull so hard I'd cry. My sister always said it's why my eyes tilted up. There. All done." She accidentally bumped into the bathroom door. It shut hard; the mirror on the back of it framed the child in a perfect rectangle.

The girl gasped so loudly it sounded as if she'd just washed up on shore. She reached out for the mirror, trying to touch the other little girl in the room.

"Have you ever seen yourself before?" Julia asked, but even as she asked the question, she knew the answer.

None of this made sense. The pieces didn't fit together. The wolf. The eating habits. The song. The toilet training. They were tiny pieces that made up the puzzle's border, but the central image, the *point*, was unseen yet. Certainly she would have seen her reflection in water, at least.

"That's *you*, honey. You. See the beautiful blue-green eyes, the long black hair. You look so pretty in that nightgown."

The girl punched her reflection. When her knuckles hit the hard glass, she yelped loudly in pain.

Julia moved in beside her and knelt down. Now they were both in the mirror, side by side, their faces close. The girl was breathtakingly beautiful. She reminded Julia of a young Elizabeth Taylor. "You see? That's me. Julia. And you."

Julia saw when understanding dawned.

Very slowly the girl touched her chest and mouthed a sound. Her reflection did the same.

"Did you say something? Your name?"

The girl stuck out her tongue. For the next forty minutes, while Julia put on a tee shirt and sweats and brushed her teeth, the child played in front of the mirror. At one point Julia left long enough to get her notebook and digital camera. When she returned to the bathroom, the girl was clapping her hands and bouncing up and down in time with her reflection.

Julia took several photographs—close-ups of the girl's face—then put the camera away. Notebook in hand, Julia wrote: *Discovery of self*. And documented every moment.

It went on for hours. The child stared at herself in the mirror long after the sky had gone dark and shown its cache of stars.

Finally, Julia couldn't write anymore. Her hand was starting to spasm. "That's it. Come on. Bedtime." She walked out of the bathroom. When the girl didn't follow, Julia reached down for a book. They finished *The Secret Garden*, so she chose *Alice in Wonderland*.

"Fitting, wouldn't you say?" she commented to herself. After all, she was alone in the room when she said it, and equally alone when she began to read aloud. "Alice was beginning to get very tired of sitting by her sister on the bank, and of having nothing to do: once or twice she had peeped into the book her sister was reading, but it had no pictures or conversations in it, and 'what's the use of a book,' thought Alice, 'without pictures or conversation?'"

In the bathroom, the jumping stopped.

Julia smiled and kept reading. She had just introduced the white rabbit when the girl came out of the bathroom. In her pretty white eyelet nightgown with pink ribbons, and her hair braided and tamed, she looked like any little girl. The only hint of wildness was in her eyes. Too big for her face and too earnest for her age, they fixed on Julia, who very calmly kept reading.

The girl came up beside her, sidled close.

Julia stared at her. "Hello, little one. You like it when I read?"

The girl's hand thumped down hard on the book.

Julia was too startled by the unexpected movement to respond. This was the first time the girl had really tried to communicate, and she was being quite forceful about it.

The girl smacked the book again and looked at Julia. Then she touched her chest.

It was the movement Julia had made to emphasize her own name.

"Alice?" she whispered, feeling a kind of awe move through her. "Is your name Alice?"

The girl thumped the book again. When Julia didn't respond, the girl thumped it again.

Julia closed the book. On the cover of this ancient, well-worn edition was a painting of a pretty, blond-haired Alice with a large, brightly dressed Queen of Hearts. She touched the picture of the girl. "Alice," she said, then she placed her hand on the flesh-and-blood girl beside her. "Is that you? Alice?"

The girl grunted and opened the book, smacking the page.

It was where they'd left off. The exact page.

Amazing.

Julia didn't know if the reaction had been to the name or the reading, but it didn't matter. For whatever reason, the little girl had finally stepped into this world. Julia almost laughed out loud; that was how good she felt right now.

The girl hit the book again.

"Okay, I'll keep reading, but from now on you're Alice. So, Alice, get in bed. When you're under the covers again, I'll read you a story."

Exactly one hour later the girl was asleep and Julia closed the book.

She leaned over and kissed the tiny, sweet-scented pink cheek. "Good night, little Alice. Sleep well in Wonderland."

ELEVEN

Ellie was alone in the police station, going through her
notes from this afternoon.

All those grieving parents and their missing children were
counting on her.

She was terrified she'd disappoint them. It was the fear that drove
her, kept her butt in this seat and her tired eyes focused on the pile of
reports on her desk.

But she'd been at it too long. She couldn't be objective anymore,
couldn't make any more notes about blood types and dental records
and abduction dates. All she saw when she closed her eyes were broken
families; people who still put up Christmas stockings every year for
their missing children.

"I could hear you crying outside."

She looked up sharply, sniffing hard. "I wasn't crying. I poked myself in the eye. What are you doing here anyway?"

Cal stood there, smiling gently, his hands shoved deeply in

his pockets. In a black Dark Knight tee shirt and faded jeans, he looked more like a high school kid than a married, fully grown father of three.

He pulled up a chair and sat down beside her. "You okay?"

She wiped her eyes. The smile she gave him was pure fiction; both of them knew it. "I'm out of my league, Cal."

He shook his head. A comma of jet black hair fell across his eyes.

Without even thinking, she pushed it away. "What do I do?"

He jerked back at her touch, then laughed awkwardly. "You'll do what you always do, El."

"What's that?"

"Whatever it takes. You'll find the girl's family."

"No wonder I keep you around." This time her smile was almost the real thing.

He stood up. "Come on. I'll buy you a beer."

"What about Lisa and the girls?"

"Tara's babysitting." He reached for his rain slicker, put it on.

"I don't need a beer, Cal. Really. Besides, I should get home. You don't need to—"

"No one watches out for you anymore, El."

"I know, but—"

"Let me."

The simple way he said it plucked at her heart. He was right. It had been a long time since someone had taken care of her. "Come on." She grabbed her black leather jacket and followed him out of the station.

The streets were empty again, quiet.

A full moon hung in the night sky, illuminating streets still damp from a late night rain. It gave off an eerie radiance that stained the trees and silvered the road.

Ellie tried not to think about the case as she drove. Instead she focused on the darkness of the road and the comforting light from the headlights behind her. Truthfully, it felt good to have someone following her home.

She pulled into her yard and parked. Before she could turn off the ignition, a song came on the radio. "Leaving on a Jet Plane."

She was plunged into a memory. Mom and Dad playing this song on the piano and fiddle, asking their girls to sing along. *My El,* Dad would say, *has an angel's voice.*

She saw her pint-sized self running for the makeshift stage, sidling up beside her dad. Later, when Sammy Barton played that song for her, she'd tumbled into love. It had been like drowning, that love; she'd barely made it out of the water alive.

"You used to love this song," Cal said, standing by her door, looking down at her through the open window.

"Used to," Ellie said, pushing the memories aside. "Now it makes me think of husband number two. Only he left on a Greyhound bus. You've got to want to get away from someone pretty damn bad to ride a bus." She got out of the car.

"He was a fool."

"I guess you're talking about every man I've ever loved. And there are a truckload of them."

"But never the right one," he said quietly, studying her.

"Thanks for that insight, Sherlock. I hadn't noticed."

"Someone is feeling sorry for herself tonight."

Ellie had to smile at that. "I won't let it last long. Thanks for letting me vent."

He slung an arm around her shoulders and pulled her close. "Come on, Chief. Buy me a beer."

They walked across the springy lawn and climbed the porch steps. Inside, Ellie was surprised to find her sister up and working.

Julia sat at the kitchen table, with papers strewn all around her. "Hey," she said, looking up.

"Julia?" Cal said. His face lit up in a smile.

Julia stood up slowly, staring at him. "Cal? Cal Wallace? Is that really you?"

He opened his arms. "It's me."

Julia ran for him, let him hold her. They were both smiling

brightly. When Cal finally drew back, he stared down at her. "I told you you'd be beautiful."

"And you still give the best hugs of any man I've ever met," Julia said, laughing.

Ellie frowned. Were they *flirting* with each other? All at once she thought about those old-time parties again. While Ellie had been center stage, singing her heart out, Julia had been on the stairs, sitting by Cal, listening from the shadows.

Julia drew back and looked at him. "You look like a rock star."

"Heroin chic. That's what they call skinny guys like me." He pushed the hair from his eyes. "It's good to see you again, Jules. Sorry it has to be under such crappy circumstances. By the way, your sister is about ready to have a meltdown."

"That'll be the day," Ellie said, opening her can of beer. She unhooked her gun belt and radio and set them on the counter. "Want one?"

"No, thanks." Julia went to the table and fished through the mess of papers. When she found what she was looking for, she offered them to Ellie. "Here, El. I have these for you."

Ellie put her beer down. "Wow. That's her?"

"It is." Julia smiled like a proud parent. "I'm calling her Alice, by the way. From Wonderland. She responded to the story."

Ellie stared at the photograph in her hand. It was of a stunningly beautiful black-haired girl in a white eyelet dress. "How'd you do this?"

"Getting her to stand still was the hard part." Julia's smile expanded. "We had a good day. I'll tell you all about it tomorrow. Now, I need to run. Will you keep an eye on her?"

"Babysit? Me?"

Cal rolled his eyes. "It's babysitting, El. Not brain surgery."

"I'd rather crack your skull open and sew it shut than watch wolf girl. I'm not kidding." She looked at her sister. "Where are you going?"

"Back to the library. I need to find out about her diet."

"Go see Max," Cal said. "The guy keeps meticulous notes. He'll be able to answer your questions."

Julia laughed. "Dr. Casanova on a Friday night? I don't think so."

"Don't worry about it, Jules," Ellie said. "You're hardly his type."

Julia's smiled faded. "That's not what I meant, but thanks for the tip." She reached for her purse and headed for the door. "And thanks for babysitting, El. Good to see you again, Cal."

"Are you a moron?" Cal said to Ellie the minute Julia left.

"I believe there's some kind of law against calling your police chief a moron."

"No. There's a law against my police chief *being* a moron. Did you see the look on your sister's face when you said she wasn't Max's type? You hurt her feelings."

"Come on, Cal. I saw a picture of her last boyfriend. Mr. World Famous scientist did *not* look like Max."

Cal sighed and stood up. "You'll never get it."

"Get what?"

He looked down at her a long time, long enough that she started to wonder what he saw. Finally, he shook his head. "I'm outta here. See you at work tomorrow."

"Don't leave mad."

He paused at the door and turned to her. "Mad?" His voice dropped. "I'm hardly mad, Ellie. But how would you know that? The only emotions you really understand are your own."

And then he was gone.

Ellie finished her beer and opened a second. By the time she emptied that can, she'd forgotten all about Cal's dramatics. They'd had plenty of fights and arguments in their time. What mattered was that tomorrow they'd be fine. Cal would smile at her as if it had never happened. It had always been that way between them.

Finally, she went upstairs. At her old room, she stopped. Turning the knob, she went inside.

The girl was sleeping peacefully, and though she looked like any other kid now, she was still curled up tightly, as if to protect herself from a cruel world.

"Who are you, little one?" Ellie whispered, feeling that weight of responsibility again. "I'll find your family. I swear I will."

FORTY YEARS AGO, WHEN THE ROSE THEATER WAS BUILT, IT HAD BEEN on the far edge of town. Old-timers still called the neighborhood Back East; it had been given that nickname when Azalea Street seemed miles away. Now, of course, it was practically in town. All around it there were small two-story homes, built in the timber rich years to house mill workers. Across the street was the library, and just down the road a block or two was the new hardware store. Sealth Park, where the girl had first shown up, was kitty-corner to it.

Max came to the movies every Friday night, alone. At first there had been talk about the weirdness of his habit, and women had shown up "accidentally" to sit with him, but in time it had settled into a routine, and there was nothing the people of Rain Valley liked better than routine.

He waved to the theater's owner, who stood at the tiny concession counter, carefully rearranging the boxes of candy. He didn't stop to chat, knowing that any conversation would inevitably circle back to the man's bursitis.

"Hey, Doc, how'd yah like the movie?"

Max turned to his left and found Earl and his wife, Myra, beside him. They, too, were at the movies every Friday night, cuddling in their seats like teenagers. "Hey, Earl. Myra. It's good to see you."

"That was some great movie," Earl said.

"You love every movie," Myra said to her husband. "Especially the romances."

They fell into step. "How's the search going?" Max asked Earl.

"It ain't no picnic, that's for sure. The phone is ringin' off the hook and the leads are pourin' in like the Hoh River in spring. There are so many lost girls out there. It breaks your danged heart. But we'll find out who she is. Chief is determined."

"That Ellen Barton is quite a woman," Myra said to Max.

He couldn't help smiling. Myra never missed an opportunity to mention Ellie. It seemed that the whole town had expected them to fall in love. For the short time they'd been an item, the gossip alert had been Defcon 4. A few die-hard romantics like Myra thought for sure there would be a sequel. "Yes, she is, Myra."

They were outside now, standing on the wide concrete path that connected the entrance of the theater to the sidewalk. On this unexpectedly dry night the other moviegoers drifted toward their cars, talking among themselves.

The crowd dissipated slowly. For a few moments people gathered in small groups along the sidewalk and in the street. Neighbors talking to one another on this beautiful night. The sound of their voices carried on the still, clean air. Earl and Myra were among the first to leave.

One by one the cars drove away, until the street was empty except for an old white Suburban and his pickup truck.

Max was halfway to his truck when a movement across the street caught his eye: a woman was leaving the library, her arms full of books. Light from a streetlamp fell down on her, made her look too alive somehow, an angel against the dark night.

Julia.

Across the street, she opened the passenger door of the Suburban and tossed her books onto the seat. She was almost to the driver's side when he said her name.

She paused and looked up.

"Hey, Julia," he said, coming up to her. "You're working late."

She laughed. It sounded nervous. "Obsessive is a word that's often been used about me."

"How's your patient?"

"Actually, I'd like to talk to you about her. Later. At the hospital."

"How about right now? We could go to my house."

Julia looked confused. "Oh. I don't think—"

"This is as good a time as any."

"I *do* have a babysitter right now."

"Then it's settled. Follow me." Before she could say no, he walked over to his truck and climbed into the driver's seat. As he started the engine, he watched her in the rearview mirror.

She stared at his truck, biting her lip, then finally got into her own car.

ON EITHER SIDE OF THE ROAD A THICKET OF BLACK TREES STOOD WATCH, their tops pressed into the starry underbelly of the night sky. Moonlight turned the ordinary asphalt into a ribbon of tarnished silver that snaked between the twin curtains of trees. At the turnoff, an old brown and yellow Forest Service wooden sign pointed the way to Spirit Lake.

Julia hadn't been out this way in years. Even now, with all the growth that had taken place on the peninsula in the two decades since high school, this was still the boonies. The locals called it the End; not only because of its location, but because of its isolation.

It was a stunningly beautiful, majestic corner of the rain forest, but she couldn't quite match it to Dr. Casanova. He definitely struck her as a big city guy. What was he doing out here in the middle of all this green darkness?

As she turned onto the gravel road, the landscape changed. The trees blocked out the pearly moonlight. No lights cut through the inky night. The ever present fog off the lake gave the forest a brooding, otherworldly feel.

It occurred to her suddenly that she was following a man she barely knew into the deep woods. And that no one knew where she was.

You're being an idiot.

He's a doctor.

Ted Bundy was a law student.

She reached into her purse and pulled out her cell phone. Amazingly, she got service. She punched in Ellie's phone number and got voice mail. "Hey, El. I'm at Dr. Cerrasin's house, talking about the girl." She glanced at her watch. "I'll be home by midnight."

She clicked the End button. "At least they'll know where to start looking for my body."

That actually wasn't funny.

In truth, she wasn't entirely sure why she was following him, anyway. She wasn't really ready for a consult, and what she did have to present as a theory would make her look like a nutcase.

Unfortunately, the past year had stolen more than her reputation. Somewhere along the way she'd lost her confidence. She needed to hear that she was on the right path.

There it was. The true reason she was here. He was the only colleague she had in Rain Valley, and he'd examined Alice.

She hated the glimpse into her own weakness, but she was not one to deny the obvious.

Up ahead, Max turned off the main road. She followed him onto the driveway that had recently been graveled. The single-lane roadway took a hairpin turn to the left and ended abruptly in a tree-ringed meadow.

Max drove into the garage and disappeared.

Julia parked alongside it. Taking a deep breath, she grabbed her briefcase and got out of the car.

The beauty of the place stunned her. She was in the middle of a huge grassy field, ringed on three sides by enormous evergreens. On the fourth border lay Spirit Lake. Mist rose from the lake like steam from a boiling pot, giving everything a surreal, fairy-tale look. Close by, an owl hooted.

She jumped at the sound.

"The infamous spotted owl," Max said, coming up beside her.

She eased sideways. "The enemy of every logger."

"And the champion of every tree hugger. Come on."

He led her past the garage and toward the house. As she got closer, she saw the craftsman-style beauty of the place. Plank cedar siding, handcrafted eaves, a big wraparound porch. Even the chairs seemed to have been handmade of clean, pure fir. It was the kind of house you didn't see in Rain Valley. Expensive and hand-tooled, yet plain. It was an Aspen or Jackson Hole kind of place.

He opened the front door and let her enter first. The first thing she noticed was the spicy aroma of bayberry; somewhere, he had a scented candle burning. Sexy music floated through the speakers. No doubt he kept the place in constant readiness for female guests.

Julia tightened her hold on the briefcase and walked into the house. A gorgeous river-rock fireplace dominated the left wall. Windows ran the length of the house, looking out from the porch to the lake beyond. Two pairs of French doors led outside. The kitchen was small but perfectly constructed; every cabinet gleamed in the soft light of an overhead fixture. The dining room was big, and bracketed on two sides by windows that overlooked the lake. A huge trestle table took up most of the space. Oddly, there was only a single chair next to it. In the living room there was an oxblood leather sofa—no chairs—and a big-screen plasma TV. A thick alpaca wool rug covered the wide-planked wood floor in front of the fireplace.

There was also a jumble of ropes and pullies by the back door. They lay in a tangled heap beside an ice pick and a backpack.

"Rock climbing gear," she said. It was too, too cliché. "Someone is into danger, I see. A man who needs extreme circumstances to feel alive?"

"Don't try to psychoanalyze me, Julia. Drink?" He turned away from her and went into the kitchen area. Opening the refrigerator door, he said, "I have whatever you want."

"How about a glass of white wine?"

He returned a moment later carrying two glasses. White wine for her, scotch on the rocks for himself.

She took the one he offered and sat down at the very end of the sofa, close to the arm. "Thanks."

He smiled. "You don't have to look so terrified, Julia. I'm not going to attack you."

For a moment she was caught by the low, soft tone of his voice and the blue of his eyes. It was a little spark, barely anything, but it made her angry. She needed to get back on solid ground. "Let me guess again, Dr. Cerrasin. If I went out to the garage, I'd find a Porsche or a Corvette."

"Nope. Sorry to disappoint you."

"Upstairs I'd find a king-sized bed with expensive silk sheets, maybe a faux fur coverlet, and a nightstand drawer full of condoms that are ribbed for her pleasure."

A frown pulled at his forehead. She got the distinct feeling that he was toying with her. "Her pleasure is always important to me."

"I'm sure it is. As long as her pleasure doesn't require any real emotion on your part, or—God forbid—a commitment. Believe me, Max, I've known men like you before. As appealing as the Peter Pan syndrome is to some women, it's lost its charm for me."

"Who was he?"

"Who?"

"The man who hurt you so badly."

Julia was surprised by the perceptiveness of the question. Even more surprising was how it made her feel. Almost as if he knew her.

But he didn't. He was just fishing, casting the kind of line that only men like him could handle. His gift was the appearance of sincerity, of depth. For some bizarre reason, when she looked at him now, she saw a kind of loneliness in his gaze, an understanding that made her want to answer him.

And then she would be caught.

"May we please keep ourselves on track?"

"Ah. Business. Tell me about the girl." He went to the fireplace and built a fire, then returned to the sofa and sat down.

"I'm calling her Alice for now. From *Alice in Wonderland*. She responded to the story."

"Seems like a good choice."

He waited for more.

Suddenly she wished she weren't here. He might be a player and a flirt, but he was also a colleague, and as such, he could ruin her with a word.

"Julia?"

She started slowly. "When you first examined her, did you see any evidence of what her diet had been?"

"You mean beyond the dehydration and malnutrition?"

"Yes."

"Facts, no. Ideas; I have a few. I'd say some meat and fish and fruit. I would guess she ate no dairy and no grains at all."

Julia looked at him. "In other words, the kind of diet that would come from living off the land for a long time."

"Maybe. How long do you think she was out there?"

There it was. The question whose answer could both make and break her.

"You'll think I'm crazy," she said after too long a silence.

"I thought you shrinks didn't use that word."

"Don't tell."

"You're safe with me."

She laughed at that. "Hardly."

"Start talking, Julia," he said, sipping his drink. The ice rattled in his glass.

"Okay." She started with the easy stuff. "I'm sure she's not deaf, and I strongly question the idea of autistic. Strangely enough, I think she might be a completely normal child reacting to an impossibly foreign and hostile environment. I believe she understands some language, although I don't yet know if she knows how to speak and is choosing not to or if she's never been taught. Either way, she hasn't hit puberty, so— theoretically, at least—she's not too old to learn."

"And?" He took another drink.

She took a drink, too. Hers was more of a gulp. Her sense of vulnerability was so strong now she felt her cheeks warm. There was nothing to do now except dive in or walk away. "Have you ever read any of the accounts of wild children?"

"You mean like that French kid? The one Truffaut made the movie about?"

"Yes."

"Come on—"

"Hear me out, Max. Please."

He leaned back into the cushions, crossed his arms and studied her. "Tell me."

She started pulling stuff out of her briefcase. Papers, books, notes. She laid them all out on the cushion between them. As Max examined each article, she outlined her thoughts. She told him about the clear signs of wildness—the apparent lack of sense of self, the hiding mechanism, the eating habits, the howling. Then she offered the oddities— the humming, birdsong mimicry, the insta–toilet training. When she'd presented all of it, she sat back, waiting for his comment.

"So you're saying she was out there, in the woods, for most of her life."

"Yes."

"And the wolf they found with her . . . that was what, her brother?"

She reached for her papers. "Forget it. I should have known—"

Laughing, he grabbed her hand. "Slow down. I'm not making fun of you, but you have to admit that your theory is out there."

"But think about it. Plug our evidence into the known fact patterns."

"It's all anecdotal, Julia. Kids raised by wolves and bears . . ."

"Maybe she was held hostage for a while and then let go to survive on her own. She's definitely been around people at some point."

"Then why can't she speak?"

"I think she's electively mute. In other words, she *can* speak. She's choosing not to."

"If that's true, even partially, it'll take a hell of a doctor to bring her back to this world."

Julia heard the question in his voice. She wasn't surprised. The whole world thought she was incompetent now; why should he be any different? What did surprise her was how much it hurt. "I am a good doctor. At least, I used to be." She reached for her papers, started putting them in her briefcase.

He leaned closer, touched her wrist. "I believe in you, you know. If that matters."

She looked at him, even though she knew instantly that it was a mistake. He was so close now that she could see a jagged scar along his hairline and another at the base of his throat. Firelight softened his face; she saw tiny flames reflected in the blue sea of his eyes. "Thanks. It does."

Later, when she was back in her car and driving home alone, she thought back on it, wondered why she'd revealed so much to him.

The only answer came buried in her own lack of confidence.

I believe in you.

The irony was that there, in that room with the soft music playing and the stairs that undoubtedly led to a huge bed, his words were what had seduced her.

TWELVE

ELLIE WAS SIPPING HER NOW WARM BEER AND PORING OVER
stacks of police reports when she heard Julia come home.
Ellie looked up. "Hey."

Julia closed the door behind her. "Hey." Tossing her briefcase on
the kitchen table, she headed for the refrigerator and got herself a beer.
"Where are Jake and Elwood?"

"See? You miss it when they don't go for your crotch. They're
camped outside your bedroom. They almost never move from there
anymore. I think it's the girl. They're crazy for her." She smiled. "So
you went to see Max."

Julia sat down on the sofa beside Ellie. "I'm hardly surprised to hear
his name in the same sentence as the words 'go straight for your
crotch.' So, what's the deal with him?"

"That's a question every single woman in town has asked."

"I'll bet he's slept with every one of them."

"Not really."

Julia frowned. "But he acts like—"

"I know. He flirts like crazy but that's as far as it usually goes. Don't get me wrong—he's slept with plenty of women in town, but he's never really *been* with any of them. Not for long, anyway."

"What about you?"

Ellie laughed. "When he first moved here, I was all over him. It's my way—as you know. No subtlety here . . . and no waiting around. If a good-looking man comes to town, I pounce." She finished her beer and set the bottle down. "We had a blast. Tequila straight shots, dancing at The Pour House, necking by the bathrooms . . . by the time I got him home, we were pretty well toasted. The sex was . . . to be honest, I don't remember it. What I do remember was telling him how easy it would be to fall in love."

"On the first date?"

"You know me. I always fall in love, and men usually like it. But not Max. He pretty much killed himself in his hurry to leave. After that he treated me like I had a communicable disease." Ellie glanced sideways, expecting to see censure in the green eyes that were so like her own. Julia couldn't know about throwing yourself at the wrong guy, about how it felt to be so desperate for love that you'd reach for anyone who smiled at you. But what she saw in her sister's eyes surprised her. Julia looked . . . fragile suddenly, as if the talk of love had upset her. "Are you okay?"

"Fine."

But Ellie could see the lie on her sister's face, and for the first time, she understood. Her sister had been broken by love, too. Maybe not as often as she had—or as publicly—but Julia had been hurt. "What happened with him . . . with Philip? You guys were together for a long time. I thought you'd get married."

"I thought so, too. I was so in love with him I ignored the signs. I found out too late that he'd been screwing around for most of the last year we were together. Now he's married to a dental hygienist and living in Pasadena. Last I heard he was screwing around on her, too. Some psychiatrist, huh? I miss the problems in my own relationship."

"He sounds like a real asshole."

"It would be easier if that were true."

"I'm sorry." For the first time, Ellie felt as if she understood her sister. Julia might be brilliant, but when it came to love, that was no protection. Every heart could be broken. "You better stay away from Max, you know."

Julia sighed. "Believe me, I know. A guy like that . . ."

"Yeah. He could hurt a woman like you."

"Like us," Julia said softly.

So she felt it, too, this new connection. "Yeah," Ellie agreed. "Like us."

THE NEXT MORNING, ELLIE WAS PARKED IN FRONT OF THE ANCIENT Grounds coffee stand when her radio beeped. Static crackled through the old black speakers, followed by Cal's voice.

"Chief? You there? Out."

"I'm here, Cal. What's up?"

"Get down here, Ellie. Out."

"Sally's making my mocha. I'll be—"

"Now, Ellie. Out."

Ellie glanced up at the woman in the coffee stand window. "Sorry, Sally. Emergency." She put the car in drive and hit the gas. Two blocks later she turned onto Cates Avenue and almost slammed into a news van.

There were dozens parked along—and in the center of—the street. White satellite dishes stood out against the gray sky. Reporters were huddled in clusters along the sidewalk, their black umbrellas open. She hadn't taken more than three steps when the reporters pounced on her.

"—comment on the report—"

"—no one is telling us where—"

"—the exact location—"

She pushed through the crowd and yanked the station door open. Slipping through, she slammed the door shut behind her and leaned against it. "Shit."

"You haven't seen anything yet," Cal said. "They were camped out there at eight o'clock when I got to work. Now they're waiting for your nine o'clock update."

"What nine o'clock update?"

"The one I scheduled to get them the hell out of here. I couldn't answer the phones with them yelling at me."

Peanut came around the corner holding a plastic mug the size of a gallon of paint. She was back on the grapefruit juice diet. A rolled-up newspaper was tucked under her arm. "You'd better sit down," she said.

Ellie immediately looked at Cal.

He nodded, mouthed, *I would.*

She went to her desk and sat down, then looked at her friends. Whatever they had to say couldn't be good.

Peanut tossed the newspaper down on the desk. The whole top half was a photograph of the girl. Her eyes were wild and crazy-looking; her hair was a nimbus of black and studded with leaves. She looked stark-raving mad, as well as filthy. Like one of those kids from *Mad Max: Beyond Thunderdome.* The byline read: Mort Elzick.

Ellie felt as if she'd been punched in the gut. So this was what he'd meant by "or else" when he'd demanded the interview. "*Shit.*"

"The good news is he didn't mention Julia," Cal said. "He wouldn't dare, without official confirmation."

Ellie skimmed the article. *Savage girl steps out of the forest and into the modern world, her only companion a wolf. She leaps from branch to branch and howls at the moon.*

"They're starting to think it's a hoax," Cal said quietly.

Ellie's anger turned to fear. If the media decided it was a hoax, they'd pull out of town. Without publicity, the girl's family might never be found. She reached into her canvas book bag and pulled out the photograph Julia had taken. "Circulate this."

Peanut took the photo. "Wow. Your sister is a miracle worker."

"We're calling her Alice," Ellie said. "Put that on the record. Maybe a name will make her seem more real."

· · ·

GIRL COMES AWAKE SLOWLY. THIS PLACE IS QUIET, PEACEFUL, EVEN though she cannot hear the river's call or the leaves' whispering. The sun is hidden from her. Still, the air is lighted and bright.

She is not afraid.

For a moment she cannot believe it. She touches her thoughts, pokes through the darkness of them.

It is true. She is not afraid. She cannot recall ever feeling like this. Usually her first thought is: *hide*. She has spent so long trying to make herself as small as possible.

She can breathe here, too; in this strange, squared world where light comes from a magical touch and the ground is hard and level, she can breathe. It does not hold on to the bad smells of Him.

She likes it here. If Wolf were with her, she would stay in this square forever, marking her territory in the swirling water and sleeping on the place she is told to, where it is soft and smells of flowers.

"Iseeyouareawakelittleone."

It is the Sun-Haired Her who has spoken. She is at the eating place, with the thin stick in her hand again, the tool that leaves blue markings behind.

Girl gets up and goes into the cleaning place, where the magical pool is now empty. She pulls down her pants and sits on the cold circle. When she is done peeing, she hits the white thing.

In the other room, Her stands up. She is hitting her hands together, making a sound like a hunter's shot and smiling.

Girl likes that smile. It makes her feel safe.

From the babble of forbidden sounds, Girl hears "Come."

She moves slowly, hunched over, holding her insides tightly. She knows how dangerous a moment like this can be, especially when her guard is down. She should always stay afraid, but the smile and the air and the softness of the sleeping place make her forget the cave. Him.

She sits where Sun Hair wants her to. *I'll be good*, she thinks, looking up, trying to force the happy face.

Sun Hair brings her food to eat.

Girl remembers the rules, and she knows the price of disobeying. It is a lesson Him taught her lots of times. She waits for Sun Hair to smile and nod, to say something. When it is done, Girl eats the sweet, sticky food. When she is finished, Sun Hair takes the rest of the food away. Girl waits.

Finally, Sun Hair sits across from Girl. She touches her chest and says the same thing over and over. "Jool Ya." Then she touches Girl.

"A lis. A lis."

Girl wants to be good, wants to stay in this place, with this Her that smiles, and she knows that *something* is expected of her now, but she has no idea what she should do. It seems as if Sun Hair wants Girl to make the bad sounds, but that can't be true. Her heart is beating so fast it makes her feel sick and dizzy.

Finally, Sun Hair pulls back her hand. She reaches into the square hole beside her and begins putting things on the table.

Girl is mesmerized. She has never seen any of these things. She wants to touch them, taste and smell them.

Sun Hair takes one of the pointed sticks and touches it to the book of lines. Behind her touch, everything is red. "Kraon. Colorbook."

Girl makes a sound of wonder.

Sun Hair looks up. She is talking to Girl now. In all the babble of sound, she begins to hear a repetition. "A lis play."

Play.

Girl frowns, trying to understand. She almost knows these sounds.

But Sun Hair keeps talking, keeps pulling things out of the secret place until Girl can't remember what she is trying to remember. Every new object seizes hold of her, makes her want to reach out.

Then, when Girl is almost ready to make her move, to touch the pointed red stick, Sun Hair pulls It out.

Girl screams and scrambles backward, but she is trapped by this cage

on which she sits. She falls, hits her head, and screams again, then
crawls on her hands and knees toward the safety of the trees.

She *knew* she shouldn't have let her guard down. So what that she
can breathe here? It is a little thing, a trick.

Sun Hair is frowning at her, talking in a haze of white noise. Girl
can make out no sounds at all. Her heart is beating so fast it sounds like
the drums of the tribe that fish along her river.

There is almost no space between them now.

Sun Hair holds It out.

Girl screams again and claws at her hair, blowing her nose. Him is
here. He knows she likes Sun Hair and he will hurt her now. All she
can think is the sound she knows best of all.

Noooo . . .

ALICE PULLED AT HER HAIR AND SNORTED, SHAKING HER HEAD. A LOW,
throaty growl seemed caught in her throat.

Julia was seeing true emotion. This was Alice's heart, and it was a
dark, scary place.

Julia opened the door and threw the dreamcatcher out in the hallway, then shut the door. "There," she said in a soothing voice, moving
slowly. "I'm sorry, honey. Really sorry." She knelt down in front of
Alice so they were almost eye-to-eye.

Alice was absolutely still now, her eyes wide with fear.

"You're terrified," Julia said. "You think you're in trouble, don't
you?" Very slowly, she reached out and touched Alice's wrist. The
touch was fleeting and as soft as a whisper. "It's okay, Alice. You don't
have to be scared."

At the touch, Alice made a strangled, desperate sound and stumbled
backward. She hid behind the plants and began a quiet, desperate
howling.

The child had no idea how to be comforted. Another of the many
heartbreaks of her life.

"Hmmm," Julia said, making a great show of looking around the room. "What shall we do now?" After a few moments she picked up the old, battered copy of *Alice in Wonderland*. "Where did we leave young Alice?"

She went back to the bed and sat down. With the book open on her lap, she looked up.

Between two green fronds, a tiny, earnest face peered at her.

"Come," Julia said softly. "No hurt."

Alice made a pathetic little sound, a mewl of sorts.

It tugged at Julia's heart, that whimper that sounded at once too old and too young. It was a distillation of longing from fear. "Come," she said again, patting the bed. "No hurt."

Still, Alice remained in her safe spot.

Julia started to read: " 'You ought to be ashamed of yourself,' said Alice, 'a great girl like you, (she might well say this) to go on crying in this way! Stop this moment, I tell you! But she went on all the same shedding gallons of tears until there was a large pool around her.' "

There was a sound across the room, a scuffing of feet.

Julia smiled to herself and kept reading.

It is a trick.

Girl knows this. She *knows* it.

And yet . . .

The sounds are so soothing.

She sits in the forest so long her legs begin to ache. Although stillness has always been her way, in this bright place she likes to move, if only because she can.

Don't do it, she thinks, shifting her weight from one foot to another.

It is a trick.

When Girl gets close, Her will beat her.

"Comeherealis."

From the jumble of sounds Sun Hair makes, Girl hears these special noises again. From somewhere, she remembers that they are words.

Trick.

She has no choice but to obey, of course. Sooner or later—sooner, probably—Sun Hair will tire of waiting; this game of hers will lose its fun, and Girl will be in Trouble.

Very slowly she steps from her hiding place. Her heart is hammering. She is afraid it will break through her chest and fall onto the floor.

She looks down at her hands and feet. Here in this oddly bright place, the ground is made of hard strips the color of dirt. There are no leaves or pine needles to soften her steps. Every movement hurts, but not as much as what will come.

She has been Bad.

Screaming is very bad. She knows this.

Out There are strangers and bad people. Loud sounds attract them.

Quiet, Damn You, she knows. As she approaches the bed, she lowers her head, then drops down to her hands and knees, looking as weak as possible. This she learned from the wolves.

"Al is?"

Girl flinches, closes her eyes. *Not a stick,* she hopes, hearing the whining sound in her own mouth.

At first the touch is so soft she doesn't notice.

The mewl catches in her throat. She looks up.

Sun Hair is closer now, smiling down at her. She is talking—always, she is talking in that sunlight voice of hers; it sounds like a river in the last days of summer, soft and soothing. Her eyes are wide open, as green as new leaves. There is no anger on her face.

·And she is stroking Girl's hair, touching her gently.

"Is okayokaynohurt."

Girl leans forward, but just a little. She wants Sun Hair to keep touching her. It feels so good.

"Comeherealis."

Sun Hair pats the soft place beside her.

In a single motion Girl leaps up and curls next to Her. It is the safest she has felt in a long time.

When Sun Hair starts to talk again, Girl closes her eyes and listens.

JULIA SAT VERY STILL, ALTHOUGH HER MIND WAS MOVING AT LIGHT speed.

What was the story with the dreamcatcher?

Had Alice understood *Come here*?

Or had she responded to the bed patting?

Either way, the response was a form of communication . . . unless Alice had simply jumped onto the bed of her own volition.

Julia's fingers itched to make some notes, but now was not the time. Instead she turned her attention back to the book and began reading where she left off.

As she finished the chapter, Julia felt a movement on the bed. She paused in her reading and glanced down at Alice, who had repositioned herself. Now the child lay curled catlike against her, Alice's forehead almost touching her thigh.

"You have no idea what it's like to feel safe in this world, do you?" Julia said, putting the book down for a moment. Her throat tightened; it took her several seconds to suppress the emotion enough to say, "I can help you if you'll let me. This is a good place to start, with you beside me. Trust is everything."

The instant the words were out of Julia's mouth, she remembered the last time she'd said them. It had been a cool, steely day in the season that passed for winter in Southern California. She'd been in the two-thousand-dollar leather chair in her office, making notes and listening to another girl's voice. In the sofa opposite her sat Amber Zuniga, all dressed in black, trying not to cry.

Trust is everything, Julia had said. *You can tell me what you're feeling right now.*

Julia closed her eyes. The memory was the kind that physically hurt. That meeting had taken place only two days before Amber's rampage. Why hadn't she—

Stop.

She refused to follow those thoughts. They led to a dark and hopeless place. If she went there, she might not be able to come back, and Alice needed her. Perhaps more than anyone had ever needed her. "As I was saying—"

Alice touched her. It was nothing at first, a movement as tentative as the brush of a butterfly wing. Julia saw it, but barely felt it.

"That's good, honey," she whispered. "Come into this world. It's been lonely in yours, hasn't it? Scary?"

No part of Alice moved except her hand. Very slowly she reached out and petted Julia's thigh in an awkward, almost spastic motion.

"It's frightening to touch another person sometimes," Julia said, wondering if any of her words were being understood. "Especially when we've been hurt. We can be afraid to reach out to someone else."

The petting smoothed out, became a gentle stroking. Alice made a sound that was low in her throat, a kind of purr. She slowly lifted her chin and looked up at Julia. Those amazing blue-green eyes were pools of worried fear.

"No hurt," Julia said, hearing the catch in her voice. She was feeling too much right now, and that was dangerous. Being a good psychiatrist was like reading a novel at forty. You needed to keep the words at arm's length or everything became a blur. She stroked Alice's soft black hair again and again. "No hurt."

It took a long time, but finally Alice stopped trembling. For the rest of the morning Julia alternated between reading and talking to the girl. They broke for lunch and went to the table, but immediately afterward Alice returned to the bed and hit the book with her open palm.

Julia cleared the dishes, then retook her place on the bed and resumed her reading. By two o'clock Alice had curled up closer to her and fallen asleep.

Julia eased off the bed and stood there, staring down at this strange, quiet girl she called Alice.

They had made so many breakthroughs in the last two days, but perhaps none held as much potential as the dreamcatcher.

Alice had reacted so violently to the trinket; it had to be of critical importance.

Julia knew what she needed now was a way to both release Alice's fear of the dreamcatcher and to explore it. Without, of course, having Alice so terrified she hurt herself. It was the best weapon in her arsenal right now—the only object she had that elicited strong emotion. She had no choice but to use it.

"Do you cry, Alice? Do you laugh? You're trapped inside yourself, aren't you? Why?" Julia drew back. She went over to her notes and wrote down everything that had transpired since breakfast. Then she read back over the words she'd written: *Violent reaction to dreamcatcher. Extreme bout of anger and/or fear. As usual, patient's emotions are entirely directed inward. It's as if she has no idea how to express her feelings to others. Perhaps due to elective mutism. Perhaps due to training. Did someone—or something—teach her to be silent always? Was she abused for speaking out or for speaking at all? Is she used to scratching and hair pulling as her only emotional display? Is this how pack animals express emotions when out of view? Is this a symptom of wildness or isolation or abuse?*

Some realization teased her, danced at the corner of her mind, moving in and out of focus too quickly for her to really see it.

Julia put down her pen and stood up again. A quick look at the video camera assured her that it was still recording. She could study the footage of the dreamcatcher incident again tonight. Maybe she'd missed something.

She checked Alice again, made sure she was asleep, then left the room. Outside, in the hallway, the dogs lay coiled together, asleep. Julia stepped over them and retrieved the dreamcatcher.

It was a poorly made trinket; the kind of thing they sold at local souvenir shops. No bigger than a tea saucer and as thin as the twigs that formed its circular perimeter; it was hardly threatening. Several cheap, shiny blue beads glittered amidst a string web. She suspected they usually came with a designer tag that detailed their importance to the local tribes of the Quinalt and the Hoh.

What was its connection to Alice? Was she Native American? Was that a piece of the puzzle? Or was it not the dreamcatcher in total that had frightened her, but rather some piece of it—the beads, the twigs, or the string?

String. A cousin to rope.

Ligature marks.

Perhaps that was the connection. The string could have reminded Alice of being tied up.

There was no way to know these answers until Alice herself revealed them.

In ordinary therapy, bound by the normal conventions of time and money, it could take months for a child to confront such fears. Perhaps years.

But this case was far from ordinary. The longer Alice remained in her solitary, isolated world, the less likely it was that she would ever emerge. Therefore, they didn't have the luxury of time. She needed to force a confrontation between the two Alices—the child lost in the woods and the girl who'd been returned to the world. These two halves needed to integrate into a single personality or Alice's future would be at risk.

Desperate times called for desperate measures.

There was only one thing to do, and it wouldn't be pretty.

She went downstairs to call her sister. Fifteen minutes later Ellie and Peanut walked through the front door.

"Hey," Peanut said, grinning broadly and fluttering her bright pink star-spangled fingernails.

Julia reached into her pocket and pulled out the dreamcatcher. "Either one of you recognize this?"

"Sure. It's a dreamcatcher," Peanut said, pulling a Baggie full of carrot sticks out of her purse. "My son used to have one hanging from his bed. I think he bought it on a field trip up to Neah Bay. They're a Native American tradition. The idea is that they protect a sleeping child from nightmares. The bad dreams get caught in the web, while the good ones slip quietly through that hole in the middle." She grinned. "Discovery Channel. Native American History Week."

"Why?" Ellie asked Julia.

"Alice had a severe emotional response to this thing. Snorting, scratching herself, screaming. It seemed to scare the crap out of her."

Ellie reached over and picked up the dreamcatcher, examining it. "You think it's the bad dream thing?"

"No. I think it's more personal. Maybe she was hurt in a room that had one, or by a person who made them. Or perhaps the string reminded her of the rope that was used to tie her ankle. I'm not sure yet. But there's *something* about it that set her off."

"I'll check it out," Ellie said. "Clues are damn few and far between. I'll send Earl up to the reservation. Maybe we'll get lucky."

"It's about time for some luck," Julia agreed, picking her purse up off the sofa. "Where could I find a bunch of them for sale?"

"Swain's General Store," Peanut answered. "They have a local souvenir aisle."

"Great. I'll be back as soon as I can."

"Better wear a mask," Peanut muttered. She and Ellie exchanged worried glances.

Julia frowned. "What's going on?"

"You remember Mort Elzik?" Ellie asked.

So it was small-town gossip. She should have known. "No." Julia glanced at her watch. She wanted to be back—with the dreamcatchers— when Alice woke from her nap. "I really don't have time for this now. I don't know how long Alice will sleep." She headed for the door.

"He published a photo of Alice in the *Rain Valley Gazette*."

"The headline called her 'wolf girl,'" Peanut said, chewing loudly.

Julia stopped. All at once she remembered Mort from high school . . . and from that night at the hospital. He'd bumped into her in the hallway. *Of course*. The bag he'd dropped held camera equipment. That was why he hadn't been at the meeting in the church; he'd used that time to sneak into the hospital. Slowly, she turned. "Any mention of me?"

Both women shook their heads. "The town is protecting you," Ellie added. "He knows you're here but no one will confirm that you're help-ing Alice."

"I knew there'd be a leak. There always is. We're fine if—"

Peanut and Ellie exchanged another worried look.

"What? There's *more*?" Julia demanded.

"Some of the reporters are leaving town. They think the whole thing is a hoax."

Julia cursed under her breath. That was the one thing they couldn't afford. If the media withdrew now, they might never find out who Alice really was. "The new photos—mine, I mean—should help. Also release some bit of information. Something scientific. Put some-one in uniform on camera to talk about the search. Use lots of missing kids' statistics. Make every word sound official. That should buy us some time."

"You need to get her talking, Jules."

"No kidding." In the old days her word would have been enough to convince the media. Now, it would mean nothing.

"You want me to go get you the dreamcatchers?" Peanut said gently.

Julia hated to bend to pressure, but she had no choice. She couldn't let Mort get a photo of her. She tossed her purse back onto the sofa. "Thanks, Pea. I'd appreciate that."

THIRTEEN

AN HOUR LATER ELLIE AND PEANUT WERE BACK IN THE CRUISER, heading for town.

"We *need* her to talk," Ellie said quietly. No matter how much evidence they accumulated, the truth always boiled down to that.

"Julia is doing her best, but . . ."

"It could take a while. I know. And what if Mort's photo ruins everything? If the legitimate media thinks we're some hicks trying to put our city on the map, it's over."

"Don't go looking for trouble, El. My Benji says—"

The car radio squawked. "Ellie? Are you there?"

"I'm not answering," Ellie said. "It's never good news anymore."

"That's a responsible choice. Probably just a ten-car pileup on the interstate, anyway. Or a hostage situation."

Another clatter of static. "Chief? Julia says you're in the car. If you don't answer, I'm going to tell everyone you wrote a letter to Rick Springfield in the eighth grade. Over."

Ellie hit the Talk button. "Don't force me to bring out the photos of you with a perm, Cal."

"There you are. Thank God, El. You need to get here now. Over."

"What's going on?"

"The kooks have landed. I swear to God."

Ellie cursed under her breath. She hit the siren and gas at the same time. In minutes she was pulling into the parking lot and getting out of the car.

There were people everywhere, though not as many as yesterday. News vans clogged the street in front of the station and a line of people snaked from the front door and down the sidewalk. They weren't the kind of people who'd shown up before. No cops from other precincts or private detectives or reporters or parents. This group looked like the Rocky Horror audience.

She brushed past them, ignoring their clamoring voices, and went into the station. Cal was at his desk, looking dazed and confused.

Earl sat at the other patrol desk. At Ellie's entrance he smiled tiredly and said, "I just took a statement from a man who lives on the planet Rebar."

Ellie frowned. "What?"

"That's who came looking for the girl. A man—no, an ambassador—from Rebar. He had a tinfoil hat and black lips."

Ellie sat down at her desk with a sigh. "Let 'em in, Earl. One at a time."

"You're going to *talk* to them?" Cal asked.

"Just 'cause they're crazy doesn't mean they don't know something."

Earl went to the door and opened it. The woman he let in wore a flowing purple dress, cowboy boots, and a blue suede headband. In her hands she held a baseball-sized crystal ball.

Another psychic.

Ellie smiled and reached for her pen.

For the next two hours she and Earl and Peanut listened to one crackpot after another tell them who Alice really was. Her favorite answer: Anastasia, reborn.

When the last man finally told his story and left, Ellie leaned back in her chair and sighed. "Where did they all come from?"

Cal answered. "Mort's picture. It makes the whole story seem unbelievable. Especially since he used words like flying and wolf girl. His story hinted that she eats only live insects and does sign language with her feet. I heard CNN pulled out of town."

"This is so not good," Peanut said, reaching for her grapefruit juice.

Cal jumped down from the desk. His tennis shoes hit with a little thump on the hardwood floor. "Use her," he said quietly. "It's our only choice."

Ellie didn't have to ask who Cal meant. She'd had the same thought herself.

"Julia?" Peanut said in a spiky voice. "But they'll only care about what happened in Silverwood."

"They'll crucify her," Ellie said, looking up at Cal. "'Wolf girl works with disgraced doctor.'"

"What choice do we have?"

"I don't know. . . ." Ellie said. "Today, when she heard about Mort's photo, she looked as fragile as I've ever seen her."

"She'll do it for Alice," Cal said.

JULIA WAS STILL TRYING TO FORMULATE A DREAMCATCHER-USE PLAN when Ellie barged into the room. Her keys and handcuffs jangled with every step. Behind her the dogs howled and scratched at the door, barking when she shut them out.

Alice ran for the plants and hid there.

Ellie clasped her keys and handcuffs, stilling them. "I need to talk to you."

Julia fought the urge to roll her eyes. The interruption had come at a particularly tender time. "Fine."

Ellie stood there a moment longer, then she said, "I'll wait for you in the kitchen," and left the bedroom.

Julia hid her pens and paper and notebooks. "I'll be right back, Alice."

Alice stayed hidden in her sanctuary, but when Julia reached for the knob, the child started to whimper.

"You're upset," Julia said softly. "You're feeling afraid that I won't come back, but I will." There was nothing else she could say. She could only teach Alice about trust by returning. One of the fundamental truths of psychiatry was that sometimes you had to leave a patient who needed you.

She slipped out of the room and shut the door behind her.

Alice's low, pitiful howling could be heard through the door. The dogs were in the hallway, sitting up on their haunches, howling with Alice.

She went downstairs and found Ellie out on the porch. It wasn't surprising. For as long as they'd been a family, important business and celebration had been taken care of outside. Rain or shine.

Ellie was sitting in Dad's favorite chair. Of course. Ellie had always drawn strength from their father, just as Julia had gotten hope from her mother. The choice of Ellie's chair meant something Big was on her mind.

Julia sat in the rocker. A soft breeze kicked up in the yard, sent drying leaves cartwheeling across the grass. The gurgling song of the Fall River filled the air. She looked at her sister. "I need to get back to her. What's up?"

Ellie looked pale, shaken even.

It unnerved Julia to see her powerhouse of a sister look beaten. She leaned forward. "What is it, Ellie?"

"The reporters are leaving town. They think the whole wild child thing is a hoax. By tomorrow the *Gazette* and maybe the *Olympian* will be the only papers still writing about the story."

Julia knew suddenly what this was about, why Ellie looked nervous.

"We need you to talk to the press," Ellie said softly, as if the timbre of her voice could remove the sting from the words.

"Do you know what you're asking of me?"

"What choice do we have? If the story dies, we may never know who she is. And you know what happens to abandoned kids. The state will warehouse her, ignore her."

"I can get her to talk."

"I know. But what if she doesn't know her name? We need her family to come forward."

Julia couldn't deny it. As painful as this decision was, the stakes were clear. It came down to her best interest versus Alice's. "I wanted to have something to tell them. A success that could be balanced against the failures. They won't—"

"What?"

Believe in me. "Nothing." Julia looked away. The silvery river caught her gaze, reflecting like a strand of sunlight against the green lawn. In that instance of brightness, she recalled the flash of the camera lights and the barrage of ugly questions. When the press went in for the kill, there was nothing that could protect you; the truth least of all. She was damaged goods now; they wouldn't listen to her opinion on anything. But they'd put her on the front page. "I guess I can't be any more ruined," she said at last, shivering slightly. She hoped her sister didn't notice.

But Ellie saw everything; she always had. Becoming a police officer had only heightened a natural skill for observation. "I'll be there with you all the time. Right beside you."

"Thanks." Maybe it would make a difference, not being so damned alone when the cameras rolled. "Schedule a press conference for tonight. Say . . . seven o'clock."

"What will you tell them?"

"I'll tell them what I can about Alice. I'll show them the pictures and reveal a few interesting behavioral observations and let them ask their questions."

"I'm sorry," Ellie said.

Julia tried to smile. "I've lived through it before. I guess I can live through it again. For Alice."

JULIA COULD HEAR THE RACKET GOING ON IN THE POLICE STATION. Dozens of reporters and photographers and videographers were out there, setting up their equipment, running sound and picture checks.

She and Ellie and Cal and Peanut were crammed into the employee lunchroom like hot dogs in a plastic pack.

"You'll be fine," Ellie said for at least the tenth time in the same number of minutes.

As he had each time, Cal agreed.

"I'm worried about Alice," Julia said.

"Myra is sitting just outside her door. She'll call if Alice makes a peep," Ellie said. "You'll be fine."

Peanut said, "They'll call her a quack."

Ellie gasped. "*Peanut.*"

Peanut grinned at Julia. "I use that technique on my kids. Reverse psychology. Now anything they say will sound good."

"No wonder your kids keep piercing their body parts," Cal remarked.

Peanut flipped him off. "At least I don't go to conventions in costume."

"I haven't worn a costume in twenty years."

Earl appeared at the door. Everything about him looked spit-shined, from his faded red comb-over to his lacquer-coated dress shoes. The creases in his uniform were laser sharp. "They're ready for you, Julia." He flushed, stammered, "I mean Dr. Cates."

One by one they peeled out of the lunchroom; the five of them collected again in the hallway.

"I'll go first to introduce you," Ellie said.

Julia nodded. *For Alice,* she thought.

Ellie walked down the hallway and turned the corner.

For Alice.

Then Earl was beside her, taking her arm.

She followed him down the hall, around the corner, and into the flash of her old life.

The crowd went wild, hurling questions like hand grenades.

"Qui-*et!*" Ellie yelled, holding her hands out. "Let Julia talk."

Gradually the crowd stilled.

Julia felt their eyes on her. Everyone in the room was judging her right now, finding her lacking in both judgment and skill. She drew in a sharp breath and caught it. Her gaze scanned the room, looking for a friendly face.

In the back row, behind the reporters and photographers, were the locals. The Grimm sisters (and poor Fred, in ash form), Barbara Kurek, Lori Forman and her bright-faced children; several of her high school teachers.

And Max. He gave her a nod and a thumbs-up. It was surprising, but that show of support helped calm her nerves. In Los Angeles, she'd always felt totally alone in facing the press.

"As all of you know, I'm Dr. Julia Cates. I've been called to Rain Valley to treat a very special patient, whom we're calling Alice. I know that many of you will wish to focus on my past, but I beg you to see what matters. This child is nameless and alone in the world. We need your help in finding her family." She held up a photograph. "This is the girl we're calling Alice. As you can see she has dark hair and blue-green eyes—"

"Dr. Cates, what would you say to the parents of those children who died in Silverwood?"

Once she'd been interrupted, all hell broke loose. The questions came at her like shrapnel.

"How do you live with the guilt—"

"Did you know Amber had purchased a gun—"

"Have you listened to the Death Knell lyrics—"

"—played the Doomsday Cavern video game?"

"Did you test her for an allergy to Prozac?"

Julia kept talking until her voice gave out. By the time it was over and the reporters had all run off to meet their deadlines, she felt utterly spent. Alone at the podium, she watched the people leave.

Finally, Ellie came up to her. "Jesus, Jules, that was bad," she said looking almost as shaken as Julia felt. "I'm sorry. I didn't know—"

"You couldn't have."

"Can I do something to help?"

Julia nodded. "Watch Alice for me, will you? I need to be alone for a while."

Ellie nodded.

Julia tried not to make eye contact with Peanut or Cal. They stood near his desk, holding hands. Both of them were pale. Peanut's bright pink cheeks were streaked with tears.

Julia walked down the steps and into the cold lavender night. At the sidewalk she turned left for no particular reason.

"Julia."

She turned.

He stood in the shadow of the street, almost lost in the shade from a giant evergreen. "I bought the motorcycle when I worked near Watts. Sometimes a man needs to clear his head. Seventy-five miles an hour on a bike will do it."

She should walk away, maybe even laugh, but she couldn't do it. In all of Rain Valley, he was probably the only person who really understood how she felt right now. How she knew that, she couldn't have said. It made no sense, but the notion stuck with her. "I think forty miles an hour would do it. I have a smaller head."

Smiling, he handed her a helmet.

She put it on and climbed onto the bike behind him, circling him with her arms.

They drove down the cool, gray streets of town, past the pod of news vans and the parking lot full of school buses. Wind beat at her sleeves and tugged at her hair when they turned onto the highway. They drove and drove, through the night, along the narrow, bumpy highway. She clung to him.

When he turned off the highway and onto his gravel driveway, she didn't care. In the back of her mind she'd known when she climbed onto this man's motorcycle where they would end up. Tomorrow, she would question her judgment—or lack thereof—but for now it felt good to have her arms around him. It felt good not to be alone.

He parked the motorcycle in the garage.

Wordlessly, they went into the house. She took a seat on the sofa while Max brought her a glass of white wine, then built a fire in the imposing river-rock fireplace and turned on the stereo. The first song that came on was something soft and jazzy.

"You don't need to go to all this trouble, Max. For God's sake, don't start lighting the candles."

He sat down beside her. "And why is that?"

"I'm not going upstairs."

"I don't remember asking you to."

She couldn't help smiling at that. Leaning back in the soft cushions, she looked at him over the rim of her wineglass. In the firelight, he looked breathtakingly handsome. A thought flitted through her mind, seduced her. *Why not?* She could follow him upstairs, climb into his big bed, and let him make love to her. For a glorious while she could forget. Women did that kind of thing all the time.

"What are you thinking about?"

She was sure he could read her mind. A man like him knew every nuance of desire on a woman's face. She felt her cheeks grow warm. "I was thinking about kissing you, actually."

He leaned toward her. His breath smelled slightly of scotch. "And?"

"As my sister pointed out, I'm not your kind of woman."

He drew back. "Believe me, Julia, your sister has no idea what kind of woman I want."

She heard the edge in his voice and saw something in his eyes that surprised her. "I've been wrong about you," she said, more to herself than to him.

"You certainly jumped to a lot of conclusions."

She smiled at that. "Hazard of the trade. I tend to think I know people."

"So you're an expert on relationships, huh?"

She laughed ruefully. "Hardly."

"Let me guess: you're a one-man woman. A hearts and flowers romantic."

"Now who's jumping to conclusions?"

"Am I wrong?"

She shrugged. "I don't know how romantic I am, but I only know one way to love."

"How's that?"

"All the way."

A frown creased his forehead. "That's dangerous."

"Says the rock climber. When you climb, you risk your life. When I love, I risk my heart. All or nothing. I'm sure it sounds stupid to you."

"It doesn't sound stupid," he said in a voice so soft it sent shivers down her spine. "You have that same passion for your work; I can tell."

"Yes," she said, surprised by the observation. "That's why today was so hard."

For a long moment they stared at each other. Max seemed to be looking for something in her eyes, or seeing something he didn't understand. Finally he said, "When I worked in L.A., we used to get gang shootings almost every night. One bleeding, dying kid after another. The first few I stayed with long after my shift was over and then talked to their brothers and sisters, trying to make them understand how their lives would unfold if they didn't change. By the end of the first year I quit giving them the speech and I quit standing by the bedsides all night. I couldn't save them all."

Their gazes locked. She felt as if she were falling into the endless sky of his eyes. "On good days, I know that. Today was not a good day. Or a good year, actually."

"Tomorrow will be better." He reached for her, pushed a thin strand of hair from her eyes.

It would have taken nothing to kiss him then; just a slight movement toward him. "You're good at it," she said shakily, drawing back.

"What?"

"Seducing women."

"I'm not seducing you."

But you are. She put down her wineglass and stood. She needed some distance between them. "Thanks for all of this, Max. You really saved me tonight. I need to get back to Alice, though. I can't be gone long."

Slowly, he got to his feet and walked her to the door. Without saying a word, he led her to the garage. They got onto the motorcycle and drove home.

FOURTEEN

THE MOTORCYCLE'S ENGINE ROARED THROUGH THE QUIET night, loud enough to rattle the nearby trees. In Los Angeles, the noise would have set off a dozen car alarms; here, it fought with the endless quiet of the dark road. Max came to the end of the driveway and slowed down, then stopped and glanced back.

Deep in the trees, the small house was made smaller by the night. All that darkness reduced it to a few lit windows.

I only know one way to love.

All or nothing.

How was it that a few quietly spoken words could hit him so hard?

He took off his helmet and jammed it onto the sissy bar behind him.

Air. Freedom. That was what he needed now. Something to clear his head and erase that moment.

He hit the gas, went faster and faster, until he was rocketing down the road.

Everything was a blur of shadows. He knew he was going too fast—there were deer and elk out here that could kill him in the blink of an eye, and potholes that would bite his tire and send him flying through the air—but he didn't care. As long as he was moving at this speed he couldn't think about her.

The minute he turned onto his road and slowed down, though, it all came back.

He parked the bike in the garage and went into his dark, quiet house, immediately turning on every light and the stereo.

Noise and light aren't life, Max.

It was Susi's voice. Though she wasn't here, had never been here, sometimes he saw his life through her eyes. Old habits were hard to break.

No dining room chairs, Max? No pictures on the wall. You can't call this a home.

He'd kept it bare on purpose. Furniture didn't matter to him; neither did decorations or comfort. He wanted a place where he could forget about all the things that made a house a home. Here, he could drink his drinks, watch sports on the big screen, and work in his woodshop.

All or nothing.

He should never have gone to her tonight, and he'd known it. After the press conference, he'd left the station as quickly as he could, intending to get on his bike and go home. Yet he'd waited outside, milled around in the darkness like a lovestruck kid.

The trouble was, he knew how hot the glare of that spotlight could be. When he'd looked at her there, behind all those microphones, trying so hard to be strong, he'd made a dangerous turn. He'd noticed her trembling lower lip and pale, pale face, her teary eyes, and his first thought had been that he wanted to kiss those tears away.

For the first time in seven years he'd been truly afraid, and not from misplacing his foot on a rock ledge or free-falling too far before pulling the rip cord. All those moments of feeling he'd accumulated in the past

years were facsimiles of an emotion. He'd thought—honestly believed—
that he couldn't feel anymore unless his life was at risk. That was what
had driven him to climb rock faces and jagged mountains: the need to
feel again, even if it lasted only a moment.

Now he'd felt something again. All he'd had to do was look in
Julia's sad eyes.

JULIA WENT INTO THE HOUSE.

Ellie was in the living room, sitting on the sofa with the dogs
spread across her lap. "It's about time," she said in a voice that held
some irritation.

"I wasn't gone that long."

"I was worried about you. The press conference was brutal."

Julia sat on the overstuffed cushion and put her feet on the coffee
table. She felt Ellie's gaze on her face, but she didn't turn to meet it.
"Yeah."

There was a long pause. Julia knew that her sister was trying to figure out what to say next.

"Don't bother," Julia said. "I just have to get through it. Again. At
least this time I have Alice."

"And me."

Julia heard a shadow of hurt in her sister's voice. "And you." At
that, Julia felt something in her chest relax.

"So where did you go tonight?"

Julia felt heat flare in her face. She glanced down at the dogs.
"Max's house."

Ellie straightened. "Really? Max *never* takes women to his house."

"I think he felt sorry for me."

Ellie was staring at her now and frowning. "Did you—"

"No," Julia said quickly. She didn't even want to hear the words
out loud. "Of course not."

"You watch out for him," Ellie said at last. "I'm not kidding, Jules.
And I'm not jealous. Just be careful."

Julia was touched by the concern. "I will be." She stood up. "I'm beat. I'm going to crash. Thanks for waiting up for me."

"Thanks for throwing yourself on the fire for us."

Julia headed for the stairs. She was just reaching for the banister when Ellie called out her name. Julia paused and turned around. "Yeah?"

"Everything will be okay, you know. Sooner or later it'll die down and they'll remember how good you are at what you do."

Julia released her breath. "That's what Mom would have said to me."

Ellie smiled.

Julia tried to hang on to those words, to let them be her armor. It was what she'd done as a child. Whenever she'd been wounded by some slight at school—or by her father's inattention—she'd gone to her mother in tears. *Everything will be okay*, her mom would say, wiping the moisture from her cheeks and enfolding her in a hug that smelled of Suave shampoo and cigarettes.

She climbed the stairs to her room and went directly to the twin bed by the window.

Julia pulled the blankets up and covered the child, then bent down slowly and kissed her sweet, soft cheek.

She meant to rise, but knelt by the bed instead. Without realizing what she was going to do, she bowed her head and closed her eyes.

Give me strength.

She kissed Alice's cheek again, then climbed into her own narrow, lonely bed and fell asleep.

SOMETHING IS WRONG.

Girl senses it the second she opens her eyes. She stands still, sniffing the air. Many things, she has learned, can be sensed if one is quiet. The coming of snow smells like apples and makes her littlest finger swell up; a hunting bear makes a sound like snoring; danger can be heard in plenty of time if one is still and quiet. This was a lesson Her could never learn. In the lazy other days that she sometimes visits in her sleep, she remembers how Her used to try talking to Girl: always the noise, and the trouble that came afterward.

Now, in her safe place, hidden by the small trees, she stares through the leaves at the Sun-Haired Her, who is so silent.

Has Girl done something wrong?

Across the room, Sun Hair looks up. She looks sad, like maybe her eyes are going to start leaking again. And tired. That was how Her looked before she got dead.

"Comeherealis." Sun Hair pats the bed.

Girl knows that movement, the touching of the bed. It means that Sun Hair will open the magic pictures and talk and talk.

Girl *loves* that. The sound of Her voice, the way she lets Girl be so close, the safety of curling up beside her.

"Comeherealis."

Girl eases around the plants and shuffles forward, trying to be as small and still as possible, just in case she has done something Bad. She wishes Sun Hair would have on the happy face again; that makes Girl feel light. She keeps her head down, careful not to make eye contact. At Sun Hair's feet, she drops to her knees.

The touch on her forehead is soft and gentle. Girl looks up.

"Thisisgoingtobedifficultalis." She sighs. "Trustmeokay."

Girl doesn't know what to do, how to show her obedience. Another little sound escapes her.

"I'msorry." Sun Hair reaches into a box on the floor and pulls out It.

For a split second Girl freezes, too frightened to move. She glances around the room expecting Him to break into this too-light place. She scrambles backward.

Finally she screams. Once she starts, she can't stop. She knows it is Wrong. Bad. Stupid to make so much noise and that the Strangers will come and hurt her now, but she is past the rules, past thinking. She hits one of the baby trees and it falls sideways, hitting the ground with a loud noise.

She screams more, gulping down air, trying to get away from it, but the white cave wall stops her. She hits it hard, feels pain thump her in the back of her head.

Sun Hair is talking to her, stringing sounds together that are as pretty as shells, but she can't hear it. Her heart is beating so fast, and It is still there, in Sun Hair's hand.

As It gets closer, Girl starts to scratch herself, drawing blood.

Sun Hair is with her now, holding her so tightly that Girl can't claw herself.

"Okayokayokayokay. Nohurt. Iknowyou'rescared. It'sokayokay-okay." Sun Hair's voice finally comes through.

Girl's screaming fades. She breathes hard and fast, trying to be strong, but she is so scared.

Sun Hair lets go of her. Slowly, as if she is the one afraid, the pretty woman lifts It up.

Girl's eyes widen. She feels sick inside, desperate. The air in the room darkens; everything smells like smoke and blood.

It catches the light. She closes her eyes, remembering his dark, hairy fingers twisting the strings . . . bending the twigs . . . threading the beads. She whimpers.

"Alis. Alis."

The touch on her cheek is so gentle that at first she thinks she's imagined it . . . that Her has come back.

"Alisopenyoureyes."

The touch feels so good. She can breathe again. Inside her chest, her heart begins to slow down.

"It'sokayalis.Openyoureyes."

Girl is beginning to hear something familiar in the garble of sounds. It pokes at her memory, makes her think of a time so long ago it turns to mist when she reaches for it. Slowly, she opens her eyes.

Sun Hair backs up a little. "Thisisadreamcatcher," she says, un-smiling now. "Youknowthis."

Dream Catcher.

She feels her tummy start to shake.

In a single motion Sun Hair breaks the dreamcatcher in half, then she rips the strings apart. The beads go flying, skitter across the floor.

Girl gasps. *Ohnoohnoohno.* This is bad. He will come now, He will hurt them.

Sun Hair reaches into the box and pulls out another one. She rips it into pieces and throws it away.

Girl watches in awe. Sun Hair ruins another and another. She takes something from the table and smashes it down on the pieces in front of her. Finally, smiling again, she holds a dreamcatcher toward Girl. "Breakit. No hurt. No hurt."

Girl understands. Sun Hair wants *her* to break His toy.

But he will hurt her.

He's not here. He's Gone. Is that what Sun Hair is trying to show her?

"Comeonalis. No hurt."

She looks at Sun Hair. The woman's watery green eyes make her feel all shaky inside.

Slowly, her hand trembling, she reaches out to touch It.

—it will burn you—

But It doesn't. It feels like nothing in her hand, just bits of string and twig. There is no blood on It, no trace of his big, angry hands.

She rips it in half, and at the motion, she feels something new grow inside her, a kind of rumble that starts deep in her belly and catches in her throat. It feels so good to break His toy, to ruin it, to reach into the box and grab another one.

She rips them all, then destroys the box. As she breaks and snaps, she thinks of Him, of all the ways He hurt her, and all the times she wanted to scream.

When the box is empty, she looks up, gulping air as if she doesn't know how to breathe.

Sun Hair takes Girl in her arms and holds her tightly.

Girl doesn't know what is happening. Her body is shaking.

"It'sokayokayokay. Nohurt. Nohurt."

Girl feels herself relaxing. A warm feeling blossoms in her chest and spreads out, down her arms and into her fingers.

"You'resafenow."

She hears that, *feels* it.

Safe.

JULIA PAUSED IN HER NOTE-TAKING TO READ WHAT SHE HAD WRITTEN.

She stands behind the plants for much of the day, staring alternately at me or out the window. Sunshine particularly engages her attention, as do bright plastic objects and dishes. Many things seem to frighten her—loud noises, thunder, the color gray, bright and shiny metal objects, dreamcatchers, and knives. The dogs' barking always sends her running to the door. It is the only time she even approaches that side of the room. Often she howls in response.

Right now, she is sitting at my feet, looking up at me. This is her new favorite spot. Since ruining the dreamcatchers, she has broken through the solitary border of the previous days. She is never more than a few inches away from me. Often, she paws at my feet and legs. When tired, she curls up on the floor beside me, resting her cheek on my foot.

Julia looked down at the girl. "What are you thinking, Alice?"

As always, there was no response. Alice stared up at her intently; it was as if she were trying to understand.

So intent was she that it took her a moment to realize that someone was knocking on the door. "Come in," she said distractedly.

The door opened just a crack and Ellie slipped into the room. Behind her, the golden retrievers were going crazy; barking, scratching, whining. She shut the door firmly. At Ellie's entrance, Alice ran to her hiding place.

"You've got to teach those dogs some manners," Julia said without looking up. She made a notation on Alice's chart. *Responds to dogs by howling quietly. Today she moved toward the door.*

"Jules?"

She heard something in her sister's voice and looked up. "What?"

"Some people are here to see you. Doctors from the state care facility, a researcher from the U.W., and a woman from DSHS."

She should have expected it. The media had hinted that Alice was "wild." Just the suggestion of it would tempt other doctors, researchers. In the old days, no one would have dared to encroach on her patient. These were not those days. Now, she would look weak; predators would begin to circle her. She got slowly to her feet and methodically put her notes and charts and pens away.

All the while, Alice watched her, looking worried.

"I'll be right back, Alice," she said to the girl hidden in the foliage, then followed her sister downstairs.

At first glance, the living room seemed full of people. On closer examination, Julia saw that there were only three men and one woman. They simply appeared to take up a lot of space.

"Dr. Cates," said the man closest to her, moving forward. He was tall and scarecrow thin with a nose big enough to hang an umbrella on. "I'm Simon Kletch, from the state's therapeutic residential care facility, and these are my colleagues: Byron Barrett and Stanley Goldberg, from the Behavioral Sciences lab at the U.W. You know Ms. Wharton, from DSHS."

Julia said evenly, "Hello."

Ellie went to the kitchen and stood by the counter.

A silence fell. They all stared at one another until Ellie asked them to sit.

And still it was too quiet.

Finally Simon cleared his throat. "Rumors are that this girl in your care is a wild child, or something close to that. We'd like to see her." He glanced up the stairs; his eyes glinted with excitement.

"No."

He seemed surprised by that. "You know why we are here."

Julia could hear his eagerness. "Why don't you tell me?"

"You're making no progress with her."

"That's hardly true. In fact, we've made huge strides. She can eat and dress herself and use the toilet. She's beginning to communicate, in her way. I believe—"

"You're civilizing her," the behavioral scientist said sharply, peering at her through small oval glasses. A sheen of sweat sparkled on his upper lip. "We need to study her, Dr. Cates. As she is. We men of science have sought a child like this for decades. If taught to talk, she can be a gold mine of information. Think of it. Who are we in the absence of one another? What is true human nature? Is language instinctive? And what is the link between language and humanity? Do words allow us to dream—to think—or vice versa? She can answer all these questions. Even you must see that."

"Even I? What does that mean?" she asked, although she knew.

"Silverwood," Dr. Kletch said.

"You've never lost a patient?" she said sharply to him.

"Of course I have. We all have. But your failure was public. I'm getting a lot of pressure to take over this girl's case."

"I'm her foster parent as well as her therapist," Julia said. She didn't call Dr. Kletch a bottom-feeder by sheer force of will. Of course he wanted to "help" Alice; she could advance his career.

"Dr. Kletch believes that the minor child belongs in a therapeutic care facility," said the woman from DSHS. "If you can't assure us that you'll get her talking and find out her name, then—"

"I will get her talking," Julia said.

"We need to study her." This from the behavioral scientist.

"And learn from her," added Dr. Kletch.

Julia stood. "You are like all the doctors who have been associated with children like this in the past. You want to use her, treat her like a lab rat so that you can write your papers and find fame. When you've sucked her dry, you'll move on and forget her. She'll grow up warehoused and behind bars and medicated beyond recognition. I won't let you do it. She's *my* foster child and *my* patient. The state has authorized me to care for her, and that's what I intend to do." She forced a thin smile. "But thank you for your concern."

No one spoke for a moment. Julia turned to the social worker. "Don't be fooled by them, Ms. Wharton. *I'm* the one who cares about this child."

Ms. Wharton bit her lip nervously and looked at the doctors, then at Julia. "Get the child talking, Dr. Cates. There's a lot of interest in this case. A lot of pressure being put on our office to move her into therapeutic residential care. Your history and the media frenzy doesn't sit well with my boss. No one wants another incident."

Ellie stepped forward. "And that's the end of the meeting. Thank you all for coming." She walked through the room, herded the crowd toward the door.

The doctors were arguing, sputtering, gesturing with their hands. "But she's not good enough," one of them said. "Dr. Cates isn't the best doctor for that child."

Ellie smiled and pushed them out the door, locking it behind them.

When it was quiet again, the dogs started to whine upstairs. Julia could hear them pacing outside the bedroom door. "Alice is upset. The dogs always respond to her emotions. I should get back."

Ellie moved forward fast, touched Julia's arm. "Are you okay?"

"Fine. I should have expected it. Mort's picture and the press conference my past. There are all kinds of doctors who would use Alice to advance their careers." On that, her voice finally broke.

"Don't let them get to you," Ellie said. "You're helping that little girl."

Julia looked down at her sister. "I . . . missed things with Amber. Important things. Maybe—"

"Don't," Ellie said. "They want you to question yourself, to lose confidence. Don't let them win."

Julia sighed. She felt as if she were melting from the inside out, shrinking. "It's not a game. It's her life. If I'm not the best doctor for her . . ."

"Go back upstairs, Jules. Do what you do best." Ellie smiled. "You hear that howling? That's her, telling you she needs you. *You.*"

"I'm afraid—"

"We're all afraid."

To that, Julia had no answer. With another heavy sigh, she left the living room and went upstairs. In the hallway, the dogs were going crazy, whining and howling and running into each other. Alice's low, keening growl could be heard through the door.

Julia paused, trying to refind her confidence. In its place she found a fake smile and shaking hands. Pushing past the dogs, she went into her old bedroom.

Alice immediately stopped howling.

"Talk to me. Please." To Julia's horror, her voice broke on that last, desperate word. All the emotions she'd tamped down and stored away rose again. All she could think about now was her failure with Amber.

She wiped her eyes, although no tears had fallen. "I'm sorry, Alice. It's just been a bad day."

She went to the table and sat down, needing the safe harbor of her profession. She studied her notes, trying to concentrate.

At first the touch was so soft that Julia failed to notice.

She looked down.

Alice was staring up at her, stroking Julia's arm. She wiped her eyes, although she wasn't crying.

Sympathy. Alice was offering sympathy. The child had recognized her sadness and wanted to alleviate it. She was *connecting*, answering in the only way she knew how.

Suddenly, none of the rest of it mattered.

Julia felt a wave of gratitude to this poor, strange little girl who had just reached out to her, reminded her that she made a *difference*. No ugly headlines or ambitious doctors or unfeeling child welfare system could steal that from her. She touched Alice's soft, scarred cheek. "Thank you."

Alice flinched at the touch. She started to pull away, probably so that she could go hide among the plants again.

"Stay," Julia said, grasping her frail, thin wrist. "Please." Her voice broke on the sharp desperation of that word.

Alice drew in a deep, shaky breath and stared at Julia.

"You know that word, don't you? *Stay*. I need something from you, too, Alice. I need to help you."

They sat that way for a long time, staring at each other.

"You're not autistic, are you?" Julia said finally. "You're worried about my feelings. Now how about I return the favor? You tell me something secret and I'll be here for you."

FIFTEEN

FOR THE NEXT TWO WEEKS THE STORY OF THE DISGRACED DOCTOR and the nameless, voiceless girl was headline news. The phones at the police station were jammed with calls from doctors, psychiatrists and counselors, kooks and scientists. Everyone, it seemed, wanted to save Alice from Julia's incompetence. Drs. Kletch and Goldberg called daily. The Department of Social and Health Services required updates twice a week. They were beginning to suggest residential care at almost every turn.

Julia worked eighteen hours a day. She was with Alice from sunup to sundown; after the child fell asleep, she went to the library and spent more hours in front of a computer screen or online.

Everything she did was for Alice. On Wednesdays and Fridays, like clockwork, she went to the police station, where she conducted a press conference. She stood at that podium, inches from the microphones that amplified her words. She told them every aspect of Alice's treatment, offered every identity hint that was revealed. None of it interested them.

They asked endless questions about Julia's past, about her regrets and failures and lost patients. They cared nothing for the milestones of Alice's recovery. Still, Julia tried. *She reached for me today.* . . . *She buttoned her blouse.* . . . *She pointed at a bird.* . . . *She used a fork.*

All that mattered to the reporters was that Alice hadn't spoken. To them, it was more proof that Julia could no longer be trusted to help even one troubled child.

But in time, even the rehashing of Julia's past began to lose momentum. The stories went from headline news on page one to a paragraph or two in the local interest or Life sections. Local water cooler conversation left the unknown girl behind; now the mini quakes shaking Mount St. Helens were on everyone's mind.

From her podium, Julia stared out at the few reporters in the police station. CNN, *USA Today,* the *New York Times,* and the national television stations weren't here anymore. Only a few of the local papers were left, and most of them were from small peninsula communities like Rain Valley. Their questions were still pointed and cruel, but they were asked in dull, monotone voices. No one expected any of it to matter anymore.

"That's all for this week," Julia said, realizing the room had gone still. "The big news is that she can dress herself. And she shows a true affinity for anything made of plastic. She can take or leave television— I think the images move too quickly for her—but she can watch cooking programs all day. Maybe that will strike a chord with someone—"

"Come on, Dr. Cates," said a man at the back of the room. He was desperately thin, with shaggy hair and a mouth made for cigarettes. "No one is looking for this kid."

There was a murmur of assent from the crowd as they talked among themselves. Julia heard the papery rustle of their laughter.

"That's not true. A child doesn't simply appear and disappear in this world. Someone is missing her."

A man from KIRO-TV stepped forward. The compassion in his dark eyes was almost harder to bear than the disinterest of his colleagues. "I don't know what's true about your past and what's media spin, Dr. Cates, but I know that you're a smart woman. There's something wrong with this kid. Big-time wrong. I think that's why her family dumped her in the woods and walked away."

Julia stepped out from behind the podium and moved toward him. "You have no evidence to support that. It's just as likely that she was kidnapped so long ago that her family has given up on her. Stopped looking."

His gaze was steady. "Stopped looking? For their daughter?"

"If—"

"I wish you luck, I really do, but KIRO is pulling out. The rumblings at Mount St. Helens are front and center now." He reached into his rumpled white shirt pocket and withdrew a card. "My wife's a therapist. I'll be fair to you. Call me if you find out something substantive."

She looked down at his card. JOHN SMITH, TV NEWS. KIRO, she knew, had a top-notch research staff and access to people and places she couldn't begin to reach. "How hard did you guys try to find out who she is?"

"Four researchers worked on it full-time for the first two weeks."

Julia nodded. She'd been afraid of that.

"Good luck."

She watched him leave, thinking, *And there goes the last of the good ones.* Next Wednesday she'd be giving her update to representatives of local newspapers, with smaller circulations than most high schools, and—if she was lucky—some low-rent stringer for the tabloids.

Peanut crossed the room, weaving through the row of metal folding chairs, picking up the discarded news releases they'd handed out. Her black rubber clogs made a thumping sound on the floor. Cal went along behind her, grabbing the chairs, clanging them shut.

Within moments the podium was the only remaining evidence of today's press conference. Soon there would be no audience for any of this. The pressure of that knowledge had been building in Julia, filling her lungs like a slow-growing case of pneumonia.

The milestones she'd reported to the media today were important.

In ordinary therapy, the amount of progress Alice had made in three weeks would be considered successful. Now the child could eat with utensils and use the toilet. She'd even come so far as to show sympathy for someone else, but none of it answered the central question of identity. None of it would get Alice back to her family and her real life. None of it would guarantee that Julia could keep working with her. In fact, with every day that passed in the child's silence, Julia felt her grasp on her confidence loosen. At night, as she lay in her bed, listening to Alice's quiet nightmares and violent moments, Julia thought: *Am I good enough?*

Or worse: *What am I missing this time?*

"You did a great job today," Peanut said, trying to force a smile. It was the same thing she'd said after each press conference.

"Thanks," was Julia's standard answer. "I better get back," she said, bending down for her briefcase.

Peanut nodded, then yelled to Cal, "I'm takin' her home."

Julia followed Peanut out of the station and into the gunmetal gray light of sundown. In the car, they both stared straight ahead. Garth Brooks's voice floated through the speakers, complaining about friends in low places.

"So . . . I guess it isn't going so well, huh?" Peanut said, strumming her black-and-white checkerboard fingernails on the steering wheel at the four-way stop.

"She's made huge progress, but . . ."

"She still isn't talking. Are you sure she can?"

The same series of questions ran like an endless monologue through Julia's thoughts. Day and night, she thought: *Can she? Will she? When?* "I believe it with my whole heart," Julia said slowly. Then she smiled ruefully. "My head is beginning to wonder, however."

"When I was a young mother, the thing I hated most was changin' diapers. So the day my Tara turned two, I set about teachin' her to use the toilet. I followed all the how-to books down to the letter. And you know what happened? My Tara stopped pooping. Just stopped. After about five days, I took her to Doc Fischer. I was worried sick. He examined my baby girl, then looked at me over his glasses. He said, 'Penelope Nutter, this girl is trying to tell you something. She doesn't want to be potty trained.'" Peanut laughed, then hit the turn signal and veered onto the old highway. "There's no metal on earth stronger than a child's will. I guess your Alice will talk when she's ready." Peanut turned down their driveway and pulled up in front of the house, honking twice.

Ellie came out of the house almost immediately; so quickly, in fact, that Julia suspected she'd been at the door, waiting.

"Thanks for the ride, Peanut."

"See you Wednesday."

Julia got out of the car and slammed the door shut. She met Ellie halfway across the yard.

"She's howling again," Ellie said miserably.

"When did she wake up?"

"Five minutes ago. She's early. How'd it go?"

"Bad," she said, trying to sound strong and failing.

"The DNA results will be back soon. Maybe they will give us an answer. If she's a kidnap victim, there will be crime scene evidence to compare to."

They'd tossed this idea back and forth like a life ring in the last few days, though it had lost its buoyancy. "I know. Hopefully she's in the system." It was what Julia always said.

"Hopefully."

They looked at each other. The word was starting to sound frayed.

Julia went into the house and up the stairs. With each step, the howling grew in volume. She knew what she'd find when she entered her room. Alice would be kneeling behind her plants, head down, face in her hands, rocking and howling. It was her only means of expressing sadness or fear. She was afraid now because she'd wakened alone. To an ordinary child, this might be frustrating. To Alice, it was terrifying.

Julia was already talking when she opened the door. "Now, what's all this racket about, Alice? Everything is fine. You're just scared. That's natural."

Alice streaked across the room in a blur of black hair, yellow dress, and spindly arms and legs. She pressed herself against Julia so closely that there was contact from waist to calf.

Alice put her hand in Julia's pocket.

This was how it was lately. Alice needed to be next to Julia always, connected.

She was sucking her thumb and looking up at Julia with a vulnerability that was both heartbreaking and terrifying.

"Come on, Alice," Julia said, pretending it was perfectly natural to have a young human barnacle attached to her hip. She got out her Denver Kit, a collection of toys that were helpful in gauging a child's development.

At the table, she set out the bell, the block, and the doll. "Sit down, Alice," she said, knowing Alice would sit down when she did. The chairs were close enough that they could still be together.

Side by side, with Alice's tiny hand still tucked in Julia's pocket, they sat down. With the Denver Kit spread out in front of them, Julia waited for Alice to make a move.

"Come on," Julia said. I need you to talk, little one. I know you can do it."

Nothing. Just the gentle in and out of the girl's breathing.

Desperation plucked at Julia's confidence, broke a tender strand of it.

"Please." Her voice was a whisper now, not her therapist-voice at all. She thought about the passing of time and the dwindling media interest and the increasingly quiet phone lines in the police station. "Please. Come on . . ."

WHEN ELLIE AND PEANUT ARRIVED AT THE POLICE STATION, THE BUILD-ing was quiet. Cal was at his desk, headphones on his head, drawing a picture of some winged creature. At their entrance, he turned the paper facedown.

As if Ellie cared to see his bizarre sketches. He'd been doing them since sixth grade. The only difference between him and every other guy she'd ever known was that Cal had never outgrown it. There were always doodles on her pink While You Were Out messages.

"Earl signed out," Cal said, pushing a lock of hair out of his eyes. "Mel is going to make one more pass out toward the lake to check on the teens, and then he's off, too."

In other words, life in Rain Valley was back to normal. The phones weren't ringing and her two patrol officers were off unless someone called in.

"And the DNA results are back. I put them on your desk."

Ellie stopped. They all looked at one another. After a long moment she went to her desk and sat down. The chair squeaked in protest.

She picked up the official-looking envelope and opened it. The pages inside had a lot of mumbo-jumbo/scientist speak, but none of it mattered. At the midsection was the sentence: *No match found.*

The second page was a lab report on the dress fibers. As expected, it revealed only that the dress was made of inexpensive white cotton that could have come from any of a dozen textile mills. There were no blood or semen traces in the fabric, no DNA present.

The final paragraph of the report outlined the procedure to be followed in the event that the DNA collected from Alice was to be tested against a found sample.

Ellie felt a wave of defeat. What now? She'd done everything she knew; hell, she'd thrown her sister to the wolves, and for what? They were no closer to an ID now than they'd been three weeks ago, and the people at DSHS were breathing down her neck.

Cal and Peanut pulled chairs across the room and sat in front of the desk.

"No ID?" Peanut asked.

Ellie shook her head, unable to say it out loud.

"You did the best you could," Cal said gently.

"No one coulda done any better," Peanut agreed.

After that, no one spoke. A real rarity here.

Finally, Ellie pushed the papers across her desk. "Send these re-sults out to the people who are waiting. How many requests have we gotten?"

"Thirty-three. Maybe one of them is the match," Peanut said hopefully.

Ellie opened her desk drawer and pulled out the stack of papers she'd gotten from the National Center for Missing Children. She'd read it at least one hundred times, using it as the only guidance she could find. The final paragraph had been burned into her brain. She didn't need to read it again to know what it said. *If none of this produces a positive identification of the child, then social services should be called in. The child will most likely be placed in a permanent foster home or a residential treatment facility, or adopted out.*

"What do we do next?" Peanut asked.

Ellie sighed. "We pray this DNA produces a match."

They all knew how unlikely that was. None of the thirty-three re-quests had seemed particularly promising. Most of them had been made by people—parents and lawyers and cops from other jurisdictions—who believed the child being sought was dead. None of them had de-scribed Alice's birthmark.

Ellie rubbed her eyes. "Let's pack it in for the night. You can send out the DNA reports tomorrow, Pea. I have another phone conference with the lady from DSHS. That should be fun."

Peanut stood up. "I'm meeting Benji at the Big Bowl. Anyone want to join me?"

"There's nothing I like better than hanging around with fat men in matching polyester shirts," said Cal. "I'm in."

Peanut glared at him. "You want me to tell Benji you called him fat?"

Cal laughed. "It'll come as no surprise to him, Pea."

"Don't get started, you two," Ellie said tiredly. The last thing she wanted to listen to was a he said/she said fight over nothing. "I'm going home. You should, too, Cal. It's Friday night. The girls will miss you."

"The girls and Lisa went to Aberdeen to see her folks. I'm a bachelor this weekend. So, it's the Big Bowl for me." He looked at her. "You used to love bowling."

Ellie found herself remembering the summer she and Cal had worked at the Big Bowl's lunch counter. It had been that last magical year of childhood, before all the sharp edges of adolescence poked through. They'd been outcasts together that summer, best friends in the way that only two social rejects can be. The next summer she'd been too cool for the Big Bowl.

"That was a long time ago, Cal. I can't believe you remember it."

"I remember." There was an edge to his voice that was odd. He walked over to the hooks by the door and grabbed his coat.

"It's karaoke night," Peanut said, smiling.

Ellie was lost and Peanut damn well knew it. "I guess a margarita couldn't hurt." It was better than going home. The thought of telling Julia about the DNA was more than she could bear.

On either side of River Road, giant Douglas fir trees were an endless black saw blade of sharp tips and serrated edges. Overhead, the sky was cut into bite-sized pieces by treetops and mountain peaks. There were stars everywhere, some bright and so close you felt certain their light would reach down to the soggy earth, but when Ellie looked at her feet, there was only dark gravel beneath her.

She giggled. For a second she'd almost expected to look down and see a black mist there.

"Slow down," Cal said, coming around the car. He took hold of Ellie's arm, steadying her.

She couldn't seem to stop looking at the sky. Her head felt heavy; so, too, her eyelids. "You see the Big Dipper?" It was directly to the left and above her house. "My dad used to say that God used it to pour magic down our chimney." Her voice cracked on that. The memory surprised her. She hadn't had time to raise her shield. "This is why I don't drink."

Cal put an arm around her. "I thought you didn't drink because of the senior prom. Remember when you puked on Principal Haley?"

"I need new friends," Ellie muttered. She let herself be guided into the house, where the dogs rammed into her so hard she almost fell again.

"Jake! Elwood!" She bent down and hugged them, letting them lick her cheek until it was so wet it felt like she'd been swimming.

"You need to train those dogs," Cal said, stepping away from their sniffing noses.

"Training anything with a penis is impossible." She grinned at him. "And you thought I didn't learn anything from my marriages." She pointed to the stairs. "Upstairs, boys. I'll be right up."

She only had to say it another fifteen times before they obeyed. Once the dogs were gone, Cal said, "You better get to bed."

"I'm sick of sleeping alone. Pretend I didn't say that." She started to pull away from Cal, then stopped dead. "Did you hear that? Someone's playing the piano. 'Delta Dawn.'" She started singing. "'Delta Dawn, what's that flower you have on?'" She danced across the room.

"No one is playing music," Cal said. He glanced over at the corner, where her mom's old piano sat, gathering dust. "That's the song you sang tonight for karaoke. One of them, anyway."

Ellie came to an unsteady stop and looked at Cal. "I'm the chief of police."

"Yes."

"I got drunk on margaritas and sang karaoke . . . in public. In my *uniform*."

Cal was trying not to smile. "Look at the bright side, you didn't strip and you didn't drive home."

She covered her eyes with her hand. "That's my bright side? I didn't get naked or commit a crime."

"Well . . . there was that time—"

"I am *definitely* making new friends. You can go home. I won't be seeing you anymore." She turned away from him too quickly, lost her balance, and went down like a tree at harvest time. The only thing missing was a cry of "Timber!"

"Wow. You really hit hard."

She rolled over and lay there. "Are you going to just stand there or are you going to hook me up to some sort of pulley system and get me up?"

Cal was openly smiling now. "I'm going to stand here. Us not being friends anymore, and all."

"Oh, damn it. We're back on." She reached up. He took her hand and helped her to her feet. "That hurt," she said, brushing dust off her pants.

"It looked like it did."

Cal was still holding her hand. She turned to him. "It's okay, big brother. I'm not going to fall again."

"Sure?"

"Semi-sure." She pulled free. "Thanks for driving me home. See you back at the station at eight sharp. The DNA will find a match. I feel it in my blood."

"That might be tequila."

"Naysayer. 'Night." She lurched toward the stairs, grabbing the handrail just as she started to fall.

Cal was beside her in an instant.

"Hey." She frowned, feeling his hold on her forearm. "I thought you left."

"I'm right here."

She looked at him. With her on the stair and him on the floor, they were eye-to-eye and so close she could see where he'd nicked himself shaving that morning. She noticed the jagged scar along his jawline. He'd gotten that the summer he turned twelve. His dad had come after him with a broken beer bottle. It was Ellie's dad who'd gotten him to the hospital.

"How come you're so good to me, Cal? I was crappy to you in high school." It was true. Once she'd sprouted boobs, plucked her eyebrows, and outgrown her acne, everything had changed. Boys had noticed her, even the football players. She'd left Cal behind in the blink of an eye, and yet he'd never made her feel bad about it.

"Old habits die hard, I guess."

She backed up one step. It was just enough to put some distance between them. "How come you never drink with us?"

"I drink."

"I know. I said *with us*."

"Someone has to drive you home."

"But it's always you. Doesn't Lisa care that we keep you out all night?"

He was looking at her closely. "I told you: she's gone this weekend."

"She's always gone."

He didn't answer. After a minute she'd forgotten what they were talking about.

And suddenly she was thinking about the girl again, and failure. "I won't find her family, will I?"

"You've always found a way to get what you want, El. That was never your problem."

"Oh? What is my problem, then?"

"You always wanted the wrong things."

"Gee, thanks."

He seemed disappointed by that. Like he'd wanted her to say something else. She couldn't imagine how she'd let him down, but somehow she had. If she were sober, she'd probably know the answer.

"You're welcome. You want me to pick you up tomorrow morning?"

"No need. I'll get Jules or Peanut to give me a ride."

"Okay. See you."

"See you."

She watched him walk away, close the front door behind him.

The house fell silent again. With a sigh, she navigated the narrow, too-steep stairway and emerged onto the second floor. She meant to turn left, to her parents'—now her—bedroom, but her mind was on autopilot and steered her right into her old room. It wasn't until she saw that both twin beds were full that she realized she'd made a wrong turn.

The girl was awake and watching her. She'd been asleep when the door opened, Ellie was certain of it. "Hello, little one," she whispered, flinching when she heard the low, answering growl.

"I would never hurt you," she said, backing toward the door. "I only wanted to help. I wish . . ."

What did she wish? She didn't know. When she thought about it, that was the problem with her life, now and always; she'd never known what to wish for until it was too late.

She wanted to promise that they'd find the girl's family, but she didn't believe it. Not anymore.

LIKE A RIVERBANK IN A SPRING THAW, THE EROSION OF JULIA'S SELF-confidence was a steady, plucking movement. No instant of it could really be seen—no giant chunks of earth fell away—but the end result was a change in the course of things, a new direction. More and more, she found herself retreating to the safe world of her notes. There, on those thin blue lines, she analyzed everything. While she still believed that Alice understood at least at the toddler level—a few words, here and there—she was making no real progress in getting the girl to speak. The authorities were breathing down her neck. Every day, Dr. Kletch left a message on the machine. It was always the same. *You're not helping this child enough, Dr. Cates. Let us step in.*

This afternoon, when she'd put Alice down for her nap, Julia had knelt by the bed, stroking the girl's soft black hair, patting her back, thinking, *How can I help you?*

She'd felt the sting of tears in her eyes; before she knew it, they were falling freely down her cheeks.

She'd had to go to the bathroom and redo her makeup for the press conference. She'd only just finished her mascara when a car drove up outside. She was halfway down the stairs when she ran into Ellie, coming up.

"You okay?" Ellie asked, frowning.

"I'm fine. She's asleep."

"Well. Peanut's waiting in the car. I'll stay here today."

Julia nodded. She grabbed her briefcase and left the house.

They drove the mile and a half to town in a heavy rain. The drops on the windshield and roof were so loud that conversation was impossible. Rain seemed to be boiling on the hood.

While Peanut parked the car, Julia opened an umbrella and ran for the station. She was hanging up her coat and walking to the podium when it struck her.

Every seat was empty.

No one had come.

Cal sat at the dispatch desk, looking at her with pity.

She glanced at the clock. The press conference should have started five minutes ago. "Maybe—"

The door burst open. Peanut stood there, wearing her department issue slicker, rain dripping down her face. "Where the hell is everyone?"

"No one showed," Cal said.

Peanut's fleshy face seemed to fall at that. Her eyes rounded, first in understanding, then in resignation. She went over to where Cal stood and tucked in close to him. He took hold of her hand. "This is bad."

"Very bad," Julia agreed.

For the next thirty minutes they waited in terrible silence, jumping every time the phone rang. By 4:45 no one could pretend that it wasn't over.

Julia stood. "I need to get back, Peanut. Alice will be waking up soon." She reached for her briefcase and followed Peanut into the car.

Outside, the rain had stopped. The sky looked gray and bruised. Exactly how she felt. She knew she should made small talk with Peanut, at least answer her endless string of questions, but she didn't feel like it.

Peanut turned onto Main Street. After a quick "Aha!" she pulled into one of the slanted parking stalls in front of the Rain Drop Diner.

"I promised Cal I'd get him dinner. It'll only take a jiff." She was gone before Julia could answer.

Julia got out of the car. She'd intended to get herself a cup of coffee, but now that she was here, she couldn't seem to move. Across the street was Sealth Park. It was where Alice had first appeared. The maple tree, now bare, sent empty branches reaching for the darkening sky. The forest in the distance was too dark to see.

How long were you out there?

Julia felt someone beside her. She pulled her thoughts back to the now and turned, expecting to see Peanut's smiling face.

Max stood there, wearing a black leather jacket, jeans, and a white tee shirt. It was the first time she'd seen him in weeks. The avoidance had been entirely intentional. And now here he was, looking down at her, taking up too much space and breathing too much air.

"Long time no see."

"I've been busy."

"Me, too."

They stood there, staring at each other.

"How's Alice?"

"She's making progress."

"Still not talking?"

She winced. "Not yet."

He frowned. It lasted only a second, maybe less; she thought perhaps she'd imagined it until he said, "Don't be frustrated. You're helping her."

She was surprised by how much those simple words meant to her. "How is it you always know what I need to hear?"

He smiled. "It's my superpower."

Beside them a bell tinkled and Peanut came out of the diner.

"Dr. Cerrasin. How are you?" Peanut said, looking from one of them to the other. She seemed certain that she'd missed something important.

"Fine. Fine. You?"

"Good," Peanut said.

Max stared at Julia. She felt a little shiver move through her; it was probably from the cold. "Well," she said, trying to follow it up with anything that made sense. But all she could do was stare at him.

"I should go," he finally said.

Later, when Peanut and Julia were in the car, driving home, Peanut said, "That Dr. Cerrasin is certainly a fine-looking man."

"Is he?" Julia said, staring out the window. "I didn't notice."

Peanut burst out laughing.

SIXTEEN

E LLIE WAS IN THE LIVING ROOM, READING THROUGH THE MISSING children reports—*again*—when Julia got home.

She knew how the press conference had gone by the disappointed look on her sister's face. It was one of those moments when Ellie wished she weren't so observant. She saw all the new lines on Julia's face, the pallor of her skin, and the pounds she'd lost. The woman was practically a scarecrow.

Ellie felt a tinge of guilt. It was her fault that Julia was disappearing. If she had done her job better, the whole burden of identification wouldn't have fallen on Julia's thin shoulders. Amazingly, though, Julia had never once blamed her.

Of course, they hardly spent any time together these days. Since the press conferences began, Julia had worked like a machine. Every hour of every day, she kept herself in that bedroom upstairs.

"No one showed," Julia said, tossing her briefcase on the sofa. There was the merest tremble in her voice; it could be exhaustion or defeat. She sat down in Mom's favorite rocker, but didn't relax. She sat stiffly; Ellie was reminded of a sliver of pale ash that had been filed too thin. There wasn't enough left to bend without snapping in half.

A silence followed, broken only by the crackling of the fire in the fireplace.

Ellie glanced up the stairs, thinking of Alice. "What do we do now?"

Julia looked down at her hands, balled up in her lap. Her sudden fragility was sad to see. "I'm making remarkable progress, but . . ."

Ellie waited. The sentence remained a fragment, swallowed by the stillness in the room. "But what?"

Julia finally looked up at her. "Maybe . . . I'm *not* good enough."

Ellie saw how vulnerable her sister was right now and knew she needed to say just the right thing; it was a talent she'd rarely possessed. "Dad used to tell me all the time how brilliant you were, how you were going to light up the world with your brightness. We all saw it. Of *course* you're good enough."

Julia made a funny sound, almost a snort. "Dad? You must be joking. All he ever thought about was himself."

Ellie was so stunned by that observation that it took her a moment to marshal a response. "Dad? He had huge dreams for us. Well, me, he gave up on by the second failed marriage, but you—you were his pride and joy."

"Are we talking about Big Tom Cates, who used up all the air in the room and squashed his wife's personality?"

Ellie laughed at the sheer ridiculousness of that. "Are you kidding? He *adored* Mom. He couldn't breathe without her."

"And she couldn't breathe beside him. She left him once, for two days. Did you know that? When I was fourteen."

Ellie frowned. "That time she went to Grandma Dotty's? She came right back." Ellie made an impatient gesture with her hand. "The point is, they both believed in you, and it would break their hearts to see you questioning yourself. What would you do right now if you were your old self and that girl upstairs needed your help?"

Julia shrugged. "I'd go up and try something radical. See if a little shaking up would help."

"So, do it."

"And if it doesn't work?"

"Then you try something else. It's not like she'll kill herself if you're wrong." Ellie realized a second too late what she'd said. When she looked at Julia, saw her sister's pale face and watery eyes, it all finally fell into place. "That's it, isn't it? This is about what happened in Silverwood. I should have figured it out."

"Some things . . . scar you."

Ellie couldn't imagine how heavy that weight was, how her sister could bear it. But there was still only one thing to say. "You've got to keep trying."

"And what if I'm not helping her *enough*? The doctors at the care facility—"

"Are assholes." She leaned forward, made eye contact. "Remember when you came home for Dad's funeral? You were in the middle of your surgical rotation. I asked you how you could stand it . . . knowing that if you screwed up, people could die."

"Yeah."

"You said, and I quote: 'That's part of being a doctor.' You said that sometimes you just kept going because you had to."

Julia closed her eyes and sighed. "I remember."

"Well, now is the time to keep going. That little girl upstairs needs you to believe in yourself."

Julia glanced up the stairs. It was a long moment before she said, "If I *were* going to do something radical, I'd need your help."

"What can I do?"

Julia's frown was there and gone so quickly Ellie thought she'd imagined it. Then Julia stood. "Find a place in the shadows, park your butt, and sit quietly."

"And?"

"And wait."

. . .

Julia felt a surprising buoyancy in her step as she went up the stairs. Until the conversation downstairs, she hadn't even realized that she'd been quietly giving up. Not on Alice; never that. On herself. More and more often, in the deepest, darkest hours of the night, she'd been questioning her abilities, wondering if she was helping Alice or hurting her, wondering about Amber and the other victims. The more she wondered about it all, the weaker she became, and the weaker she became, the more she wondered. It was a vicious cycle that could destroy her.

She squared her shoulders and tilted her chin up, adopting a winner's stance. Combined with this fledging hope of *Maybe I'm still okay*, it gave her the strength to open her old bedroom door.

Alice lay in her bed, curled up like a little cinnamon roll. As always, she was on top of the covers. No matter how cold the room got, she never pulled the blankets over her.

Julia glanced at the clock. It was nearing six o'clock. Any minute, Alice would wake from her nap. The child was like a Japanese train in the adherence to her routine. She woke at five-thirty every morning, took a nap from four-thirty to six, and fell asleep at 10:45 each night. Julia could have set her watch by it; that schedule had allowed them to conduct the press conferences.

She shut the door behind her. It clicked hard. She took her notebooks out of their storage box on the uppermost shelf of the closet and went to the table, where she read through her morning's notes.

Today Alice picked up our copy of The Secret Garden. *With remarkable dexterity, she flipped through the pages. Whenever she found a drawing, she made a noise and hit the page with her palm, then looked up to find me. She seems to want me watching her all the time.*

She is still following me like a shadow, everywhere I go. She often tucks her hand into my belt or the waistband of my pants and presses against me, moving with a surprising ability to gauge where I'm going.

She still shows no real interest in other people. When anyone comes into the room, she races to the "jungle" of hers and hides. I believe she thinks we can't see her.

She is increasingly possessive of me, especially when we are not alone. This shows me that she has the ability to make attachments and bond. Unable—or unwilling—to vocalize this possessiveness when others are speaking to me, she uses whatever is available to make noise—hitting the wall, snorting, shuffling her feet, howling. I'm hopeful that someday soon her frustration at the limitations of these forms of communication will force her to try verbalizing her feelings.

Julia picked up her pen and added:

In the past week, she's become quite comfortable in her new environment. She spends long spans of time at the window, but only if I will stand with her. I have noticed increasing curiosity about her world. She looks under and around things, pulls out drawers, opens closets. She still won't touch anything metal—and screams when an accidental contact is made—but she's edging toward the door. Twice today she dragged me to the door and then forced me to lie down beside her. She spent almost an hour in total silence, staring at the bar of light from the hallway. The dogs were on the other side, whining and scratching to be let in. Alice is beginning to wonder what's beyond this room. That's a good sign—she's gone from fear to curiosity. Thus, I think it's time to expand her world a bit. But we'll have to be very careful; I believe the forest will exert a powerful pull on her. Somewhere out there, in all that darkness, is the place that was her home.

Julia heard a movement on the bed. The old wooden frame creaked as Alice got up. As always, the girl woke up and went straight into the bathroom. She ran nimbly, almost soundlessly, across the floor and ducked into the smaller room. Moments later the toilet flushed. Then Alice ran for Julia, tucking up alongside her, putting her tiny hand in Julia's pants pocket.

She put her pen down, then gathered up her journals and notebooks and put everything on a high shelf. Alice moved soundlessly beside her, never losing contact.

Julia went to the chest of drawers and withdrew a pair of blue overalls and a pretty pink sweater. "Put these on," she said, handing them to Alice, who complied. It took her several attempts to put on the sweater—she kept confusing the neck and sleeves. When she grew frustrated and started breathing heavily and snorting, Julia dropped to her knees.

"You're getting frustrated. That's okay. Here. This is where your head goes through."

Alice instantly calmed and let Julia help her, but she drew the line at shoes. She simply would not put them on. Finally, Julia conceded defeat.

"Come with me," she said, "but your feet will be cold." She held out her hand.

Alice sidled up to Julia, put her hand in the pocket again.

Very gently, Julia eased Alice away from her. Then she held out her hand again. "Take my hand, Alice." She made her voice as soft as a piece of silk.

Alice's breathing grew heavier. Confusion tugged at her brow and forehead.

"It's okay."

Long minutes passed. They both stood perfectly still. Twice more Alice went for Julia's pocket and was very carefully rebuffed.

Finally, just when Julia was considering the viability of her plan, Alice took a step toward her.

"That's it," Julia said. "Take my hand."

Alice's reaching out was slow, unsteady, and perhaps the most courageous moment Julia had ever witnessed. The girl was clearly terrified—

she was breathing hard, trembling; the look in her eyes was of near terror—and yet she reached out.

Julia held the tiny, shaking hand in hers.

"No hurt," she said, looking down at Alice.

Alice breathed a sigh of relief.

Holding hands, Julia led her toward the door.

Alice halted as they drew close. This was the closest she'd ever really been to the door. She stared at the bright, shiny knob in horror.

"It's okay. No hurt. You're safe." Julia squeezed Alice's hand in reassurance. She didn't move, let Alice accept the moment thus far; when the girl's trembling subsided, Julia reached for the door.

Alice tried to pull back.

Julia held fast to her hand, saying soothingly, "It's okay. You're afraid, but no hurt." She twisted the knob and pushed the door open. The hallway was revealed. Long and straight, illuminated by sconces, there were no shadows in front of them, no hidden spaces. The dogs were there. At Alice's presence, they erupted into barking, prancing movements and started to run toward her.

Alice pressed against Julia. At the dogs' approach, she held out one small, pale hand and made a gurgling sound in the back of her throat.

The dogs stopped in their tracks and dropped to their haunches, waiting.

Alice looked up at Julia.

Julia couldn't make sense of it. "Okay, Alice," she said, not even sure what she was agreeing to, but she saw the question in the child's eye.

Very slowly, Alice let go of Julia's hand and moved toward the dogs. They remained perfectly still. When Alice reached them, it was as if a switch had been turned. The dogs pounced to life, licking Alice and pawing her.

Alice threw herself at the dogs, giggling hard when they nuzzled her throat.

Julia soaked in the new sight of Alice's smile.

Long minutes passed. Finally, Alice drew back from the dogs and returned to Julia's side. She tucked her hand in Julia's waistband. "Come on, Alice," Julia said.

Alice let herself be pulled slowly into the hallway. Once there, she got nervous. She looked longingly back at the plants in the bedroom. When she tried to take a step backward, Julia firmly said, "This way."

She led Alice to the top of the stairs. Here, they paused again. The dogs followed them, moving quietly.

Julia wanted to scoop Alice into her arms and carry her down each step, but she didn't dare. The girl might flail so mightily to be free that Julia would lose her hold.

Instead, still holding the little hand, Julia took one step down.

Alice gazed at her for a long time, obviously gauging this turn of events. Finally, she followed. They made their way down to the living room one step at a time. By the time they reached the sofa, it was full-on night.

She opened the porch door, revealing the darkness outside. The air smelled of coming winter, of dying leaves and rain-soaked grass and the last few roses on the bushes along the side of the house. The dogs made a beeline for the yard and started playing.

Alice made a quiet, gasping sound and took a step on her own, then another, until they were on the porch. The old cedar floorboards creaked in welcome. Mom's rocker was touched by the breeze and rocked to and fro.

Alice was easily led now, down the steps and around the corner and into the grassy yard. The sound of the river was loud; leaves whispered among themselves and floated downward. Thousands of them, all at once, though the breeze was as soft as a baby's breath.

Alice let go of Julia's hand and grabbed onto her pant leg instead; then she dropped to her knees. She sat utterly still, her head bowed.

The sound was so quiet at first, so thready, that Julia mistook it for a growing wind.

Alice lifted her face to the night sky and let out a howl that undulated on the air. It was a noise so sad and lonely that you wanted to cry, or howl along with her. It made you think of all that you'd ever loved, all that you'd lost, and all the love you'd never known.

"Go ahead, Alice," Julia said, hearing the throatiness of her voice. It was unprofessional to be so moved, but there was no way to help it. "Let it all out. This is crying for you, isn't it?"

When the howling faded, Alice was quiet again. She sat there, kneeling in the grass; she was so motionless it was as if she'd melted onto the landscape. Then, all at once, she moved. She bent forward and picked up a tiny yellow dandelion from the darkness in front of her. Julia hadn't even been able to see the flower. In a single motion she separated the root from the stem and ate the root.

"This is the world you know, isn't it?" Julia tried to get Alice to let go of her pants so the child could wander freely, but Alice wouldn't let go.

"I won't leave you, but you don't know that, do you? Someone has already left you out in these woods, haven't they?"

In the silence that followed the question, a crow cawed, then an owl hooted. Within seconds the forest at the edge of their property was alive with birdsong. The unseen branches creaked and sighed; the pine needles rustled.

Alice imitated each of the calls; each of her versions flawless. The birds answered her.

In the darkness, it took Julia's eyes a moment to notice what was happening.

The yard was full of birds; they formed a wide circle around them.

"My God . . ." It was Ellie's voice, from somewhere in the shadows.

At the sound, the birds flew away, their wings sounding breathy and fast.

Somewhere, far away, a wolf howled.

Alice answered the call.

A shiver crept down Julia's spine; suddenly she was icy cold. "Don't move," she said to Ellie when she heard a rustling in the leaves.

"But—"

"And don't talk."

Alice tugged on Julia's hand. It was the first time the girl had ever tried to lead. Julia couldn't help smiling. "That's good, little one. I'll follow."

A cloud moved away from the moon, floated across the sky. In its wake, moonlight painted the grass, lit the river. Everything looked silvery and magical.

Alice pointed at the rosebushes. They were leggy and winter bare, sorely in need of cutting back. She pulled free and approached the roses with a confidence Julia had never seen before. She straightened, lifted her chin. For once she didn't hunch over and hold an arm across her stomach. Moonlight glanced off her hair; it looked black as a crow's wing, tinged with blue.

The night felt steeped in magic, shimmering with it. Stars sparkled in the sky. Julia would have sworn she could hear the ocean. She backed away slowly, letting Alice explore this perimeter of her own world. She felt her sister's approach.

Ellie stopped beside her. "How do you know she won't run away?"

"I don't. I'm betting on her attachment to me, though. There are bad memories out there for her."

"A mammoth understatement."

Julia watched Alice draw nearer to the rosebush, wondering what the girl would do if a thorn bit her flesh. Would she turn to her for help or comfort? Had she learned at all that she wasn't alone any longer, or would she feel betrayed by this strange place and run back to the world she knew?

"Be careful, Alice," Julia said. "There are thorns."

The girl reached for a single, pink bud, plucked it from the bush.

Alice petted the rose with a gentleness that surprised Julia, then she turned away. Moving slowly, she walked toward the river. When she reached a little lip of land, she paused.

Julia and Ellie followed her, both ready to save her if she jumped. But Alice kept moving down the bank, to the place where the grass was tamped down and dead. There, she dropped to her knees and bowed her head, howling softly.

"She's calling her wolf," Julia said quietly. "Telling him her story and that she misses him."

They waited for an answer, breath held, but all they heard were the trees whispering overhead and the river's throaty laughter.

"He's at the game farm with other wolves," Ellie finally said. "Too far away to hear her."

Julia left Ellie standing there and moved toward Alice. Coming up behind the girl, Julia touched her shoulder.

Alice turned around and peered up at Julia through eyes so dark and unfathomable they seemed to reflect the endless night sky.

Julia knelt in the damp grass. "Talk to me, Alice. What are you feeling right now? You don't need to be afraid. You're safe here."

THE NIGHT IS FULL OF NOISES. SOMETIMES IT IS SO LOUD THAT GIRL HAS trouble hearing the quiet that lies beneath. It has always been like that for her. She has to work hard at not hearing the animals, the insects, the wind, and the leaves. She needs to close her eyes and listen to her own heartbeat until that's all there is. Even in the dark she sees too much—a spider crawling along the ground at her feet, a pair of crows watching her from the purple tree, a moth flying along the river. In the distance she hears the rustling movement of a hunting cat.

If only the two Hers would stop talking so loudly; then Girl could breathe again. She feels a tightness in her chest and it scares her. She should feel safe out here on the edge of her world. She could run away now if she wanted to. If she was careful and followed the river, she could find her cave again.

All those times she stood at the lying box, with her arm held out in the green-scented air, she imagined a chance like this. The moment when Sun Hair would look away and Girl would run.

But now she doesn't want to leave.

She looks down at her feet. They are planted as firmly as any tree root. This is where she wants to be. With Sun Hair.

"Talktomealis."

Sun Hair is there, in front of her, reaching a hand out to Girl. In the light of this round-faced moon, everything about Sun Hair is white.

Girl is afraid and confused. What if Sun Hair doesn't want Girl to stay? Maybe she is being let go now?

She doesn't want to go back to the cold, hungry darkness of her cave. Maybe Him is there. . . .

Sun Hair bends down. "Canyoutalktomealis?"

The other one, the big, jangling Night-Haired Her says something from the shadows. There is no color around that one, no scent. Girl cannot sense what that one feels or thinks, but she knows it is bad.

Something is wrong.

"Leavethis. Toodamnspooky," Night Hair says. She shivers as if it is cold, which confuses Girl even more. It is moons and moons away from cold.

"Goaheadandleave. Illstay." Sun Hair is looking at Girl and smiling. "Ineedyoutotalkalis. Isanyofthismakingsense?"

Girl hears something. It sneaks up on her like a hunting wolf. She frowns, trying to understand.

Need.

Talk.

Did Sun Hair *want* Girl to make the sounds that meant things?

No.

It couldn't be. That is the Bad Thing.

Sun Hair's smile slowly disappears. The color of her eyes seem to change from green to the palest gray. It is the color of lostness, of the water that leaks from your eyes. At last Sun Hair makes a sad, lonely sound and straightens.

"MaybeIwasrightElandImnottheonetohelpthisgirl."

It seems now that Sun Hair is miles away from Girl and getting farther. Sooner they will be so far apart that Girl won't be able to find her.

"Ineedyoutotalklittleone." Sun Hair takes a breath. "Please."

Please.

From somewhere, Girl remembers this sound. It is special, like the first bud in spring.

Sun Hair *wants* Girl to make the forbidden noises.

Girl gets slowly to her feet. She feels light-headed with fear.

Sun Hair is walking away now.

Leaving.

Girl's fear pushes her forward. She follows, grabs Sun Hair's hand and holds so tightly it hurts.

Sun Hair turns to her, kneels. "Itsokayalis. Itsokay. Imnotleavingyou."

Leaving. Out of the jumble of sounds, Girl hears this. It is as clear as the sound of a river rising.

Girl looks at Sun Hair. Holding tightly to her hand, she wants to look away or close her eyes so that if Sun Hair is going to hit her, she will not have to see it coming, but she forces her eyes to stay open. It will take all her heart, everything she has inside of her to think and remember and make the forbidden noise.

"Whatisit? Areyouokay?" Sun Hair's voice is so soft it makes Girl's heart ache.

She looks up into those pretty green eyes. Girl wants to be good. She licks her lips, then says quietly, "Stay."

Sun Hair makes a sound like a stone falling in deep water. "Didyou saystay?"

Girl gives her the special rose. "Peas."

Sun Hair's eyes start leaking again, but this time her mouth is curled up in a way that makes Girl feel warm inside. She puts her arms around Girl and pulls Girl toward her.

It is a feeling Girl has never known before, this holding of the wholeness of her. She closes her eyes and lets her face burrow into the softness of Sun Hair's neck, which smells of the flowers that grow when the sun comes sneaking up through nighttime.

"Stay," she whispers again, smiling now.

SEVENTEEN

ELLIE SAT IN HER DAD'S OLD CHAIR ON THE PORCH, WRAPPED UP in a heavy woolen blanket. Beside her, a cup of tea sent thin shoots of steam into the air.

Although it had been almost three hours since the Alice-in-the-woods show, she could still hear the sad, wavery notes of the girl's howling, like a mournful music of the night.

So much had happened tonight; the hell of it was, had anything changed? Alice *could* speak. That much they knew now, and it might be the open door they needed through which they could find her identity.

But for some reason, Ellie didn't believe it. She didn't think Alice belonged anywhere or to anyone. Somehow, she'd been set adrift in her life like one of those elder Eskimo women who crawl out onto the ice floes, where they remain, cold and alone and infinitely unwanted, until they simply gave up their lives.

Ellie wrapped her hands around the cup of tea. Steam pelted her face, brought with it the scent of oranges.

Behind her the porch door squeaked open.

Julia took a seat in Mom's rocker.

"Is she asleep?" Ellie asked.

"Like a baby."

Ellie tried to corral her thoughts; they were like mustangs on the open range, running wild at her approach. "Did she say anything else?" That was the starting place. Hopefully, the two words had been only the beginning.

"No. And it might be a while. Tonight was a big event, to be sure, but did you hear the way she said please? *Peas*. Like a two-year-old. And she didn't put the two words together as a sentence. To her, I believe the words were separate entities." Julia was smiling brightly. Ellie couldn't remember the last time she'd seen that.

"What does all that mean?"

It took Julia a moment to answer. "It's all very complicated and scientific, and I need a lot more information to really form a solid opinion, but in a nutshell, Alice is either electively mute—which means that she is choosing not to speak because of the traumas she's experienced—or she is developmentally delayed in her acquisition of speech. I believe it is the latter. I say this for a couple of reasons. First, she seems to understand specific, simple words, but not sentences comprised of those words. Secondly, tonight she used the two words independently, which reveals the level of syntax learning of an average two-year-old. Think of how children learn language. First it's simple word identification. Mama. Dada. Ball. Dog. Gradually, they'll string two words together to communicate a more complex idea, then three. In time, they learn to form negative sentences—'No play. No nap'—and begin to use pronouns. As they become more proficient, they will form their sentences into questions. Most scientists believe that a child can learn these complex, unvoiced rules and acquire language at any age up to puberty. After that, for some reason, it becomes almost impossible. It's why kids learn foreign languages so much easier than adults do."

Ellie held up her hand. "Slow down, Einstein. Are you saying that Alice *can* speak but hasn't been taught much, so she's got the verbal skills of a toddler?"

"That's my guess. I think she was raised in a verbal, perhaps even a caring environment, for the first eighteen months to two years of her life. It was then that she began to learn a few words and bonded physically with someone. After that . . . something very bad happened and she stopped developing her language skills."

Something very bad.

The words left a heaviness behind, a residue. "A toddler doesn't know her name. Not her last name, anyway."

"I know."

Ellie leaned back in her dad's chair and sighed heavily. "It seems like no one is looking for this kid, Jules. The NCIC has come up completely blank on any known missing or kidnapped children who match her description. The DNA had done nothing for us, and the press isn't interested anymore. And now you're telling me that even if you get her to start talking up a blue steak, she may have no idea what her name is. Or who her parents are, or what city she lives in."

"Jeez, El. I was feeling pretty good about tonight. We got her outside *and* talking."

"I'm sorry. You've done a hell of a job with her, Jules. Really. But I have responsibilities, too. DSHS thinks we should start permanent foster care proceedings."

"Don't do it, El. Please. I have a chance with her. It's not only about finding her family anymore. It's about saving her, bringing her back to the world. You reminded me of all that, of how much *good* I can do for Alice."

"You make it sound like you'll stay as long as you need to."

"Why wouldn't I? There's nothing left for me in L.A. When you don't have a husband, or kids, or a job, it's easy to walk away from your life. Just lock up your condo and go." She finally lifted her gaze. "The truth is, *I* need Alice right now. I'll do whatever I have to do to help her. Can that be enough for now? Can we just let the temporary custody agreement stand?"

"Of course." Ellie didn't know how she felt about the idea of her sister living here all through the winter. It was something she'd have to worry over later, in the dark, while she tried to fall asleep. But she knew she appreciated someone else shouldering the burden of little Alice's damaged soul. "What about . . . all that weirdness? The birds?"

Julia stared over the rim of her teacup at the moonlit river beyond. "I don't know. She's lived in a world that's different than ours, with different fundamental rules. When I was doing research on the documented cases of wild children, it was clear that in most previous centuries, these children were romanticized, seen as examples of true nature. Uncorrupted and uncivilized, they came to represent a purity of man that couldn't exist in a society that set down rules of behavior."

"And all that means what?"

"Maybe she's more a part of nature than of man, more connected to the natural world—sights, smells, plants, animals—than to us."

Ellie didn't even know what to make of that. "It looked more like magic than science to me."

"That's another explanation."

"So what now? How do we get her to start talking?"

Julia looked at her. "She needs to learn that she's safe here. I think we need to show her what a family is. Maybe it'll ring some bells with her, make her remember. And we teach her the way you'd teach any two-year-old: one word at a time."

LATER THAT NIGHT, AFTER ELLIE WENT TO BED, JULIA LAY IN HER BED, staring at the ceiling. She was too wound up to sleep. Her blood seemed to be tingling just beneath her skin.

Stay.

That moment kept repeating itself, over and over. Each time she remembered it, she felt a shiver of awe at what it meant.

Until tonight, that very moment when Alice had spoken her first word, Julia hadn't even realized how lost she'd become, how far she'd fallen. Her grasp on confidence had been fragile and slippery. But now she was *back*. She was her old self.

And she'd never give up again. First thing tomorrow morning she would call the team of doctors and scientists who wanted to study Alice and tell them to back off. Then she'd convince DSHS that they had nothing to worry about with the girl's current placement.

Maybe that was the lesson she'd needed to learn from the tragedy with Amber, the missing sign she'd been so desperate to find.

In her business, there would be failures. Heartbreaking losses. But to be the best, she had to stay strong in her belief that she made a difference.

She was strong again. No phone calls from scientists or so-called colleagues or questions from the media would ruin her again. No one would take Alice from her.

She needed to talk to someone tonight; to share her triumph, and there was only one person who would understand.

You're crazy, Julia.

She threw the covers back and got out of bed. Dressing in a pair of well-worn black sweats and a blue tee shirt, she kissed Alice's soft cheek and then left the room.

Outside Ellie's bedroom, Julia paused. There was no light from beneath the door, no sounds from within.

She didn't want to wake her sister. Besides, Ellie didn't truly appreciate the importance of tonight's events.

Without letting herself think, she moved. She went out to the car and drove toward the old highway. There were no other cars on the road this time of night; the world was dark and still. Stars splattered the sky like a Jackson Pollock painting.

Just before the entrance to the national park, she turned onto a rutted gravel road. At the final bend, she flicked off her headlights. Under cover of darkness, she pulled into his yard.

In truth, she didn't know why she was here, parked in front of his house like a teenage girl on a lonely Saturday night.

That wasn't true. She didn't want to admit why she was here, perhaps, but she knew.

No matter how often she'd told herself she was being stupid—the fly going straight into the web—she couldn't seem to stop herself.

She got out of the Suburban and walked across the dark yard, hearing the gentle lapping of the lake along the shore.

MAX HEARD THE CAR DRIVE UP AND HOPED LIKE HELL IT WASN'T A medical emergency. This was his only night off call this week and he had already finished his second scotch.

He heard footsteps on the porch. Then a knock on his front door.

"I'm out here," he called out. "On the deck."

There was a pause, a long time of quiet. He was about to call out again when he heard footsteps.

It was Julia. At the sight of him in the hot tub, she stopped dead.

She stood beneath the orangey bulb that illuminated the covered deck. He hadn't seen her since the diner, and yet—to be honest—he'd thought about her often. He couldn't help noticing how pale she looked, how thin and drawn. Her stunning bone structure now looked edgy and sharp; her chin was pointier than before.

But it was her eyes that caught him, held him as firmly as a child's grip on a favorite toy.

"A hot tub, Doctor? How cliché."

"I went climbing today. My back is killing me. Get in."

"I don't have a suit."

"Here. I'll turn off the light." He pressed the button and the tub went dark. "There's wine in the fridge. Glasses are above the sink."

She stood there a long time. So long, in fact, he thought she was going to decline. Finally, she turned and left. He heard the front door open and close. A few moments later she returned, holding a wineglass and wearing a towel.

"Close your eyes," she said.

"I can see your bra straps, Julia."

"Are you going to close your eyes?"

"What are we, eighth graders? Are you planning on spin-the-bottle later? I doubt—"

She walked away.

"Okay, okay," he said, laughing. "My eyes are closed."

He heard her return, heard the muffled thump of the towel landing in a chair and the quiet splashing of her getting in the hot tub. Water rippled against his chest; for a split second he thought it was her touch.

He opened his eyes.

She sat pressed to her side of the tub, her arms at her sides. The white lacy bra she wore had gone transparent; he saw the creamy swell of her breasts above the fabric and the water, and the dark spots of her barely covered nipples.

"You're staring," she said, sipping her wine.

"You're beautiful." He was surprised by the thready tone of his voice, surprised by how much he suddenly wanted her.

"I struggle to calculate how many times you've said that to women foolish enough to get into this tub."

"Are you foolish?"

She looked at him. "Absolutely. But I'm not stupid. Stupid would be naked."

"Actually, you're the first woman who has ever been in this hot tub."

"Clothed, you mean."

He laughed. "Those see-through scraps are hardly clothed. But no. I mean the first woman—clothed or naked—to be here."

She frowned. "Really?"

"Really."

She turned slightly, looked out at the lake. In the charcoal-hued distance, two white trumpeter swans floated lazily on the surface of the water. Moonlight seemed to make their feathers glow.

The silence turned awkward. Julia must have noticed, too, because she finally turned to him and said, "Tell me something real, Max. I don't know anything about you."

"What do you want to know?"

"Why are you in Rain Valley?"

He gave her the answer he gave everyone. "One too many gang shootings in L.A."

"Why do I think that's only part of the story?"

"I keep forgetting you're a shrink."

"And a good one." She smiled. "Jumping to conclusions notwith-standing. So, tell me."

He shrugged. "I'd been having some personal issues, so I decided to make some changes. I quit my job and moved up here. I love the mountains."

"Personal issues?"

Of course she picked up on what mattered. "That's too real," he said quietly.

"Sometimes you have to get away."

He nodded. "It was easy to leave Los Angeles. My family is crazy enough to be carnival workers, every one. My parents—Ted and Geor-gia, before you ask—are currently on leave from their jobs teaching at Berkeley. They're traveling through Central America in a motor home called Dixie. Last I heard they were looking for some bug that's been extinct for eons."

Julia smiled. "What do they teach?"

"Biology and Organic Chemistry, respectively. My sister, Ann, is in Thailand. Tsunami relief. My brother, Ken, works for a big-time think tank in the Netherlands. No one has seen him in almost a decade. Every year I get a Christmas card that says: 'My best wishes to you and yours, Dr. Kenneth Cerrasin.'"

Julia laughed so hard she snorted. At the sound, she laughed harder. Max found himself laughing along with her.

"And I thought my family was strange."

"Pikers," he said, grinning.

"Were they there for you when your . . . trouble happened?"

Max felt his smile fade. "You sure know how to throw a punch, don't you?"

"Hazard of the trade. It's just . . . I know how alone I felt during the mess in L.A."

"We're not that kind of family."

"So you were alone, too."

He put down his drink. "Why are *you* here, Julia?"

"In Rain Valley? You know why."

"Here," he said, letting his voice soften.

"Alice spoke tonight. She said *stay*."

"I knew you'd do it."

A smile overtook her face; it came all at once, as if she hadn't expected it. The porch light bathed her skin, tangled in her hair, made her lashes look spidery and fragile against her cheeks. She moved slightly. Water rippled against his chest. "The thing is . . . I've been waiting every day for weeks for this to happen. . . ."

"And?"

"And when it happened, all I could think was that I wanted to tell you."

He couldn't have stopped himself if he'd tried—and he didn't try. He closed the tiny distance between them and kissed her. It was the kind of kiss he'd forgotten about. Whispering her name, he moved his right hand down her slick, naked back and reached around for her breast. He'd barely felt the full swell of it when she eased away from him.

"I'm sorry," she said, looking as pale and shaken as he felt. "I need to go."

"There's something between us," he said. The words were out of his mouth before he knew what he was going to say.

"Yes," she said. "That's why I'm leaving."

They stared at each other. He had the strange sensation that he was losing something of value.

Finally, she climbed out of the hot tub, went into the house, and retrieved her clothes. Without even bothering to say good-bye, she left him.

He sat there a long time, alone, staring out at nothing.

JULIA DREAMT OF MAX ALL NIGHT. SHE WAS SO CAUGHT IN THE WEB that when she woke, it took her a second to realize that someone was knocking on the bedroom door.

It sounded like an advancing army.

She sat up in bed. There was no army at the door.

It was, instead, one small, determined girl, standing by the closed door.

Julia smiled. *This* was what mattered, not some near sexual encounter. "I'd say someone wants to go outside again." She swung her legs out of bed and stood up.

After finishing her bathroom routine, she came back out into the bedroom, dressed now in a pair of faded jeans and an old gray sweatshirt.

Alice stamped her foot and punched the door, grunting for emphasis.

Julia walked casually toward their worktable, where all the books and blocks and dolls were spread out. There, she sat down and put her feet on the table. "If a girl wanted to go outside, she should use her words."

Alice frowned and hit the door again.

"It won't work, Alice. You see, now I know you can talk." She got up and went to the window, pointing at the yard that was just beginning to turn pink with the dawn. "Outside." She said it over and over again, then went to Alice and took the girl's hand, leading her to the bathroom.

She pointed at herself in the mirror. "Ju-li-a," she said. "Can you say that? Ju-li-a."

"Her," Alice whispered.

Julia's heart did a little flip at the voice, whisper-soft and hesitant as it was. "Ju-li-a," she said again, pressing a hand to her own chest. "Ju-lia."

She saw when Alice understood. The child made a little sound of discovery; her mouth formed an O. "Jew-lee."

Julia grinned. This was how people must feel when they scaled Everest without oxygen. Light-headed and giddy with triumph. "Yes. Yes. Julia." Now she pointed at Alice's reflection in the mirror. "The *ya* sound is hard to make, isn't it? Now, who are you?" She touched Alice's chest, just as she'd touched her own.

Alice's frown deepened. "Girl?"

"Yes! Yes! You're a girl." She touched Alice's chest again. "Who are you? Julia. Me. And you?"

"Girl," she said again, her frown turning into a scowl.

"Do you know your name, little one?"

This time there was no answer at all. Alice waited a long moment, still frowning, then thumped the door with her fist again.

Julia couldn't help laughing at that. "You might not have much of a vocabulary, kiddo, but you know what you want and you learn fast. Okay. Let's go outside."

WHAT HAD BEGUN AS A CRISP, CLEAR MORNING WAS SLOWLY CHANGING into an ominous afternoon. Heavy gray clouds bumped into one another and formed a mass that looked like steel wool. The pale sun that had lured Max out to the mountains on this cold autumn day had all but vanished. Every now and again a beam of light would poke through the clouds, but in the last hour even those moments of gold had become infrequent.

Soon, it would rain.

He knew he should hurry, but climbing down a rock face took time. That was one of the things he loved about climbing: you couldn't control it.

He came to a drop-off. Below him, a lip of stone jutted out from the cliff; it was about the size of a kid's sled.

Sweating hard, he continued climbing slowly down and to the left, choosing his hand- and footholds with exquisite care. He was nearing the end of his climb. It was a dangerous time for climbers, the end of the day. It was all too easy to let your thoughts drift to the next step, to the packing of the supplies and the hike out, to—

Julia.

He shook his head to clear it. Sweat blurred his vision. For a moment the granite looked like a solid sheet. He wiped his eyes, blinked, until the gradations and ledges and mosses reappeared.

A raindrop hit his forehead so hard he flinched. Within moments the skies opened up and let loose. Thunder roared across the mountains. Rain hammered him.

He got to the ledge and paused, looking down. He was no more than forty feet from the ground now. He didn't need to rappel down this last distance. It would take time to set his equipment, to get ready, and it was a damned storm out here now. Wind rattled the trees and clawed his face.

He inched downward, dangled over the ledge.

He knew instantly that it was a mistake. The stone creaked and shifted, began to rotate. Tiny stones and wet dust rained down, hitting him in the face, blinding him.

He was going to fall.

Instinctively, he pushed back, trying to clear the jutting ledges and boulders below him.

And then he was connected to nothing; in the air. Falling fast. A rock smashed his cheekbone, another careened into his thigh. The boulder that had been his ledge fell alongside him. They hit the ground at the same time. It felt as if someone had just hit him in the chest with a shovel.

He lay there, dazed, feeling the rain pummel his face, slide in rivulets down his throat.

Finally, he crawled to his feet in the muddy ground and took stock. No broken bones, no extreme lacerations.

Lucky.

The thing was, he didn't feel lucky. As he stood there, beside the boulder that could have killed him, looking up at the now slick rock face of the cliff, he realized something else.

He didn't feel acutely alive, didn't want to laugh out loud at his triumph.

He felt . . . stupid.

He picked up his gear, repacked his backpack, and headed down the long, winding trail to where he'd parked his car.

All the way there—and all the way home—he tried to keep his

mind blank. Failing that, he tried to relive his near miss and enjoy it. Neither attempt was successful.

All he could think about was Julia, how she'd looked in the hot tub, how she'd tasted, how she'd sounded when she said *All or nothing*.

And how those words had made him feel.

No wonder he couldn't find that old adrenaline surge from mountain climbing today.

The real danger lay in another direction.

All or nothing.

EIGHTEEN

In the two weeks since I showed Alice a glimpse of the world outside, she has become a different child. Everything fascinates her. She is constantly grabbing my hand and pulling me somewhere so she can point to an object and say "What?" Each word I hand her, she holds on to tightly, remembering it with an ease and a will that surprises me. I can only assume that her quest for communication is so assertive because she was thwarted before. Now she seems desperate to become a part of this new world she's entered.

She is slowly beginning to explore her emotions, as well. Previously, when she was nonverbal, most of her anger was directed at herself. Now, occasionally, she is able to express her anger appropriately. Yesterday, when I told her it was time for bed, she hit me. Social acceptability will come later. For now, I am pleased to see her get mad.

She is also developing a sense of possession, which is a step on the road to a sense of self. She hoards everything red and has a special place for "her" books.

She still has not provided a name for herself; nor has she ac-
cepted "Alice." This is a task that requires more work. A name is
integral to developing a sense of self.

I am not making much progress on her past life. Obviously,
until she can communicate more fully, there can be little discovery
of her memories, but I am patient. For now, I am her teacher. It is
a surprisingly rewarding endeavor.

Julia scratched out the last two sentences as too personal, then put her pen down.

Alice was at the table, "reading" a picture-book version of *The Velveteen Rabbit*. She hadn't moved in almost an hour. She appeared spellbound.

Julia put her notebook away and went to the table. She sat down beside Alice, who immediately took hold of her hand, squeezing it hard. With her free hand she pointed to the book and grunted.

"Use your words, Alice."

"Read."

"Read what?"

"Boo."

"Who wants me to read?"

Alice frowned heavily. "Girl?"

"Alice," Julia said gently. She had spent the better part of two weeks trying to get Alice to reveal her real name. With each passing day, however, and each instance of the girl's innate intelligence being shown, Julia was increasingly certain that whoever this girl really was, she didn't remember—or had never known—her real name. Whenever Julia thought about that, it devastated her. It had to mean that, at least in the formative years, after about eighteen months to two years, no one had called this child by name.

"Alice." She said it gently. "Does Alice want Julia to read the book?"

Alice thumped the book with her palm, nodding and smiling. "Read. Girl."

"I'll tell you what. If you play with the blocks for a few minutes, I'll read to you. Okay?"

Alice made a disappointed face.

"I know." Smiling, Julia bent down and retrieved her box of blocks. She set them out on the table, arranging them carefully. They were big plastic blocks with numbers on one side and letters on the other. Often she used them to teach Alice the alphabet, but today they were going to count. "Take the block that has the number one on it. One."

Alice immediately grabbed the single red block and pulled it toward her.

"Good girl. Now the number four."

They kept at the counting for almost an hour. Alice's progress was nothing short of amazing. In less than two weeks she'd memorized all the numbers up to fifteen. Rarely did she make a mistake.

But by three o'clock she was getting cranky and tired. It was nearing nap time. She smacked the book again. "Read."

"Okay, okay." Julia leaned over and pulled Alice into her lap. She held her tightly, smoothing the silky black hair from her face. Finally, Alice popped her thumb in her mouth and waited.

Julia started to read. She had only gotten through the first paragraph when Alice tensed and let out a low growl.

A moment later there was a knock at the door.

Alice growled again, then stopped herself, as if remembering that this was a word world. "Scared," she whispered.

"I know, honey."

Ellie opened the door and stepped into the room.

Alice made a strangled sound, slid out of Julia's lap, and ran over to her hiding place in the potted plants.

Ellie sighed. "Is she *ever* going to stop being afraid of me?"

Julia smiled. "Give her time."

Ellie glanced around the room. "How's she doing?"

"She's like any developing toddler. She's learning words and reading expression and body language to pull it all together."

"How do I tell her I'm sorry? Make her understand I trapped her for her own good?"

"She can't understand that complex an idea yet."

"Thirty-nine years old and I can't make one little girl like me. No wonder I'm sterile. God saw my parenting potential."

"You're not sterile."

"If I'm not, it's over anyway. My eggs are drying up faster than fish on a barbecue."

Julia went to her sister and said softly, "That's about the fifth time you've told me you want to have kids."

"It comes out at the weirdest times."

"Dreams are like that. You can't keep 'em submerged. I'll tell you what, Ellie. Why don't you try to connect with Alice? I'll teach you how."

Ellie sighed miserably. "Yeah, right. I can't even get my dogs to heel."

"Alice will give you a chance. Just spend time with her."

"She can't stand to be in the same room with me."

"Try harder. Tonight, you'll read her a story after dinner. I'll go downstairs, leave you two alone."

Ellie seemed to think about that. "She'll stay in the fake forest."

"Then try again tomorrow night. Sooner or later, she'll give you a chance."

"You really think so?"

"I know so."

Ellie seemed to think about it. "Okay. I'll give it a try." She looked at Julia. "Thanks."

Julia nodded.

Ellie started to leave. At the door, she paused and turned around. "I almost forgot why I came in here. Thursday is Thanksgiving. Can you cook?"

"Salads. You?"

"Only meals that involve melted cheese. Preferably Velveeta."

"We're a pathetic pair."

"We are."

Julia said, "We could try Mom's old recipes. I'll order a turkey today and go shopping. How hard can it be?"

"It'll be like the old days with Mom and Dad. We can invite people over."

"Cal's family?" Julia said.

"Of course. Is there anyone else you'd like to ask?"

"What about Max? He doesn't have any family here."

Ellie's gaze was a laser beam. "No," she said slowly. "He doesn't."

"I'll . . . call him, then."

"You're playing with fire, little sister, and you burn easily."

"It's just a dinner invitation."

"Yeah, right."

"HAVE YOU *SEEN* THE AMOUNT OF BUTTER THAT GOES IN MOM'S DRESS-ing? This can't be right."

Ellie didn't bother answering her sister. She was facing issues of her own. Somewhere in this turkey (what the hell had Julia been thinking to buy a twenty-pound bird? They'd be eating turkey until Lent) was a bag of body parts she didn't want to eat, but apparently also didn't want to cook. "You think the giblet bag dissolves during cooking? If I get my arm any farther up this bird's ass, I'm gonna see my own fingers."

Julia looked down at her own task, frowning. "Do you have an at-home defibrillator?"

Ellie laughed at that. "Aha!" she said a minute later, finding the giblet bag and pulling it out. She then basted the bird with butter (to Julia's horror) and placed it on Grandma Dotty's roasting pan. "Are you going to put some of the dressing in the bird?"

"I guess so."

When the bird was stuffed and in the oven, Ellie looked around the kitchen. "What's next?"

Julia pushed the hair out of her eyes and sighed. It was only nine o'clock in the morning and already she looked as wiped out as Ellie felt. "I guess we could start on Aunt Vivian's green bean recipe."

"I always hated that. Green beans and mushroom soup? Why not just have a salad—we have a bagged one in the fridge."

"You're a genius."

"I've been telling you that for years."

"I'll get started on the potatoes." Julia headed for the porch. When she opened the door, cold air swept through, mingling with the hot air from the roaring fireplace to create a perfect mixture of warmth and crispness. On the top step, she sat down. A bag of potatoes was on the floor at her feet, along with a peeler.

Ellie poured two mimosas and followed her sister out to the porch. "Here. I think we'll need alcohol. Last year a lady in Portland served wild mushrooms at a dinner party and killed all her guests."

"Don't worry. I'm a doctor."

Laughing, Ellie handed her a glass and sat down.

Together, they stared out at the backyard.

Alice was dressed in a pretty eyelet dress and pink tights, sitting on a wool blanket. There were birds all around her—mostly crows and robins—fighting among themselves to eat from her hand. Beside her, a bag of past-their-prime potato chips provided her with endless crumbs.

"Why don't you take her a glass of juice or something? She's really calm when she's with her birds. It might be a good time to start bonding."

"She looks like a Hitchcock movie. What if the birds peck my eyes out?"

Julia laughed. "They'll fly away when you get there."

"But—"

Julia touched Ellie's arm. "She's just a little girl who has been through hell. Don't saddle her with anything else."

"She'll run away from me."

"Then you'll try again." Julia reached into her apron pocket and pulled out a red plastic measuring cup. "Give her this."

"She still gaga over the color red?"

"Yep."

"Why do you think that is?"

"No idea yet." Julia stood up. "I'll go set the table. You'll be fine."

"Okay." Ellie felt Julia's eyes on her back as she walked down the steps across the grass.

Behind her the screen door screeched open and banged shut. At the noise, the birds cawed and flew off. There were so many of them that for a second they were a dark blight against the gray sky.

Ellie stepped on a twig, snapped it.

Alice jumped up and spun around. She remained crouched, looking cornered, although the whole yard lay open behind her. Fear rounded the girl's eyes, making Ellie profoundly uncomfortable.

She wasn't used to fighting for affection. All her life, people had liked her.

"Hey," Ellie said, standing motionlessly. "No net. No shot." She held her hands out, palms up to prove it. The red measuring cup was bright in her open hand.

Alice saw it and frowned. After a minute or so she pointed and grunted.

Ellie felt the magical pull of possibility unwind between them. This was the first time that Alice hadn't run from her. "Use your words, Alice." It was what Julia always said.

As the silence went on, Ellie tried another tack. She started to sing, quietly at first, but as Alice's frown faded and an expression of interest began to take its place, Ellie turned up the volume. Just a bit. She sang one kid-friendly song after another (the kid could stay motionless *forever*). When she got to "Twinkle, Twinkle, Little Star," Alice's whole demeanor changed. It was as if she'd been hypnotized or something. A curve that was almost a smile touched her lips.

"Star," Alice whispered at exactly the right time in the song.

Ellie bit back a grin by sheer force of will. When the song was over, she knelt down and handed Alice the measuring cup.

Alice stroked it, touched it to her cheek, then looked expectantly at Ellie.

Now what?

"Star."

"You want me to keep singing?"

"Star. Peas."

Ellie did as she was asked. She was on her third go-round when Alice cautiously moved toward her.

Ellie felt as if she'd just bowled a strike in the tenth frame. She wanted to whoop out and high-five someone. Instead she kept singing.

At some point Julia came out and joined them. The three of them sat in the grass, beneath a graying November sky, while the Thanksgiving turkey browned inside the house, and sang the songs of their youth.

MAX KNEW HE SHOULD HAVE LEFT THE HOUSE A HALF HOUR AGO. Instead he'd poured himself a beer and turned on the television.

He was afraid to see Julia again.

All or nothing.

Go to her, Max.

He could hear Susan's voice in his head, gently admonishing him. If she'd been here, beside him, she would have given him one of her crooked I-know-you smiles. She knew that, for all of his running, there was a time when it all caught up to him. The holidays. He picked up the phone and dialed a California number.

Susan answered on the first ring. He wondered if she'd been waiting for his call.

"Hey," he said.

"Hey. Happy Thanksgiving."

"To you, too."

He waited for her to say something more; the quiet that crackled through the lines made him remember how easily they'd once talked.

"Hard day for you, huh?" Her voice was soft, sad. He heard talking in the background. A man's voice. A child's.

"I've been invited to Thanksgiving dinner."

"That's great. Are you going?"

He heard the doubt in her voice. "I am."

"Good."

They talked for a few minutes about little things, nothing that mattered, then came to a natural pause. Finally, Susan said, "I need to get back. We've got company."

"Okay."

"Take care of yourself."

"You, too," he said. "Tell your folks hi from me."

"I will." She paused. Her voice lowered. "Let it go, Max. It's been too long."

She made it sound easy, but they both knew better than that. "I don't know how to do that, Suze."

"So you keep risking your life. Why don't you try taking a *real* chance, Max?" She sighed and fell silent.

"Maybe I will," he said softly.

In the end, as always, it was Max who hung up first.

He sat there, staring down at his watch. The minutes ticked past.

It was time. There was no reason for him to be hiding out here, worrying, and the truth was, he *wanted* to go. It had been too long since he'd enjoyed a holiday.

As the crow flies, if one followed the river, the distance between their two houses was less than a mile. Crows, however, flew well above the dense thicket of trees. On the old highway and out along the River Road, it was slow going. The week's rainfall had left huge potholes in the road.

He parked back from the house and killed the lights and engine. Getting the wine from the backseat, he shut the car door with his hip and turned to the house. It was a pretty little farmhouse with a wrap-around porch, perched on a patch of grass that rolled gently down to the river. An old, thick-stemmed garden of roses ran the length of the house. There were no blossoms now, just dark thorns and blackening leaves. Giant trees protected the west side of the house, their tips pointed up to a velvety sky.

Susan would have loved this house. She would have run across the yard now, pointing to places only she could see. *The orchard will be there . . . the swing set goes there.* They'd spent two years looking for their dream house. Why hadn't they seen that *any* house they'd chosen would have become the very thing they sought?

He crossed the yard and slowly climbed the steps. As he neared the front door, he could hear music. It was John Denver's voice: "*Coming home to a place he'd never been before.*"

He could see them through the oval etched glass in the front door.

Julia and Ellie were dancing with each other, bumping hips and falling sideways and laughing. Alice stood by the fireplace, watching them with huge, unblinking eyes, eating a flower. Every now and then a smile seemed to take her by surprise.

He heard a car drive up behind him and then shut off. Doors opened, closed. Footsteps crunched through the gravel driveway, accompanied by the high-pitched chatter of children's voices.

"Doc!"

It was Cal's voice, calling out to him.

Before he could turn and answer, the front door opened and Ellie stood there, staring up at him. It was a cop's look; assessing.

"I'm glad you could make it," she said, stepping back to let him in. Dressed in emerald velvet pants and a sparkly black sweater, she was every inch the legendary small-town beauty queen.

He handed her the bottles of wine he'd brought. "Thanks for inviting me."

At the sound of his voice, he saw Julia look up. She was kneeling beside Alice in the living room.

Ellie took his arm and maneuvered him over to Julia. "Look who's here, little sis." With that, she left them.

He stared down at Julia, wondering if she felt as out of breath right now as he did.

Slowly, she stood. "Happy Thanksgiving, Max. I'm glad you could make it. I haven't had a real family holiday in years."

"Me, either."

He saw how she reacted to his confession; the words connected them somehow. "So," he said quickly, "how's our wild one?"

Julia seized on the subject and launched into a monologue about their therapy. As she spoke, she smiled often and looked down at Alice with a love so obvious it made him smile, too. He felt swept along by her enthusiasm and caring, and then he remembered: All or nothing.

He was looking at *all*.

"Max?" She frowned up at him. "I'm putting you into a coma, aren't I? I'm sorry. Sometimes I just get carried away. I won't—"

He touched her arm; realizing it was a mistake, he pulled back sharply.

She stared up at him.

"I've been thinking about you." The words were out of his mouth before he could stop them.

"Yeah," she said. "I know what you mean."

Max had no idea what to say next, so he said nothing. Finally, when the silence grew uncomfortable, he made some lame excuse and made his way to the makeshift bar set up in the kitchen.

For the next hour he tried not to look at Julia. He laughed with Cal and Ellie and the girls and helped out in the kitchen.

At a few minutes before four o'clock Ellie announced that dinner, "such as it is," was ready. They all hurried around like ants, moving in and out of the bathroom, clustering in the tiny kitchen, offering to help serve.

All the while, Julia was kneeling beside Alice, who stood hidden behind a potted ficus tree in the living room. The child was obviously frightened, and it was literally like seeing magic when Julia changed all that. Everyone else was seated at the oval oak table when Julia finally shuttled Alice to the table and seated her on a booster seat between herself and Cal.

Max took the only available seat: it was next to Julia.

At the head of the table, Ellie looked at them across a sea of food. "I'm so glad you're all here. It's been a long time since this table hosted a Thanksgiving dinner. Now I'd like to follow an old Cates' family tradition. Will everyone hold hands, please?"

Max reached right and took Amanda's hand in his. Then he reached left and touched Julia. He didn't look at her.

When they were all linked, Ellie smiled at Cal. "Why don't you start for us?"

Cal looked thoughtful for a moment, and then smiled. "I'm thankful for my beautiful daughters. And to be back in this house for Thanksgiving. I'm sure Lisa is really missing us all right now. There's nothing worse than a business trip over the holidays."

His three daughters went next.

"I'm thankful for my daddy—"

"—my puppy—"

"My pretty new boots."

Next came Ellie. "I'm thankful for my sister coming home."

Julia smiled. "And I'm thankful for little Alice here, who has shown me so much." She leaned over and kissed the girl's cheek.

All Max could think about was how warm Julia's hand felt in his, how steadied he was by her touch.

"Max?" Ellie said finally.

They were all looking at him. Waiting. He looked at Julia. "I'm thankful to be here."

NINETEEN

WINTER CAME TO THE RAIN FOREST LIKE A HORDE OF greedy relatives, taking up every inch of space and blocking out the light. The rains became earnest in this darkening season of the year, changing from a comforting mist to a constant drizzle.

In the midst of all this dark weather, Alice blossomed; there was no other word for it. Like a fragile orchid, she bloomed within the walls of this house where each day felt more like a home. The girl's quest for language had been both tireless and desperate. Now she strung two words together regularly—and sometimes three. She knew how to get her ideas and wants across to the two women who had become her world.

As remarkable as Alice's changes were, Julia's were perhaps even more surprising. She smiled easier and more often, she made outrageously bad jokes at dinner, and danced with them at the drop of a hat. She'd stopped running every single morning and put on a few much-needed pounds. Most important, she had reclaimed her self-confidence. She was so proud of Alice's accomplishments. The two of them still spent every waking hour together—doing art projects, working with letters and numbers, taking long walks in the woods. They seemed almost to be communicating telepathically, that's how close they were. Alice still shadowed Julia everywhere; often, she kept a hand in Julia's pocket or on her belt. But more and more often, Alice would venture a little ways on her own. Sometimes, she went to "Lellie," too, showing off some trinket she had made or found. Almost every night, Ellie read her a bedtime story while Julia wrote in her notebook. Lately, Alice had begun to curl up against Ellie for story time. On very good nights, she petted Ellie's leg and said, "More, Lellie. More."

All of it, Ellie knew, should have made her happy. It was what Mom and Dad had always dreamed of for their daughters' future, and that this closeness would finally return in the house on River Road—well, it couldn't get better than that.

It made Ellie happy.

And it didn't.

The unhappiness was pale and seldom seen, like a spider's web in the deep woods. You saw it only when you were looking for it or stumbled off the path. The new and tender closeness of their trio sometimes underscored the solitary edge of her life. A woman who'd fallen in love as often as she had didn't expect to be approaching forty alone. Even though she was happy for Julia, sometimes Ellie watched her sister's growing bond with Alice, and it made her heart ache. Whether Julia knew it or not—or admitted it or not—she was becoming Alice's mother. They would leave this house someday, find their own home, and Ellie would be alone, like before. Only it would be different now because she'd been part of a family again. She didn't want to go back to her previous life, where work and friends and dreams of falling in love made up the bulk of her life. She didn't know if it would be enough anymore. Now that she'd lived in a house where a child played games and followed you around and kissed you good-night, would she be okay again on her own?

"You don't look so good," Cal said from across the room.

"Yeah? Well, you're ugly."

Cal laughed. Taking off his headset, he put down his pencil and walked out of their office. A few moments later he returned with two cups of coffee. "Maybe you need some caffeine." He handed her the cup.

She looked up at him, wondering why she couldn't find men like him attractive—men who kept their promises and raised their children and stayed in love. Oh, no. She had to fall head over heels for guys with "issues." Guys who grew their hair too long and had trouble keeping a job and confused "I do" with "I did" pretty damned fast.

"What I need is a new life."

He pulled a chair from his desk and set it by hers. "We're getting to that age."

"You used to tell me I was crazy when I said things like that."

He leaned back in the chair and put his feet on her desk. She couldn't help noticing that the white soles of his tennis shoes were covered with purple ink. Someone had written his youngest daughter's name on the rubber, surrounded by pink hearts and stars.

It made her heart lurch, that little sight. "It looks like someone wanted to decorate Daddy's shoes."

"Sarah thought my shoes were dorky. I never should have given her a set of markers."

"You're lucky to have those girls, Cal." She sighed. "I always thought I'd be the one with three daughters. Both times I got married, I went right off the pill and started praying." She tried to smile. "I guess I have divorce lawyers instead of babies."

"You're thirty-nine, Ellie. Not fifty-nine. The game isn't over."

"It just feels that way, huh?"

He rolled his eyes. "Oh, for God's sake, Ellie. Don't you ever get tired of telling the same story?"

She sat upright. He sounded angry with her. It didn't make sense. She'd always been able to count on Cal. "What do you mean?"

"We're pushing forty, but you still act like you're the homecoming queen, waiting to be swept off her feet by the football captain. It's not like that. Love rips the shit out of you and puts you back together like a broken toy, with all kinds of cracks and jagged edges. It's not about the falling in love. It's about the *landing,* the staying where you said you'd be and working to keep the love strong. You never did get that."

"That's easy for you to say, Cal. You've got a wife and kids who love you. Lisa—"

"Left me."

"What?"

"In August," he said quietly. "We tried the old being separated in the same house—for the girls. But they were too smart for that. Amanda, especially. She's like Julia was at that age. She sees everything and isn't afraid to ask hard questions. Lisa moved out of our bedroom before Valentine's Day. Just before school started, she left for good."

"And the girls?" Ellie could hardly ask the question.

"They're with me. Lisa works too much. Every now and again she gets lonely and remembers that she's a mom and she calls or comes by. She's in love now. We haven't heard from her in weeks. Except for the divorce papers. She wants me to sell the house and split the proceeds."

"I can't believe you've never told me this. We work together every day. *Every* day."

He looked at her oddly. "When was the last time you asked about my life, El?"

She felt stung by that remark. "I always ask how you're doing."

"And you give me five seconds to answer before you launch into something more interesting. Usually about your own life." He sighed, ran a hand through his hair. "I'm not judging you, Ellie. Simply telling the truth."

The look in Cal's eyes was one of pity, and perhaps disappointment.

He stood up slowly. "Forget it. I shouldn't have said all this. You just got me on a bad day. I'm feeling low. I guess I just wanted a friend to tell me it would be okay." He headed for the door, grabbed his coat off the rack. "See you tomorrow."

She was still there, standing in the middle of the office, staring at the closed door when it hit her.

Lisa left me.

I can't believe you didn't tell me.

She'd made it about her. Cal had shared with her his pain—and it was a lion's-sized pain she knew all too well—and she'd said nothing to comfort him, nothing to help.

I just wanted a friend to tell me it would be okay.

Which she hadn't done.

For years people had made little remarks about her being selfish. Ellie had always brushed them off with a pretty smile. It wasn't true; whoever said it was either jealous of her or wasn't a friend.

You're like me, Ellie, her dad had said to her once, *a center stage actor. If you marry again, you'd best find someone who doesn't mind letting you have the spotlight all the time.*

When he'd said it, Ellie had taken it as a compliment. She loved that her dad thought of her as a star.

Now, she saw the other meaning of his words, and once she opened that door, once she asked herself, *Is it true?* she was barraged with memories, moments, questions.

Two lost marriages. Both had gone south—she'd thought—because her husbands didn't love her enough.

Was that because she wanted—needed—too much love? Did she return the amount she took? She'd loved her husbands, adored them. But not enough to follow Alvin to Alaska . . . or to put Sammy through truck driver's school with the money she earned on the police force.

No wonder her marriages had failed. It had always been her way or the highway, and one by one the men she'd married and the others she'd loved had chosen the highway.

All these years, she'd called *them* the losers.

Maybe it had been her all along.

When Mel came in to work the night shift, Ellie nodded at him, made a point of asking about his family, then raced out to her car.

She pulled up to Cal's house less than thirty minutes after he'd left the station and parked beneath a huge, bare maple tree. A pretty little birdhouse hung from the lowest branch, swinging gently in the autumn breeze. One of the last dying leaves clung to its rough hewn cedar roof.

Ellie went to the front door and knocked.

Cal opened the door. His face, usually so youthful and smiling, looked older, ruined. She wondered how long he'd looked like that, how often she hadn't noticed.

"I'm a bitch," she said miserably. "Can you forgive me?"

A tiny smile tugged at one side of his mouth. "A drama queen apology if ever there was one."

"I'm not a drama queen."

"No. You're a bitch." His smile evened out, almost reached his eyes. "It's your beauty. Women like you are just used to being the center of attention."

She moved toward him. "I am a bitch. A sorry one."

He looked at her. "Thanks."

"It'll be okay, Cal," she said, hoping late really was better than never.

"You think so?"

She felt as if she were drowning in the dark sadness she saw in his eyes. It so unnerved her, she barely knew what to say. "Lisa loves you," she said at last. "She'll remember that and come back."

"I thought that for a long time, El. Peanut kept saying the same thing. But now I'm not so sure it's what I even want."

Ellie's first reaction was *Peanut knew?* but she wouldn't fall down that trap again. This wasn't about her bruised ego. She led Cal to the sofa and sat down beside him. "What *do* you want?"

"Not to be so lonely all the time. Don't get me wrong. I adore my daughters and they're my life, but late at night, in bed, I want to turn to someone, just hold her and be held. Lisa and I stopped making love years ago. I thought I'd be less lonely when she was gone, or at least that it wouldn't make a difference, but it does." He looked at her, and in those eyes she knew so well, she saw a sadness that was new. "How can a wife in a bed down the hall be more comforting that no wife at all?"

Ellie had gone to sleep next to that kind of loneliness for more winters than she wanted to count.

"Does it get easier?"

She sighed. This was where their conversation had begun. "Be thankful for your kids, Cal. At least you'll always have someone who loves you."

MAX FINISHED HIS ROUNDS AT SIX O'CLOCK. BY SIX-THIRTY HE'D COM-pleted all his chart notations and signed out.

He was inches from the front door when they paged him.

"Dr. Cerrasin to O.R. two stat."

"Shit."

He ran to the O.R.

There, he found his patient, Crystal Smithson, in a hospital gown, in bed, screaming at her husband, who stood in the corner like a kid in a time-out, looking terrified. Crystal's stomach was huge. She pressed down on it, breathing in gasps until the contraction ended.

Trudi was beside her, holding her hand. At Max's entrance, she smiled.

"Now, Crystal, I thought I told you I didn't work Friday nights," he said, putting on his surgical gloves.

Crystal smiled, but it was frail and tired. "Tell *her* that." She rubbed her bulging abdomen.

"You might as well learn now," Trudi said, "kids never listen to you."

Another contraction hit and Crystal screamed.

"Is she going to be okay?" her husband said, taking a step toward them.

Max moved down to the end of the bed. "Let's see what we've got."

"She's fully dilated," Trudi said, moving in beside him, putting lu-bricant on his gloved fingers.

Max's examination didn't take long. He'd delivered enough babies to know that this one was going to be quick. He could feel the baby's head starting to crown.

"You ready to be a mom, Crystal?"

Another contraction; another scream. "Yes," she panted.

"The baby's crowning," Max said to Trudi. "Okay, Crystal, you can start pushing."

Crystal grunted and wheezed and screamed. Her husband rushed to her side. "I'm here, Chrissie." He grabbed her hand.

The baby's head appeared.

"Push a little more for the shoulders, Crystal, and you'll be done," Max said.

He gently pulled down on the baby's head to free the anterior, then eased up; the baby slid out, landed in Max's hands.

"You have a beautiful little girl," he said, looking up. Both Crystal and her husband were crying.

"You want to cut the cord, Dad?" Max said. No matter how many times he said those words, they always got to him.

By the time they were done, he was exhausted. He took a long hot shower, got dressed, and headed for the nurses' station.

Trudi was there, all alone. At his approach, she came out from around the desk and smiled up at him. "They're naming the baby Maxine."

"Poor kid," he said, then fell silent.

"You haven't been to the house in a while."

It would have been easy to change the subject, but Trudi deserved better than that. "I guess we should talk."

Trudi laughed. "You always said talking wasn't our best skill." She leaned closer. "Let me guess: it's about a certain doctor who had Thanksgiving dinner at the local police chief's house. Since I know you're not interested in Ellie, it must be her sister. Julia."

He shook his head. "I don't even know what the hell's going on with her. We're—"

"You don't have to tell me, Max."

"You know I wouldn't hurt you for the world—"

She silenced him with a touch. "I'm glad for you. Really. You've been alone too long."

"You're a good woman, Trudi Hightower."

"And you're a good man. Now quit being such a chickenshit and ask her out for a date. Unless I miss my guess, it's Friday night, and I know a doctor who shouldn't be going to the movies alone anymore."

He leaned down and kissed her. "Good-bye, Trudi."

" 'Bye, Max."

He climbed into his truck and headed for the theater. He had no intention of going to Julia, but when he came to Magnolia Street, he turned left instead of right, and drove down old Highway 101.

All the way to her house he told himself he was crazy.

All or nothing.

He'd had *all* once; it had practically killed him.

In her yard, he parked and sat there, staring through the windshield at the house. Finally, he got out, walked up to the front door and knocked.

Julia opened the door. Even in a pair of faded Levi's and a white cable-knit sweater that was two sizes too big, she looked beautiful. "Max," she said, obviously surprised. She eased forward and closed the door behind her, blocking the way.

"You want to go to the movies?"

Idiot. He sounded like a desperate teenager.

Her answer was a smile that started slowly, then overtook her face. "Cal and Ellie are here playing Scrabble, so yeah . . . I could go to the show. What's playing?"

"I have no idea."

She laughed. "That's my favorite."

THE MOVIE, AS IT TURNED OUT, WAS *TO HAVE AND HAVE NOT.* JULIA sat next to Max in the darkened theater, watching one of the great screen pairings of all time. When it was over, and she and Max were walking through the beautifully restored lobby of the Rose Theater, Julia got the feeling that they were being stared at.

"People are talking about us," she said, sidling close to him.

"Welcome to Rain Valley." He took her arm and led her out of the theater and across the street to where his truck was parked. "I'd take you out for some pie, but everything's closed."

"You do like your pie."

He grinned. "And you thought you knew nothing about me."

She turned, looked up at him, no longer smiling. "I don't know much."

He stared down at her; she expected him to come up with some smart-ass comeback. Instead he kissed her. When he drew back, he said quietly, "There. You know that."

When she didn't say anything, he opened the door and she got in.

All the way back to her house they talked about things that didn't matter. The movie. The baby he'd delivered tonight, the waning salmon populations and declining old-growth forests. His plans for Christmas.

At her front door she let him take her in his arms. It was amazing how comfortable she felt there. This time, when he bent down to kiss her, she met him more than halfway, and when it was over and he drew back, she wanted more. "Thanks for the movie, Max."

He kissed her again, so softly she hardly had time to taste him before it was over. "Good night, Julia."

By late December the holidays were first and foremost on everyone's mind. The Rotary Club had hung the streetlamp decorations and the Elks' had decorated their Giving Tree. On every corner in town there were tree lots set up; local scout troops were going door-to-door, selling wrapping paper.

Today had dawned bright and clear, with an ice blue sky unmarred by even the thinnest cloud. Along the riverbanks, where the ground was warmer than the air, a layer of pink fog rose from the bending shoreline to the lowest branches of the trees, turning everything beyond it to a blurry uncertainty. It was easy to picture magic in that haze; fairies and spirits and animals that lived nowhere else on Earth.

All day, as usual, Julia had been at Alice's side. They'd spent a lot of time outside in the yard.

Julia was trying to prepare Alice for the next big step. Town.

It wouldn't be easy. The first hurdle was the car.

"Town," Julia said quietly, looking down at Alice. "Remember the pictures in the books? I want us to go to town, where the people live."

Alice's eyes widened. "Out?" she whispered, her mouth trembling.

"I'll be with you all the time."

She shook her head.

Julia carefully extricated herself from Alice's clinging hold. Very carefully, she held Alice's hands in hers. She wanted to ask the girl if she trusted her, but trust was too complicated a concept for a child with such limited verbal skills. "I know you're scared, honey. It's a big world out there, and you've seen the worst of it." She touched Alice's soft, warm cheek. "But hiding out here with me and Ellie can't be your future. You've got to come into the world."

"Stay."

Julia started to respond, but before she'd formed the first word, she was interrupted by a honking horn.

Alice's face lit up. "Lellie!" She let go of Julia and ran to the window by the front door. The dogs followed her, barking out a welcome, falling over themselves in a rush. Elwood knocked Alice over. The girl's giggles rose up from the tangle of bodies on the floor. Jake licked her cheek and nudged her.

The front door opened. Ellie stood there, grinning, then dragged a Christmas tree into the house.

For the next hour Julia and Ellie struggled to get the tree in its stand, upright, and clamped down. When they were finally finished, both of them were sweating.

"No wonder Dad always drank heavily before he put up the tree," Ellie said, standing back and surveying their work.

"It's not *absolutely* straight," Julia pointed out.

"Who are we? NASA engineers? It's straight enough."

The dogs, sensing that Ellie was finally done with her task, made a run across the floor.

"Boys! Down!" Ellie said, just before they ran into her and sent her flying.

Alice giggled. The minute the sound slipped out, she covered her mouth with her hand. She looked at Julia and pointed at Ellie.

"Your Lellie needs to get control over her animals," Julia said with a wry smile.

Ellie emerged from the tangle of canine bodies. Laughing, she pushed the hair from her eyes. "I should have disciplined them as puppies, it's true." Climbing free, she stepped away from the dogs and headed for the stairs.

"Where are you going?" Julia called after her.

"You'll see."

A few moments later Ellie came back downstairs; she was carrying several huge red poinsettia–decorated boxes, which she set down on the floor by the Christmas tree.

Julia recognized them instantly. "Our ornaments?"

"Every one."

Julia moved closer. Lifting the first box top, she found skeins and skeins of lights. All the bulbs were white, because Mom said it was the color of angels and hope. She and Ellie coiled the tree in those lights, wrapped the branches in the way they'd been taught. It was the first time they'd decorated a tree together since high school.

When the lights were all in place, Ellie plugged the cords into the wall.

Alice gasped.

"You think she's ever seen a Christmas tree before?" Ellie asked quietly, standing beside Julia.

Julia shook her head. She went to the box and picked up a shiny red apple ornament. It hung from her finger on a filigree gold thread. Kneeling in front of Alice, she offered the girl the ornament. "On the tree, Alice. Make it pretty."

Alice frowned. "Tee?"

"Remember the book we read. *How the Grinch Stole Christmas?*"

"Ginch." She nodded, but her frown didn't ease.

"Remember the Who's tree? Pretty tree, you said."

"Oh," Alice said, blowing out her breath on the word. She understood.

Julia nodded.

Alice took the ornament carefully, as if it were made of spun sugar instead of bright plastic. She walked slowly across the room, stepped over the dogs and stopped, staring at the tree for a long time. Finally, she placed the gold thread on the very tip of the highest branch she could reach. Then, slowly, she turned around, looking worried.

Ellie clapped enthusiastically. "Perfect!"

A smile broke over Alice's face, transforming her for this wonderful moment into an ordinary little girl. She ran to the box, chose another ornament, then carried it carefully to Ellie. "Lellie. Prittee."

Ellie bent down. "Who is giving me this pretty ornament?"

"Girl. Give."

Ellie touched Alice's hair, tucked a flyaway strand behind her little shell pink ear. "Can you say Alice?"

She pointed emphatically toward the tree. "Put."

"You're creating a little dictator here, Jules," Ellie said, moving toward the tree.

"A nameless one," Julia said quietly. It stuck in her craw that Alice couldn't give them her name and wouldn't take the name they gave her.

Alice ran to the box and chose another red ornament. After clapping and hopping up and down at Ellie's placement of her ornament, Alice darted over to Julia. "Jew-lee. Prittee."

Alice was literally sparkling right now. Julia had never seen the girl smile so brightly. She swept down and pulled Alice into her arms for a hug.

Alice giggled and hung on. "Kiss-mas tee. Nice."

Julia twirled her around until they both were breathless. Then, smiling, they moved on to the task of decorating the tree.

· · ·

"It's the prettiest tree we've ever had," Ellie said, sitting on the sofa with a mug of Bailey's in her hand and a Costco fake mink throw rug over her feet.

"That's because Dad used to buy the biggest one on the lot, then cut off the top to make it fit in the room."

Ellie laughed at the memory. It was one she'd forgotten: The great big tree, taking up the whole corner of the room, its top hacked off; Mom frowning in disappointment, swatting Dad's arm. *You never listen, Tom*, Mom would say, *a tree isn't supposed to be trimmed on top. I should make you get us another one.*

But it took only moments, sometimes less, before he had her smiling again, even laughing. *Now, now, Bren*, he'd say in that gravelly voice of his, *why should our tree be like everyone else's? I've just given us a bit of oomph, I have. Right, girls?*

Ellie had always answered first, shouting out her agreement and then running to her dad for his hug.

For the first time, as she held a memory in her hands, she tilted it, saw it instead from a different angle. The other little girl who'd been in the room, who'd never called out agreement with her father, whose opinion had never been sought.

Ellie looked at Julia over the rim of her mug. "How come he did it every year? Cut the top of the tree, I mean."

Julia smiled. "You know Dad. He cared about what he cared about. The tree didn't matter so he didn't think about it."

"But you and Mom cared."

"You know Dad," Julia said.

"I'm like him," Ellie said. All her life she'd been proud of that fact.

"You always have been. People adore you, just as they adored him."

Ellie took a sip of her drink. "Cal accused me of being selfish," she said quietly.

"Really?"

"The correct response would have been surprise. Shock, even. Something like: how could he even *think* that?"

"Oh," Julia said, trying not to smile.

"Say what's on your mind," Ellie snapped.

"When I was little, I had a huge crush on Cal. He was everything I dreamed of when I was eleven. But he only had eyes for you. He followed you everywhere. I was jealous every time you snuck out to be with him."

"You knew about that?"

"We shared a bedroom. What am I, deaf? Just because I never told doesn't mean I didn't know. The point is, I remember when you dumped him. He kept coming around for the rest of that summer, tossing rocks at the window, but you never answered."

"We grew apart."

Julia gave her a look. "Come on. Once those football boys saw your new boobs, you were *in*. Poor Cal was left in the dust. And when you made cheerleader, well . . ." Julia shrugged. "You became royalty in this town and you loved every second. In that, you were like Dad. You . . . moved on from Cal, but somehow you kept him around like a moon caught in your orbit. It's that magic you and Dad have. People can't help loving you—even if you're sometimes too focused on your own life."

"So I *am* selfish. Is that why my marriages failed?"

"Is it?"

"Is that the kind of questions you learned in that decade of college?"

Julia laughed. "Exactly so. Here's another one: how does it make you feel?"

Ellie didn't quite know how to answer that. She'd heard this new picture of herself, but it didn't feel like a reflection yet. It felt like a possibility, one she could change or talk her way out of if she really wanted to. She'd always thought of herself as a good person who really cared about others. "I'm sorry," she said quietly.

"For what?"

"I threw you to the media wolves. All I cared about was . . ." She started to say *finding Alice's name*, but the pretty little lie caught in her throat. It was only partially true. "I didn't want to fail. I hardly thought about your feelings."

Julia surprised her by smiling. "Don't worry about it."

"If it matters, I didn't really know how bad it would be for you. Maybe if I'd known—" At Julia's look, Ellie laughed. "Okay, it wouldn't have mattered. But I *am* sorry."

"Don't be. Really. Alice is my second chance. I don't know what I would have done without her."

They were silent for a long moment.

"I want to adopt her," Julia said finally. "Alice needs to know she belongs someplace, and with someone, even if she doesn't really understand it all yet. And I need her."

"What happens if someone shows up to claim her?"

Softly, Julia said: "Then I'll need my sister, won't I?"

Ellie's throat tightened. She realized right then how much she'd missed when she and Julia went their separate ways, and how much it mattered to her that they had come back together. "You can count on me."

"Alice, you're not paying attention. We're playing with the blocks now."

The little girl shook her head and jutted her chin in stubborn defiance. "No. Prittees." She jumped up from the chair and ran around to the Christmas tree. Each ornament fascinated her, but the red ones most of all.

Julia couldn't help smiling. It had been this way from the moment they put the tree up. They'd had to work at the dining room table so Alice could always see the ornaments. "Come on, Alice. Five more minutes with the blocks. Then I have a surprise for you."

Alice turned to her. "Prize?"

Julia nodded. "After blocks."

Alice sighed dramatically and stomped back to the dining table. She plopped in her chair and crossed her arms.

This time Julia had to turn her head to hide her smile. Alice was certainly learning to express her emotions. "Show me seven blocks."

Alice rolled her eyes, but didn't say anything as she culled seven blocks from the pile beside her elbow. "Seven."

"Now show me four blocks."

Alice removed three blocks from the string she'd just created, shoving them back into the pile.

Julia frowned. "Wait a minute. Did you just *subtract* the blocks?" No. It couldn't be. The girl could only count to twenty so far. Addition and subtraction were too complex.

Alice stared at her blankly.

Before, in counting blocks, Alice had always started fresh, returning all the blocks to the pile and then choosing the newly requested number. "Are you rushing to get to your surprise or was that just a lucky guess?"

"Prize?"

"Show me one block."

Alice's smile fell. Dutifully, she removed three blocks from the pile, leaving one.

"How many more blocks do you need to have six?"

Alice held up five fingers.

"And if I take two, how many would be left?"

Alice curled down two fingers. "Free."

"You *are* adding and subtracting." She shook her head. "Wow."

"Done?"

Julia wondered what other tricks Alice had up her sleeve. Maybe it was time for an IQ test. She was about to ask Alice another question when the phone rang. Julia went into the kitchen to answer. "Hello?"

"Merry Christmas Eve," Ellie said.

"Merry Christmas Eve."

"Are you coming?"

"Hopefully. We'll try to leave in a minute or two."

"Will she make a scene?"

"She might."

"We're waiting."

"Okay." Julia said good-bye to her sister and hung up.

She went to Alice then, bent down. "Julia would never hurt Alice, you know that, right?"

Alice's face pulled into a frown.

"I want to take you someplace special. Will you come with me?" Julia held out her hand.

Alice took hold, but her frown didn't soften. She was confused, and as often happened, confusion frightened her.

"First you have to put on boots and your coat. It's cold outside."

"No."

Julia sighed. The fight over shoes never ended. "Cold outside." She reached for the fake-fur-lined rubber boots and black wool coat she'd put by the door. "Come on. I'll give you a surprise if you put them on."

"No."

"No surprise? Oh, well, then."

"Stop!" Alice cried out as Julia walked away. Frowning, she stuck her bare feet in the boots, put on her coat and clomped across the wood floor. "Smelly shoes."

Julia smiled down at her. Smelly was the word for anything Alice didn't like. "You're such a good girl." Reaching down, she took hold of Alice's hand. "Will you follow me?"

Slowly, Alice nodded

Julia led the girl out of the house and toward Peanut's truck. As she opened the door, she heard Alice start to make noises. It was the low, throaty growl she used to make.

"Use your words, Alice."

"Stay." She looked terrified.

This reaction didn't surprise Julia. She'd anticipated it. At some point in her life Alice had been taken somewhere—by someone—in a car. Perhaps that trip was the start of the bad times.

"I won't hurt you, Alice. And I won't let anyone else hurt you."

Her blue-green eyes were huge in the tiny white oval of her face. She was trying so hard to be brave. "No leave Girl?"

"Never. No." Julia tightened her hold on Alice's hand. "We'll go see Ellie."

"Lellie?"

Julia nodded, then tugged on the girl's hand. "Come on, Alice. Please?"

Alice swallowed hard. "Okay." Very slowly, she climbed into the passenger side of the truck. Julia helped her into the booster seat they'd purchased last week for this very occasion. When she snapped the seat belt in place, Alice started to whimper. At the shutting of the door, that pathetic whimper grew into a desperate howling.

Julia hurried around the car and slipped into the driver's seat. By now Alice was hyperventilating, trying to unhook the straps.

"It's okay, Alice. You're scared. That's okay." Julia said the words over and over again until Alice calmed down enough to hear her.

"I'm putting on my seat belt, see? Now I'm hooked in, too."

Alice whimpered, pulled on the strap.

"Use your words, Alice."

"Fee. Peas. Girl fee."

All at once Julia got it. *Idiot.* She should have foreseen this. The memory of those tiny pale scars on Alice's ankle. Ligature marks. "Oh, Alice," she said, feeling tears well in her eyes. Maybe she should quit now, try another time.

No.

Alice had to come into this world sometime, and in this world kids sat in car seats. But there was one concession she could make. Julia moved Alice and the car seat to the middle of the bench seat in the old truck, then held the girl's hand. "Is that better?"

"Fwaid. Girl fwaid."

"I know, baby. But I won't let you go. You're safe. Okay?"

Alice's gaze was steady, trusting. " 'Kay."

Julia started the car.

Alice screamed and tightened her hold on Julia's hand.

"It's okay, honey," Julia said over and over until Alice quieted.

It took them almost ten minutes to get down the driveway. By the time they reached the highway, she had almost no feeling left in her right hand. She ignored the pain and kept up a steady stream of comforting dialogue.

Looking back on it, Julia could pinpoint when Alice changed. It was at the corner of Azalea Street and West End Avenue.

Earl and Myra's house, to be precise. As always, the couple had decorated as if it were an Olympic event. White lights twinkled from every surface. A giant Santa and sleigh arced above the peak of the roof in a brilliant display of red and green lights. On the front door was a twinkling green wreath, and tiny green-lit trees outlined the path from street to house.

Alice made a sound of pure delight. For the first time, she let go of Julia's hand and pointed at the house. "Look."

This was as good a place as any to stop. They were a block from the police station. Julia pulled over to the curb and parked, then went around to Alice's door, opening it. Before she'd even finished unstrapping Alice, the girl was slithering out of the seat and climbing out of the truck.

At the edge of the sidewalk, Alice paused, staring up at the house. "Prittee," she breathed.

Julia came up beside her.

Alice immediately took her hand.

Julia waited patiently, knowing Alice's penchant for studying things. It was entirely possible that they'd stand here for an hour.

At some point the red door opened. Myra stood there, dressed in a long black velvet skirt and a red knit sweater. Carrying a tray of cookies, she walked slowly toward them.

Julia felt Alice's tension. "It's okay, honey. Myra is nice."

Alice slid behind Julia but didn't let go of her hand.

"Do you like cookies?" Myra said when she was closer. "My Margery liked spritz best when she was your age."

Julia turned slightly and looked down at Alice. "She has cookies."

"Cookees?"

"I made them myself," Myra said, winking up at Julia.

Cautiously, Alice peered around Julia's body. In a lightning-quick move she grabbed a red wreath cookie and popped the whole thing in her mouth. By the third cookie she'd moved out from behind Julia and stood tucked along her side.

"I brought you this, too," Myra said, offering Alice a bright red plastic purse. "It was Margery's favorite. But when I saw it, I thought of you."

Alice's eyes widened, her mouth rounded. "Red," she whispered, taking the purse in her hands, holding it to her cheek.

"How did you know she loved anything red?" Julia asked.

Myra shrugged. "I didn't."

"Well. Tell Earl Merry Christmas from me."

"He's not home yet from the men's choir practice, but I'll pass it along. And to you, too."

Holding hands, Julia and Alice walked down to Main Street and turned left. The streets were full of parked cars but empty of people on this ultimate family night. The parking lot behind city hall only had three cars in it.

Julia led Alice up the steps. "We're going to get Ellie and then we'll walk downtown. I'll show you the pretty lights."

Alice was so busy petting her purse she barely nodded.

Julia opened the door.

Inside the police station, Cal and his three daughters, and Peanut and Benji and their teenage son and daughter, and Ellie were dancing to an earsplitting rendition of "Jingle Bell Rock." Mel and his family were setting food out on the table.

Alice shrieked and started to howl.

Ellie ran for the stereo and shut it off. Silence descended. Everyone stared at one another. Cal was the first to move. He herded his girls into a group; they moved toward Julia. Alice glommed onto her side, trying to disappear. The whimpering started again; the thumb popped into her mouth.

Close, but not too close. Cal dropped down on one knee. "Hey, Alice. We're the Wallace family. You remember us, I bet? I'm Cal, and these are my girls. Amanda, Emily, and Sarah."

Alice was trembling. She tightened her hold on Julia's hand.

Peanut bustled her family forward. Her husband, Benji, was a big, burly-looking man with twinkling eyes and a ready smile. Not once during the party did he let go of his wife's hand. Their teenagers were clearly trying to appear "cool," but every now and then they grinned like little kids.

Introductions were made quietly. Benji knelt down slowly in front of Alice and wished her a very Merry Christmas, then he herded his children over to the tree.

Peanut stayed behind. "I can't go over there," she said to Julia. "Eggnog. Some people can drink a glass of it. I'd like an IV." She laughed.

At the sound, Alice looked up and smiled.

"You've really worked a miracle with her," Peanut said, showing Alice her long red fingernails. Each one sported a sparkly wreath.

"Thanks," Julia said.

"Well, I better get over to my family. But before I go . . ." She leaned close to Julia, whispered, "I have a bit of gossip."

Julia laughed. "I'm hardly the one to tell."

"Oh, you're the only one. My sources—which are FBI good—tell me that a certain doctor in town took a date to the movies. That's like Paris Hilton moving into a double wide. Some things don't happen. But this one did."

"It was just a movie."

"Was it?" Peanut gave her a wink, a pat on the arm, and she left.

For the next fifteen minutes everyone went about celebrating Christmas, but it was as if the mute button had been pushed. The laughter was quiet, the talking even more so. In the background the Vince Garibaldi trio Christmas CD came on. It was the music from *A Charlie Brown Christmas*. Mom's favorite. At some point Earl and Myra showed up with more food.

Alice was mesmerized by the opening of presents. She finally came out from behind Julia so she could see better. She didn't talk to anyone except Ellie, but she seemed content to watch it all. She dared to play alongside Sarah, who was a few years older. Not together, but side by side; Alice watched Sarah's every move and imitated it. By the time everyone started to leave, Alice could dress and undress Disco Barbie without help. After the party broke up, Ellie, Julia, and Alice walked downtown. Alice couldn't stop pointing at the various lights and decorations. She kept tugging on Julia's hand and dragging her forward. It was going better than Julia had anticipated, actually.

Julia walked beside Ellie. Alice pointed at every light, every decoration.

"She reminds me of you," Julia said to her sister. "You always had such enthusiasm for the holidays."

"You, too."

"I was quieter, though. In everything."

"So I'm a bigmouth?"

Julia smiled. "Yes. And I'm ladylike."

They walked on.

"So," Julia finally said, trying to sound casual. "I hear the gossip mill is in high gear on Max and me." •

"I've been waiting for you to bring it up. What's the story with you two?"

"I don't know," Julia answered truthfully. "There's . . . something between us."

Ellie turned to her. "I wouldn't want to see you get hurt."

"Yeah," Julia said quietly. "I've had the same thought myself."

In front of the Catholic church, Alice came to a stop. She pointed at the brightly lit manger scene set up on the yard. "Prittee."

Then the bells of the church pealed.

Ellie looked at Julia. "The service should have been out an hour ago. I called Father James myself—"

Before she'd finished the sentence, the double doors banged open and the parishioners came pouring out of St. Mark's in a rushing, chattering river of humanity. There were people everywhere, moving right at them, surging down the stairs.

Alice screamed and yanked her hand free to cover her ears.

Julia heard the scream, then a desperate howl. She turned toward Alice.

"It's okay, honey. Don't be—"

Alice was gone, lost in the sea of faces and bodies.

TWENTY

THERE ARE ONLY *STRANGERS AROUND GIRL; LAUGHING, TALK-*ing, singing strangers.

She stumbles sideways, almost falls.

Jewlee promised, she thinks.

But it doesn't surprise her, even though she can feel a ripping in her chest and a swelling in her throat.

There is something wrong with Girl. Something Bad. It has always been that way. Him told her that all the time. Why had she let herself forget? Even worse, she'd let herself *believe* in Jewlee and now Girl is afraid again. This time there are people everywhere instead of nowhere, but this makes no difference. Some words she knows now. Lost is lost; it's when you want someone to hold you but there is no one who can. Lost is alone, even when people are all around you.

She pushes through the crowd of Strangers. Any one of them could hurt her. Her heart is beating so hard and fast it makes her dizzy. They are reaching for her, trying to pull her back.

She runs until the sound of voices is funny and far away, like the roar of water in the falls at her beloved river when the snow begins to melt.

She stares out past this place called town. Her trees are there, dark now, and pointy against the sky. They would welcome her again; she knows this. She could follow the river to her cave and live there again.

Cold.

Hungry.

Alone.

Even Wolf is gone from her.

She would be too alone out there.

Now that she has known Jewlee and Lellie how can she go back to the nothing? She will miss being held, miss hearing the pretty story about the rabbit who wants to be real. Girl knows about that: wanting to be real.

That ache in her chest is back. It is like swelling up; she hopes her bones will not crack from it. A strange tightness squeezes her throat. She feels this all from far away, and wonders if finally her eyes will leak. She wants them to. It will make the hurt in her chest ease.

Then she sees the tree.

It is where she first hid in this place. Trees have always protected her. She runs to her tree and climbs up, higher and higher, until an old, bare limb cradles her.

She tries not to think about how much different—better—it felt to be held by Jewlee.

No. Leave. Girl.

She wishes she'd never believed in that promise.

JULIA SPUN AROUND, SEARCHING EVERY FACE, REACHING OUT. ALL around her people kept moving, laughing, talking, singing Christmas carols. She wanted to scream at them to shut up, to please please help her find this one little girl. Their voices were a white noise that roared in her head.

"What happened?" Ellie said, shaking Julia's shoulders to get her attention.

"She's gone." Julia almost started to cry. "One minute she was here, holding my hand . . . then the church let out and there were people everywhere. It must have terrified her. She ran away."

"Okay. Don't move. You hear me?"

Julia had trouble hearing it, actually. Her heart was pounding. All she could think about was earlier tonight, when Alice had been so afraid to get in the car and even more afraid to be strapped into the booster seat. But she'd done it. That brave, bruised child had let herself be bound and looked up at her through those sad eyes and said: *No leave girl?*

She had promised, *sworn*, not to leave Alice alone. Julia pushed through the crowd, yelling for Alice, searching every face. She knew she looked like a madwoman but she didn't care.

A breeze blew in, skudded leaves down the street and across the grass. It smelled vaguely of the not-so-distant ocean; she had no doubt that if she drew in a lungful, it would taste like tears. She stopped, trying to quell her rising panic. Now she heard Ellie yelling for Alice, too, saw flashlight beams cut through the park.

Think. What would bring Alice out?

It came to her suddenly. *Music.* Alice spent hours standing by the speakers, listening to music. She loved dozens of songs—whole Disney soundtracks. But of all the songs she listened to, one was clearly her favorite.

Julia took a deep breath and began to sing "Twinkle Twinkle Little Star."

She walked all around the empty park, singing.

" '. . . how I wonder where you are . . .' "

A bird warbled its own song. For a moment Julia didn't notice. Then it struck her that the birdsong matched her voice.

"Alice?" she whispered.

"Jewlee?"

Julia's knees buckled. She looked up into the bare branches of the maple tree. Alice was there, looking down, her face pale with fear and lined by worry, she said, "No leave?"

"Oh, honey . . . no leave."

Alice jumped down from her perch in the maple tree.

Julia scooped Alice into her arms and held her tightly. She felt the little girl tremble and knew how scared she'd been.

Julia pulled back. "I'm sorry, Alice."

A trembling smile formed on her face. "Stay?"

"Yes, honey. I'll stay."

Alice touched Julia's face, wiped her tears. "No water," she said, sounding worried.

"Those are just tears, Alice. Tears. And they mean I love you."

Ellie walked up just then and squatted down beside them. "There's our girl," she said with a sigh.

Julia looked up at her sister through a blur of tears. "What's the local lawyer's name?"

"John MacDonald. Why?"

"I want to start adoption proceedings the day after Christmas."

"Are you sure?"

Julia pulled Alice against her even more tightly. "I've never been more sure of anything in my life."

BY NOON ON CHRISTMAS DAY MAX HAD BEEN TO THE HOSPITAL TO VISIT his patients and the few children on the ward; he'd also ridden his bicycle fifteen miles, dropped off a donation at the Catholic church, and called every member of his family.

Now he stood in his quiet living room, staring out at the gray-washed lake. It was raining so hard that the entire backyard looked colorless; even the trees.

He should have put up a Christmas tree. Maybe that would have helped his mood, although he couldn't imagine why it would. He hadn't bought a tree in seven years.

He went to the sofa and sat down, but he knew instantly that it was a mistake. Ghosts and memories crowded in on him. He saw his mother sitting on her favorite chair, studying bugs through a magnifying glass . . . and his dad, sleeping on his Barcalounger, with a hand pressed to his wrinkled cheek . . . and Susan, knitting a pale blue blanket. . . .

He picked up the phone and called the hospital. "It's quiet here," he was told. "Don't come in."

Hanging up, he got to his feet. He couldn't just sit here, remembering other Christmases. He needed to do something. Go somewhere. Climb a mountain, maybe, or—

See Julia.

That was all it took: the thought of her, and he was in motion.

He got dressed, jumped in his truck, and drove to her house. Even though he knew he was being an idiot, he couldn't help himself. He had to see her.

He knocked.

Julia was laughing as she answered the door, saying something. When she saw him, her smile faded. "Oh. I thought you were going to L.A. for Christmas."

"I stayed," he said softly. "If you're busy—"

"Of course not. Come in. Would you like a drink? We have some hot buttered rum that's pretty good."

"That would be great."

She led him into the living room, then headed for the kitchen. Her gap-toothed little shadow matched her step for step. They looked almost conjoined.

A gorgeous, beautifully decorated Christmas tree dominated the corner of the room.

A rush of memories hit him.

Come on, Dan-the-man, let's put up the star for Mommy.

He turned his back on the tree and sat down on the hearth. A fire crackled behind him, warmed his back. He wouldn't be able to sit here for long, but at least he wasn't facing the tree. A coil of sleeping dogs lay at his feet.

"Well, well, well."

At the sound of Ellie's voice, he looked up. She stood behind the sofa with her hands on her hips. "It's nice to see you again, Max."

"You, too, El."

She came around the sofa and sat down beside him. "You know what I hear?"

"Trevor McAulley is drinking again?"

"Old news." She looked at him. There was no smile left. This was her cop's face. "I hear you took my sister to the movies."

"That come across the police scanner?"

"I didn't say anything at Thanksgiving, it being a holiday and all, but . . ." Ellie leaned toward him. She got so close he could feel her breath on his neck. "Hurt her and I'll cut your nuts off." She eased back, smiling again. "And you like your nuts."

"I do indeed."

"Then we understand each other. Good. I'm glad we had this little heart-to-heart."

"What if—"

Ellie frowned. "What if what?"

"Nothing."

Julia and Alice returned.

Ellie immediately stood. "I'm going to Cal's. You two be good." She picked up a box of packages and left the house.

Julia handed Max a cup.

They sat down side by side on the sofa. Neither said anything. Alice knelt at Julia's feet. She grunted at Julia and smacked the book in her lap.

"Use your words, Alice," Julia said calmly.

"Read. Girl."

"Not now. I'm talking to Dr. Max."

"*Now.*" Alice hit the book again.

"No. Later."

"Peas?"

Julia smiled gently and touched Alice's head. "In a little while, okay?"

Alice's whole body slumped in disappointment. She popped a thumb in her mouth and started turning the pages.

Julia turned to him then.

"You're amazing," he said softly.

"Thanks."

He heard the throatiness in her voice and knew how much his compliment meant to her.

She was close enough to kiss him right now, and he wanted her to.

He moved away from her slightly, as if distance could provide protection.

She noticed the movement. Of course she did.

"What happened to you, Max?"

He should have been surprised by the question, but he wasn't. "It doesn't matter."

"I think it does."

He was near enough now to see the tiny mole on her throat. Her cinnamon-scented breath fluttered against his chin. "Love," he said simply.

"Yeah," she said at last. "It'll knock the shit out of you, that's for sure. Why didn't you go home for Christmas?"

"You."

Her gaze searched his, as if looking deep for answers. She gave him a sad, knowing smile, and he wondered what it was she thought she knew. "How about a game of cards, Max?" she finally said.

"Cards?" He couldn't help laughing.

She smiled. "It's one of those things a man and a woman can do out of bed."

"No wonder I'm confused."

She laughed. "Go get the cards, Alice."

Alice looked up. "Jewlee win?"

"That's right, honey. Jewlee's gonna kick Dr. Max's ass."

· · ·

FOR THE FIRST CHRISTMAS IN RECENT MEMORY THIS HOUSE HAD BE-
come a home again. There was nothing like a child to make Christmas
a gala event. Not that Alice had understood it, of course.

Ellie and Julia had both wakened at the crack of dawn and encouraged their sleepy girl to go downstairs.

The presents had been unwrapped in the morning one at a time—
according to family tradition—and then carefully restacked under the
tree. Except for Alice's. She *loved* her packages, had carried them
around all day and hugged them to her narrow little chest. Any attempts at unwrapping them had led to hysterics.

So the toys inside remained hidden. The packages themselves were
her gifts.

In truth, Ellie hated to leave, but going to see Cal on Christmas
was one of her few traditions. She'd never missed a year. That was how
things were done in Rain Valley. Neighbors visited each other on holidays, usually staying just long enough to share a glass of wine or a mug
of hot chocolate. For all his childhood, Cal had come to the Cates'
house for Christmas, where he'd found a stocking with his name on it
tacked to the mantel and a pile of gifts under the tree. No one ever said
why it was that way, but each of them knew. For Cal, who had lived
alone with his wreck of a dad, Christmas only came to other addresses.

That tradition had remained in place for as long as Brenda and Big
Tom Cates were alive. Year after year Cal bundled up his wife and
daughters and brought them across the field and over the river for dinner. Even after Ellie's mom died and the tradition began to weaken,
Cal kept Christmas and the Cates together in his mind.

When Dad died, a subtle shift had begun. For a few years Cal and
Lisa had invited Ellie for dinner at their house. They'd tried to form a
new tradition, but nothing quite jelled. Lisa cooked the "wrong" foods
and put on the "wrong" music. It no longer felt like Christmas to Ellie;
she was an outsider somehow.

This year there had been no invitation at all. No doubt Cal assumed that she and Julia and Alice were a new Cates family and wanted to be alone. But she knew that without Lisa he would be having a rough time of it.

She packed up their presents in a pretty silver Nordstrom's bag, and headed down the driveway. On either side of her, magnificent fir and cedar trees grew tall and straight; their green tips plunged into the swollen gray belly of the sky. Although the rain had stopped, drops still fell from leaves and branches and eaves, creating a steady drip-drip-drip that matched her footsteps. There were the other sounds of the forest, too. Water rushing, needles rustling, squirrels scurrying across branches, mice running for cover. Every now and then a crow cawed or an owl hooted.

These sounds were as familiar to her as the crackling of a fire in the fireplace. Without a worry she turned onto the path and walked into the woods.

There was no way to calculate the number of times she'd crossed this bridge or walked from one house to the other. Enough so that nothing ever grew up in the path. Even in recent years, when cars and telephones were more common than walking to the neighbor's house, nothing ever grew up to hide the way.

She followed the beaten and stunted grass around the orchard and through the vegetable garden, past the old pond that used to be their childhood fishing hole. As she pushed through the cattails and heard her boots squish in the soggy ground, she heard a long-forgotten echo of their childish laughter.

There's a snake in the water, Cal—get out!

That's just an ol' twig. You need glasses.

You're the one who needs glasses—

She remembered their laughter . . . the way they'd sit on that muddy bank for hours, talking about nothing.

She followed the path back around the bend, and there was the house. For a second she expected it to look as it once had: a slant-sided shack with fake shingles; shutters hanging askew on cracked, dirty windows; a battalion of snarling pit bulls chained in the yard.

She blinked and the memory moved on. She was staring at the house Cal had built by himself, in the years after junior college and before marrying Lisa. He'd worked for a construction company back then. After a forty-five-hour workweek he'd piled on the extra hours at his own house, literally building the place around his drunken, useless father.

It was a small house that seemed to have sprouted outward, growing in a collection of sharp angles and awkward slants. Rooms had been added on as money came in, without real rhyme or reason. Cal had poured his energy into the place, trying to build for his family the home he'd never had. The end result was a quaint shingled cabin set on a patch of velvet green grass, surrounded by two-hundred-year-old evergreens.

As always, the holiday lights and decorations were world-class. Ellie always figured he went overboard to make up for all the years there hadn't even been a tree in the living room.

The porch was studded with white lights; the railings were festooned with boughs. A giant homemade wreath decorated the front door.

Ellie expected to hear music seeping through the walls, but it was oddly still. For a second she wondered if they were home. She glanced behind her and saw Cal's baby—the 1969 GTO he'd restored to perfection.

She knocked on the door. When no one answered, she tried again. Finally she heard a thunder of footsteps.

The door wrenched open and Cal's daughters stood there, huddled together, smiling brightly. Amanda, the eleven-and-a-half-year-old, looked impossibly grown-up in her low-rise jeans and studded silver belt and pink tee shirt. Her long black hair had been coiled into the haphazard braid that could only be made by a father's clumsy hands. Nine-year-old Emily was dressed in a green velvet dress that was at least a size too big, and eight-year-old Sarah—the only child to have inherited her mother's strawberry-blond hair and freckled complexion—hadn't bothered to change out of her Princess Fiona pajamas.

At the sight of Ellie, all three smiles faded.

"It's just Aunt Ellie," Amanda said.

The trio mumbled "Merry Christmas." Then Emily called out for her dad.

"Gee, thanks," Ellie said, watching them walk away.

Cal came down the stairs. He was moving slowly, as if maybe he'd just woken up. His black hair was a tangled mess. Tiny pink lines creased his left cheek. He wore a pair of Levi's so old that both knees were gone and the hemlines were foamy fringe. His Metallica tee shirt had seen better days, too.

"Ellie," he said, trying to smile. As he passed each of the girls, he hugged them, then let them go.

"You look like hell," she said when the girls were gone.

"And I was going to say how *beautiful* you are."

Ellie closed the door behind her and followed him to the living room, where a huge decorated tree took up the entire corner. She set the bag of gifts down beside it.

Cal flopped down on the sofa, put his feet on the hammered copper coffee table. His sigh was loud enough to set a tiny ornament spinning and jingling.

Ellie sat down beside him. It confused her to see Cal this way. He'd laughed his way through too many hard times to fall apart now. If Cal could become fragile, then nothing was safe. "What happened?"

He glanced behind him, made sure no little ears were nearby. "Lisa didn't come for Christmas morning . . . or dinner. She didn't send any presents. I told the girls she'd call, but I'm starting to wonder."

Ellie frowned. "Is she okay?"

"She's fine. I called her parents. She's out with her new guy."

"That doesn't sound like Lisa."

Cal looked at her. "Yes, it does."

Ellie heard the wealth of pain behind those few words. She knew it was all Cal would ever tell her about his failed marriage. "I'm sorry."

"You've been here before, right? A divorce is like a cut. It heals. That's what you always said."

The truth was, she had never been in his shoes. She'd never stayed married for more than two years, never become a love instead of a lover with her spouse. God knew she'd never had children's hearts in her grasp. "I don't think my marriages should be compared to yours, Cal. You might hurt for a long time."

"Not loving her can't be more painful than loving her was." He stared into the fire.

Ellie let him have his time. In a way, it was like the old days when they were kids. They'd sometimes sit on that bridge all day and never say more than *You got any more Bazooka?*

"How was your Christmas?" he finally said.

"Great. We made Dad's stew and Grandma Dotty's corn bread. Alice never could get the whole Santa-down-the-chimney concept. She wouldn't unwrap her presents, either. She just carried the boxes around."

"By next year she'll be a champ. Gift holidays, they learn fast. I remember the first time I took Amanda trick-or-treating."

"It was to my house."

He wanted to smile; she could tell. "Yeah. She couldn't figure out why she was dressed up like a pumpkin, but once you gave her the candy, she didn't care."

"She wore my mom's green felt hat, remember?"

Cal looked at her. In his familiar eyes she saw a longing so deep and raw she wanted to reach out for him, tell him it would be okay. "I thought you'd forgotten all that."

"How could I forget? We've been best friends for decades."

He sighed, looked over at the tree. She got the feeling that she'd disappointed him again. That was starting to happen a lot, and she had no idea why. Then again, what she knew about a truly broken heart was only slightly more than she knew about kids. It was best, probably, to change the subject, get Cal thinking about something beside his cracked family on this special day. "Julia wants to adopt Alice. She thinks the kid needs permanence."

"Good idea. How do you do it?"

"We start with a Motion to Terminate Parental Rights. If no one comes forward to claim her in the publication period, Julia's in the clear."

It was a moment before Cal said, "What if her folks finally do come forward? And they never knew she'd been found?"

Ellie and Julia had avoided that question like the plague. It was the one that could ruin it all. "That would be bad."

"Washington bends over backward for biological parents. Even if they're scum."

"Yeah," Ellie said. "I know."

"So we go from hoping they show up to hoping they don't."

"Right." Ellie paused, looked at him. They fell silent again. "It wasn't quite Christmas without you."

"Yeah," he said with a faded smile. "Things change."

Ellie didn't want to walk down that road with him. Truthfully, she was afraid that if she did, she'd start thinking about her own loneliness. Being with Cal did that to her sometimes, reminded her of how much she'd missed out on in life. She got up and went into the kitchen. She poured two tequila straight shots and set them on a tray, alongside a shaker of salt. In the living room, she set the tray down on the coffee table, pushing his feet aside.

"What the—straight shots? On Christmas day?"

"Sometimes a mood changes on its own." Ellie shrugged. "Sometimes it needs a shove." She plopped down beside him. "Bottoms up."

"What's the salt for?"

"Decoration." She clanked her glass against his and drank up. "Here's to a better year coming up."

"Amen to that." Cal downed the drink and put his shot glass on the coffee table. When he turned to her again, he seemed to be *studying* her, looking for something hidden. "You've been in love a lot."

She laughed. "And out of it a lot."

"How do you . . . keep believing in it? How do you tell someone you love them?"

She felt her smile shake. "Saying it is easy, Cal. Meaning it is practically impossible. I pity the poor guy who falls for me." She wanted to smile again but couldn't. This whole conversation was depressing her. The way Cal was looking at her made it all worse. "Enough sadness. This is a holiday."

She cleared the alcoholic evidence away and went over to the stereo. There, she put a CD in the player and turned the volume on high enough to bring the girls out of the family room, where they'd probably been watching another Hilary Duff movie.

"What's going on?" Amanda asked, tugging on her askew, falling-out braid. The girls stood close together. All of them had sad eyes on this most magical of days.

"First off, you have presents to open."

That made them smile a little, but not all the way.

"Then I'm taking you bowling."

Amanda made a very grown-up face. "We don't bowl. Mom says it's for trailer trash."

Ellie looked at Cal. "Are you telling me they don't know about secret bowling?"

Sarah took a step forward. "What'th thee-cret bowling?"

Ellie bent down. "It's bowling after hours, all by yourself, with the music blaring and all the junk food you can eat."

"Mom would never agree to this," Amanda said.

"I'll have you know," Ellie said, "that your dad and I used to work at the Big Bowl. And that's why you're the only kids in Rain Valley who get to know about secret bowling. Now, go get dressed."

Sarah tugged on Ellie's sleeve, said in a stage whisper, "C'n I be Princeth Fiona?"

"Absolutely," Ellie said. "In secret bowling, you can wear whatever you want."

Amanda looked up. "Can I wear makeup?"

Before Cal could answer, Ellie said, "Sure."

In a flurry of laughter, the girls ran up the stairs.

Cal looked at Ellie. "We haven't snuck into the Big Bowl in twenty-five years."

"I'll call Wayne and let him know. He still keeps the keys in the gnome's hat. We can leave fifty bucks in the register."

"Thanks, El."

She smiled. "Just remember this the next time I get divorced. Tequila and midnight bowling."

"Is that the magic potion?"

Her smile faded as she looked at him. "No. But sometimes it's all there is."

TWENTY-ONE

I T WAS NEARING THE END OF JANUARY, THAT MONTH WHEN THE skies were steely and tempers were lost as easily as car keys. All across town, children stood at windows, peering out at rainy backyards; their mothers spent extra hours wiping fingerprints from the glass.

Inside the Cates' house, the only light came from artificial bulbs, and the pattern of rain falling from the eaves sounded like a quickened heartbeat that wouldn't calm down.

It made Ellie uneasy.

No, it wasn't the weather that had her so unnerved. It was the company.

The woman from the Department of Social and Health Services sat stiffly erect on the sofa, as if she were terrified by the thought of an airborne dog hair finding a perch on her gray wool pants.

Julia, who looked composed and comfortable in winter white, sat beside the woman. "May I answer any other questions for you, Ms. Wharton?"

The woman's smile was as nervous as the rest of her; there and gone. All Ellie really saw was a flash of crooked teeth. "Call me Helen. And I do have some final questions."

Julia gave her the camera-ready smile. "Fire away."

Helen put down her pen and looked across the room to where Alice played by herself. She had not made eye contact with Helen once. In fact, upon introduction to the woman, she'd howled and run away. After cowering behind a tiny potted ficus tree for almost an hour, she'd finally emerged from her hiding place, only to begin eating the flower arrangement. "Obviously, this environment is perfectly acceptable. Your home study was approved for temporary foster care of . . . the minor child, and I see no deterioration that would warrant a reversal of our recommendation. As you've repeatedly reminded us, the child is flourishing in your care. My concern, actually, is for you, Dr. Cates. May I be frank?"

"I'd love to hear what you have to say," Julia said.

"Obviously she's a profoundly damaged child. Perhaps you're correct and she's not autistic or otherwise mentally challenged, but she clearly has issues. I doubt she'll ever be normal. All too often, we find that parents go into adoption of special needs children with big hearts and high hopes, only to realize that they've taken on too much. The state has some wonderful facilities for kids like . . . her."

"There are no kids like her," Julia said. "She's been uniquely harmed, I think, and there's no way to judge her future. As you know, I'm more than qualified to treat her as a patient, and I'm entirely ready to love her as a parent. What could be a better situation for her?"

Helen's smile came late and seemed as thin as nonfat milk. "She's a lucky young girl that you found her." She shot a glance at Alice, who was now standing at the window, "talking" to a squirrel. The social worker stood up and offered Julia her hand. "I see no reason to pretend anyone needs to review this. I'll certainly recommend placement with you from a home study perspective."

"Thank you."

After the social worker left, Julia's smile finally slipped.

Alice ran to her, jumped into her arms. "Scared," she whispered.

"I know, honey." Julia held her tightly, stroked her hair. "You don't like people who wear glasses. And she had an awful lot of shiny jewelry, didn't she? Still, you should have smiled at her."

"Smelly lady."

Ellie laughed. "I have to agree with the kid on that one." She headed for the coatrack by the front door and grabbed her jacket. "I'll call John and tell him you finished the home study. He can get started on the hearing date and start on the Summons for Termination of Parental Rights."

Still holding Alice, Julia moved toward her. "Once a week for three weeks, in all the area newspapers, huh? That's how we announce it to the world."

"They have sixty days from the first publication to file a Notice of Appearance. After that, you're home free."

They.

Alice's biological family.

Though they didn't speak of it, Julia and Ellie both knew that Alice wasn't like other kids who'd been lost or abandoned. Someone, somewhere, could be dreaming of her, remembering her, but not looking anymore. A parent could show up anytime, even years from now, and lay a truer claim to the child's heart than Julia had.

Ellie knew her sister had thought about that, agonized over it, in fact, and decided that she'd take the risk. It was better, Julia thought, to give Alice a home now and worry about the future, than to let the child spend a lifetime in limbo, waiting for a biological parent who might never arrive.

"Well, it's off to work for me," Ellie said. " 'Bye, Alice."

Alice hugged Ellie. " 'Bye, Lellie."

Ellie hugged her back. "Cal said it's a half day today at the girls' school. He'll bring Sarah by for a while after lunch."

"Tell him thanks. Maybe Alice will talk to Sarah this time." She nuzzled Alice's neck. "Right, little girl?"

Alice's answer was a high-pitched giggle.

Ellie left the house and went out to her cruiser. With a quick honk—Alice loved that noise—she was off.

In the weeks since Christmas and New Year's, Rain Valley had settled back into its usual midwinter routine. More often than not, the downtown streets were empty of both cars and people. The taverns filled up earlier and stayed busy longer. Ellie and Earl and Mel took turns waiting just off the highway for drivers who thought it was okay to pound beers and then operate a vehicle. Weekend matinees at the theater were jammed to the rafters with kids, and it was impossible to get a lane or a parking stall at the bowling alley.

News of the Flying Wolf Girl had all but faded from the newspapers. Even Mort had better things to write about these days, like the rumblings at Mount St. Helens and the court-sanctioned Makah tribe whale hunt.

Days at the station slid back into their comforting routine. Calm had returned to Rain Valley, and those who were charged with keeping that peace were glad. Cal had more time again to read his comics and draw his drawings, since the phone rarely rang. Peanut scheduled everyone according to their family needs and paid their paychecks on time.

In short, life was good.

Now, Ellie drove through the Ancient Grounds coffee stand, got a Grande Mocha Latte, then continued on to the station. She pulled into her parking stall behind the station and went in the back door. She was in the lunchroom, checking out what was in the fridge, when Peanut bustled into the room and slammed the door shut behind her.

"Ellen!" she said in the stage whisper she reserved for Big Gossip.

Ellie took a sip of her coffee and glanced at the clock. Eleven-thirty was pretty early for big news. "Let me guess: the wrong person was voted off *Survivor*."

Peanut smacked her. "*Survivor*'s over."

Ellie shut the fridge. "Okay, what's the skinny, big girl?"

"It's important that you keep your wits about you. Cal and I are worried."

"That I'm witless? How comforting."

"You *know* how stupid you get around certain men."

"I'm not admitting that. However, the only good-looking man in town is hot for my sister."

"Not anymore."

"Max isn't into Jules anymore?"

Peanut hit her in the shoulder. "Pay attention."

Ellie frowned. "What in the hell are you babbling about?"

"There's a guy waiting for you out front."

"So? Why the full panic?"

"He's *gorgeous*. And he won't talk to anyone but you."

"No kidding?"

"You should see the way you're smiling. This is exactly what I was afraid of."

Ellie eased out of the lunchroom and peered down the hallway. From here all she could see was a man—with his back to her—sitting in the chair opposite her desk. He was dressed all in black. "Who is it?"

"He wouldn't give his name. Won't take off his sunglasses, either." She snorted. "Must be from California."

Ellie ducked back into the lunchroom and grabbed her purse. Five minutes in the bathroom and she'd touched up her makeup and brushed her teeth. Back in the lunchroom, she turned to Peanut. "How do I look?"

"This is *so* not good. You're going to go into full slut mode now."

"Bite me. I haven't had a date in months." Ellie smoothed the wrinkles from her uniform, adjusted the three gold stars on her collar, and walked out into the main room of the station house. Peanut hurried along behind her.

Cal looked up at her approach. He immediately noticed her makeup then glanced at the man across from him and shook his head. "Big surprise," he muttered.

She kept moving. "Hello. I'm Chief Barton," she said, rounding her desk. "I understand—"

He turned to her.

Ellie forgot what she'd been about to say. All she saw were chiseled cheekbones, full lips, and a mass of unruly black hair. He took off his sunglasses and revealed a pair of electric blue eyes.

Holy Mother of God.

Ellie sat down without shaking his hand.

"I've come a long way to see you," he said in a worn, gravelly voice.

An accent. Just a hint of one, but enough. She couldn't place it. Australian, maybe. Or Cajun. She *loved* a man with an accent.

"I'm George Azelle." He reached into his pocket and pulled out a folded piece of paper, which he set on her desk.

The name registered.

"I see you remember me." He leaned forward, pushing the paper closer to her. "Don't worry about the way you're looking at me. I've grown used to it. I'm here about her."

"Her?"

He unfolded the paper he'd pushed forward. It was a picture of Alice. "I'm her father."

"ALICE, HOW MANY TIMES ARE WE GOING TO HAVE THIS SAME discussion?" Julia couldn't help laughing at her own comment. She and Alice did many things together these days. None of them could accurately be characterized as a discussion. "Put your shoes on."

"No."

Julia went to the window and pointed outside. "It's raining."

Alice collapsed to a sit on the floor. "No."

"We're going to the diner. Remember the diner? We were there last week. Yummy pie. Put your shoes on."

"No. Smelly shoes."

Julia threw up her hands in dramatic despair. "All right, then. You stay here with Jake and Elwood. I'll bring you home some pie." She went into the kitchen. With slow, exaggerated movements she gathered her keys and purse, then put on her coat. She was halfway to the door when she heard Alice stand up.

"Girl go?"

Julia didn't let herself smile as she turned around. Alice stood there, her little face scrunched in a scowl that was equal parts worry and anger. Her overalls were splattered with paint from their last art project. Julia meant to be firm, to say *I'm sorry, you can't go without shoes—not to a restaurant* and pretend to go on her way while Alice hurriedly put on her shoes. That was what she would have done with an ordinary stubborn child.

Instead, Julia went to her and knelt down so that they were eye-to-eye. "Remember our talk about rules?"

"Good girl. Bad girl."

Julia winced at the characterization, but rules of behavior were a complex idea. They took years to process and understand; it was one of the hallmarks of socialization. Societies only existed in the presence of rules that governed people's behavior. "Some places make little girls wear shoes."

"Girl no like."

"I know, honey. How 'bout this: no shoes in the car. You put them on in town and take them off when we leave. Okay?"

Alice frowned in thought. "No socks."

"Okay."

Alice dutifully crossed the room and got her shoes out of the box by the front door. Without bothering with a coat, she went outside.

As she stepped onto the porch, a cloud crossed the sky overhead, casting the yard in shadow. The drizzling rain turned to tiny flakes of snow. They kissed Alice's dark head and upturned face, immediately turning to droplets of freezing water.

"Look, Jewlee! Prittee."

It was snowing and Alice was barefooted. *Perfect.*

Julia grabbed Alice's coat and scooped the girl into her arms, carrying her to the car. She was halfway there when she heard the phone ring.

"That's probably Aunt Ellie, telling us to watch the snow." She strapped Alice into the car seat.

"Icky. Tight. Bad," Alice said, running through her words for displeasure. "Smelly."

"It does not smell and it keeps you safe."

That shut Alice up.

Julia put a CD in the player and drove away.

Alice listened to the *Pete's Dragon* soundtrack seven times without pausing. Her favorite song was "Candle on the Water." Every time it ended, she cried out "Again!" until Julia complied.

Finally, they pulled into a spot in front of the Rain Drop and parked.

The song snapped off.

"Again?"

"No, Alice. Not now." Julia leaned sideways and tried to put Alice's clammy feet into her boots. It was like trying to put surgical gloves on wet hands. "Next time, I'm going to the mat for socks."

She got out of the car and came around to Alice's side. Opening the door, she smiled. "You ready?"

Fear flashed through Alice's eyes, but she nodded.

"You're such a brave girl." Julia helped Alice out of the seat.

Alice moved slowly toward the restaurant, staring down at her feet.

"Don't be afraid, Alice. I'm right here. I won't let go."

Alice clung so tightly it hurt, but didn't say a word.

Julia opened the diner's door. A bell tinkled overhead. At the sound, Alice shrieked and threw herself at Julia.

She bent down to hug the girl, held her tightly.

The Grimm sisters were at the cash register, standing shoulder-to-shoulder. They'd obviously turned in unison at the noise, for now they were staring at Alice. Rosie Chicowski was behind them, tucking a pencil in her pink, beehived hair. To the left, an old logger sat alone in a booth.

Everyone was staring at Julia and Alice.

They should have come an hour ago, between the breakfast and lunch crowds. That was what she'd done last week, and they'd had the place to themselves. Slowly, she stood back up.

The Grimm sisters advanced, three abreast; Julia had a sudden thought about the horsemen of the Apocalypse. These days, apparently, Death rode in a battered urn in an old woman's arms.

They stared at Julia, then at Alice.

Julia stared back.

Alice snorted nervously, tugged on Julia's hand.

Violet reached into her purse and pulled out a bright purple plastic coin purse. "Here you go. My granddaughter loves these."

Alice's eyes lit up at the gift. She touched it reverently, took it in her small hand, and stroked her cheek with it. After a moment she blinked up at Violet and said, "Ank 'ou."

The three old women gasped and looked at one another. Finally they looked at Julia. "You saved her," Daisy said in a stiff voice, obviously bothered by the emotion behind the words.

"Your mom would be so proud," Violet said, nodding to her sisters for confirmation. They bobbed their heads in unison.

Julia smiled. "Thank you. I couldn't have done it without all of you. The town really protected us."

"You're one of us," Daisy said simply.

As one, the trio turned and left the diner.

Tightening her hold on Alice's hand, Julia led her to a booth in the corner. There, they ordered grilled cheese sandwiches, fries, and milk shakes from Rosie. The food hadn't been served yet when the bell over the door tinkled again.

Alice glanced up and said, "Max," matter-of-factly.

He didn't see them until he'd picked up his lunch order and turned for the door.

When he looked at her, Julia's heart did a little flip.

"Hey," he said.

She smiled up at him. "No date for lunch, Doctor?"

"Not yet."

"Then perhaps you should join us."

He looked down at Alice. "May I sit next to you?"

Her little face scrunched in thought. "No hurt Jewlee?"

Max looked surprised by that. "I wouldn't dream of it." When he saw Alice's confusion, he said softly, "No hurt Julia."

Alice finally scooted sideways to make room for him.

Max sat down across from Julia. He'd barely made contact with the vinyl seat when Rosie swooped in beside him. She was grinning from ear to ear. "It's like watching the moon landing. I *knew* it was true about you two." She set out a place setting in front of him.

"Alice is my patient," Max said evenly.

Rosie winked one heavily made-up, false-lashed eye. " 'Course she is."

When she was gone, Max said, "Before I finish my sandwich, everyone in town will know about this. Every patient I see for a week will ask about you."

A few minutes later Rosie showed up with their lunches.

"Ank 'ou," Alice said, grinning up at the waitress.

Rosie returned to the kitchen.

Julia was about to tell Alice to eat one french fry at a time when she realized that Max was staring at her.

She met his gaze and saw fear in his blue eyes. He was afraid of her, of *them*. It was a fear she understood; it had shaped much of her life. Passion was a dangerous thing, and love even more so. More often than not, it was love that had devastated her patients—either its excess or its lack. But Alice had taught her a thing or two about love . . . and courage.

"What?" he said, unsmiling.

Julia felt something new, a kind of opening wonder. She wasn't afraid anymore.

"Come here." She said it softly.

Frowning, he leaned toward her.

She kissed him. For a heartbeat of time, he resisted. Then he gave in.

Alice giggled. "Kisses."

When Max drew back, he was pale.

Julia laughed. "Might as well give the gossips something to talk about."

After that, they went back to their lunches as if it hadn't happened. Later, as they stood at the front door putting their coats on, Julia dared to touch his arm. She'd already branded him publicly with her mouth; what was a touch on the arm after that?

"I'm taking Alice to the game farm in Sequim. Would you like to join us?"

He paused just long enough to look at his watch, then said, "I'll follow you."

Julia bustled Alice out of the restaurant and back into the car. By the time they reached the entrance to the Game Farm, it was snowing in earnest. Big, fluffy white flakes fell from the sky. A few had begun to stick; a thin layer of white had formed on the fence line and on the grass.

Julia pulled up to the small wooden house where the farm's owner lived. A pair of black bear cubs sat on the porch, chewing on huge sticks of wood.

"You need to put on your boots, your gloves, and your coat," Julia said.

"No."

"Stay in the car, then." Julia bundled up and got out of the car. She joined Max, who stood by his own car. Snow peppered them, landed like bits of fire on her nose and cheeks.

"What are we waiting for?" he asked.

"You'll see."

The car door opened. Alice climbed out. She was dressed for the weather, except that her boots were on the wrong feet.

Just then Floyd came out of the house, wearing a huge arctic parka. Stepping past the playing bear cubs, he walked down the porch steps and across the snowy yard. "Hello, Dr. Cates. Dr. Cerrasin." At Alice, he bent down. "And you must be Alice. I know a friend of yours."

Alice hid behind Julia.

"It's okay, honey. This is your surprise."

Alice looked up. "Prize?"

"Follow me," Floyd said.

They hadn't taken more than three steps when the howling started.

Alice looked up at Julia, who nodded.

Alice ran toward the sound. It was sad and soulful, that cry; it floated on the icy air. Alice answered in her own howl.

They came together at the chain-link fence, the little girl in the black woolen coat and the oversized boots on the wrong feet and the wolf that was now almost half its full-grown size.

Floyd went to the gate. Alice was beside him in an instant, jumping up and down.

"Open. Play. Girl."

He worked the lock. When it clicked, he turned to Julia. "Are you sure it's safe?"

"I'm sure."

He eased the door open.

Alice slipped into the pen. She and the wolf rolled around together, playing like littermates in the snow. Every time he licked her cheek, Alice giggled.

Floyd shut the gate again. He stood there, watching them play. "This is the first time he's stopped howling since I got him."

"She missed him, too," Julia said.

"What do you suppose—"

"I don't know, Floyd."

They fell silent again, watching the girl and wolf roll around in the snow.

"It's amazing what you've done with her," Max said to Julia.

She smiled. "Kids are resilient."

"Not always." His answer was so quiet she almost missed it.

She was about to ask him what he meant, but before she'd formed the question, she heard sirens. "Do you hear that?"

He nodded.

The sound was far off at first, then it drew closer.

Closer.

When the first flashing lights appeared, cutting through the hazy snowfall, Floyd jumped into action. He grabbed Alice's coat and pulled her out of the pen, then slammed the gate shut.

Alice dropped to her knees and howled miserably.

The police cruiser drove into the yard and parked. The lights remained on, flashing in staccato bursts of color. Ellie walked toward them in the surreal light. "He's come for her," she said without preamble.

"Who?" Julia asked, but when Ellie glanced at Alice, Julia knew.

"Alice's father."

MAX CARRIED ALICE INTO THE HOUSE. SHE WEIGHED ALMOST NOTHING.

He tried not to think about how natural this felt, carrying a child, but some memories were imprinted too deeply to ever erase, and some movements felt as natural as breathing.

He tried to set her down on the sofa so he could build a fire.

But she wouldn't free him, wouldn't uncoil her arms from around his neck, and all the while, as he carried her around the house and built the fire, she was howling in a quiet way that broke his heart.

Finally, he sat down on the couch and drew her onto his lap. Her eyes were tightly shut; her cheeks were still pink with cold. The sound she made—more whimper now than howl—was the physical embodiment of loss. Too much feeling and too few words.

Look away, he told himself. *Put on a movie or turn up the music.*

He leaned back and closed his eyes. He knew instantly it was a mistake. In his mind he heard a child crying—great big crocodile tears. *My fish isn't swimming anymore, Daddy. Make him all better.*

Max tightened his hold on Alice. "It's okay, little one. Let it out. That's a good thing, actually."

At the sound of his voice, she drew in a sharp breath and looked up at him. It made him realize that it was the first time he'd spoken since they left the game farm. "Julia had to go to the police station with Ellie. They'll be back soon."

She blinked up at him through eyes that were surprisingly dry. He found himself wondering if she knew how to cry. The very idea of it—that she couldn't release her pain that way—wounded him.

"No Jewlee leave Girl?"

"No. She'll be back."

"Home Girl?"

"Yes." He tucked a straggly, still damp lock of hair behind her tiny ear.

"Wolf?" Her mouth trembled. The question was so big and complex; yet she asked it all with that one word.

"The wolf is okay, too."

She shook her head, and suddenly she appeared too old for her face, too knowing. "No. Trap. Bad."

"He needs to be free," Max said, understanding her easily.

"Like birds."

"You know about trapped, don't you?" He stared down into her small, heart-shaped face. As much as he wanted to look away—needed to look away—he couldn't. She made him remember too many moments that had passed. The surprising thing was, they were *good* memories, some of them. From a time when he'd been able to stand still . . . a time when holding a child had made him laugh instead of cry.

"Read Girl?" She pointed to a book on the coffee table. It was already open to a page.

He picked it up.

She immediately resettled herself so that she was positioned closely beside him.

He looped one arm around her and opened the book between them.

She pointed to the top of the page, very certain where she'd left off.

He began to read: "'Real isn't how you are made,' said the skin horse. 'It's a thing that happens to you. When a child loves you for a long, long time, not just to play with, but REALLY loves you, then you become Real.'"

Read to me, Daddy.

He felt Alice's hand on his cheek, comforting him. Only then did he realize that he was crying.

"Ouch," she said.

He looked down at her, trying to remember the last time he'd let himself cry.

"All better?"

He tried to smile. "All better."

Smiling at that, she snuggled up against him. He closed the book and started telling her another story, one he'd spent a long time trying to forget, but some words stayed with you. It felt good, saying it all to someone, even if, by the time he got to the sad part, the part that made him want to cry again, she was fast asleep.

TWENTY-TWO

T HE DNA IS CONCLUSIVE?" JULIA ASKED. IN THE QUIET OF THE
car her voice sounded louder than she would have liked.
Because of the snow and the falling night, it felt as if they
were cocooned in some strange spaceship.

"I'm no expert," Ellie said, "but the lab report indicated certainty.
And he knew about the birthmark. I have a call into the FBI. We'll
know more in the morning. But . . ."

"What's her real name?"

"Brittany."

"Brittany." Julia tested out the name, trying to make a match in her
mind. She thought that if she focused on little things like that—tasks—
she wouldn't think of the big things. Alice—Brittany—wasn't her
daughter; she never had been. All along, the A answer had been this
moment—Alice's reunification with her real family. It didn't matter
that she had made a fatal mistake and fallen in love with the child.
What mattered was Alice. That was the ledge Julia clung to. "Why did
it take him so long to get here?"

Ellie pulled into the parking slot marked CHIEF OF POLICE and parked.

Julia stared at the sign. The beam of the headlights seemed to set it aglow. At the same time, the falling snow obscured it. Everything about this night was conflicted, it seemed. "I understand you have a job to do, El. We both do. We let ourselves get too involved with her. I get it. But I'm a professional. Believe me when I tell you that I never lost sight of the risk I was taking, and I understand what's best for Alice."

"That's a bunch of shit, but I know why you're saying it." Ellie turned to her. In the weird mixture of light and darkness, her face seemed older and full of shadows. "There's a problem."

"Tell me."

"Do you know who George Azelle is?"

Julia frowned. It took her a moment to remember. "Oh, yeah. The guy who murdered his wife and baby daughter? Sure. He—"

"He's her father."

"No." She shook her head. There must be some mistake. The Azelle case had been a big deal. The millionaire murderer, they'd called him, referring to the dot-com empire he'd built. A circus of media attention had followed every confusing aspect of the process. The only certainty in the whole proceeding had been his guilt. "But he was convicted. He went to prison. How—"

"I'm not the one with the answers. He is."

Julia couldn't seem to move.

Ellie touched her arm. "I can go in alone, tell him I couldn't find you."

"No."

As Julia stepped out into the freezing night, she tried not to panic. Losing Alice to a loving family was something she would have made herself deal with. George Azelle was something else. "Not to a murderer," she muttered more than once on the long walk across the yard and up the stairs. All the way there, she tried to remember what facts she could about the trial. Mostly, she recalled that the jury had found him guilty.

Cotton-ball snowflakes drifted lazily from the night sky, glowing in the pyramids of light from streetlamps and windows.

Inside the station it was quiet.

Julia blinked, letting her eyes adjust slowly to the light. The main room seemed larger than usual, but that was because she'd usually seen it during press conferences. Cal was at his desk, headphones on, and Peanut stood beside him. Both looked at Julia through worried eyes.

Ellie's desk was empty. So was the chair in front of it.

"He's in my office," Ellie said.

"Oh."

Ellie looked at Peanut, then at Cal. "You two stay out here."

Peanut's eyes filled with tears. "We don't want to hear it."

Cal nodded and reached for Peanut's hand.

Ellie led Julia through the main room, past the twin jail cells with their open doors and empty bunks, to an open door. On it was a brass plaque that read: CHIEF.

Ellie went in first. Almost immediately there were voices; hers a little too fast, his gravelly and low.

Julia took a deep breath and followed her sister into the office.

There were things to notice, of course—bookcases and a desk, and family photos—but all Julia saw was George Azelle.

She might not have recognized him on the street or in a crowd, but she remembered him now. Tall, dark, and deadly. That was how the press had characterized him, and it was easy to see why. He stood well over six feet, with broad shoulders and narrow hips. His handsome face was all sharp angles and deep hollows and bruiselike shadows; the kind of face that darkened easily into anger. Black hair, threaded with gray, hung almost to his shoulders. His was the kind of face that launched a woman's dreams, although he looked worn.

"You're the doctor," he said. There was an accent in that voice, an elongation of syllables that made her think of Louisiana and bayous, of hot, decadent places and conversations that went on long into the night. "I want to thank you for everything you've done for my little girl. How is she?"

Julia moved forward quickly, almost jerkily, and held out her hand. His handshake was firm, maybe even a little more than that.

"And you're the murderer," she said, drawing her hand back. She had a sudden urge to wash the feel of him away. "A murder-one conviction, if I remember correctly."

His smile faded. He reached into his back pocket, pulled out an envelope, and tossed it on Ellie's desk. "To make an extremely long story short, the Court of Appeals reversed the trial court's denial of a Motion to Dismiss. It was a sufficiency of evidence thing. The Supreme Court agreed. I was released last week."

"On a technicality."

"If you consider innocence a technicality. I came home one day and my family was gone." His voice cracked. "I never knew what happened to them. The cops decided I was a murderer and that was it. They ignored any other evidence."

Julia had no answer to that. She tried desperately not to *feel* all this, but panic was stalking her. "She can't survive without me."

"Look, Doc, I've been locked up for years. I have a big house on Lake Washington and enough money to hire the best care for her, so let's not beat around the bush. I need to show the world she's alive, so I want her. *Now.*"

She stared at him, actually shocked by that. "If you think I'm going to just hand Alice over to a murderer, you're crazy."

"Who the hell is Alice?"

"That's what we named her. We didn't know who she was."

"Well, you know now. She's my daughter and I've come to take her home."

"You're kidding, right? For all I know, you were behind the whole thing. You wouldn't be the first man to sacrifice a child to get rid of a wife."

She saw a flash of something in his eyes. He closed the small distance between them. "I know who you are, too, Doc. I'm not the only one here with a shady past, am I? Do you really want a public fight?"

"Anywhere," she said, holding her ground. "You don't scare me."

He towered over her, whispered, "Tell Brit I'm on my way."

"I won't let you have her."

His breath was warm and soft against her temple. "We both know you can't stop me. Washington courts are pro-reunification of the family. See you in court."

As soon as he was gone, Julia sank onto a cold, hard chair. Her whole body was trembling. George Azelle was right; the Washington State courts valued reunification of the family over almost everything else.

"Do you want to talk about it?" Ellie said.

"Talking won't help."

Thinking will.

She took a deep breath. "I need information on his case."

"He gave me this." Ellie pushed a stack of papers across the desk.

Julia took the papers and tried to read. Her hands were trembling so badly that the letters shimmied on the white pages.

"Jules—"

"Give me a minute," Julia said, hearing the desperate edge in her voice. It was taking every scrap of self-control she had to not start screaming or crying, and looking into her sister's sad eyes or hearing comforting words might push her into despair. "Please."

She focused on the documents. They represented the bare bones of the procedural history. The original Motion to Dismiss the case, made by Azelle's attorney at the close of the state's case in chief; the denial of that motion; the Appellate Court's reversal and the State Supreme Court's agreement with the reversal and dismissal. Of all of them, the one that mattered most to Julia was the original certification for determination of probable cause, which outlined the facts of the state's case.

On April 13, 2002, at approximately 9:30 in the morning, George Azelle placed a call to the King County Police Department to report that his wife, Zoë Azelle, and his two-

and-a-half-year-old daughter, Brittany, were missing and had been missing for more than twenty-four hours. The Seattle Police Department responded immediately, sending officers to the Azelle residence at 16402 Lakeside Drive on Mercer Island. A countywide, then statewide search ensued. Community groups responded to the call and organized extensive search parties and midnight vigils.

Investigations conducted throughout this period revealed that Mrs. Azelle was having an affair at the time of her disappearance and had requested a divorce. Azelle was also engaged in an affair with his personal assistant, Corinn Johns.

Pursuant to their investigation, police learned the following facts:

On or about November 2001, police responded to a domestic disturbance call at the Azelle home. Officers observed bruising on Mrs. Azelle and arrested Mr. Azelle. This complaint was dismissed when Mrs. Azelle refused to testify against her husband.

On the evening of April 11, 2002, neighbor Stanley Seaman reported another disturbance at the Azelle home, although he made no call to police. He stated to his wife that the Azelles were "at it again." Seaman noted the time of the fight as 11:15 P.M.

At almost noon on Sunday, April 12, 2002, neighbor Stanley Seaman witnessed Azelle loading a large trunk and a smaller "sacklike" canvas duffel bag onto his seaplane.

Azelle asserts that he took off from Lake Washington in his seaplane, with no passengers, on or about one o'clock on April 12. According to family witness testimony, he arrived at his sister's home on Shaw Island nearly two hours later. Experts confirmed to police that the ordinary flight time for that distance would be slightly less than an hour. Azelle returned to his Lake Washington residence at 7:00 that same evening.

A local flower delivery man, Mark Ulio, arrived at the Azelle

home at 4:45 on Sunday to deliver flowers which had been ordered by Azelle, via phone, at one o'clock that day. At the time
of their delivery, no one answered at the Azelle house. Ulio reported seeing a Caucasian male in his mid-thirties wearing a yellow rain slicker and a Batman baseball cap getting into a white
van that was parked across the street from the Azelle residence.

On Monday morning, Azelle called several friends and
family members to ask if they knew where his wife and daughter were. He told several witnesses that Zoë Azelle had "run off
again." At 10:30 A.M., when Brittany did not show up at day
care and Zoë missed a meeting with her therapist, Azelle called
police and reported them missing.

Upon identifying Azelle as a suspect, police arrived at his
home with a search warrant. On a rug in the living room, they
found traces of blood. Additionally, hair samples found in the
couple's bedroom—determined to be Mrs. Azelle's—had the
roots attached, indicating a struggle. A lamp on the dresser had
a cracked base.

Throughout the search period, officers repeatedly noted
that George Azelle was either inexplicably missing during the
searches or seemingly unconcerned about his family's disappearance. Such behavior led police to consider Azelle a
suspect.

Based on the information obtained, Sergeant Gerald
Reeves placed Azelle under arrest for the murder of his wife
and daughter and advised him of his Miranda rights. State re-
quests that no bail be granted in this case. This was a brutal
and carefully planned and executed crime. Azelle's consider-
able personal wealth, in addition to his pilot's license, makes
him a serious flight risk.

Under penalty of perjury, under the laws of the State of
Washington, I certify that the foregoing is true and correct.

It was signed by the detective and dated.

When she finished, she sighed and set the papers back on the desk. Footsteps thundered in the hallway.

Peanut and Cal fought to get through the door. Peanut was first. "Well?"

"He's a scum," Julia said. "An adulterer and almost certainly a wife beater. But according to the courts, he's not a murderer. He can't be re-tried for it, either. Double jeopardy." She looked at the worried faces around her. "He's also her father. The DNA is conclusive on that: she's Brittany Azelle. Washington State courts—"

"I don't give a shit about state law," Peanut said, looking down at Julia. "What do we do to protect her?"

"We need a plan," Cal said.

"I'd stand in front of a bus for her," Julia said, and at that, she felt herself go calm.

The trembling in her hands stopped.

I'd stand in front of a bus for her.

It was true.

"Time to step into traffic," she said, and though she couldn't force a smile, couldn't in fact imagine ever smiling again, she was okay. She wouldn't think about *what if*; that would destroy her. She'd think only about Alice and how to protect her.

"Hire a detective," she said to Ellie. "Go through Azelle's records back to second grade. Somewhere, sometime, this son of a bitch hit someone or sold drugs or drove drunk. Find it. We don't have to prove he's a murderer, just an unfit parent."

IT WAS JUST PAST FIVE O'CLOCK WHEN THEY GOT HOME, BUT IT FELT LIKE the middle of the night. Clouds darkened the sky. An inch of snow frosted everything—the lawn, the roof, the porch railing. The house seemed to glow amidst all that whiteness.

Ellie parked close to the house. Neither of them made a move to get out of the car.

"I'm not going to tell her," Julia finally said, staring straight ahead.

Ellie sighed. "How will you *ever* tell her? She hates it when you leave to make breakfast."

Julia couldn't go there. Not to the imagining it place.

No leave Girl, Jewlee.

She opened the car door and stepped out into the falling snow, barely feeling the cold.

She walked up the steps, going from snow to wet wood, and opened the front door. The light and warmth hit her first. Then she saw Alice, curled up in Max's lap. At Julia's entrance, she looked up and grinned.

"Jewlee!" she squealed, sliding out of Max's arms and running for Julia.

She picked the little girl up, held her tightly. "Hey, little one." She tried to smile. Hopefully it didn't look as brittle as it felt.

Alice frowned up at her. "Sad?"

"Happy to be home," Julia said.

Relief shone in Alice's eyes. She hugged Julia again and kissed her neck.

Ellie came up behind them and smoothed Alice's hair. "Hey girlie-girl."

"Hi Lellie," she said in a muffled, happy voice.

Max was standing now. Firelight backlit him; the brightness made his face appear shadowed. "Julia?" he said. There was no mistaking the concern in his voice.

It almost undid her. She sidestepped his touch, trying to make it look like an accident, but she saw that he wasn't fooled. Of course he wasn't. She didn't know much about Max, but she knew this: he recognized heartache, understood its taste and feel and texture. And he saw it now on her face. There was no way for her to hide it, not with Alice in her arms and George Azelle's envelope in her coat pocket.

If Max touched her now, she'd cry, and she didn't want that. God knew, she would need strength for what was to come.

"He wants her back."

The sad understanding in Max's eyes was almost more than she could bear. He moved slowly toward her. For a second she thought he was going to kiss her. Instead he said, "I'll wait up for you."

"But—"

"It doesn't matter when. Come over when you can. You'll need me."

She couldn't deny that.

"I'll wait up for you," he said again; this time he didn't wait for a response. He said good-bye to each of them and left.

Silence swept in behind him.

"Max bye-bye," Alice said. "No Jewlee leave?"

Julia swallowed hard, feeling the sting of tears. She clung fiercely to Alice. "I won't leave you, Alice," she said, praying it would be true.

FOR THE REST OF THE EVENING JULIA MOVED IN A FOG. ALICE SEEMED TO sense that something was wrong. She shadowed Julia even more closely than usual.

By nine o'clock they were both exhausted. Julia gave the little girl a bath, braided her hair, and tucked her into bed. Snuggling in close on the narrow mattress, she tried to read a bedtime story, but the words kept blurring before her eyes.

"Jewlee sad?" Alice said repeatedly, her small face scrunched into a frown.

"I'm fine," Julia said, closing the book and kissing the girl goodnight. "I love you," she whispered against the soft baby-scented cheek.

"Stay," Alice murmured, her eyes heavy.

"No. It's nighttime. Alice sleeps now."

Alice nodded and popped her thumb in her mouth.

Julia stared down at the girl.

My *girl*.

An ache blossomed in her chest. She turned away from the bed and went downstairs.

Ellie sat at the kitchen table, reading through a stack of papers. The dogs lay on the floor beside her, uncharacteristically docile. "The court said—"

Julia lifted a hand as if to ward off a blow. "I can't talk about it right now. I need some . . . time. Will you watch her?"

"Of course."

Julia went to the kitchen, grabbed the car keys and her purse. Every step seemed to jostle her bones. It felt as if she were held together with old Scotch tape. "Good-bye. I'll be back soon."

Outside, she drew in a deep, shaky breath. The night smelled of wet wood and new snow and the coming night. It wasn't until she was almost to the car that she realized she'd forgotten her coat.

Freezing, she drove to Max's house. The heat came on just as she turned into his driveway.

By the time she crossed the white yard and reached the porch steps, he was there, on the deck, waiting for her. Pale light spilled through an open window and cast him in a beautiful golden glow.

She felt a powerful jolt at the sight of him. It came from somewhere deep inside of her, past muscle and bone, a place that was normally still. Coming home; that was how it felt.

She climbed the steps toward him. He started to say something else, but she didn't want to hear his words, his voice, his questions. They would be concrete, somehow, too heavy. She couldn't carry any more weight right now.

She touched a finger to his lips. "Take me to bed, Max."

He stared down at her, and for a moment—just that—she saw the man behind the smile, the man who knew a thing or two about loss. "Are you sure?"

"You're wasting time. Alice—" Her voice broke this time. She had to force a smile. ". . . might have a nightmare. I can't be gone long."

He swept her into his arms and carried her up the stairs. She clung to him, her face buried in the crook of his neck. Seconds later they were in his room. She slid out of his arms and took a step backward.

Though distance was the last thing she wanted right now, she felt awkward. Undone somehow.

She unbuttoned her shirt, let it fall to the floor. Her bra followed.

They stood there, separated by inches and yet worlds apart, undressing. Finally, both naked, they looked at each other.

When he reached for her, she said nothing, barely even breathed. He circled his hand around the back of her neck and pulled her to him. Off balance, she stumbled a bit, fell into his chest.

He kissed her slowly, with a gentleness that was both surprising and short-lived. She reached up for him, coiled her arms around him, stroking his skin, wanting him closer, closer.

It flashed through her mind to push him away, to change her mind, say, *Stop; I was wrong, you'll break my heart*, but her fear lasted no longer than an instant. Passion twisted it into something else. They moved to the bed. In a distant part of her mind she saw that he was pushing his clothes aside, making a bower of rumpled white sheeting for their bodies, and then she was on the bed with him, beneath him, her hands desperate against his bare, hot skin. She was breathing so hard and fast she felt dizzy; his name slipped from her mouth to his. Neither one of them heard it. His hands pushed past her defenses, drove her down, past pleasure and into a kind of pain and back to pleasure again. As if from far away, she heard him rip open a condom package; then her hands were on him, stroking it into place.

He groaned and covered her body with his, moving against her until she couldn't think of anything, could only *feel*.

When he entered her, with a thrust that went straight to the core of her, she cried out, terrified for a moment that she'd lost herself in all this need.

When it was over, he held her close and kissed her again. It was long and slow and gentle, and it made her want to cry.

"You're a good man, Max Cerrasin," she said throatily.

"I used to be."

She drew back just enough to look at him. In the pale light from a single lamp, she saw now what she'd refused to admit before, even to herself: she'd been lost from the moment she saw him, certainly from their first kiss. She hadn't merely stepped into love; she'd tumbled headlong, like her beloved Alice, down the rabbit hole to a place where nothing made sense. It didn't matter now whether he loved her back. What mattered was the love itself, this feeling of connecting with another heart. She could see, too, that he was worried. They'd come to a place that neither had quite expected, and there was no way to know how it would end. In the past—hell, yesterday—that would have frightened her. She'd learned a lot today. "Yesterday I was worried about a lot of things. Today I know what matters."

"Alice."

"Yes," she said softly. "And you."

Max lay beside her, holding her naked body close, and stared up at the ceiling. It had been a long time since he'd felt this way. He wanted to spend the night with Julia, to wake up beside her, to kiss her good-morning and talk about whatever came to mind.

In ordinary times that might have been possible; these were far from ordinary times. A part of her was breaking apart right now; she was holding herself together by sheer force of will.

He rolled onto his side and looked down at her. "You're so beautiful," he said, tracing her full lower lip with his finger.

"You, too," she said with a smile. Her nose brushed his chin. When she smiled, her pale green eyes made him think of misty rain-forest mornings. Cool and deep and somehow magical.

"You're turning me into a romantic," he said.

"Then you already were one."

He smiled at that. "You shrinks always know what to say, don't you?"

She stared at him a long time before she answered. "Don't lie to me, Max. That's all I ask, okay? Don't pretend to feel something if you don't."

"I've never pretended with you, Julia."

"Then tell me something real."

"Like?"

She glanced over at the bureau along the wall. There were several framed pictures displayed. Images from his life Before. "Like about your marriage."

"Her name was Susan O'Connell. We met in college. I loved her from the first moment I saw her."

"Until?"

He looked away for a second, then realized it was useless. Her keen eyes saw everything; certainly, he couldn't hide this pain by looking away. "Believe me, now isn't the right time for this conversation."

"Will there be a time for it?"

"Yes," he said softly.

She kissed him gently, then drew back. "I better go. Alice has trouble sleeping. She'll panic if she wakes and I'm gone." As she said the girl's name, her voice wavered.

"The courts will see you're best for her."

"The courts," she said with a heavy sigh.

"You don't believe they'll do the right thing?"

"The truth is, I can't think about all that right now. If I do, I'll fall apart. For now, I'm going to focus on proving that he's an unfit parent. One step at a time."

"You'll need me."

The smile she gave him was slow and steady. It released something in his chest, made breathing easier somehow. "I certainly will."

THE NIGHT PASSED FOR ELLIE IN A RIVER OF BLACK DREAMS AND FRIGHT-ening images. When she woke—at dawn—she was edgy and nervous. The first thing she did was pull out the file. Already, she'd read the words so often she'd almost memorized them. In the last twenty-four hours she'd personally spoken to every single police office who'd worked the Azelle case. In addition, she'd spent nearly an hour on the phone with the best private detective in King County.

Every person she spoke to and every report she read said the same thing.

He was guilty.

And the state hadn't proved it.

Ellie paced the living room. The dogs followed her everywhere, running into her every time she turned. They were upset by her energy. It was on *her* shoulders to prove that Azelle was a bad guy, an unfit parent, but so far all she could find was a layer of innuendo, a fog of accusation.

He was an adulterer; that was a fact. The only one she'd been able to nail down. Neighbors *thought* he hit his wife. Jurors *believed* he'd killed her, but on the basis of nothing concrete. And the media . . .

Every journalist she'd spoken to was certain he'd done it. *Guilty son of a bitch* was the label most often used to describe him. But not one story had uncovered previous bad acts. No drug charges, no DUI, not even a Drunk and Disorderly.

With a curse, she grabbed her files and left the house.

She drove straight to the Rain Drop. The diner was the only place open this early in the morning. As usual, it was full of loggers and fishermen and mill workers having breakfast before work. She stopped and talked to people in every booth as she made her way to the cash register.

Rosie Chicowski was behind the hostess desk, smoking a cigarette. Blue smoke spiraled upward, joined with the hazy cloud that was always there.

"Hey, Ellie, you're in early," she said, pulling the cigarette from her mouth and stabbing it out in the ashtray. Patrons had been smoking in the Rain Drop for fifty years. No state law was going to change that.

"I need some caffeine."

Rosie laughed. "You got it. How about one of Barb's marionberry muffins to go with it?"

"Thanks. Only one, though. Shoot me if I try to order another."

"Flesh wound or kill yah?"

"Kill me." Laughing, Ellie turned around, heading back for a booth in the empty nonsmoking section of the diner.

It was a moment before she saw him.

He sat sprawled across the burgundy vinyl booth, an empty coffee cup in front of him. He saw her and nodded.

Ellie walked over to him. "Mr. Azelle," she said.

"Hello, Chief Barton." He did not look pleased to see her. His gaze flicked over the heavy manila folder she carried.

"Can I join you? I have some questions to ask you."

He sighed. "Of course you do."

She sidled into the booth across from him. She looked at him, trying to really *see* him, but all she saw were tired eyes and deep frown lines. As she was marshaling her thoughts into a question, he said, "Three years."

"Three years what?"

Leaning toward her, he looked deeply into her eyes. "I was in prison for a crime I didn't commit. Hell, I didn't even *know* about it. I thought Zoë had left me for one of her lovers and taken our kid." The intensity in his eyes was unnerving. "Imagine how it would feel to be convicted of something terrible—horrific—and put in a cage to rot. And why? Because you made bad choices and let passion rule your life. So I had affairs. So I lied to my wife and family about that. So I sent her flowers after a knock-down and drag-out fight. It doesn't make me a killer."

"The jury—"

"The *jury*," he said with contempt. "They couldn't see past my life. Every newspaper and TV station called me guilty within five minutes. No one even looked for Zoë and Brit. *Two* eyewitnesses saw a strange van on *my* street the day my family went missing—and no one cared. The police didn't even bother to search for a white guy in a yellow slicker and Batman baseball cap who drove a grayish Chevy van. When I offered money for information, they compared me to O.J. For the last month I've been waiting every day for the DNA analysis that would give my daughter back to me. I had to get a court order to compare her DNA to the blood found at the scene. And when I get it, I race up here . . . only to find that your sister is going to fight me for custody."

Rosie showed up at the table. "Here's your coffee and muffin, Ellie. I put 'em on your tab." She grinned. "Along with a healthy tip."

When Rosie left, Azelle leaned across the table. "Do you believe me?"

She heard a crack in his voice, an uncertainty that bothered her. "You want me to see an innocent man," she said slowly, watching him.

"I *am* innocent. It'll be easier on all of us if you believe that."

"It would certainly be easier on you."

"How is she? Can you at least tell me that? Does she still suck her thumb? Does she—"

Ellie stood up quickly, needing distance between them. She didn't want to hear what he knew about their girl. "Alice *needs* Julia. Can you understand that?"

"There is no Alice," he said.

Ellie walked away, not daring to look back. She was almost to the door when she heard him call out to her:

"You tell your sister I'm coming, Chief Barton. I won't lose my daughter twice."

THE NEXT FORTY-EIGHT HOURS UNFOLDED IN A KIND OF FADED SLOW motion. The snow stopped falling. In its wake, the world was sparkling and white. Julia spent every hour working. During the day, she was with Alice, teaching her new words, taking her outside to make snow angels in the backyard. Several times during the day Alice asked about her wolf and pointed to the car. Julia gently turned her attention back to whatever they were doing. If Alice wondered why she kept kissing her cheek or holding her hand, she showed no sign of it.

But it was the nighttime hours that mattered most right now. She and Ellie and Peanut and Cal and the private detective worked all night long, poring through police reports and newspaper accounts and archived videotape. After a long shift at the hospital, Max showed up to help. They read or watched everything they could find on George

Azelle. By Monday morning, when the meetings were over, they knew every fact of his life.

And none of it would help them.

"Read Girl?"

Julia drew her thoughts back in and glanced at the clock. It was nearly two o'clock. "No reading now," she said softly. "Cal is bringing Sarah over to play with you. Do you remember Sarah?"

Alice frowned. "Jewlee stay?"

Such an ordinary question. "Not right now, honey. I'll be back, though."

Alice smiled at that. "Jewlee back."

Julia dropped to her knees. Before she could figure out what exactly to say, the front door opened. Ellie, Cal, and Sarah walked into the house.

No one bothered to say anything.

Sarah showed Alice a pair of Barbie dolls.

Alice didn't respond, but she couldn't look away from the dolls. After a few moments the girls wandered into the living room, where they played separately side by side. Alice still didn't know how to interact with other children, but Sarah didn't seem to mind.

Ellie touched Julia's arm. "You ready?"

Julia forced a smile and reached down for her briefcase. On the way out she stopped to talk to Cal. She meant to say, *When Alice feels comfortable, she'll talk to Sarah*, but when she opened her mouth, nothing came out.

"Good luck," he said softly, squeezing her arm for comfort.

Nodding, she followed Ellie out to the cruiser.

In a silence broken only by the *thump-thump* of the windshield wipers, they drove to the county courthouse. It was a tall, gray-stone building set on a hill above the harbor. The wild blue Pacific made a stunning backdrop; today, the gray sky blurred the horizon, made everything appear watery and indistinct.

Family Court was on the main floor, at the very end of a hallway. Of all the courts Julia had once frequented, Family was her least favorite. Here, hearts were broken every day.

Julia paused, straightening her navy suit, then she opened the door and went inside. Her high heels clicked on the marble floor. Ellie matched her step for step, looking ultraconfident in her gold-starred uniform. They passed Max and Peanut, who were seated together in the back row of the gallery.

George Azelle was already seated in the front of the courtroom, with an attorney beside him.

He saw them and rose from his seat, moving toward them. He wore a charcoal gray suit and a crisp white shirt. His hair had been tamed into a smooth ponytail. "Dr. Cates. Chief Barton."

"Mr. Azelle," Ellie said.

Behind them the courtroom doors banged open. Julia's attorney, John MacDonald, bustled in, carrying a worn leatherette briefcase. He looked tired, which was hardly surprising, given that they'd all been up until four o'clock that morning, looking for anything to use against Azelle. "Sorry I'm late."

George looked at the opposing counsel, no doubt noting John's brown corduroy suit and pilled green shirt. "I'm George Azelle," he said, reaching for the man's hand.

"Oh. Hullo," John said, then herded Julia and Ellie to their desk.

The judge entered the courtroom and took her seat. From there, she stared down at all of them. Without preamble, she began. "I've read your motion, Mr. Azelle. As you know, Dr. Cates has been temporary foster parent for your daughter for nearly four months and had recently begun adoption proceedings."

"That was before, Your Honor, when the child's identity was unknown," his attorney said.

"I'm well aware of the time sequence, and I understand the procedural history of this case. The question for this court is placement of the minor child. Obviously, public policy favors the reunification of biological families whenever possible, but these are far from ordinary family circumstances."

"Mr. Azelle has a history of domestic violence, Your Honor," John said.

"Objection!" Azelle's attorney was on his feet again.

"Sit down, counsel. I know he's never been formally charged with that." The judge took off her reading glasses and set them on her desk, then looked at Julia. "The white elephant in this courtroom is you, Dr. Cates. You're hardly the average foster parent seeking permanent custody. You're one of the preeminent child psychiatrists in this country."

"I'm not here in that capacity, Your Honor."

"I'm aware of that, Doctor. It would represent a conflict of interest. You're here because you won't withdraw your petition for adoption."

John started to stand up. Julia stopped him with a touch. No one could plead for Alice better than she could. She looked up at the judge, said, "In any other instance, Your Honor, I would have withdrawn if a family member had come forward. But I've read the records in this case and I'm deeply concerned for the child's safety. The mother's body has never been found and there's no finding of not guilty on the record. Mr. Azelle claims to be innocent, but in my experience most guilty people do. I just want what's best for this poor child who has already suffered so much. As you can see from my report, she's an extremely traumatized child. Until recently, she was completely mute. I'm making progress with her because she trusts me. To remove her from my care would cause her irreparable harm."

"Come on, Your Honor," Azelle's attorney said. "She's a psychiatrist. My client can afford to replace her. The truth is, my client has already suffered a tremendous loss of time with his daughter. Justice demands that he be given immediate custody."

The judge put her glasses back on and looked at them all. "I'm going to take this under advisement. I'll appoint a guardian *ad litem* to assess the child's special needs and current condition and let you know when I've reached a decision. Until then, the child will remain with Dr. Cates. Mr. Azelle is to be granted supervised visitation."

The attorney shot to his feet. "But, Your Honor—"

"That's my ruling, counselor. We're going to proceed with the utmost care here. This child has already suffered enough. And I'm sure your client only wants what's best for his daughter." She hit the bench with her gavel. "Next case."

It took Julia a moment to process what had just happened. She still had custody of Alice—for now, at least.

She heard John talking to Ellie about the logistics of visitation.

Julia knew all that. She couldn't count the number of times she'd been appointed guardian *ad litem* to protect a child's interests.

She eased away from the desk and started to leave the courtroom. In the back, by the doors, she saw Max waiting for her.

Then someone grabbed her arm. The grip was a little too tight.

George Azelle pulled her aside. His Hollywood smile was gone, watered down now by failure. In his eyes was a sadness she hadn't expected. "I need to see her."

She had no choice but to agree. "Tomorrow. But I won't tell her who you are. She wouldn't understand, anyway. We're at 1617 River Road. Be there at one." She pulled free of his arm and began to walk away.

He grabbed her again.

She looked down at his long, tanned fingers, wrapped possessively around her bicep. He was a man used to taking what he wanted; he didn't care much about crossing personal space boundaries, either. "Release me, Mr. Azelle."

He complied instantly.

She expected him to back away—cowards who were called out usually did, and men who beat their wives were always cowards and bullies—but he didn't. He stood there, towering over her and yet cowed somehow, bent.

"How is she?" he asked finally.

She would have sworn there was a fissure in his voice, that the words hurt him to say. Murderers and sociopaths were often great actors, she reminded herself. "It's about time you asked that."

"You think you know me, Dr. Cates. The whole world does." He backed away, sighing, shoving a hand through his hair and pulling his ponytail free. "Christ, I'm tired of fighting a war I can't win. So just tell me: how's my daughter? What the hell does developmentally delayed mean?"

"She's been through hell, but she's coming through. She's a tough, loving little girl who needs a lot of therapy and stability."

"And you think I'm unstable?"

"As you've pointed out, I don't know you." She reached into her briefcase and withdrew a stack of videocasette tapes, which she handed to him. "I made these for you. They're tapes of our sessions. They will answer some of your questions."

He took them cautiously, as if he were afraid the black plastic would burn him. "Where has she been?" he finally asked. This time his voice was velvety soft; she was reminded of his Louisiana roots. According to the trial transcripts, he'd been raised dirt poor in the bayou.

"We don't know. Somewhere in the woods, we think." Julia wouldn't let herself be fooled by the concern in his voice. He was playing her; she was sure of it. He wanted her to think he was a victim in this, too. "But I suspect you know that."

Ellie came up beside Julia, touched her arm. "Everything okay?"

"Mr. Azelle was finally asking about Alice."

"Call me George. And her Brittany."

Julia flinched at the reminder. "She's been Alice to us for a long time."

"About that . . ." He looked at both of them. "I want to thank you both for taking such good care of her. You literally saved her life."

"Yes, we did," Julia said. "I'll see you tomorrow at one, Mr. Azelle. Promptly."

Julia nodded and walked away. It was a moment before she realized that Ellie hadn't followed her.

She glanced back. George and Ellie were talking.

Peanut came up to her, nodded back toward Ellie and George. "That's trouble," she said, crossing her arms. "Your sister can turn to Jell-O around a good-looking man."

"I hope not," Julia said, feeling exhausted suddenly. "But maybe you should go eavesdrop."

"Glad to," Peanut said, and she was off.

Sighing, Julia walked to Max, who was waiting for her at the back door.

TWENTY-THREE

MID-AFTERNOON SUNLIGHT, AS UNCERTAIN AS TOMORROW, shone through the small barred window and landed in a puddle on the hardwood floor.

The girl on the narrow twin bed whined like any other child at naptime. "No sleep. Read."

From his place just outside the bedroom door, Max heard Julia say, "Not now, honey. Sleep."

Very quietly, she began to sing a song that Max couldn't quite hear.

It made him recall another life; in that one, the woman sitting on the bed would have had dark brown hair and the child would be a boy named Danny.

One more story, he would have said, that little boy they'd called One-More Dan and Dan the Man.

Max went downstairs. In the kitchen, he rifled through the cupboards until he found coffee. Making a pot, he then returned to the living room and made a fire.

He was on his second cup of coffee when Julia finally came downstairs. She looked worn; he would have sworn her cheeks were streaked by tears. He wanted to go to her, hold her in the way she'd held Alice and promise her that everything would be okay, but she looked too fragile to be touched. "Can I get you a cup of coffee?" he said instead.

"Coffee would be great. Lots of milk and sugar."

He went to the kitchen, poured another cup of coffee, doctored it for her, and returned.

She was sitting on the hearth, with her back to the fire. Her blond hair had come free from the twist she'd had it in. Now, pale tendrils fell around her face. The area below her eyes was puffy and shadowed, her lips were pale.

"Here." He handed her the coffee.

She gave him a fleeting look, a flashing smile. "Thanks."

He sat down on the floor in front of her.

"I want him to be guilty."

"Do you? Really?"

Her face crumbled at that. She sighed and shook her head. "How can I want it?" she whispered. "It would make her dad a monster. No child deserves that. As her doctor, I want him to be a loving parent, wrongly convicted. As her mother . . ." She sighed.

He had no words to give her. They both knew that either way, Alice—Brittany—would be wounded. She would either lose the woman who'd become her mother or be taken away from her biological father. Maybe that wouldn't hurt her now, when she couldn't understand what it meant, but someday she'd feel the loss. She might even blame Julia for it. "She *needs* you; that's all I know, and you need her."

Julia's gaze met his. She slid off the hearth and knelt in front of him. "I want to wake up and find that this was all a bad dream."

"I know."

She leaned forward and kissed him. He felt turned inside out by that kiss, broken.

Now that he'd started feeling again, he couldn't stop. Didn't want to. He drew back just enough to look at her, and whispered, "You told me once I could have all or nothing from you. I choose all."

She tried to smile. "It took you long enough."

WHEN GIRL WAKES UP, SHE GOES TO THE *WINDOW* AND STANDS THERE, staring out at the *yard*. She loves these new words, especially when she adds *my* in front of it. This word means something is hers.

There are hundreds of birds in her yard right now, though not so many as there will be when the *snow* is gone and the sun is hot again. Down below, lying on top of the melting snow, is a pink flower.

Maybe she should bring it inside. That would make Jewlee smile, maybe, and Jewlee needs to smile more.

She tries not to think about that, but already it is too late. She is remembering last night, when Jewlee held Girl so tightly she had to push her away . . . and how Jewlee's eyes had watered at that.

Lately, Jewlee's eyes water all the time. This is a Bad Thing. Girl knows this. Although it now seems long ago that Girl was in the deep forest, she sometimes remembers Him. And Her.

Her's eyes watered more and more . . . and then one day she was DEAD.

The memory of it is terrifying. Before, in days past, Girl would have howled now, called out to her friends in the deep woods.

Use your words.

This is what she must do now. Using her words is a Good Thing that makes Jewlee happy. But which words? And how can she put them together? How can she tell Jewlee how it feels to be warm . . . to not be afraid anymore. These words are too big; too many are needed. Maybe she'll just hold Jewlee extra tightly tonight and kiss her cheek. She loves it when Jewlee does that to Girl at bedtime. It is like a bit of magic that makes Girl dream of the pretty things in her yard instead of how she used to sleep in her cave, freezing cold and all alone.

She hears the door to the bedroom open and close. Hears footsteps.

"You've been standing at that window a long time, Alice. What do you see?"

Is that a bad thing? There are so many rules in this place. Sometimes she can't remember them all.

She turns to Jewlee, who looks like a princess in one of the *books* they read. Still, Girl can see the water trails on Jewlee's cheeks and it makes her feel sad inside, like the rabbit who'd been forgotten by his little boy in the story. "Bad?" she wonders. "No window stand?"

Jewlee smiles, and just like that, Girl feels happy again. "You can stand there all day if you like." She goes to the bed she sleeps in and sits down, putting her legs out on top of the covers.

"Book time?" Girl hopes, reaching for the story from last night. Grabbing it, she rushes over to the bed. "Teeth, first?" she says, proud of herself for remembering. It is hard to think of such things at story time.

"And pajamas."

Girl nods. She can do it all—go potty, brush her teeth, and put on the pink *jammies* with the stiff white feet. Then she is on the bed beside Jewlee, tucked in close.

Jewlee pulls her sideways, settles Girl on her lap so they are nose-to-nose. Girl giggles, waiting for kisses.

But Jewlee doesn't do that. She doesn't smile. Instead, very softly, she says: "Brittany."

The word hits Girl hard. It is what Him used to say when he was mean and wobbly from the stuff he used to drink. What does Jewlee mean? Girl feels the panic growing inside her. She scratches her cheek and shakes her head.

Jewlee holds Girl's hands in hers and says it again.

"Brittany."

This time Girl hears the question in the word. Jewlee is asking her something.

"Are you Brittany?"

Had those other words been there all along, only drowned out by Girl's heartbeat?

Are you Brittany?

Brittany.

The question is like a fish swimming downstream. She grabs onto its tail, swims with it. She gets an image of a little girl—tiny—with short, curly black hair and huge white plastic underwear. This baby lives in a white world, with lights everywhere and a soft floor. She plays with a bright red plastic ball. Someone always gives it back to her when she drops it.

Where's Brittany's ball? Where is it?

She looks at Jewlee, who is so sad now it makes Girl's heart hurt.

How can Girl tell her how happy she is here, how this is her whole world now and nothing else feels right?

"Are you Brittany?"

She understands finally. *Are you Brittany?* Very slowly, she leans toward Jewlee, gives her a kiss. When she pulls back, she says, "Me Alice."

"Oh, honey . . ." Jewlee's eyes started leaking again; she seems to shrink. She pulls her into her arms, holding her so tightly that *Alice* can hardly breathe. But she laughs anyway. "I love you, Alice."

She says it again, just because she can, and because it makes her feel like she can fly. She isn't just Girl anymore. "Me Alice."

AT HER DESK IN THE STATION HOUSE ELLIE STARED DOWN AT THE HUGE array of papers spread out in front of her. The tiny black letters swarmed the pages, blurred. She shoved the pile aside, feeling a ridiculous satisfaction when the papers fluttered to the floor.

She got up from her desk and left her office. There, alone amidst the empty desks and quiet phones, she paced back and forth.

Back and forth.

What now?

All of their investigations had led them nowhere. There was no way they could convince the court that George Azelle was an unfit parent.

Julia—and Alice—were going to lose.

Ellie went to the secret cabinet in the back room and grabbed a bottle of scotch so old it had once belonged to her uncle. "Thanks, Joey," she said, nodding as she poured herself a drink. At the last minute she decided to take the bottle back with her. Switching on the light, she sat down at her desk in the main room and sipped her drink.

What now?

It kept coming back to that, like bits of flotsam circling a drain.

She was just pouring another drink when the door opened.

George Azelle stood there, wearing faded designer jeans and a black suede shirt that was open just enough to reveal a triangle of thick black chest hair.

"Chief Barton," he said, stepping in. "I saw the light on."

"It *is* the police station."

"Ah. So you're always here at midnight, are you? And drinking?"

"These are hardly ordinary times."

He nodded toward the bottle. "Do you have a second glass?"

"Sure." It wasn't exactly professional, but she was off duty and right now she didn't care. She went into the kitchen, got him a glass and ice and returned to her desk. In her absence, he'd dragged a chair over to sit across from her. She handed him the glass. The ice clinked against the sides.

She studied him closely, noticing the shadows beneath his eyes that told of sleepless nights; the thin strips of scarring that lined the inside of his left wrist. Sometime, long ago, he'd tried to kill himself. "I love her, you know. Regardless of what you think you've learned from all those reports on the floor."

His words struck her deeply, found a soft place to land. They were compelling; no doubt as he'd intended. She leaned back from him, needing distance between them. "Tell me about your marriage."

He gave a negligent flick of the wrist. The movement was strangely seductive. She was reminded of some rich, idle Lord of the Realm. "It was terrible. She slept around. I slept around. We fought like crazy people. She wanted a divorce. It would have been my third." He smiled disarmingly. "I'm a romantic, in my way."

Ellie knew about that kind of faith. *A believer*, she thought, *like me*. She pushed that comparison away. "And where is your wife now?"

"I don't know. If you're wondering why I sound so emotionless when I answer, remember that I've been answering that question for years. No one ever likes my answer. I thought she took Brittany and ran off with some new man."

Ellie watched him talk. There was something deeply seductive about him. Maybe it was in the tone of his voice, so soft and confident, or the way his lilting accent made every word sound carefully consid- ered. "Did you testify in your own defense?"

"'Course not. The lawyers said there was too much to cross- examine me on. I wanted to. I would have been convincing, too. I thought about that a lot in prison. Regrets keep you company in there. I paid a fortune to private investigators. The best lead came from that flower delivery man who reported seeing a man in a yellow slicker and Batman baseball cap sitting in a van across the street from my house."

"And?"

"And we never found him."

"So you wish you would have testified."

"I didn't know how it would . . . stay with me. People think I'm a monster."

"Is that why you're here? To use Alice—I'm sorry, Brittany—to prove your innocence?"

He gazed at her; there was no smile on his face now, no hint of it in his eyes. He looked as honest as a man with a deeply troubled past could look. "When the world sees that she's alive, they'll have to ques- tion all of it."

"But she's already been so hurt."

"Ah," he said quietly, sadly. "So have I."

"But she's a child."

"My child," he reminded her, and at that, she saw past the regret, past the sadness, to a wounded man who would do anything to have his way.

"I don't think you understand how traumatized she's been. When we found her, she was practically wild. She couldn't talk or—"

"I've read the newspaper accounts and watched the tapes. Why do you think I'm talking to you? I know your sister saved Brittany. But she's my daughter. You have to know what that means. I'll get the best help for her. I promise you."

"My sister *is* the best, that's what I'm trying to tell you. If you love Alice—"

He stood up. "I should leave now. I thought if you knew how much I love my daughter, you'd be a cop. But you're Julia's sister, aren't you? This is one more place I won't find justice."

Ellie knew she'd gone too far in questioning his love for his daughter. "You'll ruin her," she said quietly.

"I'm sorry you feel that way, Chief Barton. I truly am." He walked over to the door, yanked it open. Then he paused, looked back. "I'll see you—and Brittany—tomorrow."

Ellie let out her breath in a sigh. His words—*I thought you'd be a cop*—stayed with her for a long, long time.

In all the tussle of facts and emotions and fear of the past few days, she'd been focused on Alice and Julia. She'd forgotten that she had a job to do. She was the chief of police. Justice was her job.

THE NIGHT FOR JULIA WAS ENDLESS. FINALLY, SOMETIME AROUND THREE o'clock, she gave up on sleep and went to work. For hours she sat at the kitchen table, in the glow from a single lamp, reading about George Azelle.

His life was a web of innuendo and speculation. Nothing had ever been proven.

Pushing the papers aside in frustration, she put on her jogging clothes and went outside, hoping the cool air would clear her head. She would need her wits about her today. She ran for miles, down one road, up another, until she was aching and out of breath. Finally, near dawn, she found herself back on her own driveway, coming home.

She went to her father's favorite fishing spot and stood there, breathing hard, watching sunlight creep over the treetops. Though the world was inky dark and freezing cold, she could remember how it had felt to be here in the summer with him, how his big, callused hand had swallowed her smaller one and how protected she'd felt by that.

She heard footsteps behind her.

"Hey," Ellie said, coming up beside her. "You're up early." She handed Julia a cup of coffee.

"Couldn't sleep." She took the mug, wrapped her fingers around the warm porcelain.

In silence, they stared across the silvered field to the black forest beyond. Cal's house was a twinkling of golden lights in the early morning mist.

"He's going to get custody, Jules."

"I know." Julia stared down at the river, watching the pink dawn light its surface.

"We need to *prove* him guilty." She paused. "Or innocent."

"You watch too much *CSI*. The state spent millions and they couldn't prove it."

"We have Alice."

Julia felt a shiver run down her spine. Slowly she turned to face her sister. "She doesn't remember anything. Or she can't tell us, anyway."

"Maybe she could lead us back to where she was kept, or held."

Lead us back.

"You mean . . . My God, Ellie, can you imagine what that could do to her?"

"We might find evidence."

"But, El . . . she could . . . snap. Go back into herself again. How could I live with that?"

"How traumatized is she going to be when Azelle takes her away? Will she ever understand that you didn't abandon her?"

Julia closed her eyes. This was precisely the image that stalked her. If Alice felt abandoned again, she might simply fade back into silence and next time there might be no escape.

"I've thought it through from every angle. I was up all night. This is my job, Jules. I have to follow the facts. If we want to know the truth, this is our only hope."

Julia crossed her arms, as if that simple movement could ward off this deepening chill. She walked away from her sister. Ellie didn't understand what her proposal could mean. How fragile a child's mind could be, how quickly things could turn tragic.

But Julia knew. She'd seen it happen in Silverwood.

Ellie came up behind her. "Jules?"

"I don't think I could survive if Alice . . . cracked again."

"All roads lead to Rome," Ellie said quietly.

Julia turned to her. "What do you mean?"

"No matter what we do—or how we do it—Alice gets hurt. No child should grow up without a father, but losing you would be worse. You've got to trust my instincts on this. We need to *know*."

To that, there was no answer. Ellie put her arm around Julia and pulled her close.

"Come on," Ellie finally said, "let's go make our girl breakfast."

MAX WAS GETTING OUT OF THE SHOWER WHEN HE HEARD THE DOOR-bell ring. He toweled off, put on an old pair of Levi's, and went downstairs. "I'm coming."

He opened the door.

Julia stood there: he could see how hard she was trying to smile. "Ellie wants to take Alice into the woods. To see if . . ." Her voice wavered. ". . . if she can find . . ."

He pulled her into his arms and held her until she stopped trembling, then he led her into the living room. On the sofa, he once again took her in his arms.

"What do I do?"

He touched her face gently. "You already know the answer to that. It's why you've been crying." He wiped the tears from her cheeks.

"She could regress. Or worse."

"And what will she do if Azelle gets custody?"

She started to say something, then paused, drawing in a deep breath.

In the silence that followed, he said, "This is the time to be her mother, not her doctor."

She looked up at him. "How is it you always know what to say to me?"

He tried to glance away, couldn't. Very slowly, he pulled away from her and went upstairs. On the bureau he found what he was looking for: a five-by-seven framed photograph of a little boy in a baseball uniform, smiling for the camera. His two front teeth were missing. He took the picture downstairs and resettled himself on the couch.

Julia sat up, alarmed. "Max? What is it, you look—"

He handed her the picture. "That's Danny."

Frowning, she studied the small, shining face, then looked at Max again, waiting.

"He was my son."

She drew in a sharp breath. "Was?"

"That's the last picture we have of him. A week later a drunk driver hit us on the way home from a game."

Her eyes filled with tears; the sight of it should have broken him, plunged him into his loss, but instead it strengthened him. It was the first time he'd said Danny's name out loud in years, and it felt good.

"I would do anything . . ." He stared down at her, not caring that his voice was breaking or that his eyes were watering. "*Anything* to have one more day with him."

Julia looked at the picture for a long time, and then slowly she nodded in understanding. "I love you, Max."

He took her in his arms and held her tightly. "And I love you." He said it so quietly that he wondered if she'd heard, or if he'd only imagined the words; then he looked in her eyes and he knew: she'd heard him.

"Someday you'll tell me about him . . . about Danny," she said.

He leaned down to kiss her. "Yeah. Someday."

TWENTY-FOUR

ALICE, HONEY, ARE YOU LISTENING TO ME?"

"Read Alice."

"We're not going to read right now. Remember what we talked about this morning and again at lunchtime?" Julia tried to keep her voice even. "A man is coming to see Alice."

"No. Play Jewlee."

Julia stood up. "Well. I'm going downstairs. You can stay up here by yourself if you'd like."

Alice immediately made a whimpering sound. "No leave." She got up from her chair and raced to Julia's side, tucking a hand into her skirt pocket.

Julia's heart swelled painfully. "Come on," she said quietly.

Down the stairs they went, side by side, Alice's hand tucked firmly in Julia's skirt.

Ellie was standing by the fire, apparently reading the newspaper. Unfortunately, it was upside down. "Hey," she said, looking up at their entrance. Though she wore full makeup and had curled her hair, she still looked tired somehow, and scared.

"Hi Lellie," Alice said, pulling Julia toward her sister. "Read Alice?"

Ellie smiled. "The kid's like a bloodhound on the scent." She ruffled Alice's black hair. "Later."

Julia dropped to her knees and stared at Alice, who was smiling brightly.

"Read now?"

"When the man comes, you don't need to be scared. I'm right here. So is Ellie. You're safe."

Alice frowned.

The doorbell rang.

At the sound, Julia almost jumped out of her skin.

Upstairs, the dogs—who were barricaded in Ellie's bedroom—went crazy; jumping and barking.

Julia slowly rose.

Ellie walked toward the door. She paused for only a moment, long enough to straighten her shoulders, then opened it.

George Azelle stood there, holding a huge, stuffed teddy bear. "Hi, Chief Barton," he said, trying to look past her.

Ellie stepped aside.

Julia watched it all as if from far away. She felt like a ghost in the room, recently dead, watching her family gather after her funeral. Everything was quiet and slow. No one knew quite what to do or say.

He stepped past Ellie and came into the living room. His curly black hair had been pulled back into a ponytail again. He wore ordinary Levi's and an expensive white shirt, with the sleeves rolled up to just below his elbows.

Looking at them now, in the same room—the man with the dark, curly hair and the chiseled face and the little girl who was his carbon copy—there was no mistaking the link between them.

He stepped forward, let the teddy bear slide down his hip. He held it negligently by one arm. "Brittany." He said the name softly. There was no mistaking the wonder in his voice.

Alice slid behind Julia.

"It's okay, Alice," Julia said, trying to ease away from her, but Alice wouldn't let her go. "She's got a strong will," Julia said to him. "She doesn't like to be away from me."

"She gets her stubbornness from me," he said.

For the next hour they were like some terrible tableau in a French film. In the beginning, George tried to communicate with his daughter, talking about nothing, making no sudden moves, but none of it worked. Even reading aloud didn't draw Alice out. At some point she streaked over to the potted plants and crouched there, watching him through the green, waxy leaves.

"She has no idea who I am," he finally said, closing the book, tossing it aside.

"It's been a long time."

He got up, began to pace the room. Then, on a dime, he stopped and turned to Julia. "Does she talk at all?"

"She's learning."

"How will she tell people what happened to her?"

"Is that what matters most to you?"

"Fuck you," he said, but the words held no sting; were, in fact, kind of desperate-sounding. He went around the couch and moved toward the potted plants. He moved cautiously, as if he were approaching a wild and dangerous animal.

A low growling came from the leaves.

"That means she's scared," Ellie said from the kitchen.

Upstairs, the dogs began to howl.

George was less than five feet from the plants now. Squatting down, he was almost eye level with his daughter. Long moments passed like this, with him silent and frowning; his daughter growling in fear.

Finally, he reached out to touch Alice.

She threw herself backward so hard she could have been hurt. A plant fell over, crashed to the floor.

He immediately pulled his hand back. "Sorry. I didn't mean to scare you."

Alice crouched on all fours, staring up at him through an opening in the leaves, breathing hard.

George took a deep breath, let it out slowly. Julia heard his resignation. It was over. At least for the day. *Thank God*. Maybe he'd give up.

He surprised her by starting to sing: " 'Twinkle, Twinkle, Little Star.' "

It was Julia's turn to draw in a sharp breath. His voice was beautiful and true.

Alice stilled. As the song went on, repeating, she sat back on her heels, then got to her feet. Cautiously, she neared the plants and started humming along with him.

"You know me, don't you, Brittany?"

At that, the name Brittany, Alice spun away and ran upstairs.

The bedroom door slammed shut.

George got to his feet. Shoving his hands in his pockets, he looked at Julia. "I used to sing that song to her when she was a baby." He came closer.

Julia was going to say something when she heard a car drive up. "Who's here, El?"

Ellie went to the front door, opened it. "Holy *shit*." She slammed the door shut and turned around. "It's KIRO TV and CNN . . . and the *Gazette*."

Julia looked at George. "You called the press?"

He shrugged. "You spend three years in prison, Doctor, and then judge me. I'm as much a victim here as Brittany is."

"Tell it to someone who'll believe it, you selfish son of a bitch." She tried to rein in her anger. It wouldn't do any good to scream at him with the press right there. "You've seen her. Becoming the object of media attention could destroy her. You and I know what it's like when they make you the story. There's nowhere to hide. Don't do that to Alice."

"Brittany." His gaze softened. She thought she saw true concern in his eyes. Or hoped she did. It was all she had to seize on to. "And you've left me no other choice."

The doorbell rang.

"Do you really want to prove your innocence?" Julia said, hearing the desperate edge in her voice. As she said it, she thought: *God help me. God help her.* Then she looked at her sister, who nodded in understanding.

"I've spent a fortune trying to prove it."

Ellie pushed away from the kitchen counter. "You have something you didn't have before."

"A small-town police chief on the case? That's not gonna cut it."

"Not me," Ellie said, moving toward him.

The doorbell rang again.

"Brittany," Julia said. The name tasted bitter on her tongue, or perhaps it was more than that; perhaps it was the taste of true fear and she hadn't known it until now. "I think she lived in the forest for a long time. Years, maybe. If she did, your wife may have been held there also. Whoever took them might have left evidence behind."

George went very still. "You think Brittany could lead us there?"

"Maybe," Ellie answered. Julia could barely manage to nod.

"Is it . . . safe? For Brittany, I mean?"

Julia couldn't have answered that question; not even for Alice. Her throat was too full of tears. *This is wrong, even if it's for the right reason.*

"Julia won't let her see the actual site . . . if we find it, that is." Ellie's gaze was steady. "You asked me to do my job, George. Was that another lie?"

Julia drew in a sharp breath. The room felt full of words unspoken, fear denied. A guilty man would say no. . . .

"Okay," he finally said. "But we go tomorrow. No dragging it out."

Julia honestly didn't know how to feel. "Okay." The word was barely louder than a whisper.

"And no media," Ellie said.

George looked from one of them to the other, as if trying to gauge their honesty. "Okay. For now."

The doorbell rang again. There was pounding on the door.

"Hide," Ellie said sharply to George, who stumbled into the kitchen and crouched behind the cabinets. "Come with me," she said to Julia.

The two of them walked to the door, opened it.

There were several reporters on the front steps, including Mort from the *Gazette*. They were already talking when the door opened.

"We're here to interview George Azelle!"

"We know that's his car."

"Can you confirm that the wolf girl is his missing daughter?"

"Doctor Cates—have you cured the wild child? Is she speaking now?"

Julia stared out at the faces in front of her, feeling distant from them, disconnected. Only a few months ago she would have given anything to be asked the last question, to be able to answer it in the affirmative. Then, the reformation of her reputation meant everything to her, but now her world was infinitely different.

She felt Ellie's gaze on her. No doubt her sister was thinking the same thing.

Julia looked out at the reporters who were staring at her, microphones at the ready, willing—now—to believe her. She could be the one again, the doctor to whom they listened. She knew it was true. Alice could be her living proof, just as she was George's. All she had to do was use Alice—show the tapes and then present the girl. The progress they'd made was nothing short of miraculous. The journals would be clamoring for articles on her therapy techniques.

In the end, after all the times she'd dreamt of her triumphant return, it was surprisingly easy to smile coolly and say: "No comment."

ELLIE, CAL, EARL, JULIA, AND ALICE WERE IN THE PARK. THEY NEEDED to set out before dawn. There could be no witnesses to this trek of theirs; a media trail would ruin everything. George stood apart from the rest of them, his arms crossed, talking to his lawyer.

"Can she do it?" Cal asked, voicing everyone's concern.

Ellie had no answer to that. "I don't even know what to hope for."

She reached out for Cal, held his hand. The warmth and familiarity of his touch made her breathe easier.

She had been up most of the night, going through procedural manuals and e-mailing law enforcement colleagues around the country. She'd put together an evidence gathering kit and invited Cal along to be their official photographer. Everything had to be done exactly right. If they actually found anything, she needed to preserve the site for county and maybe even federal crime scene investigators.

It was dark and quiet out here. Cold. The icy breath of late January scraped their skin and chapped their lips. They'd been here beneath the maple tree for almost a half hour. In all that time, no one had said a word except Julia, who was kneeling in front of Alice. In the darkness, they all looked like apparitions; Alice most of all, with her black hair and dark coat and red boots.

"Scared." She gave a halfhearted growl.

"I know, honey. I'm scared, too. So is Aunt Ellie. But we need to see where you were before. Remember what we talked about? Your place in the woods?"

"Dark," Alice whispered.

Ellie heard Alice's whimper, her trembling voice, and she wanted to stop this thing right now. How could they do this?

"No leave Alice?"

"No," Julia said. "I'll hold your hand all the time."

Alice sighed. It was a harrowing, heart-wrenching sound. "'Kay."

Behind them a car drove up. It was the final member of their party.

Ellie walked over to the sidewalk, where Peanut and Floyd now stood alongside a game farm truck. Beside them, on a leash, was the wolf, muzzled.

"You sure about this?" Floyd asked.

"I'm sure." Ellie took the leash from him.

"Wolf!" Alice cried out, running for them.

The wolf jumped at Alice, knocked her down.

"Are you going to bring him back?" Floyd asked, watching the pair play on the icy grass.

"I don't think so. He belongs in the wild."

Floyd's gaze landed on Alice. "I wonder if he's the only one." Then he walked back to his truck and drove away.

Ellie looked down at her watch, then went to her sister, who stood alone now, staring into the forest. "It's time."

Julia closed her eyes for a moment and drew in a deep breath. Releasing it, she went to Alice and knelt down. "We need to go now, Alice."

Alice pointed to the muzzle and the leash. "Bad. Trap. Smelly."

Ellie exchanged a worried look with her sister. Last night they'd decided to use the wolf to help Alice find her way back to her old life. It had seemed less dangerous in the abstract.

"She needs him," Julia said.

"Okay, but I've got to keep the muzzle on." Ellie bent down and unhooked the leash. The wolf immediately nuzzled up against Alice.

"Cave, Wolf," the girl whispered, and off they went, the two of them, toward the woods.

"Tell me that's not a damned *wolf*," George said, coming up to Ellie.

"Let's go," was Ellie's answer.

By the time the sun crested the trees, they were so far from town that the only noise was their footsteps, crunching through the underbrush, and the silvery bells of the river rushing alongside them.

No one had spoken in more than an hour. In a ragged formation, with Julia and Alice and the wolf in the lead, they kept moving, deeper and deeper into the woods.

The trees grew denser here, and taller, their heavy boughs blocking out most of the light. Every now and then sunlight slanted through to the forest floor; it looked solid, that light, so dappled with motes that you weren't entirely sure you could walk through it.

And still they went on, toward the heart of this old-growth forest, where the ground was spongy and always damp, where club mosses hung from leafless branches like ghostly sleeves. A pale gray mist clung to the ground, swallowing them all from the knees down.

Around noon they stopped in a tiny clearing for lunch.

Ellie didn't know about everyone else, but she was uneasy out here. They seemed so small, this band of theirs; it would be too easy to make a wrong turn and simply disappear. The only noise now was the ever constant breeze. It brushed thousands of needles overhead. They heard the rustling long before they felt the cool touch of the wind on their cheeks.

They sat in a rough circle, clustered at the base of a cedar tree so big that they could all hold hands and not make a complete circle around its trunk.

"Where are we?" George asked, stretching out one leg.

Cal unfolded his map. "Best guess? Well past the Hall of Mosses in the park. Not far from Wonderland Falls, I think. Who knows? A lot of this area isn't surveyed."

"Are we lost?" George asked.

"She's not," Ellie said, getting to her feet again. "Let's go."

They walked for another few hours, but it was slow going. Thick undergrowth and curtains of hanging moss blocked their way. At a clearing beneath a quartet of giant trees, they made camp for the night, pitching their Day-Glo orange pup tents around the fire.

All the while, as they set up camp and cooked their supper from cans, no one said much of anything. By nightfall the sounds of the forest were overwhelming. There was endless scurrying and dropping and cawing. Only Alice and her wolf seemed at ease. Here, in all this green murkiness, Alice moved easier, walked taller. It gave them all a glimpse of who she would someday become, when she felt at home in the world of people.

Long after everyone else had gone to bed, Ellie stayed up. Sitting by the river's edge, she stared out at the black woods, wondering how Alice had made this trek alone.

She heard a twig snap behind her and she turned.

It was Julia, looking worn and tired. "Is this the insomniacs meeting place?"

Ellie scooted sideways, making room for her sister on the moss-furred nurse log. On either side of them fragile green sword ferns quivered at the movement of their bodies.

They sat side by side; at their feet, the river rushed by, almost invisible in the darkness. The night air smelled rich and green. Overhead, the Milky Way appeared in patches between the trees and clouds.

"How's Alice doing?" Ellie asked. It flashed through her mind that soon they'd have to start calling her Brittany. Another in a long line of things they didn't want to face.

"Sleeping peacefully. She's completely at ease out here."

"It's her hometown, I guess. Her own backyard."

"Is she leading us somewhere . . . or just walking?"

"I don't know."

"I hope we're doing the right thing." Julia's voice cracked on that.

They fell silent; both of them questioning their choices. Ellie wanted to avoid talking about George, but out here, where there was nothing but her and her sister and the night sky, it was easy to see things more clearly. "Have you seen how George looks at her?" Ellie said the words quietly, in case he was awake and listening. Hopefully the sound of the river would drown out their voices.

"Yes," Julia answered. There was a pause before she said, "He looks like a man with a broken heart. Every time she ignores him or turns away, he winces."

"It's making me nervous. What if we find—"

"I know." Julia leaned against her. "Whatever happens, El, I couldn't have handled it without you."

Ellie slipped an arm around her baby sister and drew her close. "Yeah, me too."

Behind them a twig snapped.

Ellie jerked around.

George stood there, his hands jammed in his pockets. "I couldn't sleep," he said, walking toward them.

Ellie studied him. "I guess only Alice can."

George stared out at the forest. Quietly, not looking at them, he said, "I'm afraid of what we'll find."

If it was an act, it was Oscarworthy. Ellie glanced at Julia and saw the worry in her sister's eyes. So Julia saw it, too. "Yeah," Ellie finally said, tightening her hold on Julia. "We're all afraid."

ELLIE WOKE AT DAWN AND STARTED THE FIRE. IN A HEAVY SILENCE THEY ate breakfast and broke down camp. By first light they were on their way again, fighting through deeper, denser undergrowth, pushing through spiderwebs as taut as fishing wire. It was just past noon when Alice stopped suddenly.

In this shadowy world of towering, centuries-old trees and ever present mist, the little girl looked impossibly small and afraid. Looking at Julia, she pointed upriver. "No Alice go."

Julia picked Alice up, held her tightly. "You're a very brave little girl." To Ellie, she said, "Make good notes and take pictures. I need to know everything. And be careful."

Julia carried Alice over to the base of a behemoth cedar tree. They sat down on the soft carpet of moss at its feet. The wolf padded to their side and laid down.

Ellie looked ahead, into the green and black shadows that lay ahead. Cal, Earl, George, and his lawyer came up beside her, one by one. No one said a word. It took a surge of courage to move forward, to lead them all deeper into the woods, but she did it.

They followed the river around a bend and over a hill and found themselves in a man-made clearing. Stumps created a perimeter; fallen logs were the boundaries. Empty tin cans were everywhere, lying on the hard ground, their silvery sides furred by moss and mold. There were hundreds of them—years' worth. Old magazines and books and other kinds of garbage lay in a heap beside the cave. Not far away, tucked back in a grove of red cedar trees, was a small, shake lean-to with no door.

To the left a dark cave yawned at them, its open mouth decorated with ferns that grew at impossible angles, their lacy fronds fluttering in the breeze. In front of it a shiny silver stake had been driven into the ground. A nylon rope lay coiled around it; one end was attached to the stake by a metal loop.

Ellie knelt by the stake. At the end of the ragged nylon rope was a leather cuff that had been chewed off. The cuff was small—just big enough to encircle a child's ankle. Black blotches stained the leather. *Blood.* She closed her eyes for a split second and wished she hadn't. In the darkness of her thoughts she saw little Alice, staked out here. It had been the girl's small, bare feet that had worn the circular grove in the dirt. How long had she been out here, going round and round this stake?

Cal bent down beside her, touched her. She waited for him to say something, but he just squeezed her shoulder.

Slowly, Ellie pushed to her feet. "Gloves on, everyone." Then she made the mistake of looking at George.

"Jesus," he said, his face pale, his mouth trembling. "Someone tied her up like a damned *dog*? How—"

"Don't—" Ellie could feel the tears streaking down her cheeks; it was unprofessional, but inevitable. "Let's go," she said to Cal.

In a silence so thick it was hard to walk through and harder to breathe in, Ellie conducted her first true crime scene search. They found a pile of woman's clothes, a single red patent leather high heel, a blood-spattered knife, a box of half-finished dreamcatchers, and a small ratty baby blanket so dirty they couldn't be certain what color it had once been. Appliquéd daisies hung askew from the trim.

When George saw the blanket he made a strangled, desperate sound. "Oh my God . . ."

Ellie didn't dare look at him. She was hanging on by a thread here. If the look on George's face matched the sound of his voice, she'd lose it. "Catalogue everything, Earl," she said.

Behind the lean-to was another stake with another leather ankle strap; this one was bigger; it too was caked with dried blood. Someone else had been staked out here. An adult.

Zoë.

"She couldn't even *see* her daughter," Ellie whispered. Zoë's rope was longer; it allowed her to reach the mattress in the lean-to.

Cal touched her again. "Keep moving."

She nodded, hearing the thickness in his voice; it matched the stinging in her eyes. She moved forward slowly, studying everything from the pile of junk by an old moss-furred stump to the dirty, stained mattress that lay between two Douglas firs. There were animal signs everywhere—this camp had been vacant for a long time; the scavengers had come in.

Back in the trees, not far from the dirty mattress, Ellie found an old trunk, rusted almost shut. It took her a few tries, but she finally opened it. Inside she found piles of old Spokane newspaper clippings—most of them were about prostitutes who'd disappeared from the city streets and never been found. The last clipping was dated November 7, 1999. There were also several guns and a blood-encrusted arm sling.

Down at the bottom, buried beneath the bandages and newspapers and dirty silverware, was a yellow plastic raincoat and a ratty Batman baseball cap.

Behind her George let out an anguished cry. "He *saw* it. That flower delivery guy saw the kidnapper parked in front of my house."

Ellie didn't turn around; she couldn't see George right now. But she heard him drop to his knees in the muddy dirt.

"If they'd listened, maybe they could have found them before he did . . . this. Oh my *God*."

When he started to cry, Ellie closed her eyes. She'd done her job, found the truth.

But it wasn't the truth she'd wanted to find.

ALICE'S HEART IS POUNDING IN HER CHEST. SHE KNOWS SHE SHOULD RUN! But she can't leave Jewlee.

Still, she hears the voices here. The leaves and the trees and the river. These are the sounds she remembers, and though there is fear in her chest, there is something else, something that makes her get to her feet.

Wolf brushes up against her, loving her. Not far away, his pack is standing together, waiting for his return. This Alice knows. She can hear their padding footsteps and growling at one another; these are the sounds below, softer than the rustling leaves and the rushing water. The sounds of life that fill all this darkness.

She bends down. It takes a long time, but she finally frees Wolf from the smelly, icky trap on his face and around his neck.

He looks up at her in perfect understanding.

She feels sad at the thought of losing him again, but a wolf needs his family.

"Fwee," she whispers.

He howls and licks her face.

"'Bye," she whispers.

Then he is gone.

Alice looks back up at Jewlee, feeling such a swelling in her heart that it almost hurts. She knows what she wants to tell Jewlee, but she doesn't have the words. She takes Jewlee's hand, leads her well around the place (she doesn't want to see the cave again; oh no). They climb over one of the trees Him cut down and push through a patch of stinging nettles.

There it is.

A mound in the earth, covered with stones.

"Mommy," Alice says, pointing to the rocks. It is a word she thought she'd forgotten. Once, long ago, her mommy had kissed Alice the way Jewlee does . . . and tucked her into a bed that smelled like flowers.

Or maybe these are dreams. She can't be sure. She remembers a glimpse, a moment: Her bending down, kissing Alice, whispering *Be good for Mommy. Remember Her.*

"Oh, baby . . ." Jewlee pulls Alice into her arms and holds her tightly, rocking her back and forth.

Alice wishes her eyes would water like a real girl's, but there is something Wrong with her. Her heart hurts so much she can hardly stand it. "Love Jewlee," she says.

Jewlee kisses Alice, just the way the mommy used to. "I love you, too."

Alice smiles. She is safe now. She closes her eyes and falls asleep. In her dreams she is two girls—big girl Alice who knows how to count with her fingers and use her words to make herself understood. On the other side of the river is baby Brittany, wearing the pants called diapers and playing with her red ball. The old mommy is there with her, waving good-bye.

Alice knows she is sleeping. She knows, too, that in the world where she is only Alice, she is in Jewlee's arms, and she is safe.

Julia stood beneath the maple tree in Sealth Park with Alice asleep in her arms. No one had told her where to go or what to do after the Search and Rescue team dropped them off at the fire station, and yet somehow she and George had ended up here, like shells washed ashore, at this place where the search had begun. The *whop-whop-whop* of the helicopters and the peal of the sirens were finally fading away.

"What now?" George asked, looking dazed and confused, as if he weren't really waiting for an answer.

"I don't know. Ellie is going back to the crime scene tomorrow with all kinds of experts."

"Did you hear what he did to my baby? How he tied her like a dog and—"

"Stop." Julia turned to him, seeing the pain in his eyes, the tears. They didn't have all the facts yet—there were tests to run and results to wait for—but all of them knew the truth.

George hadn't done this to his family.

"I'm sorry, George." She wanted to say more but couldn't. She felt as if she were made of chalk and crumbling away bit by bit.

"I guess we'll talk later. When it all . . . fades."

"I don't think it will fade for us, George, but yes, later would be

good. Right now I better get my girl home." Despite her best inten-
tions, her voice caught on that. *My girl.* "Our girl, I mean."

He reached out cautiously, touched Alice's back. His dark hand
looked huge between her shoulder blades. "I never stopped loving her."

Julia closed her eyes.

She couldn't think about this now or she'd fall apart. With a
mumbled apology, she turned away from him and walked briskly
toward her truck.

She was almost to the sidewalk when she saw Max.

Light from the nearby street lamp cascaded down on him, made his
hair look silvery white. His face was all shadows.

Slowly, he crossed the street toward her. His boot heels were loud
on the worn, bumpy asphalt; each step matched the beating of her
heart.

He moved in close, the way lovers did. "Are you okay?"

Try as she might, she couldn't stop the tears from flooding her eyes.
"No."

He took Alice from her and put the sleeping child in her car seat.
Then he did the only thing he could do: he took Julia in his arms and
let her cry.

By the time Ellie finished writing her report and sending out
faxes and e-mailing the right agencies, she was exhausted.

She pushed away from her desk, sighing heavily. It was only ten
o'clock, but it felt much later.

There was nothing more she could do tonight, so she got up slowly
and walked through the station, turning off lights as she went. The off-
site 911 service was probably besieged with questions. It was something she'd deal with tomorrow.

Outside, the night was still and quiet. A slight breeze tugged at her
hair and made the fallen leaves dance along the rough sidewalk.

She was almost to her cruiser when she noticed George. He was
leaning against a streetlamp. He wore no coat; he must be freezing.

She went to him.

He didn't look up at her approach.

Ellie had never been good with words and none came to her now.

He looked at her. "All the big city cops who followed me around, and it was you who found the truth."

"I had Alice." Ellie remembered a moment too late. "Brittany."

He leaned down and kissed her on the lips. It wasn't a romantic kiss, but still she felt its impact.

In other days, other times, this feeling would have been enough to make her reach for him, to deepen the kiss into Something. Now, instead, she drew back.

"Thank you," he whispered.

"It doesn't change everything," she said, hearing the crack in her own voice. "Alice needs my sister. Without her . . ."

"She's my daughter. Can you understand that?"

Ellie's voice, when it finally arrived, was barely there. This was the place truth had sent them. "Yeah. I know."

TWENTY-FIVE

BY THREE O'CLOCK THE NEXT DAY ALL OF THE MAJOR NETWORK and cable news channels were interrupting regularly scheduled broadcasts to report on the discovery of Zoë Azelle's body in the deep woods of Washington State. Crime lab analysis had confirmed her identity, as well as that of the man who'd been there, too. His name was Terrance Spec, and he'd had a long history of problems with the law. He'd been convicted of first-degree rape twice. He'd also been a suspect in all those Spokane prostitute disappearances a few years ago, but no solid evidence had ever turned suspicion into probable cause. He'd been killed in September—a hit-and-run accident on Highway 101.

Every newspaper and radio station and television show proclaimed George Azelle's innocence.

The jury system had failed, they said. A man everyone from waitresses to senators had blown off as a "guilty son of a bitch" had been innocent. Pundits from CNN and Court TV—especially Nancy Grace, who'd called him a vicious sociopath with a killer smile—were busy wiping the egg from their made-up faces.

Now, George stood at the podium in the police station with his lawyer. They'd been answering the same questions all afternoon. The revelation that the wolf girl—so easily discarded as sensationalism by them only a few weeks before—was his daughter only fueled the fire. The headline LIVING PROOF was even now being inked across millions of newspapers.

Ellie stood at the back wall, shoulder-to-shoulder between Cal and Peanut, watching the show.

She felt Cal's gaze on her. In fact, he'd been watching her too closely all day. Wherever she went, he was there, standing by but saying nothing. "What?"

"What what?"

Peanut laughed. "You two are gonna have to quit with the philosophical discussions. I can't keep up."

Ellie ignored her friend. "What, Cal?" she said, irritated.

"Nothing."

"If you've got something on your mind, you might as well spit it out. We've been friends long enough that I know when you're pissed off about something. What did I do?"

She expected him to smile at that, maybe make some smart-ass geek boy response, but he just stared at her. After a second or so she started to feel uncomfortable.

Finally, he smiled, but it didn't light his eyes. "I don't think that's true, El. In fact, I think you hardly know me." With that, he walked away, went back to his desk, and sat down. Putting on his headset, he pulled a sketch pad out and began drawing.

Ellie rolled her eyes.

Peanut didn't smile.

"He's going all Napoleon Dynamite again," Ellie said, irritated.

"There's a rumor going 'round town," Pea said. "I heard it this A.M. myself. From Rosie at the diner who heard it from Ed at The Pour House."

"I'm guessing it's about me."

"It seems a certain female police chief was seen kissing a certain famous out-of-towner last night. Right in the parking lot in front of everyone. Oh, and did I mention his track record with women?" She made a tsking sound. "Not good."

Ellie winced. "Actually, he kissed me."

"Well, that makes a world of difference." Peanut sighed and shook her head. It was exactly how she responded when one of her kids was making her crazy. "Ellie, you're a fool. There, I finally said it. I've been waiting for you to wake up and see what's in your own backyard—we both have—but clearly that isn't going to happen. A good-looking felon comes to town and you're all over him like gray on Seattle. In fact, I hear wedding bells now. Who cares that he's going to take Alice away from Julia and break all our hearts? What matters is he's got a great smile and a big dick and he knows how to use them both."

"In the first place, it was a kiss, not a blow job. In the second—"

Peanut walked away from her.

Ellie ran after her. "Come back here, damn it. You can't say something like that to me and just walk away." She grabbed Peanut's arm and spun her around. There were reporters clustered around them, but Ellie didn't care. "I didn't go for him, Peanut."

"From what I heard—"

"Did you *hear* me, damn it? *I didn't go for him.* Zero. Zip. Nada. He did kiss me—and I could have turned it into something, but I didn't. He's going to take Alice from us, for God's sake. How can you think I'd sleep with him?"

Peanut frowned. "Really? You didn't—"

"Kept my jeans zipped, as my dad used to say."

"Why?"

It was Ellie's turn to frown. "Alice is more important."

"Nothing used to be more important to you, El, than a good-looking man."

"Things change." Ellie thought about that; it made her smile. Feel free.

"I'm proud of you." Smiling, Peanut slung an arm around her. Together, they headed back to Peanut's desk.

"Hey. What did you mean *we*? You said *we* both have been waiting for you to see."

Peanut shrugged. "Someday you should think about the people who love you, El." She looked down at her watch. "Hey, aren't you supposed to be in court?"

Ellie glanced at the clock. "Shit. George is already gone." She ran for the door.

By the time she reached the courthouse, it had started to rain. Cold, icy drops that fell from a sad gray sky. She parked on the street out front and ran up the steps.

At the closed door of the judge's chambers, Ellie knocked.

"Come in."

She opened the door to a large, austerely decorated room. Books lined all the walls. A huge desk dominated the center of the room; behind it sat the judge.

Julia stood near the corner beside a huge potted plant. Both attorneys were seated in front of the judge's desk. George stood all alone on the left side of the room.

"Everyone is here," the judge said, putting on her glasses. "The circumstances have changed since the last time you came to me."

"Yes, Your Honor," said George's attorney.

The judge looked at Julia. "I know how much you care about Brittany, Dr. Cates. You also know how the system works."

"Yes." The word seemed to deplete Julia, leave her smaller. "I know Mr. Azelle is a victim here, as much as Alice is, and I hate to further hurt him, but . . ." She paused, as if gathering her courage, then looked up at the judge. "His needs must be second to hers."

The judge frowned. "In what way?"

"She needs more time with me. She loves me . . . trusts me. I can . . ." Her voice slipped, caught on desperation. "Save her."

Ellie went to Julia, stood beside her.

"Will she always be a special needs child?" the judge asked gently.

"I don't know," Julia answered. "She's come so far. She's extremely bright, though. I believe she can rise above her past, but for many years she'll need constant care and treatment."

"There must be special schools for kids like her," George said.

"There are," his attorney answered. "And other doctors who could treat her. Your Honor, Mr. Azelle is a victim here. We can't compound his tragedy by taking his daughter away again."

"No," the judge said. "And I'm sure Dr. Cates knows that."

Julia turned to George. "She has no idea who you are, George. I sympathize with you, honestly I do—I was up all night thinking about what you've suffered—but the truth is, your daughter is what matters now. Father is a concept she can't understand yet, and if she were taken away from me now—abandoned again—she could regress. She'd almost certainly retreat back into silence and howling and self-mutilation. She isn't ready. I'm sorry." She stared at him, willing him to believe her. "Maybe you could move here for a few years. I would keep working with her. We could slowly—"

"Years?" George looked shaken by that, as if he'd never considered it. "You want me to stay here for *years* while my daughter lives with you? While she learns to call you Mommy? And I get to be whom? The man next door? Uncle George?"

It was Julia's turn to look shaken. "I could move to Seattle. . . ."

"You don't get it, Dr. Cates." His voice was gentle but firm. "I love my daughter. All those days behind bars, I dreamed of finding her, of taking her to the park and teaching her to play the guitar."

"You love the *idea* of a daughter. I've read everything there is to know about you, George. When Alice lived with you, you were always gone. She was in day care five days a week. Zoë said you were never home for dinner or on weekends. You don't even know your daughter. And she doesn't know you."

"That's not my fault," he said softly.

"I . . . love her," Julia said, her eyes filling with tears.

"I know you do. That's the problem. That's why she can't keep living with you or be your patient, here or in Seattle."

"I don't understand. If I can help—"

"She'll never love me," he said, "not as long as you're around."

Julia drew in a sharp breath. Slowly, she closed her eyes, battling for control, then she looked up at George. Everyone in the room knew there was nothing she could say to that.

"I'll do everything for her," George promised, "get all the best doctors and psychiatrists. I'll make sure she's taken care of. And later, when she loves me and knows who I am, I'll bring her back to see you. I'll make sure she never forgets you, Julia."

IN A SMALL TOWN LIKE RAIN VALLEY THE ONLY THING MORE PREVALENT than gossip was opinions. Everyone had one and couldn't wait to share it. Max figured that the meeting in the courthouse had barely finished when people started talking about it.

He called Julia every ten minutes; there was never an answer. For almost an hour he waited for her to call him, but his own phone remained silent.

Finally, he couldn't stand it anymore. She might think she needed to be alone; she was wrong. He'd made that mistake for too long—thinking that heartache had to be borne alone. He wouldn't let her make the same error.

He got in his car and drove to her house. With every turn, he pictured her. She'd be sitting on the sofa right now—or lying in bed—trying not to cry, but one memory of Alice laughing . . . or eating the flowers . . . or giving butterfly kisses . . . and the tears would fall.

He knew.

She might try to forget it, to outrun it, as he'd done. If so, years might pass before she'd realize that those memories needed to be held on to. They were all you had left.

He pulled up to her house and parked. From the outside everything looked normal. The rhododendrons that guarded the porch were huge and glossy green in this rainy season. A pale green moss furred the roof. Empty planters hung from the eaves. Behind and around the house, giant evergreens whispered among themselves. He crossed the yard and went to the front door, knocking softly.

Ellie answered, holding two cups of tea. "Hey, Max," she said.

"How is she?"

"Not good."

Ellie stepped back, letting him enter the house, and handed him the cups. "She's up in my room. First door on the left. Alice is asleep so be quiet."

He took the cups from her. "Thanks."

"I'm going to the station. I'll be back in an hour. Don't leave her alone."

"I won't."

She started to leave, then stopped and turned to him. "Thanks. You've helped her."

"She's helped me," he said simply.

He watched her leave, heard her car start up. Then he put down the tea—there would be a time for that later; making tea was for a relative who wanted to help but didn't know how—and went upstairs. At the closed bedroom door he paused, then drew in a deep breath and opened it.

The room was full of shadows. All of the lights were off.

Julia lay on her back in the big king-sized canopy bed, her eyes closed, her hands folded on her stomach.

He went to her, stood beside the bed. "Hey," he said softly.

She opened her eyes and looked up at him. Her face was red and swollen, as were her eyes. Tears had scrubbed the color from her cheeks.

"You know about Alice," she said quietly.

He climbed into the big bed and took her in his arms. Saying nothing, he held her and let her cry, let her tell him her memories one by one. It was something he should have done long ago; formed all his memories into solid, durable things that would last.

She paused in her story and looked at him, her eyes shimmering with tears. "I should stop rattling on about her," she said.

He kissed her gently, giving her all of himself in that one kiss. "Keep talking," he said when he drew back. "I'm not going anywhere."

THE STREETS DOWNTOWN WERE EMPTY. EVERY STOREFRONT ELLIE passed, she got a sad, tired wave from someone inside. Four people had hugged her in the diner while she waited for her mocha. None of them bothered to say anything. What was there to say? Everyone knew that by this time tomorrow their Alice would be gone.

It was late when she finally left the station and headed for the river. As she climbed the porch steps to the front door that had always been hers, she felt as if she were carrying a heavy weight on her back. This was as bad as she'd ever felt in her life, and for a woman who'd been divorced twice and buried both of her folks, well, that was saying something.

Inside, everything was exactly as it always had been. The overstuffed sofa and chairs created an intimate gathering place in front of the fireplace, the knickknacks were few and far between and mostly handmade. The only difference was the collection of ficus plants in the corner.

Alice's hiding place.

Only a few weeks ago the girl had rushed to that place at the drop of a hat—or the start of a big emotion. But lately she'd hidden less and less in her leafy sanctuary.

The thought of it was almost more than Ellie could bear, and if it hurt her to imagine, what was Julia feeling now? Every tick of the clock must be a blow to her.

She went over to the stereo and popped the *Return of the King* CD into the player. It was a day for sad, desperate songs and emotional music.

She tossed her purse on the dining room table. It hit with a jangly thump. She'd just made herself tea when she saw her sister.

Julia was out on the porch, in the freezing cold, wrapped in their father's old woolen hunting coat.

Ellie made a second cup of tea and took it out to the porch.

Julia took the drink with a quiet "Thanks" and "have a seat."

Ellie grabbed one of the old quilts from the trunk on the porch and wrapped it around her. Sitting on the porch swing, she put her feet on the trunk. "Where's Max?"

Julia shook her head. "He had an emergency at the hospital. He wanted to stay . . . but I sort of needed to be alone. Alice is asleep."

Ellie started to rise. "Should I—"

"No. Please. Stay." At that, Julia smiled sadly. "I sound like Alice. Brittany, I mean."

"She'll never really be Brittany to us."

"No." Julia sipped her tea.

"What will you do?"

"Without her?" Julia stared out at their backyard. In the darkness, they couldn't see much past the river. Moonlight brightened the water. "I've been thinking a lot about that. Unfortunately, I don't have an answer." Her voice softened, trembled. "It's like watching Mom die all over again."

She started to say more, but fell suddenly silent. "Sorry. Sometimes . . ." She stood up, turned away. "I need to be with her now," she said in a small, breaking voice, and then she was gone.

Ellie felt the start of tears. She tossed the blanket aside and got up. What good would it do to sit here by herself and cry?

She walked down into the damp grass toward the river. Across the black field she saw the twinkling yellow lights of Cal's house. *Someday you should think about all the people who love you, El*, Peanut had said. Cal had always been on that list. Through both her marriages, all her disastrous affairs, and the deaths of her parents, Cal had always been the one constant man in her life.

Even though he was mad at her for something, he was the one man on the planet who saw her as she was and loved her anyway. She needed a friend like that now.

She was at his door in no time. She knocked.

And waited.

No one answered.

Frowning, she glanced behind her. Cal's GTO was there, hidden beneath a tan canvas cover and a smattering of fallen leaves.

She opened the door, poked her head in, and said, "Hello?"

Again, there was no answer, but she saw a light on down the hall. She followed it to the closed door of Lisa's study.

Suddenly she wondered if Lisa was back. The thought made her frown deepen. Nerves twisted her stomach, made her feel panicky, but that made no sense. She knocked on the door, "Hello?"

"Ellie?"

She pushed the door open and saw that Cal was there alone, sitting behind a drafting-like table with papers spread out all around him.

For no reason she could quite touch, Ellie felt a rush of relief. "Where are the girls?"

"Peanut took them to dinner and a movie so that I could work."

"Work?"

"I thought you'd be out with George tonight."

"I need new friends." She sighed. "He was wrong for me. What do I need to do? Take out a billboard?"

"Wrong for you?" Cal leaned against his desk, studying her. "Usually you don't figure that out until you're married."

"Very funny. Now, really, what are you doing?"

She crossed the room toward him, noticing the smudges on his cheek and hands. When she sidled up behind him, felt the touch of his arm against hers, she immediately felt less alone, less shaky.

There was a pile of papers in front of him. On the top page was a faded, working sketch of a boy and girl holding hands, running. Overhead, a giant pterodactyl-type bird blotted out the sun with its enormous wingspan.

He pushed the sketch aside; beneath it was a full-color drawing—almost a painting—of the same two kids huddled around a pale, glowing ball. The caption beneath them read: *How can we hide if they see our every move?*

Ellie was stunned by the quality of his artwork, the vibrant colors and strong lines. The characters looked somehow both stylized and real. There was no mistaking the fear in their eyes.

"You're a talented artist," she said, rather dumbly, she thought, but it was so *surprising*. All those days while she'd been sitting at her desk, doing paperwork or reading her magazines or talking to Peanut, Cal had been creating Art. She'd blithely assumed it was the same doodling he'd been doing since Mr. Chee's chemistry class. She felt suddenly as if she were losing her hold on herself. How could she have been with him every day and not known this? "Now I know why you said I was selfish, Cal. I'm sorry."

He smiled slowly. It transformed his face, that smile, reminded her of a dozen times long past. "It's a graphic novel about a pair of best friends. Kids. He's a good kid from the wrong side of the tracks with a mean drunk for a dad. She hides him in her barn. Their friendship, it turns out, is the last true innocence, and it falls to them to destroy the wizard's ball before the darkness falls. But if they kiss—or go farther— they'll lose their power and be ruined. I just started submitting it to publishers."

"It's about us," she said. At the realization, it felt as if a doorway somewhere opened, showed her a glimpse of a hallway she'd never seen. "Why didn't you show me before?"

He tucked a strand of hair behind his ear and stood up to face her. "You stopped seeing me a long time ago, El. You saw the gangly, screwed-up kid I used to be, and the quiet always-there-for-you guy I became. But you haven't really looked at me in a long time."

"I see you, Cal."

"Good. Because I've waited a long time to tell you something."

"What?"

He took her by the shoulders, held her firmly.

And he kissed her.

Not a friendly peck or an I-hope-you-feel-better brushing of the lips. An honest to God, send the blood rushing to her head, kiss. Tongue and all.

Ellie resisted at first—it was all so unexpected—but Cal wasn't letting her run the show this time. He backed her up against the wall and kept kissing her until her breathing was ragged and her heart was beating so fast she thought she'd faint. It was a kiss that held back nothing and promised everything.

When he finally drew back, making her whimper at the sudden loss, he wasn't smiling. "You get it now?"

"Oh my *God*."

"Everyone in town knows how I feel about you." He kissed her again, then drew back. "I was beginning to think you were stupid."

She didn't know how a nearly forty-year-old twice-divorced woman could feel like a teenage girl again, but that was exactly how she felt. All giddy and breathless. In an instant her whole life had clicked into place. It all fit now. *Cal*.

Behind them the door opened. Ellie turned around slowly, still feeling dazed.

Peanut stood in the doorway. Like flowers from a single stem, three little faces hovered beside her. Peanut said, "Go put on your jammies. Daddy will be up in a minute to put you to bed." When they were gone and their footsteps on the stairs had faded to nothing, Peanut's gaze moved from Cal to Ellie and back to Cal.

A smile finally tugged at the corners of her mouth. "You kiss her?"

Ellie had the thought: *Peanut knew?* and felt a flash of irritation. Then Cal was pulling her toward him and she forgot about everything else. In those eyes she'd known forever, she saw love. True, this time; the kind that began on a cold day between two kids and lasted for a lifetime. He squeezed her hand. "I did."

Peanut laughed. "It's about damn time."

Ellie put her arms around Cal and kissed him. She didn't care if Peanut was watching. It wouldn't have mattered if she'd been on Main Street, in uniform, during a traffic stop. All her life she'd been looking for love and it had been there all along, across the field, waiting for her. "It is," she whispered against his lips. "About damn time."

· · · ·

JULIA KNEW SHE WAS HOLDING ALICE TOO TIGHTLY, BUT SHE COULDN'T seem to let go. Neither could she think of her as Brittany. For the last hour, no matter what she did—or appeared to be doing—Julia was also watching the clock, thinking *Not yet*. But time kept moving on, slipping past her. Every second that passed brought her closer to the time when George would drive up to the house and knock on the door and demand his daughter.

"Read Alice." The child thumped her finger on the page. Somehow she knew exactly where they'd left off.

Julia knew she should close the book quietly, say that it was time to talk of other things, of families that had been split up and fathers who came back, but she couldn't do it. Instead she let herself hold her little Alice and keep reading, as if this were any other rainy January day. "'Weeks passed,'" she read, "'and the little rabbit grew very old and shabby, but the boy loved him just as much. He loved him so hard that he loved all his whiskers off, and the pink lining to his ears turned grey, and his brown spots faded. He even began to lose his shape, and he scarcely looked like a rabbit anymore except to the boy.'" Julia's voice gave out on her. She sat there, staring at the words, watching them blur and dance on the page.

"Want Alice real."

She touched Alice's velvety cheek. Every time they read this story, Alice said the same thing. Somehow the poor little girl thought she wasn't real. And now there was no time to prove otherwise to her. "You're real, Alice. And so many people love you."

"Love." Alice whispered it softly, as she always did, with a kind of reverence.

Julia closed the book and set it aside, then pulled Alice onto her lap so they were looking at each other.

Alice immediately looped her arms around Julia's neck and gave her a butterfly kiss. Then she giggled.

Be strong, Julia thought.

"You remember Mary and the secret garden and the man who loved her so much? The man who was her father? He'd been gone, remember?" Julia lost steam. She stared into Alice's worried face and felt as if she'd fallen into the turquoise pools of her eyes. "There's a man. George. He's *your* father. He wants to love you."

"Alice loves Jewlee."

"I'm trying to tell you about your father, Alice. Brittany. You have to be ready for this. He'll be here soon. You *have* to understand."

"Be Mommy?"

Julia almost gave in, but a glance at the clock reminded her how short time was. She had to try again.

Alice had to understand that she wasn't abandoning her, that she had no choice. She glanced over at the suitcase she'd packed so carefully last night. In it were all of the clothes and toys the town had gathered for "their" girl. Additionally, Julia had packed all of Alice's favorite books and a few of her own childhood favorites that they hadn't gotten around to yet. And there were the boxes that had been donated by the local families. Everyone in town had given their Alice something.

How would she button Alice's—*Brittany's*—coat, kiss her on the cheek, and say good-bye? *You'll be fine. Go off with this man you don't know and who doesn't know you. Go live in a big house on a street you can't cross without help in a city where you'll never quite be understood.*

How could she do it?

And how could she not? No matter how she tussled with all of this, she couldn't escape the fact that George Azelle was a victim in this, too. He'd lost his daughter and found her again, against all odds. Of course he wanted to take her home. And he'd hired all the best medical professionals to care for her. Julia was terrified that it wouldn't be enough, but she didn't know how to stop the inevitable.

She drew in a ragged breath and tightened her hold on Alice. Outside, she heard a car drive up.

"Mommy?" Alice said again. This time it was her little girl's voice that sounded wobbly and afraid.

"Oh, Alice," she whispered, touching her soft, pink cheek. "I wish I could be that for you."

· · ·

ALICE HAS A VERY BAD FEELING. IT IS LIKE THE TIME WHEN HIM FIRST left and she was so hungry that she ate the red berries off the bush by the river and threw up.

Jewlee is saying things that Alice can't make herself understand. She is trying hard; she knows these words are important. Father. Chance. Daughter. Jewlee says them all slowly, as if they weigh down her tongue. Alice knows they mean something important.

But she cannot understand and the trying is hurting now.

Jewlee's eyes keep watering.

Alice knows this means Jewlee is sad. But why? What has Alice done wrong?

She has tried so hard to be Good. She showed the grown-ups the Bad Place in the woods, even went to the rocks that covered Her, even though it made Alice feel so sad. She let herself remember things she'd tried to forget. She'd learned to use forks and spoons and the toilet. She'd let them call her Alice, and had even learned to love that word, to smile inside when someone said it and meant her.

So what is left, what has she not done?

She knows about Leaving. Mommies who are soon to be DEAD have pale cheeks and shaking voices and leaking eyes. They try to tell you things you don't understand, hug you so tightly you can't breathe.

And then one day they're gone and you're alone and you wish your eyes would leak and someone would hold you again, but you're alone now and you don't know what you did wrong.

Alice feels that sick stomach feeling coming back, the panic that makes breathing hurt. She keeps trying to figure out what she has done wrong.

"Shoes!" she says suddenly. Maybe that is it. She never wants to wear her shoes. They pinch her toes and squish her feet, but she will *sleep* in them if Jewlee will keep loving her. "Shoes."

Jewlee gives Alice a sad, sorry smile. From outside comes a sound, like a car driving into the yard. "No shoes now, honey. We're inside."

How can she say *I'll be good, Jewlee?* Always. Always. *I'll do every-thing you say.*

"Good girl." She whispers it as a promise, meaning it with every piece of her.

Jewlee smiles again. "Yes. You're a very good girl, honey. That's why all this hurts so much."

It isn't enough, being a good girl. That much she understands.

"No leave Alice," she says desperately.

Jewlee looks toward the glass box that holds the outside. The *window.*

She is waiting, Alice knows. *For Something Bad.*

Then Jewlee will Leave.

And Alice will be Girl again . . . and she will be alone. "Good girl," she says one more time, hearing the crack in her voice. There is nothing else she can say. She runs across the room and picks up her shoes, trying to put them on the right feet. "Shoes. Promise."

But Jewlee says nothing, just stares outside.

TWENTY-SIX

ELLIE SAW THE CLOT OF NEWS VANS PARKED ON EITHER SIDE OF the old highway. A white police barricade had been set up across her driveway, barring entrance. Peanut stood in front of it, her arms crossed, a whistle in her mouth.

Ellie hit the lights and siren for a second; the sound cleared the street instantly. Reporters parted into two groups and went to either side of the road. She pulled around the barricade and rolled down her window to talk to Peanut.

"They're a roadside hazard. Get Earl and Mel out here to disperse the crowd. This day is bad enough without the media."

A bright red Ferrari pulled up behind the cruiser. Ellie looked in her rearview mirror. George smiled at her, but it was faded, less than real. There was a sad, haunted look in his eyes.

Reporters swarmed his car, hurling questions.

"What are you going to do now?"

"Will there be a funeral?"

"Who did you sell your story to?"

"Get them out of here, Peanut," she said, then stepped on the gas.

The Ferrari followed her down the potholed gravel road.

Ellie kept looking in her mirror, hoping he'd turn around or disappear.

By the time she pulled up in front of the porch, her stomach was coiled into a tiny ball.

She parked and killed the engine, then got out of the car.

George walked over to her. "How do I look?" he said, sounding nervous. He tucked a wavy strand of hair behind one ear.

"Good." She cleared her throat. "You look good."

He smiled and it took over his face, wiping away the nervousness, lighting those blue, blue eyes. Then his smile faded. He looked at the house and said, "It's time." His voice was soft, seductive. She wondered how many women had been drawn into the darkness by it and left there, alone, wondering vaguely how they'd gotten so lost. "I told your sister I'd pick up Brittany at three."

Brittany.

With a sigh, she led him across the yard. They were almost to the steps when a gray Mercedes pulled up behind them and parked.

"Who's that?" she asked George.

"Dr. Correll. He's going to work with Brit."

The man got out of his car. Tall, thin, almost elegantly effete, he walked toward them. His lean face showed plenty of lines but no hint of personality. "George." He nodded at George, then he shook Ellie's hand. "I'm Tad Correll."

He had the grip strength of a toddler. Ellie had an almost overwhelming urge to coldcock him. "Nice to meet you." She was about to turn away when she noticed the hypodermic needle sticking out of his breast pocket. "What's that for? You a heroin addict?"

"It's a sedative. The girl might be upset by the transition."

"You think?" Ellie couldn't help looking at George. She knew it was in her eyes—the pleading, the desperate *don't do this*—but she didn't say it again.

"She's my daughter," he said quietly.

There was no answer to that. Ellie knew that if she were in his shoes, no force on Earth would keep her from her child.

She nodded.

The three of them headed for the house. At the front door, Ellie knocked.

Anything to put off the inevitable.

Then she opened the door.

Julia sat on the sofa with Alice tucked beside her. At the foot of the sofa was a small red suitcase.

Julia looked up at them. Her beautiful face glistened with tear tracks; her eyes were puffy and bloodshot. She didn't move. Ellie was pretty sure she couldn't. At the knock, Julia's legs had probably given out on her. Max stood behind her, his hands resting on her shoulders.

"Mr. Azelle," Julia said in a shaky voice. "I see you've brought Dr. Correll." She nodded at the doctor and got to her feet. "Your reputation precedes you, Doctor."

"As does yours," Dr. Correll said. There was no hint of sarcasm in his voice. "I watched the tapes. Your work with her has been phenomenal. You should publish it in the journal."

Julia looked down at Alice, who looked scared now.

"Jewlee?" Alice said, her voice spiking up in fear.

"It's time for you to go now," Julia said in a voice so quiet they all moved a little closer to hear.

Alice shook her head. "No go. Alice stay."

"I wish you could, honey, but your daddy wants to love you, too." She touched Alice's tiny face. "You remember your mommy? She would have wanted this for you."

"Jewlee Mommy." There was no mistaking the fear in Alice's voice now. She tried to hug Julia more tightly.

Julia worked to uncoil the girl's spindly arms. "I wanted to be . . . but I'm not. No Jewlee Mommy. You have to go with your father."

Alice went crazy. Kicking and screaming and growling and howling. She scratched Julia's face and her own.

"Oh, honey, don't," Julia said, trying to calm the child, but she was crying too hard to be heard.

Dr. Correll swooped in and gave Alice a shot.

The child howled at that. A huge, desperate wail that came from all the dark places she'd seen in her life.

Ellie felt tears in her own eyes, stinging, blurring everything.

Julia held onto Alice, who slowly quieted as the sedative took effect.

"I'm sorry," Julia said to her.

Alice's eyes blinked heavily. She coiled her arms around Julia and stared at her. "Love. Jewlee."

"And I love Alice."

At that, Alice started to cry. It came with no sound, no shuddering, no childlike hysterics, just a soul deep release that turned into moisture and dripped down her puffy pink cheeks. She touched her tears, frowning. Then she looked up at Julia and whimpered two words before she fell asleep. "Real hurts."

Julia whispered something none of them could hear. She looked ruined by those quietly spoken words and Alice's tears.

They all stood there a moment, staring at each other. Then Dr. Correll said, "We should hurry."

Julia nodded stiffly and carried Alice out to the Ferrari. She looked down into the passenger seat, then turned to George. "Where's her booster seat?"

"She's not a baby," he said.

"I'll get it," Ellie said, going to the truck. Somehow that did it to her, after all she'd just seen; unhooking the booster seat—Alice's seat—and yanking it out of the truck made her cry. She tried to hide her face from George as she fit the seat into the Ferrari.

Very slowly, Julia bent down and put the sleeping child into the car. She whispered something into Alice's tiny ear; none of them heard what it was. Then she kissed her cheek and backed away, shutting the car door gently.

Julia stood face-to-face with George. She handed him a thick manila envelope. "This is everything you need to know. Her naptimes, bedtimes, allergies. She loves Jell-O now—but only if it has pineapple in it—and vanilla pudding. She tries to play with pasta, so unless you want a real mess, I'd keep it away from her. And pictures of bunnies with big ears will make her giggle; so will tickling the bottoms of her feet. Her favorite book—"

"Stop." George's voice was harsh, throaty. He took the envelope in shaking hands. "Thank you. For everything. Thank you."

"If you have problems, you'll call. I can be there in no time—"

"I promise."

"I want to throw myself in front of your car."

"I know."

"If you—" Her voice cracked. She wiped her eyes, said, "Take care of my—*our*—girl."

"I will."

Overhead, a cold breeze rustled through the leaves. In the distance, a crow cawed, then another. Ellie half expected to hear a wolf howl.

"Well," George said. "We need to go."

Julia stepped back.

Ellie went to her sister, put an arm around her. Julia felt frail and too thin suddenly, like someone who has been hospitalized for a long time and had only recently gotten out of bed. Max came up, too; they bookended her. Without their steadying presence, Ellie thought her sister might collapse.

George got into his car and drove away. Dr. Correll followed.

For a few moments their tires crunched on the gravel driveway, their engines purred. Then there was no sound left, no trace of them.

Just the wind.

"She cried," Julia whispered, her whole body trembling. "All the love I gave her . . . and in the end all I did was teach her to cry."

Max pulled Julia into his arms and held her tightly. There was nothing more they could say.

Alice was gone.

· · ·

She is in a car.

But it is not the kind of car she knows. This one is low—almost on the ground—and it darts around like a snake. The music is so loud it hurts her ears.

She opens her eyes slowly. She feels funny, kind of wobbly and sick and tired. Her stomach might throw everything out her mouth if she's not careful. Wetting her dry lips, she looks around for Jewlee or Lellie.

They are not here.

She feels the panic start deep inside her and blossom out. The only thing that stops her from screaming is how tired she is. She can't seem to make a big noise. (He can probably hear her heartbeat. It is so loud he will probably yell at her. She covers her heart with her hand to quiet the sound.)

"Jewlee?" she says to the man.

"She's back in Rain Valley. We're long gone. But you're with me now, Brittany, and everything will be good."

She doesn't understand all his words. But she knows *gone*. Her eyes start watering. It hurts, this crying. She wipes the tears away, surprised a little that they are clear. They should be red as her blood; that's how it feels. As if she has been poked with the sharp knife again and is bleeding. She remembers bleeding. "Jewlee Mommy gone. Alice bad girl."

The man looks at her. He is frowning. She knows he will hit her now, but she doesn't care. Jewlee can't make it all better anymore.

Just thinking it makes her eyes water more. She starts howling, softly, though she knows there is no one to hear. She is too far from her place. Her howling grows louder, more desperate.

"Brittany?"

She says nothing. The only way to protect herself is in the quiet. She has no one to care for her anymore so she needs to be small and still.

She closes her eyes, lets the sleep come for her again. It is better to

dream of Jewlee, to pretend. In her dreams she is a good girl and has a
Jewlee Mommy to love her.

SOMETIME LATER—JULIA HAD NO IDEA WHEN; SHE'D LOST HER GRIP ON
time—she sent Max downstairs and Ellie back to work. They'd both
been smothering her all day, trying to offer a comfort that didn't exist.
Frankly, it took all her strength, every bit she had, to stay here and not
scream until she was hoarse. She couldn't let herself look at the people
she loved—and who loved her. All of it just made her think of Alice.

She stared out the bedroom window at the empty yard.

Birds.

Come spring, those birds would come looking for Alice. . . .

Behind her the dogs chuffed softly to one another; they'd spent almost an hour looking for their girl. Now they were quiet, lying beside
Alice's bed, waiting for her return. Every now and then howls would
fill the air.

Julia glanced down at her watch and thought about how long
they'd been gone. A few hours, and already it felt like a lifetime.

It was five-thirty. They would be nearing the city now. The majestic green of Alice's beloved forest would have given way to the gray of
concrete. She would feel as alien there as any space traveler. Without
her, the little girl would regress, retreat once more into her frightened
and silent world. Her fear would be too big to handle.

"Please, God," she whispered aloud, praying again for the first time
in years, "take care of my girl. Don't let her hurt herself."

She turned away from the window . . . and saw the potted plants.
Before Alice, those plants had been separate, placed as they'd been in
various places throughout the house. Now they were the forest, the
hiding place.

She knew she should stay where she was, keep her distance, but
she couldn't do it. She walked over to the plants, stroked their glossy
green leaves. "You'll miss her, too," she said throatily, not caring that
she was talking to plants. It didn't matter now if she went a little crazy.

She wasn't Dr. Cates now. She was just an ordinary woman missing an extraordinary girl.

It was almost six now. They were probably on the floating bridge, crossing Lake Washington, nearing Mercer Island; Alice would see the snowcapped mountains in the distance and see where she'd come from. The air would smell different, too; of smog and cars and the tamed blue sound.

She finally left the room. Downstairs, the house was quiet except for the clang and rattle of Max's cooking.

She went to the table that was set for two, pretending not to see the blank space where the third place mat belonged. "What're you making?" she asked Max, who was in the kitchen, chopping vegetables.

At the sound of her voice, he looked up.

Their gazes met. "Stir fry." He set down the knife and moved toward her.

"The phone keeps ringing."

"It's Ellie," he said. "She wants to make sure you're okay."

He put an arm around her and led her to the window. Together they stared out at the dark backyard. The first star of evening looked down on them.

She leaned against him, loving the heat of his body against hers; it reminded her how cold she was. He didn't ask how she was or tell her it would be okay. He simply put his hand around the back of her neck, anchoring her. Without that touch, she might have drifted away, floated on this sea of emptiness. But with the one simple gesture he'd reminded her that she hadn't lost everything, that she wasn't alone.

"I wonder how she's doing."

"Don't," he said softly. "All you can do is wait."

"For what?"

"Someday when you think about her howling or eating the flowers or trying to play with spiders, you'll laugh instead of cry."

Julia wanted to be helped by his words. As a psychiatrist, she knew he was right; the mother in her couldn't believe it.

Behind them the doorbell rang.

To be honest, she was thankful for the distraction. "Did you lock Ellie out?" she asked, wiping her eyes and trying to smile. "I shouldn't have sent her to work anyway. I thought being with Cal would help."

"Does it help?" Max asked. "Being with someone who loves you?"

"As much as anything can."

He nodded.

Julia let go of him and went to the door, opening it.

Alice stood there, looking impossibly small and frightened. She was twisting her hands together, the way she did when she was confused, and she had her shoes on the wrong feet. The sound she made was a strangled, confused howling. Seeping, bloody scratches lined her cheeks.

George stood behind Alice. His handsome face was pale and seamed with worry lines she hadn't seen before. "She thinks you let her go because she was bad."

It hit Julia like a blow to the heart. She dropped to her knees, looked Alice in the eyes. "Oh, honey. You're a *good* girl. The best."

Alice started to cry in that desperate, quiet way of hers. Her whole body shook, but she didn't make a sound.

"Use your words, Alice."

The girl shook her head, howled in a keening, desperate wail.

Julia touched her. "Use your words, baby. *Please.*"

The loss wrenched through Julia again, tore her heart. She couldn't go through this again. Neither one of them could. She knew that Alice wanted to throw herself at her, wanted a hug but was afraid to move. All the little girl could think was that she was bad, that she would be abandoned again, just like before. And once more she was afraid to talk.

George climbed the creaking porch steps.

Alice darted away from him, pressed her body against the side of the house. Her feet hit the metal dog bowls. The clanging sound rang through the chilly night air, then dissipated, leaving it quiet once more.

George looked at Alice, then at Julia. "I tried to buy her dinner in

Olympia. She went . . . crazy. Howling. Growling. She scratched her face. Dr. Correll couldn't do shit to calm her down."

"It's not your fault," Julia said softly.

"All those years in prison . . . I dreamed she was still alive. . . ."

Julia's heart went out to him. Slowly, she stood. "I know."

"I imagined finding her again . . . I thought she'd run into my arms and kiss me and tell me how much she missed me. I never thought . . . never realized she wouldn't know me."

"She needs time to remember. . . ."

"No. She's not my little girl anymore. I guess you were right when you said she never was. When she was a baby, I was never home. . . . She's Alice now."

Julia's breath caught. Hope flickered inside her. A tiny flame of light in the dark. She heard Max come up beside her. "What do you mean?"

George stared down at his daughter. He looked older suddenly, a man lined by hard choices and harder living. "I'm not who she needs," he said in a voice so quiet Julia almost missed it. "She's too much for me to handle. Loving her . . . and parenting her are two different things. She belongs here. With you."

Julia reached for Max's hand, clinging to it. But she looked at George. "Are you sure?"

"Tell her . . . someday . . . that I loved her the only way I knew how . . . by letting her go. Tell her I'll be waiting for her. All she has to do is call."

"You'll always be her father, George."

He backed up, went down a step, then another. "They'll say I abandoned her," he said softly.

Julia gazed down at him, wishing she could tell him it wasn't true, but they both knew better than that. The media *would* judge him harshly for this. "Your daughter will know the truth, George. I swear to you. She'll always know you love her."

"I can't even kiss her good-bye."

"Someday you'll be able to kiss her, George. I promise you."

"Keep her close," he said. "I made that mistake."

Julia's throat was so full of emotion she could only nod. If this were a Disney movie instead of real life, Alice would give her father a hug right now and say good-bye. Instead she was huddled alongside the house, trying to disappear. Her cheeks were marred by scratches and streaked with blood and tears.

George turned and walked away. In the driveway, he waved one last time before he got in his car and drove away.

Julia knelt in front of Alice.

Alice stood there, her little arms bolted to her sides, her hands curled into fists. Her mouth was trembling and tears washed her eyes, magnifying her fear.

Julia's tears started again. There was no way to stop them, even though she was smiling now, too. Her emotions were almost too big to handle; her whole body was trembling.

Alice looked terrified. She watched George drive away, then turned to Julia. "Alice home?"

Julia nodded. "Alice is home."

Alice whispered, "Jewlee Mommy!" and threw herself into Julia's waiting arms.

They fell backward onto the hardwood floor, still locked together. Julia held Alice tightly, kissing her cheeks, her neck, her hair.

Alice buried her face in the crook of Julia's neck. She felt the whispers of her breath as she said, "Love Jewlee Mommy. Alice stay."

"Yes," Julia said, laughing and crying. "Alice stay."

EPILOGUE

As always, September was the best month of the year. Long, hot, sunny days melted into cold, crisp nights. All over town the grass was as thick as velvet and impossibly green. Scattered randomly throughout the towering evergreens were maple and alder trees dressed in their red and gold autumn finery. The swans had left Spirit Lake for the year, although the crows were everywhere, squatted on phone lines above every street, cawing and squawking at passersby.

At the corner of Olympic and Rainview, Julia stopped walking.

Alice immediately followed suit, tucking in close, putting her hand in Julia's pocket. It was the first time in weeks she'd done it. "Now, Alice," Julia said, looking down at her. "We've talked all about this. There's nothing to be afraid of."

Alice blinked up at her. Though she'd gained weight in the past nine months, and grown at least an inch, she still had a tiny, heart-shaped face that sometimes seemed too small to hold those wide, expressive eyes. Today, wearing a pink corduroy skirt with matching cotton tights and a white sweater, she looked like any other girl on the first day of school. Only the careful observer would have noticed that she had too many missing teeth for a kindergartener and that sometimes she still called her Mommy Jewlee. "Alice not scared."

Julia led Alice to a nearby park bench and sat down beneath the protective umbrella of a huge maple tree. The leaves overhead were the color of ripe lemons; every now and then one fluttered to the ground. Julia sat down, then pulled Alice onto her lap. "I think you *are* scared."

Alice popped a thumb in her mouth for comfort, then slowly withdrew it. She was trying so hard to be a big girl. Her pink backpack—a recent present from George—fell to the ground beside her. "They'll call Alice wolf girl," she said quietly.

Julia touched her puffy, velvet soft cheek. She wanted to say *No, they won't,* but she and Alice had come too far together to tell each other pretty lies. "They might. Mostly because they wish they knew a wolf."

"Maybe go school next year."

"You're ready now." Julia eased Alice off her lap. They stood up, holding hands. "Okay?"

A car pulled up on the street beside them. All four doors opened at once, and girls spilled out of the car, giggling and laughing. The older girls ran off ahead.

Ellie, in uniform, looking deeply tired and profoundly beautiful, took Sarah's hand in hers and walked toward Julia.

"Of course you're on time," Ellie said. "You have one kid to get ready. Getting these three organized is like herding ants. And forget about Cal. His deadline's made him deaf." But as she said it, she laughed. "Or maybe it's me, always telling him to listen up."

Sarah, dressed in blue jeans and a pink tee shirt, carrying a Shark Tales backpack, looked at Alice. "You ready for school?"

"Scared," Alice said. When she looked up at Julia, she added, "*I'm* scared."

"I was scared on the first day of kindergarten, too. But it was fun," Sarah said. "We had cake."

"Really?"

"You wanna walk with me?" Sarah asked.

Alice looked up at Julia, who nodded encouragingly. "Okay."

Alice mouthed: *Stay close*. Julia nodded, smiling.

The two girls came together, began walking toward the school.

Ellie fell into step beside Julia. "Who'd have thought, huh? You and me walking our daughters to school together."

"It's the start of a new family tradition. So, how's the new bathroom coming?"

"Cal ordered a Jacuzzi tub." Ellie grinned. "It's big enough for two. He's going to start on the addition next spring. Three girls in our old bedroom is a nightmare. They fight every second."

"Have you met your new neighbors?"

"Yeah. A couple from California. They have two sons who already follow the girls around like lovesick puppies. I find it hilarious. Cal is not so amused. But I think he's glad Lisa made him sell the house. Too many memories."

"He always belonged in our house anyway."

"Yeah," Ellie said, sounding like a woman head over heels in love. After two expensive weddings, complete with all the trimmings, she'd finally gotten lucky in a tiny chapel on the Vegas strip.

They crossed the street and climbed the steps to Rain Valley Elementary. All around them women were holding onto their children's hands. Julia noticed the woman beside her, a beautiful redhead with bright, teary eyes. When she saw Julia look at her, the woman smiled. "It's my first time," she said. "Walking Bobby to school. I hope I don't embarrass him by bursting into tears."

"I know what you mean," Julia said. It was hard to let Alice go out in the world, but she had to do it.

As they moved down the hallway, a bell rang. Kids and parents scattered, disappeared into classrooms.

Alice looked nervously at Julia. "Mommy?"

"I'll sit right out front all day, waiting for you. If you get nervous, all you have to do is look out the window, okay?"

" 'Kay." She didn't sound okay.

"You want me to walk you in?"

Alice looked at Sarah, who was motioning for her to hurry, then back at Julia. "No." *I'm a big girl*, she mouthed.

"Come on, Alice," Sarah said. "I'll show you to Ms. Schmidt's room."

Following Sarah, Alice walked down the last bit of hallway to room 114. She gave Julia one last worried wave, then opened the door and went in. The door shut behind her.

Julia let out her breath in a sigh. She wanted to smile and cry at the same time.

"Yours can't stand to leave and mine can't wait."

"Yours didn't live through what Alice did. Maybe it *is* too early—"

Ellie looped an arm around Julia, drawing her close. "She's going to be fine."

Arm in arm, they walked out of the school and down the stairs and across the street to the park. There, they sat down on the cold wooden bench and stared out at the town that had shaped their lives. The maple tree that had first welcomed Alice was a blaze of bright yellow leaves.

"What are you going to do, now that she's in school?" Ellie asked, leaning back. "Next year it'll be all day."

Lately, the question had arisen in Julia's mind, too. She'd had to ask herself who she was now, what she wanted. The answers had surprised her. For almost half of her life she'd been driven by her career. It had meant everything to her. Yet, she'd lost it in a heartbeat. Perhaps she'd had some blame in that—she didn't know, would never know if she could have changed Amber's future—but the blame wasn't what mattered; that was the lesson she'd learned. Life was impossibly fragile. If you were lucky enough to have a loving family, you had to hold onto them with infinite care. Never again would she be afraid of love. She turned to her sister. "Max asked me to marry him."

Ellie shrieked and pulled Julia into her arms, holding her tightly.

"I thought I'd open an office here, too. Work part-time. There are kids who need me."

Ellie drew back. "Mom and Dad would be so proud of you, Jules."

That made Julia smile. "Yeah." She closed her eyes for just a moment, a breath, and remembered all of it—the woman she'd been less than a year ago, afraid of her own spirit and the danger of sharp emotions . . . the little girl named Alice she'd taken into her heart . . . and the man who'd dared to push past his own darkness, toward the light they'd found deep in this old-growth forest. For years to come she knew that the people of Rain Valley would talk about this special time, when a child unlike any other had walked out of the woods and into their lives and changed them all, and how it had begun in mid-October, when the trees were dressed in tangerine leaves and danced in the chilly, rain-scented breeze, and the sun was a brilliant shade of gold that illuminated everything.

Magic hour.

For the rest of her life she'd remember it as the time she finally came home.

MAGIC HOUR

KRISTIN HANNAH

A Reader's Guide

A CONVERSATION WITH KRISTIN HANNAH

Random House Reader's Circle: What inspired you to write this story?

Kristin Hannah: *Magic Hour* is a rare thing for me: a story inspired by actual events—with my spin on them, of course. One day, when I was reading the newspaper, I came across a local story that immediately captivated me. Two young men (in their early teens) had walked out of the deep woods one day and claimed that they'd never seen civilization before. This took place on rugged Vancouver Island. The townspeople immediately flocked around the boys, took them in, and provided them with everything they needed. Well, it turned out that the boys were actually runaways from Southern California and it was all a big hoax. But the seed was planted for me. I know these forests well, you see, and I know that it's entirely possible to live completely off the grid in that green darkness. One day, I found myself thinking of a little girl with no name . . .

RHRC: I read somewhere that *Magic Hour* is one of your favorite books. Why?

KH: The answer to that is easy: Alice. I have written a lot of characters over the years, but few of them have stayed with me the way that Alice has. I fell in love with everything about her—the way she perceived the world, her remarkable courage and strength, her capacity to love. I did a lot of research on feral and abused children in the creation of Alice, and honestly, the stories of these children were absolutely heartbreaking. I felt a real burden to make Alice true to her circumstances and yet give her the tools for a normal life.

RHRC: How did you get into the character of a little "wild" girl?

KH: The key to Alice was a combination of research and insight. I read countless terrible stories of similarly situated children, many of which were tragic. By the conclusion of the research, I really felt that I understood her psyche as much as an outsider can. Once I knew what was "normal," I began to inhabit Alice, to see the world in the way that she would, to "start over," in a way. I tended to think of Alice as a visitor from another place, another world. I think that was the key to understanding her. Julia's job, therefore, was to teach Alice how to be of this world and not detached from it.

RHRC: This book has so many moving scenes and touching moments that are sure to stay with a reader for a long time. Do you have a favorite moment in this book?

KH: Actually, I do have a favorite moment in the book. It's the scene in the back garden at night, when Julia takes Alice outside for the first time. There, Alice howls like a wolf in pain and perfectly imitates the sounds of other animals. I loved this idea that

Alice was more a part of the natural world than the civilized one. I remembered the whole Locke/Rousseau debate on the nature of man from my college days, and I called upon that for a great deal of Alice's creation. I particularly loved the semi-magic of the birds coming to Alice.

RHRC: Julia and Alice bond with each other over classic books: *The Secret Garden, Alice in Wonderland, The Velveteen Rabbit.* Were these some of your favorite books as a child? Were you a voracious reader as a child?

KH: I think most authors were voracious readers as children, and I am no exception. *The Secret Garden* was one of my childhood favorites, but I had never read *The Velveteen Rabbit* until I began *Magic Hour.*

RHRC: Did George Azelle want Alice back to prove his innocence or because he loved and missed her? What was more important to him?

KH: I think it's both, actually. As a nonpracticing lawyer, I am extremely fascinated by the workings of our legal system. One of the things we see repeatedly is how the justice system is both helped and hindered by the aggressive reporting in today's media. Julia was hounded by the media for not seeing her patient's intent, while George was convicted in the press for a murder he didn't commit. Both of their lives were arguably ruined by the media's scrutiny, and both used Alice as their redemption. I do believe that George loved his daughter and wanted her back—but he wanted the daughter of his memory, not the damaged, frightened girl he found.

RHRC: How much research went into this book? Did you encounter anything in your research that really struck a chord with you?

KH: This book was more research-intensive than most of my books, to be honest. In addition to doing the obvious research about feral and abused children, I worked hard to understand the impact of complete isolation and growing up without any of the trappings of civilization. There was also the research into speech and communication in isolated individuals and the potential ramifications of lost speech. Beyond all of that, there were the legal, moral, and ethical questions that concerned both the media coverage and the previous trial.

RHRC: When you describe Rain Valley you make it sound so beautiful yet you're also very honest about its drawbacks. Do you think it takes a special kind of person to live and thrive in a place like Rain Valley?

KH: I do, actually. Rain Valley is a rather stylized version of a real town in the Olympic rain forest—one you might have heard of lately: Forks, Washington. That's right; it's the same setting as the Twilight series. I went to school not far from the area and I know it well, and yes, you do need to be a certain kind of individual to thrive in an old-growth forest. It's staggeringly beautiful, and very, very damp. You learn to love the mist. I was really glad to be able to bring this exquisite corner of the world alive for readers.

RHRC: Out of all your books, which book was the most difficult to write?

KH: Hmmm . . . that's a toss up. I'm going to have to break the rules and give you two answers. The two most difficult books to write were *Firefly Lane* and *Winter Garden*. *Firefly Lane* was a deeply personal book that touched on some of the most painful issues in my life. In a way, the book was therapeutic to me, but all of that therapy came at a price. It was really difficult sometimes to find the strength to write about my memories of my mother. *Winter Garden*, on the other hand, was difficult to write because the subject matter, while completely unlike anything I have ever experienced, touched me in a profound way. Quite simply, I fell in love with the story in *Winter Garden* and I felt a true pressure to get it right. It is a powerful, heartbreaking story that I didn't want to screw up.

RHRC: Do you ever find yourself disliking your characters?

KH: I never dislike my characters, but I often want to hit them on the head and tell them to snap out of it. Personally, I have a really difficult time with dishonesty and conflict, so I am constantly trying to make my characters act nicer or more honorably.

RHRC: How do you celebrate completing a book?

KH: I've gotten to the stage in my life where I celebrate all of it— starting a book, writing a book, coming up with an idea, editing a book, finishing a book. As I've gotten older, I have begun to realize how important it is to celebrate your choices in life. I really try to not miss an opportunity to kick back and have some fun and simply enjoy how lucky I am to be a professional writer. And when I'm really, really lucky, I get to do that celebrating on the beach in Hawaii. Preferably with a few girlfriends around me.

RHRC: What's next for you?

KH: I can't say yet what's next for me. So I guess I'll tell you a little more about the book I have out now. *Winter Garden* is probably my best book to date. It's the story of two grown women who discover that their cold, distant mother has a secret past. I find that idea fascinating. What if you found out that your mom had been a super spy? Or had had another family? Or that her whole life story was a lie? I just love the idea that you can live with someone for decades and never really know them. *Winter Garden* is a unique novel for me—part contemporary family drama, part historical novel, part epic love story.

QUESTIONS AND TOPICS
FOR DISCUSSION

1. Kristin Hannah writes that "the modern world no longer believed in senseless tragedy." Why do you think people often need to hold someone accountable when something goes wrong? Is it human nature to play the blame game? Would a guilty verdict have offered the parents of those killed some solace? Do you think it's ultimately better to seek justice or to simply forgive in a situation like this one?

2. After seeing Amber Zuniga for three years, should Julia have been able to foresee the events that unfolded? What kind of culpability should a psychiatrist have for the crimes of their patients? Is it really possible to predict human behavior?

3. Before the tragedy, Julia was considered to be one of the best psychiatrists in the country. Would you trust Julia with your children after everything that happened?

4. Was Julia's mom wrong to tell her then thirteen-year-old daughter the secrets of her marriage, especially since she only told her one side of the story? Why do you think her mother told her those things?

5. With all the milestones that Alice reaches under Julia's care, why is speech the one that everyone is so focused on? Do people value talking over most other abilities?

6. Kristin includes a lot of research in this novel about feral children. How do you think Alice is like a feral child? How is she different?

7. Hannah writes "A name is integral to developing a sense of self." Why? What does this mean?

8. Why doesn't Alice think she's real?

9. Obviously, Alice learns a lot from Julia. But what does Julia learn from Alice? How does meeting Alice change her life?

10. Julia connects with Alice in a way that is completely unprofessional. Do you think Julia is wrong to try to keep Alice away from George? Is she choosing what's best for Alice or what's best for herself? George doesn't have the necessary skills to deal with Alice, perhaps, but he is her father. How important is that in this case?

11. The media plays a huge part in this novel. Press coverage ruins Julia's life and arguably helps to convict George. Do you think the media goes too far these days? Do you believe that cases are in effect tried in the press? How could we better balance free speech with blind justice? Can you think of any recent case that mirrors George's trial?

12. How would this story have been different if it had been told from George's point of view?

13. Did George give up on Alice too easily or was it right for him to realize he couldn't take care of her in the way she needed to be?

14. Do you think Alice will be able to grow up and live a normal life?

Read on for an exciting preview of
Kristin Hannah's wonderful novel

ANGEL FALLS

ONE

IN NORTHWEST WASHINGTON STATE, JAGGED GRANITE MOUNTAINS reach for the misty sky, their peaks inaccessible even in this age of helicopters and high-tech adventurers. The trees in this part of the country grow thick as an old man's beard and block out all but the hardiest rays of the sun. Only in the brightest months of summer can hikers find their way back to the cars they park along the sides of the road.

Deep in the black-and-green darkness of this old-growth forest lies the tiny town of Last Bend. To visitors—there are no strangers here—it is the kind of place they'd thought to encounter only in the winding tracks of their own imaginations. When they first walk down the streets, folks swear they hear a noise that can only be described as laughter. Then come the memories, some real, some manufactured images from old movies and *Life* magazine. They recall how their grandmother's lemonade tasted . . . or the creaky sound of a porch swing gliding quietly back and forth, back and forth, on the tail end of a muggy summer's night.

Last Bend was founded fifty years ago, when a big, broad-shouldered Scotsman named Ian Campbell gave up his crumbling ancestral home in Edinburgh and set off in search of adventure. Somewhere along the way—family legend attributed it to Wyoming—he took up rock climbing, and spent the next ten years wandering from mountain to mountain, looking for two things: the ultimate climb and a place to leave his mark.

He found what he was looking for in Washington's North Cascade mountain range. In this place where Sasquatches were more than a campfire myth and glaciers flowed year round in ice-blue rivers, he staked his claim. He drove as close to the mighty Mt. Baker as he could and bought a hundred acres of prime pastureland, then he bought a corner lot on a gravel road that would someday mature into the Mount Baker Highway. He built his town along the pebbly, pristine shores of Angel Lake and christened it Last Bend, because he thought the only home worth having was worth searching for, and he'd found his at the last turn in the road.

It took him some time to find a woman willing to live in a moss-chinked log cabin without electricity or running water, but find her he did—a fiery Irish lass with dreams that matched his own. Together they fashioned the town of their combined imagination; she planted Japanese maple saplings along Main Street and started a dozen traditions—Glacier Days, the Sasquatch race, and the Halloween haunted house on the corner of Cascade and Main.

In the same year the Righteous Brothers lost that lovin' feeling, Ian and Fiona began to build their dream home, a huge, semicircular log house that sat on a small rise in the middle of their property. On some days, when the sky was steel blue, the glaciered mountain peaks seemed close enough to touch. Towering Douglas firs and cedars rimmed the carefully mowed lawn, protected the orchard from winter's frozen breath. Bordering the west end of their land was Angel Creek, a torrent in the still gloaming of the year, a quiet gurgling creek when the sun shone high and hot in the summer months. In the wintertime, they could step onto their front porch and hear the echo of Angel Falls, only a few miles away.

Now the third generation of Campbells lived in that house. Tucked tightly under the sharply sloped roofline was a young boy's bedroom. It was not unlike other little boys' rooms in this media-driven age— Corvette bed, Batman posters tacked to the uneven log walls, *Goosebumps* books strewn across the shag-carpeted floor, piles of plastic dinosaurs and fake snakes and *Star Wars* action figures.

Nine-year-old Bret Campbell lay quietly in his bed, watching the digital clock by his bed flick red numbers into the darkness. Five-thirty. Five thirty-one. Five thirty-two.

Halloween morning.

He had wanted to set the alarm for this special Saturday morning, but he didn't know how, and if he'd asked for help, his surprise would have been ruined. And so he snuggled under the Mr. Freeze comforter, waiting.

At precisely 5:45, he flipped the covers back and climbed out of bed. Careful not to make any noise, he pulled the grocery sack from underneath his bed and unpacked it.

There was no light on, but he didn't need one. He'd stared at these clothes every night for a week. His Halloween costume. A sparkly pair of hand-me-down cowboy boots that they'd picked up at the Emperor's New Clothes used-clothing shop, a fake leather vest from the Dollar-Saver thrift shop, a pair of felt chaps his mom had made, a plaid flannel shirt and brand-new Wrangler jeans from Zeke's Feed and Seed, and best of all, a shiny sheriff's star and gun belt from the toy store. His daddy had even made him a kid-sized lariat that could be strapped to the gun belt.

He stripped off his pj's and slipped into the outfit, leaving behind the gun belt, guns, chaps, lariat, and ten-gallon hat. Those he wouldn't need now.

He *felt* like a real cowboy. He grabbed the index card with the instructions on it—just in case—and went to his bedroom door, peeking out into the shadowy hallway.

He peered down at the other two bedrooms. Both doors were closed and no light slid out from underneath. Of course his sixteen-year-old sister, Jacey, was asleep. It was Saturday, and on the day after a high-school football game, she always slept until noon. Dad had been at the hospital all night with a patient, so he'd be tired this morning, too. Only Mom would be getting up early—and she'd be in the barn, ready to go, at six o'clock.

He pushed the flash button on his Darth Maul watch. Five forty-nine.

"Yikes." He flicked up the collar on his flannel shirt and bounded down the last set of stairs. Feeling his way through the darkened kitchen, he hit the "on" button on the coffeepot (another surprise) and headed for the front door, opening it slowly.

On the porch, he was spooked by the black shape of a man beside him, but in the second after he saw the outline, he remembered. It was the pumpkin-headed farmer he and Mom had made last night. The smell of fresh straw was strong—even a day later.

Bret picked his way past the decorations and jumped off the porch, then he ran up the driveway. At the empty guest cottage, he zagged to the right and slithered between the fence's second and third rail. Breathing hard, he clambered up the slippery grass pasture.

A single floodlight lit up the huge, two-storied barn his granddad had built. Bret had always been in awe of the famous grandfather he'd never met, the man who'd left his name on streets and buildings and mountains, the man who'd somehow known that Last Bend belonged right here.

The stories of granddad's adventures had been told and retold for as long as Bret could remember, and he wanted to be just like him. That's why he was up so early on this Halloween morning. He was going to convince his overprotective mother that he was ready to go on the Angel Falls overnight trail ride.

He grabbed the cold iron latch on the barn door and swung it open. He loved the smell of this old barn; it always made him think of his mom.

Sometimes, when he was away from home, he'd smell something—hay or leather or neat's-foot oil—and he'd think of her.

Horses nickered softly and moved around in their stalls, thinking it was feeding time. He flicked on the lights and hurried down the wide cement aisle toward the tack room. He struggled to pull his mom's jumping saddle off the wooden tree. He dropped it twice before he figured out how to balance it on his arm. With the girth dragging and clanging behind him, he headed to Silver Bullet's stall.

There he stopped. Jeez, Bullet looked bigger this morning . . .

Granddad would never *chicken out.*

Bret took a deep breath and opened the stall door.

It took him lots of tries—*lots* of tries—but he finally got the saddle up on the horse's high back. He even managed to tighten the girth. Not enough, maybe, but at least he'd buckled the strap.

He led Bullet to the center of the arena. He couldn't see his boots—they were buried in the soft dirt. The lights overhead cast weird shadows on him and Bullet, but he liked those slithering black lines. They reminded him that it was Halloween.

Bullet dropped her head and snorted, pawing at the ground.

Bret tightened his hold on the lead rope. "Whoa, girl," he said softly, trying not to be afraid. That was the way his mom always talked to animals. She said you could talk down the craziest animal if you were patient and quiet.

The barn door shuddered, then let out a long, slow creaking sound. Wood scraped on cement, and the door opened.

Mom stood in the doorway. Behind her, the rising sun was a beautiful purplish color and it seemed to set her hair on pink fire. He couldn't quite see her face, but he could see her silhouette, black against the brightness, and he could hear the steady *click-click-click* of her boot heels on the concrete. Then she paused, tented one hand across her eyes. "Bret? Honey, is that you?"

Bret led Bullet toward Mom, who stood at the edge of the arena with her hands planted on her hips. She was wearing a long brown sweater and black riding pants; her boots were already dusty. She was staring at him—one of those Mommy looks—and he sure wished she'd smile.

He yanked hard on the rope and brought the mare to a sudden stop, just the way they'd taught him in 4-H. "I saddled her myself, Mom." He stroked Bullet's velvet-soft muzzle. "I couldn't get her to take the bit, but I cinched up the saddle just like I'm s'posed to."

"You got up early—on Halloween, your third favorite holiday—and saddled my horse for me. Well, well." She bent down and tousled his hair. "Hate to let me be alone for too long, eh, Bretster?"

"I know how lonely you get."

She laughed, then knelt down in the dirt. She was like that, his mom, she never worried about getting dirty—and she liked to look her kids in the eyes. At least that's what she said. She pulled the worn, black leather glove off her right hand and let it fall. It landed on her thigh, but she didn't seem to notice as she reached out and smoothed the hair from Bret's face. "So, young Mr. Horseman, what's on your mind?"

That was another thing about his mom. You could *never* fool her. It was sorta like she had X-ray vision. "I want to go on the overnight ride to Angel Falls with you this year. Last year you said maybe later, when I was older. Well, now I'm a whole year older, and I did really good at the fair this year—I mean, hardly *any* nine-year-olds got blue ribbons—and I kept my stall clean and kept Scotty brushed all down. And now I can saddle a big old Thoroughbred by myself. If I was at Disneyland, I would *definitely* reach Mickey's hand."

Mom sat back on her heels. Some dirt must have gotten in her face, because her eyes were watering. "You're not my baby boy anymore, are you?"

He plopped onto her bent legs, pretending that he was little enough to still be held in her arms. She gently took the lead rope from him, and he wrapped his arms around her neck.

She kissed his forehead and held him tightly. It was his favorite kind of kiss, the kind she gave him every morning at the breakfast table.

He loved it when she held him like this. Lately (since he'd started fourth grade) he'd had to become a big boy. Like he couldn't let Mom hold his hand as they walked down the school corridors . . . and she definitely couldn't kiss him good-bye. So now they only had times like this when he could be a little boy.

"Well, I guess any kid big enough to saddle this horse is ready to go on an overnight ride. I'm proud of you, kiddo."

He let out a loud *Whoopee!* and hugged her. "Thanks, Mom."

"No problema." She gently eased away from him and got to her feet. As they stood there together, she let her gloved hand sort of hang there in the space between them, and Bret slipped his hand in hers.

She squeezed his hand. "Now I've got to work Bullet for an hour or so before Jeanine gets here to worm the horses. I've got a zillion things to do today before trick-or-treating."

"Is she giving any shots?"

"Not this time." She ruffled his hair again, then reached down for her glove.

"Can I stay and watch you ride?"

"You remember the rules?"

"Gee, no, Mom."

"Okay, but no talking and no getting off the fence."

He grinned. "You just *have* to tell me the rules again, don't you?"

She laughed. "Sit down, Jim Carrey." Turning her back to him, she tightened the girth and bridled the mare. "Go and get me my helmet, will you, Bretster?"

He ran to the tack room. At the chest marked *Mike's stuff*, he bent down and lifted the lid, rummaging through the fly sprays, brushes, lead ropes, buckets, and hoof picks until he found the dusty black velvet-covered helmet. Tucking it under his arm, he let the lid drop shut and ran back into the arena.

Mom was on Bullet now, her gloved hands resting lightly on the horse's withers. "Thanks, sweetie." She leaned down and took the helmet.

By the time Bret reached his favorite spot on the arena fence, Mom was easing Bullet toward the path that ran along the wall. He climbed up the slats and sat on the top rail.

He watched as she went 'round and 'round. She pushed Bullet through her paces as a warm-up: walk, trot, extended trot, and then to a rocking-horse canter. Bret watched as horse and rider became a blur of motion.

He knew instantly when Mom had decided it was time to jump. He'd watched so many times, he knew the signs, although he couldn't have said what they were. He just *knew* that she was going to head for the first two-foot jump.

Just like he knew something was wrong.

He leaned forward. "Wait, Mommy. The jump is in the wrong place. Someone musta moved it . . ."

But she didn't hear him. Bullet was fighting her, lunging and bucking as Mommy tried to rein the mare down to a controlled canter.

"Whoa, girl, slow down. Calm down . . ."

Bret heard the words as Mom flew past him. He wanted to scramble down from his perch, but he wasn't allowed to—not when she was working a horse over jumps.

It was too late to yell anyway. Mom was already at the fence. Bret's heart was hammering in his chest.

Somethingiswrong. The words jammed together in his mind, growing bigger and uglier with every breath. He wanted to say them out loud, to yell, but he couldn't make his mouth work.

Silver Bullet bunched up and jumped over the fake brick siding with ease.

Bret heard his mom's whoop of triumph and her laugh.

He had a split second of relief.

Then Silver Bullet stopped dead.

One second Mom was laughing, and the next, she was flying off the horse. Her head cracked into the barn post so hard the whole fence shook. And then she was just lying there in the dirt, her body crumpled like an old piece of paper.

There was no sound in the big, covered arena except his own heavy breathing. Even the horse was silent, standing beside her rider as if nothing had happened.

Bret slid down the fence and ran to his mom. He dropped to his knees beside her. Blood trickled down from underneath her helmet, smearing in her short black hair.

He touched her shoulder, gave her a little shove. "Mommy?"

The bloodied hair slid away from her face. That's when he saw that her left eye was open.

* * *

Bret's sister, Jacey, was the first to hear his scream. She came running into the arena, holding Dad's big down coat around her. "Bretster—" Then she saw Mommy, lying there. "Oh my God! *Don't touch her!*" she yelled at Bret. "I'll get Dad."

Bret couldn't have moved if he'd wanted to. He just sat there, staring down at his broken mommy, praying and praying for her to wake up, but the prayers had no voice; he couldn't make himself make any sound at all.

Finally Daddy ran into the barn.

Bret popped to his feet and held his arms out, but Daddy ran right past him. Bret stumbled backward so fast, he hit the fence wall. He couldn't breathe enough to cry. He just stood there, watching the red, red blood slither down his mommy's face. Jacey came and stood beside him.

Daddy knelt beside her, dropping his black medical bag into the dirt. "Hang on, Mikaela," he whispered. Gently he removed her helmet— should Bret have done that?—then Daddy opened her mouth and poked his fingers between her teeth. She coughed and sputtered, and Bret saw blood gush across his daddy's fingers.

Daddy's hands that were always so clean . . . now Mommy's blood was everywhere, even on the sleeves of Daddy's flannel pajamas.

"Hang on, Mike," his dad kept saying, over and over again, "hang on. We're all here . . . stay with us. . . ."

Stay with us. That meant don't die . . . which meant she *could* die.

Dad looked up at Jacey. "Call nine-one-one *now.*"

It felt like hours they all stood there, frozen and silent. Finally red lights cartwheeled through the dim barn, sirens screamed; an ambulance skidded through the loose gravel alongside the horse trailer.

Blue-uniformed paramedics came running into the barn, dragging a bumping, clanking bed on wheels behind them. Bret's heart started beating so loud he couldn't hear.

He tried to scream *Save her!* but when he opened his mouth, all that came out was a thick black cloud. He watched the smoke turn into a bunch of tiny spiders and float away.

He clamped his mouth shut and backed away, hitting the fence so hard it knocked him dizzy. He covered his ears and shut his eyes and prayed as hard as he could.

She is dying.

Memories rush through her mind in no particular order, some tinged with the sweet scent of roses after a spring rain, some smelling of the sand at the lake where she tasted the first kiss that mattered. Some—too many—come wrapped in the iridescent, sticky web of regret.

They are moving her now, strapping her body to a strange bed. The lights are so bright that she cannot open her eyes. An engine starts and the movement hurts. Oh, God, it hurts . . .

She can hear her husband's voice, the soft, whispering love sounds that have guided her through the last ten years of her life, and though she can hear nothing from her children, her babies, she knows they are here, watching her. More than anything in the world, she wants a chance to say something to them, even if only a sound, a sigh, something . . .

Warm tears leak from the corners of her eyes, slide behind her ears, and dampen the stiff, unpleasantly scented pillow behind her head. She wishes she could hold them back, swallow them, so that her children won't see, but such control is gone, as distant and impossible as the ability to lift her hand for a final wave.

Then again, maybe she isn't crying at all, maybe it is her soul, leaking from her body in droplets that no one will ever see.

PHOTO: © CHARLESBUSH.COM

KRISTIN HANNAH is the *New York Times* bestselling author of eighteen novels, including the blockbuster *Firefly Lane*. She lives in the Pacific Northwest and Hawaii with her husband.

For more information, please visit
www.KristinHannah.com